BY HANNAH BONAM-YOUNG

Next of Kin

Next to You

Out on a Limb

Set the Record Straight

Next of Kin

Next of Kin

a novel

Hannah Bonam-Young

DELL BOOKS

NEW YORK

2024 Dell Trade Paperback Edition

Copyright © 2022, 2024 by Hannah Bonam-Young
Excerpt from *Next to You* by Hannah Bonam-Young
copyright © 2022 by Hannah Bonam-Young

Published in the United States by Dell, an imprint of
Random House, a division of Penguin Random House LLC, New York.

Dell and the D colophon are registered trademarks
of Penguin Random House LLC.

Originally self-published in slightly different form in the United States
by the author in 2022.

Library of Congress Cataloging-in-Publication Data
Names: Bonam-Young, Hannah, author.
Title: Next of kin: a novel / Hannah Bonam-Young.
Description: Dell trade paperback edition. | New York: Bantam Dell, 2024.
Identifiers: LCCN 2023039962 (print) | LCCN 2023039963 (ebook) |
ISBN 9780593872109 (trade paperback) | ISBN 9781778027710 (ebook)
Subjects: LCGFT: Romance fiction. | Novels.
Classification: LCC PR9199.4.B6555 N46 2024 (print) |
LCC PR9199.4.B6555
(ebook) | DDC 823/.92—dc23/eng/20230915
LC record available at https://lccn.loc.gov/2023039962
LC ebook record available at https://lccn.loc.gov/2023039963

Printed in the United States of America on acid-free paper

randomhousebooks.com

4 6 8 9 7 5 3

Book design by Jo Anne Metsch

This book is dedicated to those who think
Jess was Rory's best boyfriend.
The rest of you are wrong.

AUTHOR'S NOTE

Dear Reader,

Thank you for picking up *Next of Kin*! I wanted to include a list of content and themes throughout the book that may be distressing to some readers.

Content Warnings:
- Foster care and adoption
- Past parental neglect and abandonment
- Past death of a parent (drug overdose)
- Drug and alcohol consumption
- Descriptive sex scenes
- Anxiety, PTSD, and anger management issues
- Medically fragile infant in NICU (fetal alcohol syndrome)
- References to ableism

Chloe and Warren were both in foster care growing up. Chloe was eventually adopted but Warren and his younger brother, Luke, were not. The topics of foster care and adoption were written with the utmost care. I, with the employment of sensitivity readers, worked diligently to portray this subject in a balanced, honest manner.

Luke, Warren's teenage brother, is Deaf. He communicates exclusively in American Sign Language (ASL). I'm very grateful to the sensitivity readers from the Deaf community who partnered with me to portray Luke's experience accurately.

I hope you enjoy Chloe and Warren's love story.

Wishing you peace,

HANNAH BONAM-YOUNG

Next of Kin

ONE

MY PHONE RINGS, FLASHING A NUMBER THAT IMMEDI-ately sends a chill down my spine. I follow my instincts, ditching my cart and spot in the checkout line to find quiet in the grocery store's bathroom, which, thankfully, is empty.

"Hello, this is Chloe." My voice is already shaking.

"Hi, Chloe, this is Rachel Feroux calling from Child Protective Services. Is this a good time to talk?"

I close the toilet stall and lock it behind me as an all-too-familiar feeling of dread creeps into my chest. I paw at my collarbone with my free hand. A nervous rash is most likely already spreading. "Sure." *Connie . . . it has to be Connie.* She's hurt, or worse. Why else would CPS call? I haven't heard from a social worker in over six years.

"Okay, great." Rachel clears her throat, then seems to brace herself with a loud inhale. "In your file, it states that you're open to your birth mother contacting you. Is that still accurate?"

Do I want to know? "Yes . . ."

"It is sort of an unusual call, I suppose. Your mother . . . sorry, Constance. Constance has put in an urgent request that you visit her. She's at the hospital."

My body goes entirely still, and the blood pumps slower in my veins. As much as I have tried to distance myself from her, the need for Connie to be okay still sits lodged in my throat.

"She has just, entirely unexpectedly, given birth."

"I'm sorry, what?" I fight for my next breath.

"Your mother had a baby." My palm hits the stall's wall before my back does, and I slide down to sit on the floor. *I'll burn these clothes later.*

"No. That—but—*what?*"

"I understand that it must be a lot to process. I wish there was a way for me to deliver this news that wouldn't give such a shock. I know that it's been over ten years since you have seen or heard from your mother."

That is not *entirely* true. There were plenty of times in high school when she showed up without my adoptive parents' permission, and I never told.

"Is she— Is Connie okay?"

"Yes, she's fine. A colleague of mine is with her right now. The baby was premature. The doctor who called us earlier said they will make a full recovery, probably after a two- or three-month NICU stay. The baby . . . will not be placed with your mother. We are looking into different care options."

Colleague. Placed. Care. Social workers are all over this—why would Connie want to see me? Wouldn't she understand how messed up that is? To need me while she sends another kid into foster care? *No, not just another kid . . . my sibling.*

She clears her throat. "Constance has listed you as a possible caregiver. She's willing to sign over her parental rights to you. If not, the baby, after making a full recovery, will be placed in foster care."

I pull the phone away from my face and stare blankly at the screen for a moment. I must have a bad signal or be imagining this entirely. A possible caregiver? For a baby. *Me?*

"But . . . I'm twenty-four." I'm not sure why that's the thought that escapes when there are about two thousand others bouncing around in my head, but for whatever reason, it's what comes out. Twenty-four, recently graduated, no idea what I'm doing . . . Hell, I had been crossing my fingers that my bank card wouldn't be declined for my groceries.

"Chloe, I understand that this is a lot to ask of you. Especially considering your . . . distant relationship with your birth mother. However, it's only appropriate that we follow up with each possible contact she provides. You have every right to say no, and there could be visitation options with your sibling if you were to want that."

I gasp softly as an undeniable rush of joy curves my lips into a smile, another thought breaking through the heavy silence. *I have a sibling.* I'd have given anything for a sibling growing up, someone familiar and known. Someone to love and be loved by unconditionally. "Would I even be allowed?" I ask hesitantly. "If I wanted to?"

"That would require a much larger conversation . . . one that may be best to have at my office."

"Yeah . . . okay."

"There would be lots to discuss. I think, right now, we should just digest this news." Rachel's voice remains cool yet determined.

"Right." I pinch the bridge of my nose. My eyes are closed, but the room keeps spinning.

"Constance *is* asking to see you regardless."

"Okay." I don't know if it's the prospect of seeing Connie or the thought that she chose not to reach out before now that causes my lips to tremble, but either way, they do.

"But to be perfectly clear, the choice is ultimately yours." Rachel's gentle confidence reassures me somewhat.

"Yeah . . ."

"How about I give you the phone number of my colleague who is with Constance now? If you decide you want to see her, you can get the information from her. Then we can go from there, whatever you decide."

My head aches and pounds, feeling like it would on a relentlessly humid day before a thunderstorm.

After Rachel gives me her colleague's details, I hang up the phone and press it into the space between my eyes. Focusing on that spot of slight discomfort, one I'm choosing to cause and not receive unwillingly, seems to help. I think of Connie, or at least the latest version of her I have in memory, and transfer that image to a hospital bed.

Sympathy swells despite my impulse to shut my emotions down and get out of this bathroom without causing a scene. I imagine the similarities between where she is now and the picture that used to sit on her bedside table. Our first photo together, taken as she lay in a different hospital bed almost twenty-five years ago. She had been alone then too and only seventeen.

My thoughts hold on my birth mother until an unwelcome memory rises to the top of the pile. I was four years old, waiting on an empty school bus that had already made a second loop back to my street. Sitting alone with the bus driver and my kindergarten teacher, I remember thinking that they both looked at me with the same expression my mom had when I'd fallen out of a tree a few days before. I asked myself why they did that—I wasn't hurt.

"Mommy didn't mention any plans she had for today?" Ms. Brown had asked me.

"Nope," little me answered.

"Do you know your grandma's phone number? Or where she might work?"

"I don't have a grandma. I have an uncle, but he lives on a big boat."

"And your . . . dad? Do you know your dad's name, sweetie?" Ms. Brown was making me nervous, and I wanted my mom. Mostly so I could show her the artwork I'd made and ask if I had a dad like my friend Sara did. Sara's dad seemed nice. Maybe, I had thought, he could be my dad too.

"Nope," I answered.

"Okay, all right. Well, I think you and I are going to go on a little adventure today! Would you like to see where Ms. Brown lives?"

"Don't you have a dog?" I asked.

"Uh . . . yes, I do."

"I don't like dogs. They're stinky."

"Well, how about we put him outside and the two of us can play inside?"

Ms. Brown had taken me back to her house for two hours before CPS workers arrived and placed me in emergency care.

I've read in my file since—the one I was "gifted" on my eighteenth birthday—that the police tracked Connie down a few days later. She was high, drunk, and angry to have been found. I bounced around foster care for a year until my mom proved successful enough in her sobriety that I was able to move back in with her. I knew she had worked hard for that. Counselors, social workers, and teachers—they'd all told me how much my mom had worked to get me back.

I've never understood why they needed to tell me that, as if any five-year-old should be grateful to be with their own mother. As if I was a sobriety chip and not a human.

When Connie relapsed ten months later, my head was so filled up with forced gratitude that I felt worse for her than for myself. I should have been told I didn't deserve to eat nothing but dry Froot Loops for three days straight—but I wasn't. Instead, I felt sad for her. I still do.

Now, she's brought another kid into this mess.

Determination fills my chest, and I open my eyes, bringing myself back into the fluorescent-lit bathroom and into my adult body that shakes as waves of nausea cause goosebumps to spread. I know that I need to go see my mother. I won't let my sibling go through what I did. I can't.

TWO

I STEP OUT OF THE TOILET STALL AND WASH MY HANDS.
Once I'm positive I have scrubbed every last piece of public
bathroom off me, I bring some cold water to my face. The water
droplets run down into the neck of my T-shirt as I lean over the
sink, bracing myself with a firm grip on either side. *Do not throw
up in a grocery store bathroom.* I look at my reflection in the clouded
mirror resting above the basin.

My mother's eyes look back at me. Deep green with amber
flecks. Thick, dark eyelashes and even thicker eyebrows. The
women in our family were built to battle the elements, carry children on our backs, live through famine—survive. *Strong brows,
strong noses, strong bodies, strong hearts.* Connie has written that on
each of my birthday cards—the years she remembered.

I always thought it was a batshit crazy thing to write, but now
the familiar sentiment is sort of nice. I became far less insecure
about my soft-edged figure when I realized my body had evolved

to hold weight and strength because of what my Polish lineage—on Connie's side—had to survive.

My chestnut-brown hair is getting far too long, falling almost to the ends of my fingertips, but I like it that way. Mostly because my adoptive mother would hate it—it's not practical. I tie it up now to allow my neck to breathe. Everything feels too close to my skin.

Outside the grocery store bathroom, crowds of shoppers go about their day. Announcements on the overhead speaker include a promotion on paper towels. The beeps of the cash registers are steady and jarring. The smiles of the cashiers plastered and polite. A woman uses a coupon on cat litter that gets her a whole twenty cents off. The world hasn't turned upside down for anyone else.

I abandon my cart of groceries and make a mental note to never return to this store in case I was spotted doing so. There is frozen stuff in the cart, after all.

I pass by a picture-perfect family entering the store as I leave. Two parents, two kids. They're giggling with one another. The dad makes a silly face at the little girl balancing on the end of the cart, holding on for dear life. I push down the resentment that threatens to burn its way up my throat and turn into tears. I envy them, deeply, in my gut.

Finally outside, I lean on the concrete wall of the building and take a much-needed breath of the mid-June air. When I woke up this morning, my to-do list consisted of buying groceries, watching a documentary my father recommended, and possibly getting tipsy enough on wine to download yet another dating app. Now, bigger things to tackle.

I pull out my phone to call Rachel's colleague.

"Hello, this is Odette."

"Hi, Odette, it's Chloe, Connie's . . . daughter."

"Oh, yes!" Odette sings out. "Hi, hon. Good to hear from you." Her tone is so warm it builds an ache in my chest. The longing to be comforted by her is outweighed by my need to keep this day progressing forward at top speed. I need to remain a moving target.

"I was wondering if you could tell me where Connie is and how to see her."

"Of course. Is this a mobile number? It may be best to text the details to you. Is that okay?"

"That would be great, thanks."

"Okay, hon, talk soon," Odette says softly.

I copy the address of the hospital from Odette's text and paste it into the GPS on my phone. There is no way I'm paying for a cab ride across the city, but I also don't have any change for the bus. I'd go inside and use the ATM, but they could be waiting for the owner of the abandoned grocery cart to return or beginning to hang wanted posters, so I won't be doing that.

I do have my expired student bus pass, however, given to me by my alma mater. It's only been one month since graduation. That has to count for something. Perhaps the pass is sort of like expired yogurt: You can still try it if you're too broke to afford more—which I am.

The bus driver waves me on without reading the fine print—*thank god*—and I take a seat toward the back next to a window. I shut down thoughts of where I'm headed, hoping to not add "cried on public transport" to today's list of achievements.

The ride passes far too quickly. The back doors open to a crowded stop filled with scrub-wearing folks clamoring to get on. I make my way through them and up the ramp to the visitor entrance of the hospital.

As I get into the empty elevator, it dawns on me that, prior to ninety minutes ago, I hadn't thought of Connie in a few weeks. Not since Mother's Day. The guilt comes in an unexpected and tsunami-sized wave.

Without pausing, I frantically search the collection of buttons on the wall and push the emergency stop button. The elevator immediately halts. I place my hands around the base of my neck, apply pressure with my forearms against my chest—as my adoptive parents taught me when I was experiencing anxiety, or what they affectionately called *nerves*.

I haven't seen Connie for six years. I hadn't known if she was alive, though I always suspected I would feel it if she passed. What do I say to her? Call her? Should I have stopped at the lobby gift shop first? Do you get flowers for the new mother who will be leaving alone?

"Hello, is something wrong?" A muffled male voice comes through the elevator's speaker. *Shit.*

"Oh no, sorry, I pressed it accidentally," I stammer.

"No problem." The elevator hums and starts back up.

Two floors later, I step off and follow the purple arrows on the floor to the maternity ward, per Odette's instruction. There is a phone hanging on the wall outside the entrance of locked double doors. A sticker next to it reads INFORM THE CHARGE NURSE WHO YOU ARE HERE TO VISIT AND WAIT FOR THE DOORS TO OPEN. I pick it up, and it trills a few times before a rather crabby-sounding woman answers.

"Hi. I'm here to see Constance Walden." I haven't said my pre-adoption surname out loud in a long time.

"One moment, please." The line clicks, and the doors open slowly with a hum. I walk in and nod at the nurse at the front desk. She barely looks up as she points over her shoulder toward, presumably, Connie's room.

"End of the hall on your left," another, kinder nurse chimes in from behind, offering me a sympathetic grin.

"Thanks." At this point, to keep me upright, my feet have to keep moving faster than my fears can grow.

I knock three times, shifting my weight from one foot to the other, before a towering woman steps out. She is probably in her midsixties, dressed in purple from head to toe, and has dreadlocks that rest past her shoulders. She has dark skin, painted-on red cheeks, and kind eyes that she uses to look me up and down adoringly.

"Oh, Miss Chloe . . . look at you." She clasps her hands in front of her face. "I'm sure you don't remember me, but I have known your mother for a long time. We met when you were only five years old." She lowers her hands and holds one palm out for me to take, which I do willingly. "It's so nice to see you again, my dear. Though I wish it was under different circumstances." We both let go.

I do remember her, or her kind eyes at least, and I feel a little safer for it. "It's nice to see you again, Odette." I force out a smile, and she puts one hand on my shoulder, the comfort of which almost sends me into a fit of tears. I resist.

"How are you holding up?"

"Weird morning." My voice, despite my efforts, has no ease to it.

"Mmm, I can believe that," she says. "Well, hon, I'm here to be your mama's friend right now. Is it okay if I call her your mama?"

I shrug, but before I speak, she continues, "Connie and I have kept in touch over the years . . . when she's doing well. I've helped her with rehabilitation programs, a sponsorship group, things like that. Mostly, I try to be a listening ear. Before last night, when she asked me here, I hadn't heard from her in two years. The hospital staff had been less than friendly. She hadn't even seen the baby before I got here this morning. Connie—"

She stops speaking, exhales, and rubs her eye with a closed fist. "Connie had gone into the ER, complaining of stomach pains. She was . . . drunk. They discovered she was in active labor, and they performed a C-section. She hadn't known she was pregnant." Odette's face turns solemn. "I'm a children's support worker, but the hat I'm wearing through this door is Connie's friend first. I want to be clear, sweet girl, that I know she has made many mistakes. I know they have impacted you greatly. But she is having a hard time, and we need to be as compassionate as we can be right now."

Guilt wraps tightly around my heart as it beats a little faster. "Understood." I swallow thickly.

"Okay, hon. You ready to go in?"

I hesitate to ask, but I have to know before my feet will move me. "Is . . . is the baby in there?"

"No. She's in the neonatal intensive care unit. She's safe."

I have a sister. "Can I see her?" I ask with trepidation. "After?"

Odette's expression clouds, and she nods a few times. "Sure, hon."

I press my mouth into a hard line and adjust myself to stand straighter, inhaling deeply. "Okay. I'm ready."

THREE

"MISS CONNIE? I HAVE SOMEONE HERE FOR YOU. . . ."
Odette pulls back the curtain wrapped around the hospital bed
in the otherwise empty room. "Chloe has come to visit."

I blink at the person lying in front of me. This woman shares
almost no recognizable features with the mother I remember.
Connie's face is hollow, with circles under her eyes that are almost black. Her lips are cracked and dry, and her hair is no longer
dark brown, like mine, but bleached blond and fraying.

If I saw her on the street, I wouldn't have thought twice as I
passed her by. Maybe I have. A tear falls onto my cheek, but I
wipe it away before Odette or Connie sees it.

"Hello . . ." I sincerely cannot think of any other word to say.

Connie looks me up and down, face neutral, shrinking me to
two feet tall. Even now, as she looks like this, I still crave her approval.

"You really came." Her voice is more familiar than her face,
but gruff. She wipes her nose with the back of her forearm.

"I did." All my energy is concentrated on keeping my tone and expression neutral.

"Well . . . good." Connie already sounds annoyed. *Off to a great start.*

I look toward Odette, and she takes my cue.

"Connie . . . Chloe has agreed to visit you out of the kindness of her heart. We talked about this, my dear. I know you're grateful she agreed to come."

The woman in the bed nods, looking between Odette and me rapidly. Her movements gain momentum as the emotional energy in the room shifts to an unpredictable intensity.

"So this is the part, huh? The part where you two team up on me? Mock me? Dismiss me? Well, *dear*"—she spits this word back at Odette—"don't forget that I made *her*." She gestures to me with a limp wrist. "I know how to talk to her."

"You asked for me?" I step in front of Odette, shielding her the best I can, though my height does little to hide her broad shoulders and towering figure.

"Yeah . . ." She leans back, calming her body down physically, but her eyes remain wild. "I . . . I didn't know." She looks at her lap, wringing her hands. "I didn't know I was pregnant. I didn't know. . . . I wouldn't have done it again."

"But you have." The harsh reply escapes me before I think to take Odette's words of caution. Connie's face falls, looking like a scorned child. How can someone so physically worn look so young?

"Yeah, I have." The room stills, the tension lowering. Odette glides over to the chairs sitting next to the bed and gestures for me to sit with her, and I do.

"Why don't you tell Chloe why you've asked her here?" Connie doesn't look up but shakes her head. "Connie." Odette reaches for her hand. "She came . . . it's your turn now."

"Chloe . . . baby . . ." My mother's voice shifts to the tone I remember. "I'm so—I'm so sorry." Her lips tremble, but no tears appear.

I nod and cautiously raise my hand before deciding where it's safest to rest. I choose her knee that's covered by a thin hospital sheet.

"I don't want her to go through what you did. I couldn't live with myself if—"

Odette interrupts. "Let's try to keep all expectations manageable and free from guilt." She raises an eyebrow at Connie, a reminder, it seems.

"I want you to take the baby until I can get clean. . . . I know you're still so young but—" She looks up toward me, tears in her eyes. "You're *you*. You're way more responsible than I have ever been."

I lean back in my chair; my hand moves to my knee instead. "Because I had to be," I say.

"Yeah, I guess so," she whispers.

I look to Odette, who, despite having no idea what I plan to say, gives me an encouraging nod.

I straighten and rock back and forth until the motion comforts me enough to speak. "I'll do it. But only if you promise to give up custody completely." I turn toward Odette. "That's what Rachel said on the phone."

Odette purses her lips.

I lick my lips before speaking. "I'll do it, if I even can. I don't know if I'll be allowed . . . but you won't get custody again. You can visit with her when you're sober. You can see her often, when you are . . . but . . . she is not going to live with you—ever. Do you understand?" My voice pitches louder with the last question, and I regret it immediately.

Connie wipes a single tear away, but the look on her face is one of accepted defeat instead of hurt.

I jump on the defensive. "They may not let me. I don't know . . . I just finished school. I have tons of student loans and started freelancing less than a month ago. I'm living alone right now. I can't move . . . home." No need to add *My adoptive parents left the country and we aren't particularly close.*

Odette speaks up. "But we appreciate your willingness to try."

I offer an awkward but appreciative smile. I look back toward Connie and study her for a moment, my heart filling with worry. "I really hope things turn around for you."

She fumbles to gather a tighter hold on Odette's hand. "Me too," Connie whispers.

We sit in awkward silence until Odette stands and gracefully turns to me. "Chloe, would you like to go meet your sister?"

I nod, rising to stand next to her. I move away from the hospital bed and around the back of the chair I'd been sitting in. I choose to give a parting gift to Connie. "Good to see you, Mom."

She reaches for my hand, and I gently touch the back of hers before tensing and moving away. "Goodbye," I say.

I follow Odette into the hallway. She places a hand on my back after shutting the door. I blankly look off to the white walls with metal panels across the hall as she uses a heavy palm to pat me. "No rush, hon."

I smile unconvincingly over my shoulder to Odette, who stands behind me. She continues her soothing motions as I catch my breath and unclench my jaw.

Who was that woman?

Sober or not, my mother has always looked like herself—warm, familiar, like me. Now, I'm perhaps the only version of who my mother used to be that's left in this world. She's a stranger now, in all ways. A stranger my heart breaks for. A stranger I still need the approval of, love from . . . but I will have to settle for trust. The trust she is giving me to look after my sister.

FOUR

ODETTE LEADS ME BACK PAST THE ELEVATORS AND toward the NICU. Eventually, we arrive at another entryway with a video camera above the door. Whoever is watching must have noticed Odette is wearing a visitor's pass around her neck since the doors open before she reaches for the phone on the wall. She waves politely at the nurses' station as we pass, going toward a dimly lit hallway.

I feel out of place here, like I'm trespassing in someone else's life. I make an effort to not look into the rooms with other families. I'm glad Odette walks with such force, otherwise I may turn and run.

Odette slows, nearing the end of the hall. A man wearing blue scrubs, the same as the nurses at the front desk, sits at a computer in an alcove outside the room. He's facing a large window that looks into one of the many private suites.

From where we stop in the hallway, I can look through it to see an incubator with a dual-monitor stand towering above it. Odette clears her throat, and the nurse looks toward us as he switches off the computer he'd been typing on. He stands and reaches out a hand to shake with Odette and then me.

"Hi. I'm Calvin. I'm looking after Baby Walden this afternoon. I'll be here till seven." Calvin is probably a few inches taller than me and has olive-toned skin and dark hair and eyes. He reminds me of a classic World War II soldier, short in stature but strong-looking, with broad muscles in his upper body, a wide stance, and coifed black hair.

"Hi, Calvin, this is Chloe, baby girl's older sister, and I'm Odette from CPS."

Something beeps, and I turn to look at the monitors, trying to decipher what any of it means.

"Good to meet you both." Calvin steps beside me and points toward the window. "The top line is her heart rate, the middle is her oxygenation level, the last is the feeding tube's input."

I nod. The other screen is a baby monitor, a live feed of my sister. *My sister.*

"If you have any questions, don't hesitate. It can be really overwhelming. There are a lot of beeps and alarms and wires, but it all looks far worse than it actually is."

I smile at him through the fog of my overstimulation. He has clearly given this speech thousands of times, but I do find myself settling at the sight ahead of me. I can barely make out the shape of a baby under each wire, bandage, and wrap.

"Let's go inside." Odette reaches for the glass sliding door.

"What's her name?" I blurt.

Odette doesn't slow as she opens the door and guides me in with a steady hand on the small of my back. "No name yet."

I walk over and look down at the incubator. Her tiny body is nearly transparent. She has a monitor on her right foot, which is sticking out from under a blanket.

"I love her little toes. Oh my goodness," Odette coos from behind me.

I agree, but fail to speak or move closer. I didn't know humans could be so small. I feel worried just looking at her.

An alarm sounds, and Calvin comes inside.

"Looks like someone is a little overexcited to meet her sister." He opens the incubator and turns her, rubbing her back with what seems like far too aggressive a motion. I look at the screens; the top line is flashing in rhythm with the blaring alarm.

Another nurse pops her head in as the monitor continues sounding. "Hey, folks, would you mind stepping outside for a minute?" She looks at me before continuing, "Might be a good time to get you a visitor's badge? Baby girl just needs some extra help right now." She glances at the monitor and then back at us. "And we need to get more staff in here." She ushers us out the door quickly, and I crane my neck to look back toward Calvin.

The nurse leads us to the opposite side of the hall, where she has a standing desk on wheels.

"She's going to be okay, right?" I ask as three medical staff walk past us, pushing a cart in front of them.

"She's been putting up an amazing fight so far. Her heart is proving more challenging than we had originally hoped, but she's strong and is doing great otherwise." She shuffles around, trying to catch my eye as I glance around the hallway. "Hey . . . she has a great team in there. She's in good hands."

I nod, but my heart is beating so loud it competes with the quickened rhythm of the beeping monitor inside the room.

"You're the big sister, right?" the nurse asks me.

"Yeah," I think I answer, but I can't be sure.

"Wonderful . . . and you'll be attempting next-of-kin care adoption?"

"Yes." I'm guessing what she's saying for the most part, since I can barely hear. My adoptive parents called it "selective hearing" growing up, but I can't help it. When I'm anxious, it's like I've put earmuffs on, and voices all seem to dim.

"Good for you. In that case, there is some paperwork I need you to fill out. Starting with family medical history, stuff like that."

Odette reaches for my hand and wraps both of her hands around it. "We can do our best, but we don't have a lot of background history of mom's side of the family, and none of the father's."

The nurse grimaces. "Right, well. Okay." She hands a file folder to Odette.

I notice the monitor is no longer ringing and turn to see all the staff except Calvin leave the room. Calvin waves for us to come back in, and a huff of breath escapes me as my body springs toward the door.

"All right! So!" Calvin claps his hands once. He stands straight but relaxed—confident yet approachable. "Baby Girl was taking the new medication well—a little too well. We have adjusted, and now we should be able to avoid any more tachycardic episodes. No need to worry. She's a tough little one."

I let my shoulders fall back—they're a lot heavier than they were this morning.

"Otherwise, she's doing fantastic. Not a single thing to note other than needing to catch up on some lung development and weight gain, which is normal for preemies."

I push the pads of my feet into my shoes and twist them, trying to ground myself back into this room. I've never been scared out of my body before.

"I'll be outside if you need me." Calvin cleans his hands, disposes of his outer gown, and goes to sit at the window desk, out of view from where I stand. I slump into the armchair next to my sister.

"Quite the day . . ." Odette's voice is soft as she looks lovingly into the incubator.

"I don't know where to start." I place my forehead into my palms.

"Well, is there someone you might want to call? This is a lot to take in all at once."

"Nope." If I needed a reminder of how lonely I have become—this is perfect. My university roommates all left after graduation, leaving me a great big (but thankfully rent-controlled) apartment to myself. My adoptive parents went to live in Barcelona to care for my aging abuela, and the guy I was seeing ghosted me a few weeks back. On top of that, I freelance, so I don't have co-workers.

The plan was to start a life after graduation. I had a lot of plans, though I had no actual idea how to begin. Regardless, I was going to find my sitcom-style chosen family and welcome in my mid-twenties alongside them. I was going to get new roommates. I was going to tell them everything this time, be honest, be genuine. I was going to find love.

"Well, then allow me to keep you company." Odette sits down next to me in the other armchair. The one set up here for the other parent, I suppose. I look over at the cot in the corner of the room—am I expected to sleep here? I look toward my sister. Would she know she's alone?

"I think we start with giving this sweet baby a name." Odette breaks the silence.

"Am I—am I supposed to do that?" I stammer.

"That's what Connie wants. She thought it would be better that way."

I don't have the energy to try to psychoanalyze why Connie wouldn't even bother to name her because, truthfully, I'm grateful for the chance.

I stand and slowly approach the incubator. In all the action, her lilac hat was pulled back slightly, and I can make out more of her little face. Her name hits me instantly, as if her soul speaks to my own. "Willow."

"Mmm. I like that." Odette rises and stands beside me.

"There was this song my abuela used to play for me, 'Little Willow.' I think Paul McCartney wrote it."

"Willow it is." Odette's smile is so warm. She really found the right career. Smiles like that belong with people in crisis.

"Will she have Connie's last name? Or mine?"

"I would presume Connie's until custody is final. Then, if possible, it would be your choice."

"Right." I sniffle into my sleeve.

There is no way they're going to let me have her. Do I even want her? Her little hand twitches. *Yes, yes, I do.* I reach out to brush her fingertips. The way her hand curls around my pinkie finger spurs me on. "What's next?"

"We get you to see Rachel. She'll be Willow's caseworker. Then we start your application process. They'll do a home and finance assessment, psych evaluation, things like that."

"You make it sound so easy." My chest rises impossibly high with a breath that does nothing to soothe me.

"Oh, hon, it is not easy. Not in the slightest. But you have me, Rachel, and a whole team of people behind you who want to make it easier for you and Willow."

I nod repeatedly, trying to convince myself that I agree but fail. All of today's shock runs up my body and climbs up my throat. A muffled sob comes out, then another and another. "I don't know what to do." Odette rubs my back as I lean forward in the chair.

"Chloe, if this is what you want, you can do it. You will do it. But if it's too much, if you aren't ready to be a full-time care-giver . . ."

"I can't leave her. I can't," I interrupt, blubbering still.

"Okay then, okay. Then we do our best."

FIVE

"I HAVE GOOD NEWS AND SOME BAD NEWS—"

"As usual, then," I interrupt Rachel, who sits across from me in her cubicle—one of thirty in this large room alone.

The first time I came here, I found out each caseworker has about twenty kids under their supervision. There are three floors with rooms like this one. That is a lot of kids. *A lot.*

Rachel's desk is covered in file folders, Post-it notes, and disposable coffee cups. She has a professional exterior, but her personality sneaks out once in a while through small smirks, cleared throats, and muffled laughs.

"Your apartment was found suitable for care, and you passed both the psych evaluation and the background screening. . . ." There's a definite *but* coming on. "However,"—*close enough*—"we are still concerned about your income and financial security. We do not have a clear indicator that you'll be able to keep up with your rent and bills if Willow is placed in your care."

I flatten my dress out with my palms and tug at the fabric on my lap. "But since graduation, I've picked up enough work to pay all my bills, put money aside, and make loan payments." Graphic design work, thankfully, pays well when you can find it.

"Right, and we appreciate your efforts. But we don't have enough proof that this will continue, and you do not have enough savings, as of right now, to fall back on. Additionally, if Willow was to be placed with you, you would need to either cut back on work or make childcare arrangements, which can be costly."

I know Rachel isn't enjoying having to deliver this news—her face says she'd rather crawl into a hole—either way, I can't help but feel annoyance settle between us.

I bite the inside of my cheek, my eyes narrowing on the edge of Rachel's desk where a chewed piece of gum sits. "So I'm screwed then? No chance?" The tip of my nose and my eyes begin to burn, warning of tears. I choose not to stop it. I don't have the energy.

"No. I said there was good news too, remember?" I blink rapidly at Rachel, willing her to continue. "We have this new program, a new initiative . . . TeamUp." Her lip twitches with the hint of excitement.

My mind wanders to whomever is making marketing decisions for Child Protective Services. What a shitty gig and what terrible work they do. Every program I attended as a kid had an awful name. "Found Children," my least favorite, was a support group for adopted kids.

"TeamUp?" I purposely raise a brow to show my distaste.

"Yes, TeamUp." Rachel opens a desk drawer and pulls out a pamphlet with a design somehow worse than the name. I take it anyway.

"The program was designed to partner up prospective guardians who will mutually benefit from one another. Both members would make fantastic foster or next-of-kin care providers; they would have passed the evaluations with flying colors, except for an element such as housing or income. In your case, you would be a wonderful contributor to housing. Having a three-bedroom apartment in an accessible building is really great. Someone with steady work and consistent income would be a good counterpart in your particular case."

"So we'd live together? At my place?" I ask, my brows pressed together with disdain.

"Yes." Rachel shifts in her seat, her tone sympathetic but strained, her patience thinning.

"Is that not . . . a little strange? I mean . . . I won't know this person."

"It is new, a little unusual—sure. But it could be the difference between Willow being placed with you and needing to go into temporary care until your re-evaluation in January. If you were to agree, it would be a short-term arrangement. Enough time for you to prove consistent income and for your TeamUp partner to find appropriate housing elsewhere. There would be a visit beforehand, and I would be available for support throughout."

"It sounds like you have someone in mind," I say.

Rachel's mouth raises at one corner—she needs to work on her poker face.

"I suppose I do, yes. Another one of my cases. Similar situation to yours—a sibling guardianship."

I nod, imagining another woman who is also trying to navigate this process and raise her sibling. We could figure it out together. Maybe it could even be fun. . . . "Can I meet her?"

"Well, actually, it's a him," Rachel replies matter-of-factly, but her eyes shift between mine, trying to gauge a reaction.

My jaw drops. "A man? You want me to live with a man I don't know?"

She gives me an exasperated look as she adjusts her glasses.

"I'm not trying to end up on the news." I raise my voice slightly, laughing unconvincingly.

Rachel scoffs, smiling. She is certainly letting her mask slip today.

"Warren is one year younger than you and trying to get legal custody of his fifteen-year-old brother. He has also passed all the evaluations other than housing. He has a one-bedroom apartment at the moment, and any child above the age of ten is required to have their own room. However, he's a mechanic's apprentice and has over two years of work at a consistent rate of pay."

"I . . . I don't think I would feel safe."

"Your safety, Willow's, and all my cases are my top and only priority. The psych evaluations have been extensive. I'd never ask you to consider it if I wasn't confident everyone would be safe."

Perhaps Warren is safe, considering he had to undergo the same evaluations I did. But a fifteen-year-old boy who grew up in the system? I can't help but wonder if there are similar evaluations in place for the older kids too.

"And his brother?" I ask nervously.

"A great, sweet kid," Rachel continues. "Warren has been trying to locate housing but has struggled to find a two-bedroom apartment that would be close to his work and his brother's school—which is a necessity."

"He can't just change schools?" I ask abruptly.

"The school is for Deaf children, and it's the only one in this area."

I avoid eye contact and nod. I know that school; it isn't too far from me, actually. I breathe in, preparing to mentally weigh the pros and cons.

"Willow has about seven weeks left until she will be out of the NICU. You have time to make another arrangement. It would need to be someone willing to commit to the evaluation process and be certified by our office." She pauses, studying my reaction. "There may be another guardian who decides to try TeamUp, but I would presume most would be looking for income assistance and not housing, as housing tends to be more flexible."

There's a plea in Rachel's tone, whether she intends it or not. Her job is to be an advocate, but it must be a tricky balance when she is representing both Willow and this older boy. They both need a win.

"Warren is looking for something immediate. The sooner the better. His brother is currently placed in a group home that is"— Rachel hesitates and shakes her head—"unfortunately unable to meet the needs of a Deaf child."

They don't know sign language? My heart drops. That must be so lonely. "And if I say yes . . . will I be approved to bring Willow home? As soon as she's ready?"

"Yes, if Warren agrees to the arrangement as well."

"Okay . . . I'm in." *Anything for Willow.*

"Wonderful." Rachel's face remains nearly neutral, but she does tap with the tips of her index fingers as if she is drumming on her desk's edge.

"I will let Warren know, and we can arrange a meeting. Would you prefer to meet here?"

"You can give him my address. He may as well see where he might be living for the next few months." I sit straighter in the chair, nodding to provide myself reassurance.

Rachel grins. "Okay. I'll ask if that's comfortable for him and let you know."

I stand. "Great."

"Thank you, Chloe, for being open to this. I think it will be really beneficial for you both."

"Let's hope so." *It's only until January. How hard could it be?*

SIX

WARREN IS LATE. I PACE BACK AND FORTH IN FRONT OF my building's front entrance and check my phone yet again. It's 10:52 AM. *Twenty-two minutes late.* I have been standing outside for thirty, like a reasonable person would when about to meet a potential roommate. Not simply a roommate, but someone who stands to make or break my sibling's placement. He better be pulling a car off an old lady or rescuing a cat from a tree.

I checked my appearance three times before leaving the apartment and changed my outfit twice, settling on my favorite yellow jumpsuit. I paired it with my clay cherry earrings and red headband. People like bright colors, right? This outfit says, "I'm safe, approachable. We can be a team."

A black car pulls up into the semicircular driveway of my apartment building, and I adjust my posture to stand straighter as I expect to meet Warren and direct him to the visitors' parking. The music from the car is far too loud for it to be a ride service, but I look behind me to see if someone is waiting for one. It's only me outside.

The car turns off and the door opens. I notice a buzz-cut first, and then the sheer height of the stranger as he shuts the car door and surveys the building. He moves toward me, paying me no mind. Not Warren, I suppose. I allow my eyes to follow him as he passes me. He has the face of a handsome movie villain—devastatingly sharp.

"Hey!" I yell, but the stranger doesn't turn. "Hello? You can't park here!" I project my voice louder.

The guy looks over his shoulder and narrows his eyes ever so slightly before turning back toward the front entrance.

"Hey!" I say, exasperated.

"I'll be just a minute." He lifts a hand to literally wave me off. His voice is deep and smug—a deadly combination.

"Excuse me? No!" I look around, no sign of another car approaching. Perhaps it's because I'm bored waiting around for Warren to show, but I choose this hill to die on. I follow the brooding stranger inside the lobby. He presses the call button on the intercom next to the inner door as I enter.

"Listen, *Prison Break,* you can't park out front. You're blocking the entrance." He turns and looks down at me, more out of necessity than patronization—but the effect is the same. He opens his curled lips to speak as my phone rings.

I reach into my back pocket and lift a hand in front of his broad chest to silence him. He raises his eyebrows at my palm as I pull up my phone.

"Huh?" My buzzer is ringing. Oh, shit. *Of-freaking-course* . . . I silence my phone and let out a long sigh, lowering my hand to my jumpsuit's pocket.

"Warren, I take it?"

A deep, brief laugh escapes him. "Chloe?"

I pucker my lips and give him a single nod. "Yup." We both look out to his car.

"I guess I should go move that, then." He isn't taking this seriously, and it fuels my annoyance. I open the front door for him and make a show of waving him through.

He ducks out of the lobby, and I push my forehead into the heel of my hand. Almost thirty minutes late, parked in a no-parking zone, villain's cheekbones . . . this is a disaster.

He returns, wearing a bashful expression that is entirely put on for my benefit and dripping with arrogance. "Can we start over? Nice to meet you, Chloe." He extends a hand to me.

"Why were you late?" I open the inner door with my key fob and let him step in front. He lowers his unshaken hand.

"Traffic?" He doesn't even attempt to mask the lie. He's amused for some reason.

I narrow my eyes at him, wearing my best *screw you* expression that I've been perfecting since puberty.

"Fine . . . I slept late. It's my day off." He raises both hands.

"Great . . ." We step into the elevator.

"Why does that make you so mad?" he asks, eyes narrowed.

"I think people should be on time? Like the normal societal expectation?"

"Noted." He blows out his mouth as if to say *geez,* and it only adds to the rage threatening to spill out of my mouth.

I'm not normally an angry person. I avoid conflict. I don't usually let people get under my skin. Or, more accurately, I don't usually let them know they have. I take a few deep breaths. *Start over.*

He follows me off the elevator and toward my apartment door. I fiddle with my keys, trying the first three on my lanyard before I notice him watching.

"Did you just move in?" He places his forearm on the wall next to my door to support his leaning frame.

"No." I don't look up as I insert a fourth key.

"Wondering, since you seem to have keys to the whole city there—but none of them are marked for this door." His voice is heavy with sarcasm, his smirk audible.

The fifth key turns the lock, and I widen my eyes at him as I push the door open. My shoes land on the mat next to the door, but he leaves his on—another strike.

The entry of my apartment has a door on the right, which leads to a bathroom, and another on the left, leading to the first of the unoccupied bedrooms. The hallway ends as it bends into the kitchen on the right before opening up into the living area. The space has brick walls and high ceilings that meet where I sleep in the loft above.

"I had two roommates for university. They both moved out in the spring, but I kept the lease. What I pay here is what a one-bedroom seems to be going for these days." I flick the lights on in the empty bedrooms, and he glances around, nodding but silent.

We enter the main living area, and he looks around at my furniture. Most of it is thrifted or from a big-box store, and it definitely has a feminine vibe. There's a pink couch, fluffy off-white carpet, and a purple velvet armchair in the living room. He looks toward it as if he's hearing one long joke.

"What?" I ask.

"Nothing, just . . . cutesy." He shrugs.

My head involuntarily retracts at his use of *cutesy* when, clearly, he meant *girly* in a derogatory way. I count another strike against him.

"My room is up there." I point toward the spiral staircase that leads to the loft, open to the downstairs but not in view. "You wouldn't fit—slanted ceilings." I blurt out that last part as I look up at him. He tightens his lips and looks away, silently taking in the apartment.

I wait for him to speak, but he doesn't, and the silence grows uncomfortable. I tap my foot and cross my arms in front of my chest. I might not like this guy right now, but I'm going to have to learn to.

"I figured the front bedroom would be a better fit for you, and the other one for . . ." I don't know if Rachel told me his brother's name.

"Luke," he adds but doesn't turn to face me as he walks toward the collection of art prints hanging on the wall of the dining area opposite the kitchen.

"Luke," I repeat, nodding.

He turns over his shoulder to speak. "What is this?" He points to the middle frame, which houses a poster I made in a screen-printing class in third year. I grin to myself as he faces forward.

"It—uh—it's what I imagine tampon advertisements would look like if they were used by men. I made it in school." The image is a vintage-style 2-D animation of a box of tampons surrounded by slogans and quotes as if it were plucked out of a 1940s housewife magazine.

"Real men bleed on Tampax," he reads and tilts his head at me. "This is what they teach you at university?" He turns and points at the sofa. I nod and he sits.

I choose to let the loaded comment slide. What does he have against higher education? Or is it only me he has an issue with?

"Does Friday work?" Warren asks bluntly as I sit at the opposite end of the couch.

"Friday? Hmm. Should I expect you on Saturday, then?" I stare blankly. Perhaps his comment about university upset me a little. *What's gotten into me today?*

The corner of his mouth raises. "For someone who takes a good hour to find a key, you sure care about tardiness."

"Tardiness? You were thirty minutes late. If I had another choice, you—"

He interrupts, "If either of us had another choice, we wouldn't be agreeing to this." He uses both pointer fingers to gesture to the space between us. "But here we are. Subjects of the CPS's whim and approval." I shift in my seat, responding to the annoyance in his voice as he continues. "Look, this is probably going to suck. I'll clean up after Luke and myself. He'll be in school most days. My work hours fit into his schedule. I'll pay my half of the rent, and I'll make our own food. I don't expect help from you outside of letting us crash here."

"Okay . . ." Not much of a *team,* then.

"And your sister—Willow, right?" I nod. "She'll be sharing a room with you?"

"She will be. Once her NICU stay is done. Hoping she'll come home in three weeks."

Warren holds the bridge of his nose. "A baby?"

"Yes." My smile washes off.

"I didn't know that." Warren sighs.

"Well . . . sorry?"

"It's fine."

"Oh, I'm so glad it's fine for *you,*" I reply, eyes narrowing.

He looks up from the floor and makes eye contact that is far too intense. I look away immediately. "Sorry," Warren says, throwing out that word like it's nothing.

I choose the uncomfortable silence over an insincere response, and the quiet lingers.

"I'm hoping Friday is all right. It gives me the weekend to get Luke's room set up. Once Rachel does a house visit and gives the all clear, he can move in. She said Monday, hopefully." There's a shift of emotion in his voice—desperation, maybe.

"Sounds good." I try to match his brief and curt demeanor, but I continue despite myself. "I bet Luke is really excited."

Warren studies me for a brief moment, and then speaks only in sign language. "He is mostly excited to live with a hot older girl."

I lean back in my seat and meet his stare. "Well, I hope he isn't too disappointed," I sign back.

Warren laughs and raises a fist to wipe his expression away. I feel a sense of pride rising in my chest, having gotten a real reaction out of someone who seems very unwilling to give them away.

"Rachel didn't mention you could sign. I—"

"She didn't ask," I interrupt. His brows crease, waiting for an explanation. "My adoptive father is Deaf."

He slips back to boredom. "Cool." He stands. "See you Friday, then."

Before I can stop him or get any of my planned speech out, all the house rules and expectations I'd spent hours writing down, he's out the front door.

"Cool," I say, mimicking him to the empty apartment. It doesn't feel as satisfying that way.

SEVEN

"THIS IS BRYCE. BRYCE, THIS IS CHLOE." WARREN INtroduces his friend to me, face as indifferent as ever.

I reach out for Bryce's hand with a polite smile, and he extends his own. His eyes are fixed on my chest. In the time I take to look at our hands, to Warren, then back to Bryce, his eyes still haven't left my cleavage. I rip my hand away with a startling force that makes him realize he has been caught. Warren smirks, and I glare at him too.

"I work with War at the shop," Bryce sputters out.

I won't be engaging with Bryce anymore.

"So where do you want to start?" I ask, turning my focus solely to Warren.

He furrows his brow. "Thanks, but I'm good. I've moved a lot . . . don't need more than a second set of hands." His *Thanks* comes across as confused annoyance without any sense of genuine appreciation.

"Oh, well, I get that. It might go faster if I grab a box or two."

"No. Really . . . all good." He glances up and down my body far too quickly for it to be anything inappropriate—just enough to make me feel utterly useless. I dressed practically today so I could help—bell-bottom jeans with a striped mustard-and-red T-shirt tucked in, bandanna in my hair. Cute, obviously, but a working outfit nonetheless.

"All right . . . I'll be upstairs if you need anything." I have work to do anyway.

He doesn't even acknowledge my response before he tilts his head up to Bryce, and they make their way back toward the front hall. For the next ninety minutes, I work at my desk that's propped up against the railing of the loft, a few feet from the end of my bed. They don't talk much at all except for directions when the object they're carrying is blocking the other's view.

Male friendships are strange. Though I suppose I'm no expert on friendships of any kind. Elementary school had been a write-off, being transferred among schools when I moved from my mom's to a foster family, then back to Connie, then to my now-parents' place as a foster placement, then, after my adoption, to our new home.

I was perpetually the new kid. High school was hard friendship-wise too. I had strict parents who insisted it was better for me to struggle through all the advanced-level classes and have a tutor than to make time for socializing with my peers. University *had* been better.

A renewed sense of freedom meant I went a little too hard on the socializing my first year, but none of those friendships stuck. The two friends I lived with, Lane and Emily, both came from the other side of the country and had returned home. The group chat

has definitely slowed down with each passing day since graduation, but I do miss them. How would I even catch them up at this
point? I never even told them I had been adopted.

I finish up my work and can no longer ignore my nagging bladder, which is now full because I've been trying to remain out of
the way of the two men downstairs. I try to listen but hear nothing below. It seems this is my chance to sneak in and out of the
bathroom. If I'm lucky, I might have time to snag a bag of chips
out of the pantry before retreating once again.

I run downstairs, but I'm not fast enough. Hearing the sound
of the elevator announcing its arrival as I get into the hallway, I
make a dash to the bathroom right as the front door swings—
"Ow!"—into my face.

"What? Oh, shit." Warren drops his side of the mattress and
pushes past Bryce, who stands in the doorway—blankly staring at
me and my bloody nose.

"Let me see." Warren reaches up to my face and tries to move
my hand away.

"No—that's okay. I got it. I'm just going to—" I try to step
around him to get into the bathroom, but he doesn't budge. "I
actually get nosebleeds a lot. It may be a coincidence!"

Warren looks back at me, confused. "The door slammed into
your face. I don't think it's a coincidental nosebleed." I try to
squeeze around him again, but he steps into my path.

"Let me see." He's frustrated, and his voice has lowered. I find
myself following his instructions, despite my desire to suffer in
private.

"Yeah . . . ouch. Well, it doesn't look broken." He tilts my face
with a grip on my jaw. His thumb is pressed into the front of my
chin, and his fingers are curled underneath. It's the most physical
contact I've had in months, from a cute guy, that is. My stomach

swirls. He lowers his hand and looks at Bryce. "Nice one, jack-ass."

"How was I supposed to know she was standing there?" Bryce asks, voice dripping with derision.

"Could I?" I gesture to the bathroom door behind Warren, and he steps out of the way.

I rush in, shut the door, and look at myself in the mirror. Dried blood is already forming around my neck, and my top is definitely ruined. A shower will be the fastest way to get it all off, and an excuse to hide out a little longer.

When I'm finished, I have to pull my bloodied clothes back on for the sole purpose of getting me upstairs, lest I endure another embarrassing incident today. Once I'm upstairs I change and look toward the full-length mirror in the corner of my room as I sit on my bed. Without blood obscuring my view, I see that my nose is purple and rough-looking.

"Chloe?" a deep voice calls from the dining room below. I walk to the railing and lean over to see Warren looking up.

"Uh, yep?" I retreat out of view slightly—he has a strong, focused stare, and I'm not used to being seen.

"Do you need a ride?"

"Huh?"

"To the hospital?"

"Oh, uh, no. No thanks." I doubt it's broken. He doubted it too. There's a pregnant pause, and I glance back over the edge to see Warren rubbing his palm back and forth over his shaved head.

"Bryce is gone." He sounds cautious, as if he intended to say something else.

"Okay." I try to speak loud enough for him to hear from below while also juggling a tone of indifference.

"Sorry, uh, about him . . . earlier." So he *did* see.

I peek over, and he looks up as I look down. Our eyes meet for what I think may be the first time. I don't immediately pull back. I might like viewing him from up here. *Not so tall now, are you?*

"Can I look at your nose?" he asks.

"What?"

"I want to make sure it isn't broken."

"I didn't realize you had a medical degree." I feign surprise.

"I fix cars, not people. But I've been in enough fights to know a broken nose when I see one." How many fights would that take? I think back to the psych evaluation given by the CPS. How extensive had it *really* been?

"Fine," I squeak.

I make my way down the spiral staircase as he watches each placement of my feet. I stop in front of him as he leans on the dining table. Even with him in an almost-sitting position, I still have to look up at his face. I salute as I stomp my feet to signal my position, as if I were lining up in front of an army general. The side of his lip curls up slightly, but his eyes grow weary. I tire him, I think.

The all-too-familiar feeling of embarrassment over being "too much" flares. My adoptive mom did that too—made me feel like I was being too much at all times. She spent most of my adolescence trying to tone me down. It's been a few weeks since they video-called me from some random bar in Barcelona to tell me there was a drink called The Chloe. Damn, I should probably call them.

"It may not be broken, but it's not looking good." Warren's thumb is placed down on the apple of my cheek, his words and touch bringing me back from my trailing thoughts. I resist the urge to close my eyes.

"Well, it's probably for the best. Wouldn't want Luke thinking

I'm too hot right out of the gate. Better to pace myself." I make the joke to set him at ease, but he doesn't look any less concerned. "Seriously, it doesn't hurt that bad. All good," I say.

He studies me, and I swallow without meaning to.

"When did you start making your feelings smaller for other people's benefit?" he asks, his narrowed eyes focused intently on me. My head involuntarily retracts, jarring my nose. *Ow.*

"I—I wasn't." *Shit, I might have been . . . but how does he know that?*

Warren pushes his lips into a frown as he nods. "Okay." He rises from the table's edge. "I'm gonna get my shit put away." He walks directly to his room without looking back once.

I'm stuck in the spot he left me in, contemplating a question I had never once considered before.

EIGHT

I SPENT MOST OF THE DAY AT THE HOSPITAL WITH WILLOW. The hundreds of wires she started life with have now diminished to one tube split between her nostrils, forcing air into her little lungs to help them expand. Cautiously optimistic, her team and I have made a plan for her to come home next week. My notebook has begun filling with medications, doses, and specialist appointments that she will continue to need for the foreseeable future.

On my bus ride home, most of the women my age are with a gaggle of friends. A few of them toward the back pass around a flask and giggle as they check to see if the driver is looking. Another group is scrolling on their phones and dressed to go dancing. None of them, it seems, are headed home at eleven on a Saturday night to sit by themselves and wallow.

When I finally arrive at my apartment's front door a half hour later, there's music playing from inside. Not loud enough to upset the neighbors but loud enough for me to recognize it from the hall. The unmistakable sounds of "I Think We're Alone Now," by Tiffany. I smile to myself, knowing I'm most likely about to catch Warren jamming out to an eighties classic.

As I slip off my shoes, I can't help but speed-walk down the hall toward the sound coming from the TV. Warren is sprawled out on the sofa. The TV remote is resting on his chest, and his hands are raised out in front of him, playing an invisible drum set. A laugh escapes me, and he opens his eyes. He scans me briefly before giving me a polite upward nod and lying back down, his hands finding the rhythm again.

Warren isn't even a little embarrassed, and I'm a little disappointed. Where does all his confidence come from? *Can I get some of it?*

I don't move—I like this song, and his sporadic but intentional drumming motions are sort of mesmerizing to watch. His eyes clench tighter as he commits to the drum solo, and I can't help but smile. Maybe there's a guy under the hardened exterior who likes to have fun. Someone who likes eighties music and couch-drumming.

After the last few bars, Warren opens his eyes, and I watch him notice that I'm still here. Then, all the fun energy blows out of the room like dust in the wind, which is coincidentally the song that begins playing. With an exasperated sigh, he lowers one hand to the remote, quieting the music a few notches. "You need something?" Warren asks flatly.

"Oh, uh. No." *Just watching, like a weirdo. A lonely creep.*

"Thought you were out for the night. . . ." He looks me up and down with a raised brow, eyes focusing on his second pass. I think he's trying to decide where I've been in my purple jean skirt and polka-dot blouse that don't give him much of an idea.

"Have fun?" he asks. His eyes give up trying to make sense of my clothes and look up to me, his expression bored.

I can't help but wonder what he thinks of my outfit. Since university, my style could be defined as *oversized toddler*. And, truthfully—it's the most me I've ever felt. I like color and patterns. Sue me.

"Yeah." I shrug.

"Not too much fun, I suppose," he continues as I narrow my eyes. "If you're home before midnight . . ."

"Well, the hospital visiting hours end at ten."

"Ah." I swear I see a small smile form before he looks back at the TV.

I walk around the couch and gesture to the cushion where his feet are. "May I?"

Warren shifts up to a sitting position, his legs bent and between us. I'm content to listen to the music playing from the TV, but he doesn't turn the volume back up. I look toward him and watch him stiffen, his energy no longer relaxed or comfortable. His eyes glaring and fixed on me.

"What?" I ask, suddenly aware of every inch of space I occupy.

"We aren't going to be friends, Chloe." His voice is low and full of unadulterated arrogance as he tilts his head in confusion.

I huff, making an effort to form a look of bemused shock that is totally unreflective of the rejection I'm feeling. "Well, damn. Okay."

"I don't mean to be an asshole . . . but I think that there isn't any reason to try and force it for only five months."

I don't know what to say at first, so I wistfully look back toward the TV as the song ends and another ballad begins.

"We might have different definitions of friends, Warren. Usually, sitting on a couch next to someone doesn't mean they're looking for a BFF . . . unless you want to make friendship brace-lets? I did that at summer camp once."

His jaw flexes. "I want to make sure we're on the same page. I don't expect anything from you, for Luke or me."

"Nor do I," I retort. He rolls his eyes in response.

"What?" I sharply ask.

"I doubt that."

I laugh without joy, my jaw working. "Why?"

"Because girls like you have had help your entire life." Warren gestures around the apartment with an amused sort of annoy-ance. His eyes widen as if to say, *look around you!*

"Girls like me?" I scoff. "Please, do tell me more about myself, Warren."

He drapes his arms over his knees. "You got the adopted, two parents, nice house, university, fancy-ass apartment experience. We don't have anything in common."

I actually feel stunned. When did he even learn these things about me? It isn't even me, really—no one can be condensed into list form. "I'm sorry. I must be hallucinating. Are you seriously—"

"You disagree?" he interrupts. "You think you didn't have it easier?"

"Well, no . . . but . . ." I stop myself as Warren leans back to rest his arm along the back of the couch.

"I'll stay out of your way; you stay out of mine. That's all I ask." He looks at me, and his blue eyes look more gray than they have before. Clouded by judgment, it would seem.

I try to think of a clever comeback, something that will con-vince him I'm not some stuck-up, privileged debutante. Then it hits me. Why? Why do I feel the need to explain myself to this near perfect stranger? He doesn't know anything about me. He's asking *not* to know more. . . . It actually feels a little freeing. I've had so many people expect so much of me for a long time.

"Fine." I look at him and match his stare, our eyes fusing a connection that grows steadier each time it occurs. "Get off my couch then."

And, to his credit, he does.

NINE

"Hi, Luke. Nice to meet you. I'm Chloe." I finger spell *Luke,* since Warren never taught me his name sign. I do show him the sign my father has given me for my name.

Luke is about my height with thin brown hair that falls into his glasses. He's the spitting image of his brother, piercing eyes with a sharp jaw and hollow cheeks, but there is a warmth to him that Warren is missing.

"Nice to meet you, Chloe." He turns toward Warren, stern-faced. "Why didn't you tell me she could sign? I could have really embarrassed myself."

Warren slyly looks toward me, then back to his brother as he signs, "I already did. It seemed only fair."

I try to hide my grin as Luke looks toward me for an explanation. "He called me hot."

"That is embarrassing." Luke raises an eyebrow at his brother, then looks back to me as if to see if his brother was right. I think, based on the fact that he had to check again, he was not.

"Anyway, I'm sorry about my signing. I haven't practiced much in the last four years. My father is Deaf, but we haven't talked much since I moved out for school."

"What did you do in school?" Luke signs.

Warren taps him on the shoulder to get his attention before he looks back at me, wearing an expression that immediately signals he's going to try to get under my skin. Warren leads his brother by the shoulder to the tampon ad hanging in my dining room—his favorite piece, apparently.

"Graphic design. Her work is all around the house. I'm so sorry."

"Prick," I say as Luke faces the wall.

Warren smiles over his shoulder. He's teasing me. *Huh, I'm pretty sure that's what friends do, isn't it?* Trying to hurt my feelings is different from trying to rile me up. Maybe he's in a good mood because of Luke's arrival.

"I like it." Luke turns to me, wearing a polite smile.

"Thank you, Luke. At least one of you has good taste." I make a point to not look at Warren. "I'm sure you and your brother have got lots to do. I'll get out of your way."

I walk to the kitchen to make a snack as they sink down onto the couch. They both laugh every once in a while, and I can't help but smile each time. The group home must have been really lonely for Luke.

As I head toward the stairs, snack in hand, I catch Luke's wave from the corner of my eye. "Is your room up there?" He points at the spiral staircase.

"Yes."

"That is so cool! Can I see?" He looks genuinely interested. I suppose the novelty of the loft has worn off on me.

"Oh, sure."

"What are you doing?" Warren circles around to stand next to me, stopping Luke from reaching the bottom step.

"I want to see the loft." Luke points to my room.

"That is Chloe's space." His hands are moving so fast I can barely make out what's being signed.

"I don't mind," I sign to Warren. I appreciate his concern, but it isn't necessary.

"Well, I do." He glares down at me, and my feet glue to the floor as my heart stops for a moment. Someone signing at you with anger in their eyes lands far more pointedly.

"Oh, okay." I attempt my best polite smile at Luke to both comfort him and avoid eye contact with Warren.

"Luke." I make note of Luke's sign name as Warren uses it.

"What?" Luke glares. I think it's time for me to head upstairs as both brothers make faces at each other.

"Come on, we have grocery shopping to do." Warren speaks at the same time he signs, knowing he's out of my view.

I turn as the stairs curve back toward them and reply both in speaking and signing, "Oh, I'm going later. If you want to write down what you need, I can get it."

"No," Warren says sternly.

Frustration fills my chest, and I let the energy out through an exasperated sigh as I follow the rest of the steps to my room. *Warren is such an asshole.* Then again, most good-looking men tend to be. They're granted the permission, apparently, when they hit the age of maturity. I throw my headphones on and get back to my work assignment, a boring but well-paying job for a local tech company looking for new business cards.

Hours pass as I complete three style options. I send the mockups over and check the time. Before my brain has registered that it's 8 PM, my stomach signals it.

I take my headphones out and listen to the apartment below. No one seems to be around. I make my way downstairs and begin assembling ingredients for dinner from a now fully stocked fridge. I notice a lot of *L* and *W* scribbles written on several of the contents. Sharing is also off the table, I presume. Luke knocks on the cabinet, and I turn to him, feeling myself easily slip back into the routines of living with a Deaf household member again.

"What are you making?" Luke signs.

"Taco bowl." I shimmy in excitement.

"Nice." Luke doesn't move. I'm not sure if he is looking for company or food.

"Am I in the way? Did you need the fridge?"

"No, thanks."

"Want one?" I gesture to the ingredients.

"Sure."

"Cut the peppers?" I ask.

"Okay." Luke sets himself up next to me, and I pass him a knife and a cutting board, along with the red peppers. "Sorry Warren was such an ass earlier."

I wince. I wish he didn't feel like *he* had to apologize. "You don't need to be sorry."

"He is a good guy, really." Luke offers me a genuine smile, his eyes curving into crescent moons.

"He doesn't seem to like me very much."

"It isn't you. I actually think he does like you. He hates that this is the only way I could live with him." He shrugs and pushes the core of a pepper to the side of the cutting board. "Not a big fan of CPS or their rules."

Luke reminds me a lot of myself at his age. Eerily aware of the world around him and intent on keeping the peace—a skill children shouldn't have to learn so young.

"What about you? Rachel mentioned your group home staff didn't speak ASL . . . that must have sucked."

"Well, my handwriting definitely improved." Luke grins, but his eyes hold the weight of his words.

"Right." *Oof.* We both pick up our ingredients and get to work.

As Luke places the last piece of pepper into the hot pan, he turns to me. "If my brother hasn't already said it—thank you."

"Don't. Please don't. I needed you guys just as much, probably more."

We both nod and go about our tasks for a few moments. I shred some cheese as the veggies cook.

"Your sister is Willow, right?" Luke signs.

"Yeah."

"Warren said she's moving in sometime next week."

"Hopefully. She has to have her breathing tube out for at least seventy-two hours." I force out an uneasy smile.

"She's been sick?"

"Yeah. She was born prematurely. She also has fetal alcohol syndrome, which damaged her heart. My birth mother didn't know she was pregnant."

"Shit."

I'm not sure if I should raise an eyebrow at his use of a curse word, but I let it slide. It might be worth checking with Warren what *his* house rules are. "Yeah."

"Do you see her a lot? Your mom?" Luke's face isn't heavy with emotion. These aren't unusual conversations for him to be having, I suppose. They must have been pretty frequent at group homes, especially.

"No. She's not well."

"Where is she now?"

"I don't know. Once she left the hospital, she . . . hasn't reached out to anyone." I avoid eye contact. Too much sympathy from others often makes tears start flowing, and I don't want to freak the kid out.

"Sorry." Luke contorts his mouth into an anxious frown.

I serve up our bowls, and we move to sit at the table. Shortly after, Warren appears back at the front door with a shopping bag from the local pharmacy. Things for Luke, I presume, as he places it inside his room. He looks toward the table and slows his steps and tenses as he sees our dinner. Passing us, he goes to the kitchen, grabs a glass of water, and heads back down the hall.

The shower turns on, and my brain flips to a thought of him shirtless before I have a moment to stop myself. What does he hide under those loose-fitting black shirts he seems to have bought in bulk?

It has been a long time since I saw someone naked. My baby sister moving in is certainly not going to help that situation. Should I try to get laid before she moves in? To tide me over? Gross . . . I need to think about something else. Something much more table-conversation appropriate. *What were we talking about before?*

"What about your mom? Do you see her?" I ask Luke.

"Our mom died when I was a baby. Our dad comes and goes as he likes."

Well, that's sobering. "I'm sorry . . ." I sign, wrists limp.

If Luke was a baby, Warren must have been eight or so when his mom passed. I think of myself as that four-year-old sitting on the bus and wince. I lost my mom, but not forever. Even during the hardest parts, deep down, I always knew that.

"It wasn't so bad when Warren and I were together, but we haven't lived in the same house since I was nine."

"I'm glad you're together now."

"Me too."

The bathroom door opens, and Warren walks toward the living room . . . in only a towel. *Avert eyes. Avert eyes. Avert—shit.* My breath hitches in my throat as my heart hums in my ears. His upper body is all muscles and smooth skin.

I heard once you could imagine what something would feel like on your tongue by simply looking at it. Does that apply to the line up the center of his chest? The dip of his collarbones where water droplets still remain? My eyes fall lower. His abdomen narrows into a V-shape, pointing down to his . . . *damn, am I ovulating or something? Keep it together, Chloe.*

"Hey. All good?" Warren signs to Luke, paying me no mind yet again. I swallow and focus my attention on the last bites of my dinner.

"Yeah. We're talking shit about you," Luke signs back, grinning.

"Funny. It's time for bed. Fifteen minutes, okay?"

I check the clock on the stove; it's barely nine. Little early for a fifteen-year-old, no?

"Okay."

"We gotta be out of here by seven-thirty. Set your alarm, okay?"

Luke rises from his seat and takes his dishes to the sink, cleaning up after himself, while Warren traces his every move. He dries his hands on the tea towel on the stove, then meets Warren, where he has stayed planted at the end of the hallway, and pulls him into a hug. Warren resists, stiff as a board for a brief moment, before he dips his chin downward and wraps the crook of his elbow around Luke's head to pull him in closer. I stand and quietly tidy up the kitchen. This doesn't seem like a moment Warren would want me to witness.

TEN

"I HEAR CONGRATULATIONS ARE IN ORDER." CALVIN'S voice enters before the rest of him as the sliding door of Willow's room opens. I shuffle her up my chest as she rests on me, and I look toward him with a smile.

"I was wondering if you'd be working today," I say.

"I'm not supposed to be. I wanted to catch my favorite patient before she goes." He reaches out and tickles the bottom of Willow's foot. Calvin is usually with Willow four shifts a week. I've taken a lot of comfort knowing he's been here when I can't be.

"Willow, don't be rude. Thank Calvin for all his hard work." I lean in closer to her ear, but project my voice so Calvin can hear too. "You owe him, kid." I tilt my head up and see Calvin watching us, a fond look in his eye.

He clears his throat against a fist. "Since I'm not technically working today, and since Willow is no longer my patient, I was wondering . . . if I could give you my number," he says.

My eyes widen, but I'm not shocked, to be honest. I know how special Willow is to him—he told me he started in the NICU the day Willow was born, transferring from a different department. She has been his first and only patient here. "Of course!"

He smiles but looks surprised. "I honestly didn't think that would work." He hands me a piece of paper with his number on it.

I turn to lay Willow down in her car seat for the first time. "What? Why not?"

"Well, it's a little unusual, and you're way out of my league."

I stiffen. Thankfully my back is turned to him as I buckle Willow in. Oh, he meant to give me his number, like, *give me his number.* I scroll through my Rolodex of memories with him over these past eleven weeks.

He's cute, around my age, and seems kind. Also, he knows the tiny, precious baggage I now carry fairly well. All right, I'm cool with it. I turn around and offer him a playful eye roll with a smile. "I'm not out of your league."

He looks down at the suitcase in my left hand, the diaper bag around my shoulder, and the car seat on my right. "Want help to your car?"

"Oh, actually, we're taking a cab." I'm working on saving for a car, considering how many specialist appointments Will is going to have, but I'm also hoping to have enough saved up so as not to take on more debt, in an effort to not displease the CPS gods.

Calvin looks down to his feet as he speaks. "I . . . I drove here. Can I give you two a ride? I don't want to stick around here too long anyway—I'll get roped in to work." He looks toward my face with trepidation.

Thirty-three dollars. That's how much the cab company quoted me. "Yeah, that would be great. Thank you."

He reaches out for the bag, and I hand it over, our fingers brushing briefly.

"All right, well, allow me the pleasure of Willow's first car ride." He slides open the door, and I say a silent goodbye to the room that has housed my sister for the past eleven weeks.

"No pressure." I wink as we enter the hallway side by side.

We stop at the nurses' station to say our goodbyes. Calvin receives more than a few suspicious smiles and widened eyes as he stands behind us in street clothes, holding Willow's suitcase. I blush, wondering how far the other nurses' imaginations are going.

Calvin leads us toward the elevator and down to the parking garage below the hospital. After checking at least three times that the seatbelt is properly laced through the car seat, I sit next to Willow in the back of Calvin's sporty SUV.

"It's okay if I sit back here, right? I'm a little nervous," I say.

"Of course. I would be too."

It suddenly dawns on me that I know nothing personal about Calvin. Perhaps I missed the part of stranger danger lessons when they tell you to not accept rides, even from kind nurses.

We made small talk for the entire twenty-minute ride to my apartment building fairly effortlessly. Calvin insisted on parking and helping us up to my door, which felt like a very gentlemanly thing to do. He carries the diaper bag and Willow in her car seat while I pull the suitcase behind me.

"Yeah, right?" he's saying. "That is the last time I ever let a patient talk me into an extra Jell-O. It was horrible. I won't eat anything lime-flavored ever again." Laughter bubbles out of me as we step off the elevator.

"This is us." I unlock the door on my third try and place the suitcase to hold it ajar, turning back to face Calvin, standing in the hallway of our floor.

"Right. Well, thanks for letting me give you a ride, and thanks for—" Calvin stops, looking over my shoulder. I turn to see Warren leaning against the wall behind me, past the bathroom entrance. He's staring at us with a teasing gleam in his eye and arms crossed in front of his chest. I look at Calvin, who is smiling awkwardly at the man behind me.

"This is my roommate, Warren. Warren, this is Calvin."

Calvin steps around me, places Willow's car seat down, and reaches to shake Warren's hand. Warren does so reluctantly. "Nice to meet you, man."

"Yeah, you too," Warren responds, looking him up and down.

I look between the two men, who seem to be exchanging words that are silent to the female ear. I think this is the part of *West Side Story* when they start snapping and walking toward each other. Why, I have absolutely no idea.

"Okay, well. Thanks, Calvin," I say, interrupting the awkward exchange.

He turns to me and nods. "Anytime." He looks briefly past me and then down to Willow. "See you soon, Will." He stretches out one arm, and I pause like an idiot—not realizing he was inviting me into a side hug. I lunge forward, and our bodies awkwardly meet. We pull away, giggling softly. "All right, well, I'll see you soon."

"Yeah!" I answer a little too eagerly.

"Nice to meet you." Calvin waves to Warren, who raises a hand before shoving it deep into his jeans pocket.

"Bye," I say as I move the suitcase away from the door and let it shut. I turn and notice that Warren is leaning in the same spot, looking at me like I have something on my face.

"What?" I huff.

"Who is *that* guy?"

"That guy," I mimic his mocking tone, "is Calvin. Willow's nurse and my . . . friend."

"Do nurses usually provide a door-to-door service, or is that reserved for the hotter single guardians?" His grin is teasing, but his voice is deadpan.

I'll skip over the fact that he called me hot—again—but my heart *does* skip a beat. I choose not to respond to Warren and instead kneel down to take Willow out of her car seat.

I stand and curl Willow into my chest. "Willow, meet Warren. Our grumpiest roommate."

Just then, Luke pops out of his room. His face beams as he steps quickly toward me. He signs hello a few times and reaches out for Willow's hand. I look at Warren, who must literally be glued to the floor in order to resist taking a closer look at the world's cutest baby.

Eventually, he moves to tap Luke on the shoulder. "Let's clear the hallway. Let Willow see the rest of the apartment." They filter out into the living room; Warren sinks into the armchair and Luke onto the couch.

I look down at Willow and up at the apartment around me. I have wanted her here for so long—the moment feels surreal. A wave of anxiety passes through me as I realize that what was a team of nurses, pediatricians, cardiologists, and respiratory therapists is now only me. I'm incredibly unsupervised.

I sit down on the sofa and lay Willow between Luke and me. She is shy of three months, but she is the size of a one-month-old, weighing only ten pounds.

"Can I hold her?" Luke asks. I look at Warren for permission, hoping to avoid another loft incident, and he nods.

"Of course. Remember to support her neck." I reach down to lift Willow into Luke's lap.

Luke's smile widens as he looks down at her in the crook of his arm. He's a natural. Perhaps he's had younger foster siblings before. I glance toward Warren, who watches Luke with a worried expression. I try to meet his eye to reassure him, but he doesn't look away from them.

After a few minutes, Willow fusses, and Luke tenses before looking at me to take her. I smile and lift her onto my chest, leaning her on me so I can make use of my hands.

"You did great. She's a little fussy because it is time to eat."

I move toward the bouncer chair in the corner of the room, placing her gently inside so I can go make a bottle. Taking the formula out of the diaper bag, I get to work in the kitchen. The gurgles and grunts get progressively louder.

Looking back toward Willow, Warren and Luke are nowhere to be seen. My heart sinks. I can't help but think humans aren't meant to do this alone. Still, I won't ask for help—not after Warren's judgments and comments. I'll have to do this by myself—but how hard could it be?

ELEVEN

I HAVEN'T SLEPT LONGER THAN TWO CONSECUTIVE hours in a week. Willow hates sleep. She also hates the bassinet, my bed, her bouncer chair, her play mat. Pretty much everything except my arms.

I didn't know how good I had it before, when I could lie in bed until my bladder forced me up. I could fall asleep without worrying about not getting at least six hours—even if I stayed up way too late. My body is no longer 80 percent water. It's now mostly coffee sloshing around in my veins.

I bring Willow's bouncer chair into the kitchen so I can make my breakfast. She fusses as I bounce the seat with my foot, trying to stretch across the kitchen to find ingredients. I'm out of milk. As well as eggs, bread, cheese, and basically everything else—though I knew that yesterday. I close the fridge and grab a granola bar from Luke's box on the counter.

Not my finest moment, stealing from a minor, but I'll pay him back.

The coffee pot fills, and I'll have to drink it black. I've never had the taste for black coffee before, but now I can't seem to function without it. I make Willow a bottle, and for a desperate second, consider splashing some into my mug. *No,* I tell myself, *you can't use formula in place of creamer.* I bring both of our liquid breakfasts to the couch. Watching the sunrise may be the only perk of guardianship so far. *And Willow too . . . obviously.*

Warren's door opens, and I count the fourteen steps he takes from his room to Luke's. Same thing every morning. Warren wakes up long before the 7:30 alarm he insists they both set, walks to Luke's door, opens it, flips the lights on, then waits about twenty seconds before entering. Luke showers while Warren makes them both breakfast, usually cereal or toast and eggs.

Afterward, he makes their lunches while Luke tidies up. Then, without saying or signing a word to me or each other, they're out the door by half past eight. Today will be no different, I'm sure.

Someone speaks. "Uh. You okay there?"

I stare out the window as the pink sky grows more orange.

"Chloe?" the voice says. *Oh, that's me.*

"Mmm. What?"

"You all right?" Warren stands at the back of the couch. I don't have the energy to look up to his face, but there's judgment in his tone all the same—and something new. Pity, I think.

"Yeah . . . why?"

"Because you're attempting to feed the couch cushion a bottle."

Huh? Oh, shit. I look down at my right hand, where the bottle is, and realize Willow is on my left, fast asleep.

"Oh . . ." I put the bottle on the coffee table. A small whimper makes its way out of my mouth as a few tears break loose. *Boy, am I tired.* "Sorry . . . haven't slept." I don't turn toward Warren. I would rather not read his expression right now. No doubt it's something along the lines of *poor spoiled girl, not so easy now, is it?*

My eyes close involuntarily to accept a few moments of rest as Willow sleeps beside me. I startle awake at the sound of a creak coming from the arm of the couch. Turning, I find Willow resting comfortably along Warren's forearm.

He nods at me, a half smile pushing out his lips, then turns to walk toward Luke's room. He opens the door, pauses, and leaves after waking Luke up with Willow still curled around him like a koala cub. My eyes follow him intently as he walks toward the kitchen and pulls out two bowls for cereal.

He speaks to me without turning. "You want to go shower or something?"

I could cry tears of happiness. "Uh, sure. Okay. Um, is that all right?"

Warren turns to look at me with pity and nods.

I will probably pay for this later, but I need this far too much to have pride right now. I run upstairs to get baby-vomit-free clothes, the last set I can find, and practically sprint to the bathroom. I let the hot water from the shower hit my back for a full minute before I even start washing myself. It is glorious. Does Warren picture me in here involuntarily the way I've pictured him? Nope, not wasting precious shower time on that.

As I pull my clothes on, there's a faint knock at the door. I zip up my jeans and open it to find Luke in the hallway.

"Morning," I sign.

"Hey." We step around each other, and I make my way back toward the kitchen, my hair still in a towel. I feel like a new person.

"Thank you so much." I reach to take Willow from Warren's arms, and he presents her to me like a trophy. "I really needed that shower. Thank you."

He smiles mischievously. "The shower was mostly for our benefit."

I roll my eyes but can't seem to shake off my grin. "Well, either way, thank you. Really, thanks."

"You can stop saying that now."

"What?" I ask, confused.

"Thank you," Warren replies flatly.

"Well, I just want to be clear. You made it pretty obvious help was off the table, so I want to show my appreciation—before you start resenting me, that is." Am I tired or is it simply easier to be honest when you know someone already doesn't like you? *Either way* . . .

Warren takes a bite of his toast and stares me down, pinning me to the spot. I wait for him to speak, but he doesn't, as usual.

"What?" I ask, again.

"Nothing." Warren's eyes glance down my frame and back up slowly until our eyes lock on each other.

"You're staring," I force out, quiet but determined.

"You're nice to look at—especially when you're clean." He winks, and somewhere, an angel gets its wings.

"Don't say stuff like that," I fire back.

He tilts his head, managing to chew toast and smile devilishly. "Why?"

"Because friends compliment each other. You don't want to be friends, remember?"

"Yeah, you're probably right." He doesn't look away though.

"Well, thanks again." I turn and take Willow upstairs to get her dressed.

As soon as I lay her down on the edge of my bed to get her diaper off, I hear my phone begin ringing downstairs. They'll have to leave a voicemail. Hopefully it's not a prospective client—I need the work.

I change Willow into her clothes for the day, and she fusses from the cold air of the apartment hitting her skin. I grab a spare outfit, diaper, and pacifier and throw them into an old tote bag to bring with me to the store before heading back downstairs. "We're venturing out today, Will, whether you like it or not. Big sisters have to eat too."

I reach into the side of the couch and pull out my phone—Calvin called. The second time since he dropped us at home. *Not a fan of texting, I guess.* I add *call Calvin back* to today's list of tasks, alongside groceries, laundry, work, and sleep. *Please.*

"Where are you going this morning?" Luke asks from the dining table.

"Grocery store. I owe you a granola bar, by the way."

"Don't worry about it."

I glance toward Warren, whose back is fortunately turned. "Thanks."

"You're welcome to anything with an *L* on it." He gestures toward the fridge. "I don't mind sharing."

"Neither do I." I smile.

Warren clears his throat, and Luke follows my glance toward him. He signs to Luke, "You ready to go?"

Luke takes his bowl to the sink, giving it a quick wash before placing it in the dish rack. I haven't lived with any fifteen-year-old boys before, but this one seems particularly easy. I feel bad for the presumptions I made before we met. He's a good kid. His brother might not be so bad either.

I got out the door as the boys were getting their shoes on. It's not a competition, but I did win. I hit the sidewalk outside our building, pushing Willow's stroller ahead of me with one hand and a to-go cup of nasty black coffee in the other. The woman who tried to feed her couch a bottle this morning is long gone. *I have my shit together, world. Look at me!*

There is a fifteen-minute walk ahead of me to the grocery store, so I give Calvin a call back. Efficiency is my new middle name.

"Hey, sorry I missed your call," I say quickly as soon as he answers.

"No worries. I thought maybe it was too early anyway, but I was leaving work."

"Headed home to sleep?" I couldn't contain the sound of my jealousy, even if I tried.

"I have a couple of errands to run, but then yes. What is your day looking like?"

"We've finally left the house today. Going to get groceries and do some laundry if Will cooperates. I have a project that is nearing overdue, and I need a good nap." I'm rambling. "So . . . errands too, I guess."

"Well, next time, let me know, and I'll tag along." He means help, which is sweet because he doesn't say it.

"Yeah, thanks. I'd like that," I say.

"I have to go, but while I have you . . . I was wondering if you were free next weekend. I don't work either day, which is rare. I was thinking we could watch a movie while Willow sleeps?"

"She doesn't sleep, she rests. It's sort of her thing."

"Oh, I remember. She kept me on my toes at night. I envied the nurses with older kids many times."

I laugh. "But yes, that sounds nice."

"Okay. Talk soon," Calvin says.

"Bye." I hang up and slip the phone into the stroller's caddy. Showered, on my way to get groceries, have a potential date lined up—today is going my way.

TWELVE

I SQUEEZE A WEEK'S WORTH OF GROCERIES INTO THE bottom of Willow's stroller and hook a few bags on the handle-bars before heading back out into the early-autumn day. Just under three months ago, I left this parking lot to meet my sister for the first time, and today, I left the store with her. If anyone had labeled me as the local grocery-cart abandoner, they didn't show it. There were no wanted posters, at least.

I still feel as unqualified to be a guardian as I did that day, but I haven't questioned my decision once. I won't. Willow should be with family. Everyone should be, if they have a choice.

I decide to take the long way home through the park since the stroller seems to be the one thing Willow doesn't vocalize her ha-tred toward. *Another victory*. The trees are browning, and crisp leaves crackle under the spinning wheels of the buggy. The air is still and peaceful. I talk out loud to Willow—I read somewhere that it's a good thing to do with babies.

"Someday we'll come here to go on the slide at the playground,

Will. Would you like that?" She isn't much of a conversationalist, but I persevere. "You're going to love the park. You can go on the swings, climb ladders. You'll do it all." I look down at her, still so small but growing every day. "I'm so proud of you, Will. You're doing so well."

Strong brows, strong noses, strong bodies, strong hearts. Another woman born into this family—already proving our mother right with her ability to survive all she threw at her.

I pass by a group of teenagers huddled together and spot a familiar face resting against a fence post. From the path, I can see Luke clearly, but I doubt he can see me. He's with some friends, a few girls, but mostly guys—they all look to be his age. The girls are signing back and forth, though I can't make out what they're saying from here. I should probably keep going and mind my own business. But is he allowed to leave school property mid-morning?

"Willow, don't look now, but your friend Luke is over there. Do you know what a group of teenagers is called? Hooligans."

I step back to get momentum to push the heavy stroller forward after stopping to look. I notice one of the girls handing Luke a cigarette. Actually, based on the smell that's wafting around the park—it's not a cigarette at all. *I know that smell, kid.* I spot a picnic table about fifteen feet away from their group and push Willow toward it. I won't shame him in front of his friends, but I do want him to know he's busted.

I sit at the table and take my coffee out of the stroller caddy. Simply a mom sitting with her daughter at the park. Luke's friends will be none the wiser. Luke spots me, and I do a polite wave. He stiffens but plays it cool for the sake of his comrades, who are now looking my way as well. I pull out my phone to appear unaware. When I look back up, the group is making their way to the park's exit, which, if I remember correctly, is at least in the direction of their school.

I rise from the table, feeling victorious. "We're going to have to talk to Grumps later, Willow. Your friend Luke was up to no good." These are probably not the phrases the mommy blogs would recommend, but they'll have to do.

A few hours after we've returned home, I get Willow down for her nap and throw myself dramatically back on the couch. As I twiddle my thumbs, I try to decide whether to work, eat, nap, or do laundry. Option *E,* scrolling on my phone, seems like the obvious choice. As I pull it out of my back pocket, the apartment door unlocks and opens. Luke's backpack hits the floor, and I check the time—it's far too early for him to be home. No sign of Warren either. I sit up so I can see the hallway from the couch.

"Hey."

"Hi." Luke walks around to sit on the floor in front of the armchair.

"You all right?"

"No." His eyes are blank.

"Want to talk about it?"

"I know you saw me earlier." Luke bites his cheek.

I shuffle my leg under me, bracing for a tricky conversation. "Yeah, I did."

"Are you going to tell Warren?"

"I think I should."

Luke leans, placing the back of his head onto the seat of the chair. His eyes stare up at the ceiling far above us. He has one benefit that most teenagers don't have, I suppose, being able to tune out adults whenever he wants.

I throw a couch pillow on his lap. "You know, Warren will probably go easier on you if you tell him first."

"I think I'm fucked either way."

"Okay, dial it back. I'm also fairly certain you're not supposed to be home from school right now."

"I don't feel well."

Luke's skin is paler than usual. There's a slight sheen to his forehead, and his eyes are red. "Nauseous?" I ask.

"Yeah."

"Was that your first time, Luke? Getting high?" I have no idea if I signed that right—it wasn't something I'd expect my dad to teach me.

"Yeah."

"Is that the truth?" I ask.

"No."

I can't help but grin. "When Warren gets home, I'll go upstairs and give you guys some room to talk." I stand to make some lunch. Luke is staring at the ground in front of him, picking at the carpet. "Hungry?"

"Yes." Luke pushes his lips into an exaggerated frown as he signs.

"All right, come on." I gesture to the kitchen, and he follows close behind.

I make Luke a grilled cheese sandwich, and he carries it off to his bedroom after a quick nod of appreciation. I don't imagine Warren will go easy on him, but then again, I probably wouldn't either if it was Willow. I wish, with all of my heart, that I never have to find out. Smoking pot is one thing, but with our family history? Anything is a risk.

I've stayed far away from anything addictive. Well, besides caffeine. And sugar. And the occasional glass of wine too. Thankfully, I've never been inclined to enjoy in excess—though perhaps my current coffee intake could be cut back.

I hope, wherever she is, that Connie is okay. I hope her stitches healed, and I hope she kept them clean. When Odette called the day after I brought Willow home, she hadn't heard from her. "Not yet," she had said, as if Connie's reappearance was inevitable. We'd talked for an hour or so. Odette is a great listener—someone I would trust with the deepest parts of me, if I knew how to access them all. We talked about the loneliness I didn't expect to feel while having a constant companion. She assured me that it's normal.

I'm only one week into parenting, and I know I should allow myself more time for these feelings to pass, but I'm tired down to my bones. The loneliness that has been hanging over me for years threatens to swallow me up. I miss a life I never got to live—the one with the found family and friends I didn't get the chance to find. I grieve for it.

Odette suggested making a list of all the things I'll get to do, now that I have Willow, but it would be a long list of disingenuous hopes. All the milestones I look forward to, but none of my own. Only Willow's. Perhaps parenthood is always putting yourself on the back burner.

Maybe that's why my adoptive parents don't take kindly to the choices I've made. Namely, graphic design, self-employment, fostering Willow—I'm on a roll in recent years of messing up my mother's vision for my life. If I can do anything for Will, it'll be supporting her choices as she grows up. They'll be *hers,* after all.

THIRTEEN

"CHLOE!" WARREN'S AGITATED VOICE BOOMS THROUGH the floor of my loft. I roll my computer chair over to the side of my desk and pop my head over the ledge.

"Yes?" My tone mistakenly comes out more confused than concerned.

"Can you come down here?" His voice is stern, a command in the form of a question. Luke better not have thrown me under the bus—I made him a sandwich!

"Okay." Willow's no longer asleep but chewing on her fist with enthusiasm. I'll use her as a human shield. *She sorta owes me.*

"What's up?" Luke is sitting with his head hanging. Warren stands at the end of the table, arms crossed and scowling.

Warren speaks and signs at the same time, even though Luke isn't looking up at him. "So I hear that you had a run-in with Luke at the park today."

I'm not sure when to speak, so I wait.

"Luke also told me he came home three hours early from school, and the two of you had a lovely lunch together."

My lips curl slightly. I'm nervous, and something about Warren saying *lovely* is amusing. Evidently, my nervous smile pisses him off. His jaw tenses and his foot begins to tap in sporadic movements against the hardwood floor.

"Really appreciate you taking the time to tell me." Warren glares as he signs.

"I told Luke I thought it would be best for him to talk to you. That I would if he didn't." Luke watches me as I speak, but I don't sign. I shuffle Willow, repeat myself, then continue while signing, "I didn't want to get between you two."

"You did the moment you decided to not tell me he was skipping school. I didn't know where he was. Well, I thought I did! I thought he was at school!" Warren's face is turning red. "But then his teacher called me saying he missed the last two periods. Imagine my surprise when I rushed home to see him passed out in his bed, smelling of skunk, with a nicely prepared grilled cheese next to his pillow."

I bite my tongue. *Do not laugh.*

"This is not funny." Warren's low timbre sends a cold wave of air over the room. I bring Willow closer to my chest, tucking her against me fully.

"I know. I'm sorry. I laugh when I'm nervous."

Warren pinches the bridge of his nose. "I knew this would fucking happen."

"What?" I respond, frustrated.

Warren shifts his weight, and for a moment, it seems as if he's going to turn and walk away. Instead, he plants himself so every part of him is facing me. He rubs a hand over his head furiously, as if he is trying to calm himself through his own skull.

"We are not teammates, okay?" Warren yells. My body stiffens, and my joints lock in response. There is nothing handsome about Warren's face as he loses his temper. There is no glint in his eye or warmth to the edge of his mouth. "This isn't good cop/bad cop. You do not get to make any sort of decisions when it comes to my brother. You should have called me the moment you saw him at the park."

I look down at my feet. I haven't felt at the mercy of someone's temper since I moved out for university. There was a reason I chose to move away from home and stay away. I hate it. I hate feeling like I've let someone down. Like I'm inherently bad or wrong. Tears brim my eyes. "I know. I'm—"

Warren interrupts, more flustered than before. "You don't have any say over our lives." His tone switches toward the end, sounding like someone reaching their breaking point—voice pitching higher and shaky.

I step backward until the backs of my legs find a chair; I sit. Maybe if I show him I'm not a physical threat, he'll relax, like a bear or something. "I know that, Warren."

"Okay." He throws his hands up, exasperated, but hesitates as some familiarity falls back into his expression. His eyes fall to the floor as he wipes his nose with a knuckle before putting his hands on his hips. He shakes his hanging head.

When he looks up, there is no arrogant mask or anger. His face tells me a different story—he's embarrassed. After a moment of looking between Luke and me, trying to form words, he turns away and storms down the hall to his bedroom.

When my parents would punish me, they'd dismiss me after. Usually by saying, "Go to your room" or "We're done talking," and I would know what to do, at the very least, to not make things worse. Now, I have no idea. . . . I guess it's up to me. I take Willow back to our room, feeling a profound sense of defeat.

Two silent hours pass. After composing and deleting several lengthy text messages about roommate boundaries, emotional outbursts, and a sprinkling of apologies, I carry Willow downstairs. I place her on the play mat in the living room, then go to make dinner.

Warren and Luke are still shut away in their rooms, and there are no signs of life other than the sound of Willow's coos and jingling toys. I decided upstairs that the best strategy would be to make enough spaghetti and meatballs for the house—a peace offering of sorts. An olive oil–infused branch.

The expression that fell over Warren before he shut himself away told me everything I needed to know. He was far more upset with himself for blowing up than he was at Luke or me.

Having Willow with me has its challenges, but at least I have over a decade of time before being thrown into raising a teenager. Warren is doing his best in an impossible situation, though he *could* be less of a jerk about it.

I'm straining the pasta when the sound of Warren's door opening disrupts the otherwise quiet apartment. I take a deep breath in, reminding my nervous system that I have every right to take up space here. He can be pissed, but he can't make me uncomfortable in my own home—I won't give him that power.

I scoop three portions of pasta into the bowls laid out on the counter as Warren approaches from down the hall. His footsteps stop at the corner of the kitchen, and I hear him softly shut a drawer that I'd left open. He doesn't move. I turn, two servings in hand, and walk toward him.

For the one who did the yelling this afternoon, he does an ex-

tremely convincing impression of a scorned child. His head hangs
until he can probably see my feet, then he slowly looks up. Eyes
heavy and hesitant. There is possibly even fear. Of me? Strange.
Not once, even during his yelling, was I fearful of him. Nervous,
sure . . . but not scared.

I tilt my head toward the living room while holding up the two
bowls, gesturing for him to follow me, and we sit next to each
other on the couch.

"Thanks." He takes his dinner from me, and then we sit in silence while I try to slurp my noodles back as quietly as possible.

When I place my empty bowl on the coffee table, I turn to see
that Warren has barely touched his food. He catches my eye
briefly before speaking. "I'm sorry for earlier. That was not okay."

I nod, almost missing the uncomfortable silence.

"I get angry sometimes. It . . ." He hesitates. "I'm working on
it, among other things . . . in therapy." His voice is low and raspy,
sounding like the ghost of his usual self.

"It's all right."

"But it isn't." He tucks one bent leg up on the couch cushion so
his body faces mine. His eyes are deep in thought and not entirely
looking my way. I swear a person could spend years trying to decipher all the inner workings behind Warren's eyes. "It's not okay,
and I'm sorry." His nostrils flare as he looks down at his lap. I can
practically hear the lecture he's giving himself. No need to pile
on. "Fuck . . . I—"

I interrupt. "I should have called you. I know that now. I think
I was trying to balance being Luke's roommate and yours—but
that was wrong. He's a kid. Even though we aren't a . . . team, I
should have placed your interests above his."

Warren chews his lip as he looks toward my face.

I choose to speak instead of thinking about the swirling in my chest that occurs when he looks at me so carefully. "*Team* is a weird term, right?"

"Mutually beneficial cohabitants." His stare doesn't relent as he responds, but his voice is less grave.

"MBC for short?" I jest.

"You could redesign those god-awful pamphlets Rachel had." The usual confidence in his voice returns somewhat.

I smile. "I would really like to."

Warren picks at the skin around his thumb and seems to be collecting his thoughts. I look away to give him the space to do so.

"I'm glad you care about Luke though. Not many people have. He's a good kid. He makes poor judgment calls when he's trying to impress people—a family trait." Warren continues before I can get a word in: "I do ask that you don't get too close. In just over five months, we'll be out of each other's lives. I've been looking at another school a few cities over—housing is a bit easier to find around there, and I could commute or find another shop to work at."

He pauses to look up from his hands in his lap. "I don't want to see him lose anyone else." His expression is full of weariness that tightens his jaw.

I take a moment to consider carefully what to say next. "I won't overstep again but . . . what you're asking doesn't really feel fair. For any of us. This is my home too, and I don't want to be walking on eggshells or live this . . . distantly."

I hold his eye contact timidly. "If I'm being honest, I could use some backup. Today was the first time since Willow has been home that I even felt a little bit like me, simply because of a shower. I don't want to feel scared to ask for help every now and then. We can keep things separate but still be human."

"Human?" A glint of teasing returns to his eyes.

"Think hunter-gatherer style. For the betterment of our young and our survival."

"What do you suggest?" Warren asks.

I'm happy to see a small curl return to the corner of Warren's lip.

"One grocery list—we can still label items, but there's no point doing two trips. You make breakfasts, and I'll make dinners. We'll split the bill fifty-fifty. I won't interfere with Luke, but I will be his friend—because I like him, and because he might need a friend other than his grumpy older brother."

I give him a coy smile. "Sometimes I'll ask you or Luke to hold Willow when I need ten minutes to myself. We can stop orbiting and perhaps start checking in with each other—so we don't blow up when shit gets hard."

"Okay . . . that can work." Warren pushes out his bottom lip as he nods softly.

"Okay, good," I respond triumphantly. *I honestly thought it would take a lot more convincing.*

Warren takes both of our dishes and opens Luke's door. A moment later, they both step out, and Warren pats Luke, who is now carrying my bowl, on the back.

Warren signs, "And Luke will do the dishes."

Luke seems to be relieved—cleaning duties might be less harsh a punishment than he was expecting.

FOURTEEN

"WHERE ARE YOU TWO HEADED SO EARLY?" WARREN takes Willow from me, freeing my hands so I can lift the car seat and diaper bag onto the dining table. He boops her nose when he thinks I'm not looking.

"We have Willow's first cardiologist follow-up at ten at the hospital. It wouldn't take so damn long if the buses were back to back, but we have a thirty-minute wait between our second and third bus." I shove another baby bottle of water into the diaper bag and go to the kitchen to fill up the formula container.

"Three buses?"

Warren sounds as if he's asking Willow, but I answer for her. "Yep."

He shifts Willow onto his chest, holding her head against him with one palm while her bum rests in the bend of his arm. Something about the way he can carry her with one hand and how small she looks in his arms makes me swoon. How natural it is for him to hold her, like she weighs absolutely nothing at all. He takes a long sip of his water and watches me go around the kitchen. *Always staring.*

"What?" I ask incredulously.

Warren grins into his glass and shakes his head before replying, "Can you drive?"

"I'm saving for a car—you know that."

"That isn't what I asked," he says, smirking.

"Yes, I can drive," I huff.

"Safely?" Warren is almost mocking in tone.

"I think so?"

I glare at him, and his stupid smirk grows in response. *He enjoys my annoyance.* Warren tilts his head back and forth, deciding *something.* "Fine."

"Fine, what?"

He pulls a set of car keys out of his jeans pocket and rattles them. "You'll have to drop Luke and me off and pick us up, but you can have my car . . . for today."

Before I think, I'm crossing the kitchen and throwing my arms around his waist. I press the side of my head into his chest, opposite from Willow's. "Thank you!" *I really didn't want to take the bus.*

The cotton of his shirt is soft under my fingers, but nothing else about him is. The hard lines of his chest are all solid muscle and bone. He smells like the softest hint of fuel and rust—sort of like an old penny. Not something I'd normally find sexy, but *damn* if it isn't wafting straight from my nose into my pulse. I'm suddenly aware of my breasts as they push into his side, pressing farther with each inhale I take of his intoxicating scent. I've been here for far too long. *Move away, Chloe.* I pause and lift my chin to see his face.

He looks down at me with a pained expression that makes me

step back until my hands find the countertop behind me. "Sorry," I mumble.

He frowns after clearing his throat. "Don't be."

"When, um, when do you get off?" I ask.

His eyes widen, and one side of his lip curls up.

"Off work! When do you get off work?" My cheeks heat.

"Four."

I nod, take the keys from him, and put them into the diaper bag. "I guess we have time for breakfast after all, Will." I avoid eye contact with Warren like my life depends on it.

I reach for her as Warren speaks. "Yes. Duty calls."

He makes us scrambled eggs and toast. Luke joins us at the table, and we all eat breakfast together, as we have since our negotiations last week. Whether Warren wants to admit it or not, I think Willow and I are both growing on him. He picked her up out of her bouncer chair last night, then read a book on the couch as she slept on his chest.

I hadn't even asked, and it gave me a chance to catch up on work. Moments like that, and these breakfasts together, keep the loneliness at bay. I'm starting to dread the end of these five months.

"I'll clean up." Luke gathers all of our plates and heads to the kitchen.

Warren faces me. "So, I have a favor to ask." I think about the car keys sitting in my diaper bag, perhaps not a kind gesture as much as a bribe.

"Yes?" I ask skeptically.

"It's my birthday next weekend, and I was wondering if I could have a few people over on Saturday."

I raise an eyebrow. "Bryce?"

Warren smirks. "Yes, he would be one of them."

I sigh. "I mean, this is your house too. You can have people over. Let me know when to make myself scarce."

"Oh, right." Warren's face falls. Was he going to ask me to hang out with him and his friends? *Surely not.* "Thanks." *Didn't think so.* Still, a twinge of disappointment rises up. I want to be invited, even if it's out of pity.

Oh, wait, Saturday—I forgot. "I actually have someone coming over Saturday too. Sorry, I should have asked."

"Nurse boy?" It's better than last week's nickname—*Scrubs.*

"Calvin, yes." I stand to get Willow ready to leave.

"And, I mean, you'll be hanging out upstairs. . . ." He says this as if it is a question despite there not being one at all.

I nod, studying his expression that tells me nothing.

Warren purses his lips. "Cool." He turns to grab his lunch from the kitchen, and my eyes follow him for a change as he putters around. He reaches for the top cupboard where he keeps his snacks—knowing full well the rest of us can't reach them. His shirt raises a little, and I catch a glimpse of his toned abdomen. My thighs squeeze together.

Warren is hot. There is no denying it. Unfortunately, he's also well aware of that fact. I wonder if one of these friends coming over is a girlfriend. I bet she's gorgeous. I bet she also has a Pavlovian response to the smell of fuel now too.

Luke clears his throat, and I snap my attention toward the end of the hallway where he's standing, looking at me with amused annoyance. "You're drooling," Luke signs as he waltzes past me to grab his backpack.

"Shut up," I fire back. He raises an eyebrow as he slings the backpack over his shoulder.

"No I was not!" *Shit, was I?* That's the second time this morning I've felt all . . . wound up . . . because of Warren. I can't go there.

There's no safety net with Warren. He's too close, too gorgeous, too brooding, too intriguing. Plus there's the whole *if he leaves, Willow goes into care* thing. That little fact alone is enough to wash my attraction away.

"Time to go, Will." I gently buckle her into the car seat on top of the stroller, and we all funnel out of the apartment in silence.

We step out of the elevator and take the side exit out of the building. If I get a car within the next few months, we'll have to fight over who gets the parking spot. I put Willow's car seat in the back and strap her in. Luke sits next to her, and Warren slips into the passenger side.

I try to act casual as I get into the driver's seat. His car is as sexy as he is—perhaps more so—I can't ride Warren to the other side of town, after all. *Do not go there, brain.*

The car has a smooth, black leather interior, built-up stereo, and the driver's seat tilted back to the heavens. Why do men always think the farther they sit from the steering wheel, the cooler they are? *Why are they a little right?* I make quick work of adjusting the seat and mirrors as Warren grins my way.

"Whenever you're ready." He huffs out a laugh at my expense. The electronic seat hums as it moves closer to the front. I fight the urge to flip him off as the seat stops at a comfortable distance for my short legs.

Warren's car is far more powerful than my parents' Mitsubishi I learned to drive in, so I may have pressed a little too hard on the gas pedal as we exited the parking lot. To his credit, he didn't react other than a quick glance at the speedometer.

We drop Luke off first and watch him walk toward a group of friends outside the main set of doors of the school. "Those are the ones I saw him with—at the park," I say.

Warren scratches his chin as he tilts to get a better view.

"They look relatively harmless," I suggest, hoping to ease Warren's furrowed brow. "He's a good kid." I send him my best encouraging smile, subtle but warm. Warren sighs before he starts to direct me to his work.

About ten minutes later, I pull into a mechanic's garage at the end of an industrial road. Warren points to a parking space with a peace sign spray-painted onto the fence in front, and I pull in.

"Like *War and Peace*?" I ask. "That's what they call you, right? War?"

He blinks rapidly before tilting his head to answer, but he's interrupted by a double knock on my window. I glance quickly at Warren, who nods, before I roll it down.

"Well, hello." An older man, probably around sixty, is standing next to the car, his body turned to the side. He has a long gray beard and is stout in stature.

"Hi," I reply, looking back briefly toward the passenger seat, which is now vacant.

"I take it you're the roommate?"

An awkward laugh finds its way out before Warren steps up next to the man. "Morning, Ram," Warren says. Another nickname? *I kinda want one.*

"War," Ram acknowledges Warren's greeting, but his eyes shift between me and the backseat—where he focuses, a small smile falling under his thick beard and mustache. "I'm Ram. This is my shop."

"Nice to meet you, I'm Chloe."

"Good to meet you, Chloe. Heard a lot about you."

I look toward Warren. *Heard a lot about me?* Surely he'd hate to admit that he's been talking about me . . . but Warren doesn't react in the slightest, not even a little embarrassed.

"Belle!" Ram shouts, and I watch in the rearview mirror as a woman a similar age to his own steps out of the garage. She's dressed head to toe in denim, and her bleached-blond hair could land a plane. I instantly love her.

"Chloe doesn't have all day, Ram," Warren pipes up, but he looks resigned. Belle steps up next to Ram.

"Well, hello, darlin'." Belle could be a Dolly Parton impersonator, in voice and body.

I smile so wide that my cheeks push into my eyes. "Hello, I'm Chloe."

She nods and looks at the backseat, then toward Warren, as she points to Willow. "And this must be . . . ?"

Warren nods and opens the car door, allowing her in. I truthfully thought that no one in his life would know we exist, let alone be excited to meet us. *Or have heard a lot about us.* My heart flutters a little at that thought.

Belle slips into the backseat and gasps as she looks Willow over. "Oh my! Well, aren't you the most beautiful babe I've ever seen? Hello, little one!"

Warren stands back, arms crossed and smiling to himself. He looks proud—of what, exactly, I'm not sure.

"All right, really. Willow has an appointment she needs to get to." Warren looks at Ram for backup, as if he'd need to be the one to pull Belle away.

"Well, all righty then. You take care of her now. 'Kay, Chloe? And yourself." Belle taps me gently on my shoulder.

"Will do."

"Good girl. Nice to meet you." She shuts the door of the backseat, and I lean out the window to respond.

"Nice to meet you too!"

Ram and Belle walk back to the shop, hands in each other's

back pockets, and Warren takes a step toward the car, lowering his head to my window.

"They seem nice." I don't bother to hide the gleam in my eyes or my *you do care about us!* shit-eating grin.

"They are, yeah." He studies my expression and rolls his eyes. He looks as if he's going to say something, but he changes his mind, smiling as he taps the roof of the car. "See you at four." He walks away as I roll up the window. I drive all the way to Willow's appointment wearing an unwavering smile.

FIFTEEN

"NOT THE BEST NEWS, I'M AFRAID." DOCTOR O'LEARY flips a chart two times, then hands me the page. I have no idea what I'm looking at. It's a graph with a subtle curve heading upward.

"We would hope to see this line, which represents the blood pressure in her lungs, going down or flattening out. With patent ductus arteriosus, we need to make sure the opening isn't allowing too much blood to flow into her lungs. The higher her blood pressure, the higher the risk is of that happening. She isn't in dangerous territory right now—for hypertension, that is—but we need to be cautious that her blood pressure doesn't keep trending upward."

I scan the page back and forth. I understood a solid 60 percent of what he said. "So what should I do?"

"We'll adjust her medications slightly, and you'll need to bring her in at least once a week until her condition stabilizes. Most likely in a few months' time, we'll see her heart as healthy as it can be. However, if the upward trend in her blood pressure continues or if the opening in her artery doesn't begin closing, we may need to discuss surgical options."

My lips part as I suck in too much air. "Okay."

"Otherwise, she's doing well." He puts his hand out for the chart, and I give it back. "Her weight gain is trending perfectly; her development seems unimpacted by the fetal alcohol syndrome or premature birth. You are doing a terrific job, Chloe." He plants a steady hand on my shoulder, and I take a breath in, a single tear falling down my cheek. It's nice to be told that. Most of the time, I feel absolutely clueless.

"Talk with the front desk on your way out. Our outpatient clinic days are Fridays. You can set a schedule for appointments at the same time each week. Tell them to book for the next eight weeks, and we'll go from there."

I nod and gather our bag and place Willow in her car seat, fighting the tremble of my jaw and putting on a brave face.

After my brief stop at the front desk, I get us both buckled into Warren's car and finally allow the tears to flow freely. I suddenly have so many questions I didn't think to ask the doctor. I text Calvin a few of them. I also add that I'm excited to see him this weekend so he doesn't think I'm using him for his medical database.

CALVIN: Shit, I'm so sorry. I actually have a thing Saturday I can't get out of. Can we reschedule for next week? As far as the medical stuff, I will ask Cardiology and get back to you.
CHLOE: Oh, bummer. No worries. Next week should be fine. Thanks!

I gather myself as best I can and drive home. I think of Connie while I do. I wonder where she is, if she is okay and . . . mostly, I want to know if she understands the impact she's had on Willow's life. On her heart. Possibly forever. I doubt the drinks were worth it.

I think of Willow's dad too—whoever he is. Connie hadn't mentioned him at all, to me or Odette, but I'd love to find out if she knows. Or if she has told him that out there somewhere, he has a kid. I hope not. I wouldn't want anyone coming to find her. Her court hearing is still eight months away, and I'm fairly sure a biological father could contest it if he wanted to—delaying it, at least. I hold my breath at a red light until my lungs hurt just enough. Little doses of control do nothing to help the actual problem. But it feels good. For a moment.

Once home, I get Willow down for her nap. I snuggle her a little longer than usual and lean my ear down to listen to her tiny chest, feeling it rise and fall gently. *I love her so much.* Her wide nose and strong brow match my own. Most strangers will presume I'm her mother. I will benefit from that, I'm sure.

Willow settles in her bassinet after a few minutes of back rubs, and I begin working on my newest commission; posters for an upcoming music festival. I haven't had to cut back on work so far—only sleep. Until I'm confident that Rachel and CPS will be satisfied with my average monthly income, I'll need to keep finding as much work as possible. I can rest when my re-evaluation is over. Or, if not then, when Willow's custody is final.

The time passes slowly until my phone alarm goes off, announcing that it's time to wake Willow and leave to get Luke from school. I allow myself a brief moment of pride as I juggle work, parenting, appointments, and roommate duties while buckling Willow into Warren's car.

I figure out how to turn the stereo on, and a CD begins playing a rock ballad that I don't recognize. It sort of sounds like a mix of Rush and Led Zeppelin, but it's definitely new. I love it. I'll ask Warren who the band is later, or figure out how to eject the CD. *Why does this thing have so many damn buttons?*

As I pull in front of Luke's school and spot him, I honk twice before realizing most of the kids can't hear me, including Luke. A teacher glares, and I offer an embarrassed wave in the form of an apology. Eventually, Luke sees me and waves goodbye to a girl who fiddles with her hair as she looks toward him. I smile to myself. Is that a hint of a crush in her eyes as she watches him throw his bag and body into the front seat?

"Hey! Who is that?" I ask, gesturing out the passenger window.

Luke looks at the girl, already knowing who I mean. "Stephanie."

I nod, pulling the car out of the school's parking lot. I've never had to drive and sign before, and I won't attempt it. Warren's car outranks most people in his life. I absolutely cannot damage it. I claim my chance to speak at the next red light.

"And? Tell me about her."

Luke blushes. "Warren has a no-signing-in-the-car rule." This could be a convenient excuse, but I take the kid at his word. We drive to get Warren from work in silence, other than Willow's gurgles from the back.

"Hey," we all sign in unison as Warren slides himself into the backseat.

"I don't think I've ever sat back here."

"Did you want to switch?" I sign and speak, turning to the backseat as Warren buckles himself in and pushes up the sunshade on Willow's car seat to take a peek at her.

"No. All good." He switches to a silly British accent as he says, "Home please, driver." I roll my eyes and put the car into drive.

Luke turns over his shoulder, and out of the corner of my eye, I can see him signing to Warren—though I can't make out what is being said.

I toss the keys to Warren as we all exit the car, and he does a full loop around, scouring for any damage. I can't even blame him—the fact that he let me borrow his car when I needed to is enough. He won major roommate points today.

"Don't check the front too closely. I did hit a few elderly people on my way out of the hospital's parking lot."

"Mercy kills, really," Warren replies flatly, his eyes creasing as he struggles to contain his amusement. I snort in response, which is in and of itself a mortifying sound, but Warren doesn't react; he's too focused on the car.

I take the stroller out of the trunk as Warren unbuckles Willow's car seat. Luke walks ahead, playing the part of a mopey teenager well. Perhaps his conversation with Warren had been a lecture.

"So how did Willow's appointment go?" Warren holds the door open for me and the stroller.

"Not great. They're adjusting her medications. Her doctor is worried that her blood pressure is increasing. They'll need to see her more often. Every Friday." I look to meet his eyes. Warren has given a lot more than I would have expected him to this past week. I can't bring myself to ask for more.

"Fridays?" He nods, and I do so in return. "Okay," Warren says calmly.

"Okay?" My eyes well up with gratitude.

"Yeah—today worked, didn't it?" Warren is so matter-of-fact it's as if he's forgetting the hard-and-fast rules he tried to put into place over two weeks ago.

"Yes. Um, thank you, Warren." I don't know what possesses

me, but I reach for his hand as we wait for the elevator. I wrap my palm around the back of his knuckles and give a small squeeze. I have got to stop touching him—it does terrible things to my brain. For example, I was momentarily convinced he was turning his hand around to hold mine before the elevator sounded off and I moved to push the stroller inside.

SIXTEEN

I TOLD WARREN NOT TO WORRY ABOUT THE NOISE DURING his party tonight, that if Willow woke up, I would deal with her—it's not like she's a great sleeper anyway—but *fuck,* his friends are loud.

I take a peek over the balcony, the third I've allowed myself since they all arrived. There are six people: Bryce, another guy I saw at the garage on Monday morning but didn't meet, and two ladies and their boyfriends, I presume, since they sit draped over the men's laps. One of the women is particularly loud and possibly drunk. She has squealed several times that she wants to "go dancing" and she's "too hot not to be out on a Saturday." I *briefly* find myself envying Luke.

It seems as if Warren didn't know what kind of party he was setting up for this evening, despite it being his own. He ordered a few pizzas and put out a few bottles of cheap alcohol, then a nice bottle of wine and a playlist fit for an indie coming-of-age movie. The wine threw me off the most. Warren doesn't strike me as a wine guy. He put out a few of my wineglasses too, next to the red plastic cups.

I've been putting up a good fight for over an hour, but my bladder, once again, betrays me. I check myself in the mirror of my room. I may have put on an outfit that wouldn't stand out at a party, just in case I was invited to stick around. A long-sleeve sheer black blouse tucked into my best pair of jeans that really show off the curve of my . . . *assets.*

The bra underneath is a bright purple, and you can make out the shape, color, and texture of the lace from under the thin material of my shirt. It's nothing compared to what the other women downstairs are wearing; they look like models. *Gorgeous, half-naked models.* I'm simply trying to blend in, right? Not compete.

I descend the spiral staircase, and the loud one squeals, "Oh my god! Have you been up there the whole time?"

I look past her to Warren, who blinks rapidly at me as he leans forward in his chair. Before I answer her, Warren says, "This is my roommate, Chloe." His eyes slowly trace my body from the floor to the top of my head, and his jaw ticks. Goosebumps form on my arms under the intensity of his stare. *The shirt is working.* "She has a hot date tonight." He takes a swig of beer as his brow creases.

I hesitate, enjoying his reaction, but decide to correct him anyway. "Actually, I don't. I have to use the bathroom. Sorry to interrupt." I glide past them all, doing my best to seem casual, and catch my breath when I close the bathroom door. After I wash up, I reapply some mascara.

Bryce speaks as I head back upstairs, passing behind the couch. "Hey, Chloe, join us." A few people echo their approval, and I look to Warren, who gestures to the empty seat next to him. A tiny rush of pride at being invited to sit streaks through me, like I got invited to sit at the cool kids' lunch table.

I sit, and the loud woman brings me a beer.

"Thanks." I smile up at her.

"I'm Giorgianna. You can call me GiGi. That's my boyfriend, Tyler." The man in the darkened part of the room closest to the dining table raises his cup in lieu of a greeting. "That's Cassie and her boyfriend, Caleb. OMG! I just realized your names both start with a *C*!" Cassie and Caleb both wave, so I do as well. I give a quick sideways glance to Warren, who is reading the label of his beer like it's revealing the secrets of the universe.

"I'm Matt. Nice to meet you." The man sitting next to Bryce leans forward to shake my hand. He seems the safest person to talk to, the most approachable. Handsome too. His eyes are piercing like Warren's, but there's less weight to them. He's got long black hair with a slight wave to it, a full beard, and warm brown skin.

"And you remember Bryce," Warren pipes up from next to me. I smile politely but turn my flaming eyes to Warren. He smirks into the top of his beer.

"Nice to meet you all." I swallow my pride. "Nice to see you again, Bryce."

GiGi sits back down after fetching a drink and goes back to her conversation with Tyler and C squared. Bryce stands and goes to the dining table to pour himself another drink. The music blaring from the stereo doesn't quite fit the vibe. More *acoustic chill* versus *low-key frat house*. But it's the most action this living room has seen in a long time. It's good for the apartment's soul.

Matt slides down the couch to the seat closest to me, facing the center of the living room. Warren perks up next to me.

"So, Chloe, what happened to your date?" Matt is definitely a little tipsy, slurring his words, but his warm smile is comforting.

"He had plans he couldn't get out of." I shrug.

"Her guy is a nurse." Warren says *nurse* like it's a dirty word.

"I wouldn't call him *my guy*. . . ." We haven't even been on a date yet. "Tonight was going to be the first time we hung out. Takeout and a movie—nothing major."

Matt raises an eyebrow to Warren, and I look between them, trying to determine what's being said without them speaking. Matt, kindly, puts me out of my misery. "We're trying to figure out why someone would pass on a date with"—he stops to rub his chin—"well . . . with a girl like you." He gestures to me with an open palm. "You know, because you seem so nice!" His voice pitches way up.

Warren stifles a laugh at Matt's expense.

"Especially since you invited him *here*. To your bedroom. On a first date," Warren says pointedly, confidently leaning back into his chair. Smirking, as per usual.

Calvin didn't think I invited him over for sex, right? No, he knew the location was for Willow's sake . . . I think. I lift my bottle to my lips, looking for any sort of distraction.

Ew, warm beer. "It was not, um. I wasn't going to—" I cut myself off. There's no point arguing my intentions. So what if I wanted to have sex with Calvin anyway? That's no one else's business.

Matt's eyes drift to my lips, and my back involuntarily straightens. He tilts his head and focuses, deep in thought. By the look in his eye, I'd guess it involves me. My eyes flick to Warren, whose eyes are laser focused on Matt, glowering at him. I think my outfit's working *too* well.

I clear my throat. "I'm going to get some wine. Do either of you want some?" I stand and walk away before they have a chance to answer.

Warren stands abruptly, following close behind as I fetch a bottle opener from the kitchen drawer. "I think I might take this to go," I say over my shoulder. He seems as if he's going to say something, but then we both turn to the dining room and stop still entirely.

I put the corkscrew down on the kitchen counter and use the ledge to balance myself. *Oh, hell no.* I watch as Tyler, GiGi, and Bryce divide white powder on a tray with a credit card. My lips tremble as I will myself not to burn these idiots where they stand.

"Absolutely fucking not," I mutter, mostly to myself.

Warren's expression falls, his lips tight and pale. He puts a gentle hand on my shoulder, but I shrug him off and storm toward the dining table.

"Pack that shit up right now and get out." I barely recognize my own voice. "You cannot do that here."

I spend so much energy every day keeping myself pleasant. My clothing is approachable, my hair tucked away, my voice pitched up and calm, my posture hunched, head tilted down or legs crossed to take up as little space as possible. But not now.

It feels good to let a little rage out. Surprisingly so.

The three of them look briefly at Warren, who stands in the kitchen as if his body is stuck in wet cement, then back to me. Bryce towers in front of me, stupid as ever, with a *can you believe this* expression toward the rest of the guests over my shoulder. I don't wait for Warren's backup. This is my house too. My baby sister is upstairs.

I'm going to cause a fucking scene.

"There are two minors here that we would never get to see again if you assholes do something stupid or their caseworker finds out. This is a drug-free zone." I lower my brows farther as I step closer to Bryce and slow my speech. "I said Get. The *fuck.* Out." I might literally have stomped my foot. Embarrassing, but I give myself a pass—confrontation is new for me.

"Warren, man, are you gonna let this *bitch* talk to us like that?" Bryce sneers, head turned toward the kitchen.

My fists close at my sides. I don't turn to see Warren's reaction. I can't seem to bring my attention away from the table. I stare down GiGi, who is wide-mouthed and seems amused. I raise an eyebrow at her. *You don't want to mess with me right now.*

To her credit, GiGi nods rapidly, picks up the tin box they were using as a tray, and slips it into her purse. Her boyfriend, less agreeable, sucks his teeth as he knocks over a pile of cups on his way out the door.

Bryce follows behind, glaring eyes not leaving me, but I give him no response. I don't move at all until the front door shuts behind them. I sink into a dining chair, the momentum leaving me alongside the breath in my lungs.

There are several shuffles and steps behind me as I hold my cheeks in my palms. The door shuts with a thud. Matt, I think, mumbles something to Warren about celebrating on a different day but doesn't wait around for a response before making his exit as well.

I check behind me. *Yeah, all gone.* I cleared out Warren's entire party within twenty minutes of joining. Shit. I run two hands over my hair until my forehead rests in the crooks of my forearms.

Warren walks slowly from the kitchen to sit backward on the dining chair across from me where the three idiots stood a few seconds ago. His broad chest spreads out on either side of the backrest. His jaw is flexed, and his wide eyes are fixated on something across the table. He tightens his hands on the edges of the chair, knuckles as white as his blanched cheeks.

I brace myself for a difficult conversation.

SEVENTEEN

I WORK UP THE COURAGE TO SPEAK FIRST. "LOOK, I WOULD say sorry for ruining your birthday but—"

"No." Warren's voice is low and forceful. He clears his throat as he wipes a hand over his face, dragging eyelids and lips in his path. "Sorry, just . . . give me a minute." The sound of his foot tapping the leg of the table fills the quiet apartment as one song transitions into another from the far side of the living room.

"Are you okay?" I'm completely unsure how to read him right now. At least he doesn't seem angry with me.

"I'm—I'm trying to calm down . . . so I don't follow Bryce." His chest heaves a few times.

Warren stands and paces between the dining chair and the wall with his favorite art piece of mine. I watch him move as my heart beats in my ears. He's brimming with focus, with intensity, with angst.

Once his body relaxes and he sits, I pour two glasses of wine and push one over to him.

"Thanks." He throws it back in a series of gulps before placing the glass back down empty.

I pour him another.

He takes a small sip before speaking. "Chloe, I didn't know they had drugs on them. I want you to know that. I wouldn't have—" His jaw clenches as his eyes shut. "I froze. I'm sorry."

I place my hand on top of his on the dining table, and he meets my eyes, finally.

"I say this with love, Warren, but you have shitty friends."

He smirks and lifts his thumb between my index finger and thumb. He rubs his calloused thumb across the side of my finger, in what appears to be an almost unconscious movement. Tingles flood my veins, starting from the side of my knuckle and shooting to the swelling organ in my chest that beats faster with every swipe.

"I think *friends* is a rather strong term for most of them. Bryce invited Tyler and Caleb, who brought their girlfriends. I don't know them. Bryce is a piece of shit. I do know that."

"I'm sorry I ruined your party." I hadn't planned on apologizing, but I can't help it. He looks so sad. Like the kid who invited the whole class to his birthday and no one showed.

"It wasn't fun anyway. I don't know what I was thinking." He looks at me, but not with his usual arrogance. There is no gleam in his eye, no confidence pressed into the corner of his lips. I miss it, actually.

He takes a long sip, puts the glass down, and moves his hands to his lap. "My mom died of an overdose."

My stomach drops and tightens, though I try not to react outwardly. I haven't been allowed much of Warren's inner world, and I don't want to be kicked out too soon by responding poorly.

"I'm so sorry." He waves off my apology, but his face falls as he lets his bravado slip back down. His eyes fall to his lap.

"She, uh, actually died on my birthday." *Fucking hell.* I don't even try to stop my jaw from lowering this time. Words fail. "It's always a weird day for me. Then that, tonight?" He scoffs as he takes a large sip of wine. "I'm sorry you had to be the one to intervene but . . . thank you."

His hands lift to the table as if he's going to reach for me. He hesitates and goes for his glass instead, finishing it off. As he sets his wineglass back down, he looks directly into my eyes with intent—I don't turn away.

It feels like granting permission. I'm letting him see me fully in return for his vulnerability. I don't usually allow people in like this. Being open has never gotten me anywhere but heartbroken.

My parents didn't do emotions. Connie had failed me. Kids were cruel and teenagers self-involved. It left me with shallow relationships and empty connections. It taught me to favor polite over real.

This isn't empty. This is vast, full, abundant. Warren's eyes swirl with a pain that matches my own. Here, I could choose to exchange part of my hurt for his. We could hold on to it for each other. Ease some.

"While I'm hoping for a gold star from my therapist, I wish I'd decked Bryce for what he said." His voice is low, quiet. I break our eye contact to watch as his hands form fists against the table.

"I've been called worse," I offer pathetically.

Warren tenses before he speaks. "I used to have a real problem with fighting. It's why I didn't stay with Luke until I aged out. I got into a fight with another kid at the home we were at. . . . I don't even remember why." He flexes his hands—straightening his fingers before laying flat palms down. "Still . . . I'd really like to have hit him for what he called you."

"Tell you what. Next time I'll hit him, and you can enjoy it from afar." He watches my mouth part as I take the last sip of wine from my glass. "But I'm glad you didn't. You're better than that."

I'm hyperaware of his stare as I lick the last drop of wine off my top lip. Something within me screams to get some distance between us. I take both of our empty glasses to the sink and begin washing up. There's room to breathe over here. Room from that look in his eye. *Like I'm edible.*

After the glasses are sparkling, I turn and lean back on the sink. Warren collects empty pizza boxes, plates, and cups from around the living room, appearing deep in thought as he sets them down next to the stove.

I think he can see me out of the corner of his eye as I focus my gaze on his profile. I can't help myself; the tension in his expression only further accentuates his sharp edges that draw me in. I follow the hard line of his jaw to his neck—which does nothing to cool the heat building in me.

I think I could choose to look away, if I wanted to, but I don't. My breasts rise and fall as my breathing becomes labored. My clothes feel far too tight on my skin. The moment he turns his head to lock eyes with mine, I know what we're about to do.

"Chloe . . ."

He walks toward me, puts his hands on my waist, and uses them to effortlessly lift me onto the edge of the sink. My hands land flat above his collarbones, fingers curling into his T-shirt. He keeps one hand on my waist and moves the other across my jaw. Still, he doesn't bring his mouth down on mine. His eyes shift be-

tween my own half-closed eyelids and then focus in on my lips—
which pout in response.

"You've got to stop looking at me like that." He brushes his
thumb across my bottom lip, and my eyes fully close. He groans.
"Don't do that either."

"Do what?" My voice is breathier than I've heard it before.

"Act like you want my touch that much." He brushes my lip
again, longer this time, from one corner to the other. I reel from
it, but I hold still so he doesn't pull away. I don't want him to stop.

My tongue finds the pad of his thumb. Rough and salty. Pos-
sessed by whatever force there is between us, I nip his thumb
gently as I look up at him. Warren's eyes close this time. It is immeasurably rewarding to make him react. *I want to see what other
reactions I can pull from him.* My heart stammers at that thought.

He slides his hand into my hair, holding the base of my skull in
his palm before he smiles at me so wide I hardly recognize him.
Not a look of desire, but something more—excitement, joy, gratefulness. Alarm sirens sound off somewhere in my mind. This
could go wrong. Terribly wrong. I barely know Warren, and he is
the only person standing between Willow and foster care. *What
am I doing?*

"I-I think we sh-should just be friends," I stutter out while my
aching hands rub the front of his shoulders and neck, speaking to
the contrary. My better judgment is saying this is a bad idea. But
the rest of me screams that this bad idea would feel so, so good.

Warren tilts his head with a smirk. His eyes narrow in on my
chest as it heaves upward, then toward my hands, which fist his
T-shirt.

He licks his lips as he opens them, speaking in a hushed tone,
"I said I didn't want to be your friend."

Then his lips are on mine, steady and encompassing.

My brain melts away. The version of me that suggested we do anything but *this* is gone. She was a fool. He parts my lips with his tongue, and I place my hand on the back of his neck to pull him closer in.

My fingers brush the base of his shaved hair, and it's softer than I expected. His hand on my waist loosens and trails down the side of my body until he brings it around to grab my ass. His hands fill with my body wherever they land. He's greedy and I love it.

Warren lets out a small groan as he readjusts and brings his other hand to my ass as well. He can kiss, like *really* kiss. Perhaps I have never been truly kissed before. I nip at his top lip and pull away slightly to take it with me. He smiles against my mouth as he repeats in kind. We kiss like we bicker—trying to one-up each other.

My lips are buzzing against his. Kisses like a welder's torch hitting metal. Our mouths clash and soothe with such ease, it's as if we've been doing this all along. A fire lights in my belly thinking of all the time we've wasted not kissing since he walked through my front door. *I'm going to make it up to you, body.*

He tastes of wine and licorice, and I can't seem to get enough. He must feel the same, as the tip of his tongue licks across my lips again and again. I can't help but moan into his mouth as I imagine him doing that elsewhere on my body.

Warren's hold on me tightens in response. He pulls away to speak but seems to shake it out of his system and comes back to my mouth. I smile against his lips, thinking of the man who wouldn't even let me sit next to him a few weeks back—now lost for words.

"What?" His voice is full of amusement and sensuality. I kiss the corner of his mouth, then jaw, which he raises with a huff of air, allowing me access to his neck.

"I was thinking about how much I must've won you over . . . to be here now." I kiss his earlobe, and he releases a staggered moan. "I thought you hated me." I nip at his neck, and he takes a long breath in.

"Chloe, you're not at all who I thought you were. But fuck my opinion. I'm a judgmental ass." As he says the word, he spreads his palms. "Yours is amazing, by the way."

I pull away from his neck to find his mouth, but he rests his forehead on mine. It feels more intimate than the kissing somehow.

My panting breaths slow as he gathers himself and goes on. "But I never hated you. Not even close. You're not the problem here." With that confession, he moves to find my lips again, building until we're back in the rhythm and feverish wanting of before—except now, there's an additional layer of something left unspoken.

I part my legs farther around his hips, and he steps closer, leaving no gaps between us as our hands travel each other's bodies. I run my hand over the top of his head again, loving the feeling of it under my palm. My chest presses into his, serving as a reminder to him, it seems. He trails one hand up my back, then up the side of my body in a painfully slow, delicate movement. My shirt is doing nothing to separate my skin and his touch. He moves to cup my breast and bites my lip in sequence.

I want him to carry me to his room. Without speaking, I think he knows this. He moves both hands to the back of my thighs, preparing to lift me. I brace to be picked up, wrapping both my arms around his neck, when there is a clanging of dishes from the edge of the room. We startle back from each other, and I fall into the sink as Warren turns to face the noise. *Shit.*

"What is happening?" Luke can't decide where to let his eyes land. I look at Warren, who is attempting to adjust the bulge in the front of his jeans. I push out of the sink and lower myself down off the counter. *No, no, no.*

"I think you're old enough to understand what is happening," Warren signs back to Luke, hands practically smoking from their speed.

"Yeah, thanks." At first, I thought Luke was shocked, but he's angry. I try to decide how quickly I could reach the bottom of my stairs if I run. I take a small step to the left, edging closer to my exit route, as Luke continues, "What happened to not getting too attached? If you mess this up, I'll be in another group home before you can get your dick back in your pants." Luke is fuming, and Warren doesn't look too far behind.

"I'm going to go." I don't look at either of them as I walk between them and hurl myself up the stairs. I sit on the edge of my bed, desperately wishing I could eavesdrop on sign language from a safe distance. The lights downstairs don't turn off for another hour. A slow, torturous hour. They must have had a lot to say.

I check my phone and open my texts with Warren. Ellipses appear and disappear from him. I don't know what to say either, but fine, I'll start.

CHLOE: Luke okay?
WARREN: Yeah, he's fine.
CHLOE: Good.
WARREN: Helluva kiss . . . Definitely saved my birthday.
CHLOE: Well, happy birthday.

WARREN: Sure you don't need the bathroom? You know, before bed . . .

CHLOE: I think I'm good.

WARREN: Glass of water, perhaps?

CHLOE: Not a good idea.

WARREN: Staying hydrated is very important.

CHLOE: Good night, Warren.

WARREN: Good night, dove.

CHLOE: Dove?

He doesn't respond before I can no longer fight my closing eyes. I settle back onto the bed and touch my lips with my finger. They're swollen and warm, even still. *Helluva kiss indeed.*

EIGHTEEN

SLEEP, IN COMBINATION WITH THE LACK OF ALCOHOL in my system, has brought rational thought back into the loft. There's no sense denying it was a great kiss—incredible even— but it will be just the one. That is final. Even if my vagina begs to differ. *I'm in control here, dammit.*

Willow coos from the bassinet beside my bed, and I bring her onto my lap to lie lengthwise against my thighs, raising my knees to take a good look at her little face. She has been much more expressive lately, giving smiles that I know are only for me.

"I won't mess this up for you, kiddo. I promise," I whisper to her as I brush her soft cheek with my finger. No amount of strikingly handsome men in this world could make me risk this little girl's well-being. Even if they happen to live downstairs. Even if they happen to kiss like *that*.

My strategy is to be bold, direct, and clear. I have repeated those three words to myself a dozen times this morning already.

"Bold, direct, clear," I mutter once again, as I step off the stairs into the dining room.

Annnd he's shirtless. Well played, Warren.

I don't put Willow down in her chair as I normally do to make her bottle. Instead, I carry her to the kitchen, holding her tightly in my grasp. This poor baby is a human shield far too often.

"Morning." Warren glances up and down my body, grinning wide, as he flips a pancake on the stove. Pancakes too? *He's playing chess while I play checkers.*

"Sup." *Sup?* Breathe, Chloe. Keep it simple. Get a bottle. Mix it. Sit on the couch. Feed Willow. The couch faces away from the kitchen—get there, and you'll be safe. *Safe from the view of his abs—sweet mercy.*

"How was your night?" Warren asks as he takes Willow from my arms as I struggle to open the formula. *Shit, my shield . . .*

"Fine." I project my voice with the confidence of an unbothered woman, but I still don't look at him. He's far too close and far too naked.

"Mine was fantastic, thanks for asking. I had this amazing dream . . . maybe you could translate it for me?" Warren's smugness is radiating off him, and whether I choose to look at him or not, I can see it. He wants to get under my skin *and* into my bed, apparently. "Imagine it. This woman and I were kissing, right? And it was incredible, like damn near perfect, but then—"

"Shit!" I interrupt, having spilled a good three bottles' worth of formula all over the kitchen counter and floor. I try to brush as much as possible back into the container with the back of my hand—this counter's clean enough, right?

Warren grimaces as he shifts to hold Willow in one arm, using his free hand to flip another pancake onto the plated stack next to the stove.

As I finally finish sweeping the last of the formula off the floor, Warren is feeding Willow a bottle he must've made when I was cleaning up. Her little hand fiddles with the black corded necklace around his neck as she drinks. He carries both her and the plate of pancakes to the dining table. I have about fifteen seconds before this morning is so perfect—minus the spill—that I won't be able to bring myself to say anything at all.

"We need to talk about last night," I blurt out as I fall into the dining chair across from Warren.

"Go for it." Warren adjusts the bottle in Willow's mouth. The side of her head is pressed into his bare chest. *Lucky.*

I clear my throat. "Okay. So . . . obviously we both agree that last night was—"

"What part?" Warren is a good actor. I'll give him that. I almost believe he doesn't know what I'm referencing, but the twitch of his lip gives him away.

"The kissing part?"

"Oh! Right, *that*. Nice work, by the way." Warren's smirk is sexy and not helpful.

"Mm-hmm, thanks. Anyway, I want to be clear—"

"Don't you mean bold, direct, *and* clear?" My stomach drops. He heard—*that's embarrassing.*

"Yes . . ." I gather my courage, letting out a breath. "Kissing can't happen again." There, I said it. No taking it back. I look at Warren and focus in on his lips briefly. *Goodbye, dear friends.*

"Well . . . I hear you . . ." Warren says, patting Willow's back until she lets out a little hiccup.

Once Willow has finished, he stands up and walks over to her play mat, lays her down, and pushes the toy that hangs overhead into action.

My eyes follow him as he saunters around the apartment. Any

arrogance missing last night is back in full force. He smirks over the top of his mug as he sits back down across from me. His eyes focus on mine, and I swallow air as he swallows coffee. I don't speak, knowing he hasn't finished his thought yet and because I've said all I needed to say.

"I do disagree, though." *There it is.*

"Warren—"

"Chloe," he interrupts. He's not taking this seriously.

I let the frustration show on my face, and he sees it. His eyes narrow, and he pauses, maybe to plan his next words more carefully than before.

He tries again. "We can both say we won't kiss again, fine. I can be as pious as the next guy. But that won't change the way you look at me. It certainly won't change how I look at you. We'll definitely be doing it again at some point—probably a lot more than kissing too. So, as far as I see it, we can either fight it—feel this tension grow and grow until we can't control ourselves like horny teenagers—*or* we can call it."

I close my mouth—*shit, when did I let my jaw drop?* I look down at my plate, unable to think while looking at him. I hesitate to even attempt to speak, but too much time is passing. I look up to face him. "No."

Warren jerks backward in response, eyebrows raised. He's surprised. . . . At least I can say I did that.

I look over at Willow as I begin to speak. "Sorry, but no. If we . . . if we become more . . . *intertwined* and then mess it up somehow, and you and Luke leave before my review with Rachel . . . I would lose Willow. I just—I don't know you well enough yet to know that wouldn't happen. I wouldn't forgive myself if she ended up going into care because I couldn't stop myself from . . ." I choose not to finish that thought out loud.

A heavy silence fills the space between us. With a deep breath, I gather the strength needed to look at him. He's chewing his bottom lip and looking above my shoulder, to the spiral staircase behind me.

He nods to himself, slowly at first, and then with increased determination as he says, "January fourteenth, right?"

How does he remember the day of my re-evaluation? Perhaps he did check the calendar I hung next to the front door after all.

"Yes . . ." I answer skeptically.

"Okay." Warren licks his lip as he nods.

"Okay?" I ask.

His eyes are lost in thought as he shifts to look over his shoulder at Willow's play mat.

"Let's make a deal, then." He turns to me, and as his eyes fixate on mine, it sends a cool shiver down my spine.

"I'm listening . . ." I say suspiciously.

"January fifteenth. . . . I get to take you on a date," Warren says. I roll my eyes, but he doesn't let up. I pause.

He'd plan a date four months in advance? A date with me? He didn't even want to be my friend five weeks ago. "Really?"

Warren nods once. He parts his lips to speak as my phone begins buzzing on the table. Calvin is calling. I watch Warren look down and notice too.

"Unless you have another reason, that is?" His eyes aren't as warm as they had been. His jaw has tightened too.

The phone buzzes again, and I feel paralyzed with indecision. Everything in me wants to dive across the dining table toward Warren, but I've already missed Calvin's call once. I don't want him to think I'm ignoring him.

"I, um, I should get this." I can't meet Warren's eyes as I stand and take my phone to the bathroom with me. I need a moment to gather myself. I shut the door and look at myself in the mirror. I'm flushed, and the remnants of last night's makeup darken my eyes.

"Hey, Calvin, it's not a good time. Can I call you back?" My voice cracks, pitched higher than normal.

"Hey, sorry," he says.

I bring the back of my hand to my cheek, trying to cool and comfort myself. I can barely make out what Calvin is saying.

"I got called into work, but I'll be off at seven. Can I call you after my shift is done? Or I can come over?" Calvin is walking, his voice fast and jostled by the sound of movement.

"Sure, yeah." I pull the phone away and stare at the screen with a grimace. I *may* have agreed to a full-blown date instead of a call while my thoughts were wrapped up somewhere in the dining room.

"Sweet. I'll see you tonight then. I'll bring some food. Text me what you'd like later."

Shit, shit, shit. Too late to back out now. "Okay, see you later."

I hang up and push the phone to my temple. What did I agree to? Calvin is nice, sure. He is definitely cute. But I don't feel tension pulling in my belly when I look at him. *I don't feel edible.*

Also, how do you tell someone you won't date them because you might have plans four months from now? You can't. I push open the bathroom door the same moment Warren shuts his across the hall. I knock on his door.

"Occupied," he responds from inside.

"Can we talk?" I ask.

"Can you wait? I'm changing. Or you can come see for yourself."

I lean back against the wall next to his door, head tilted up to the ceiling, willing myself to calm down. As if all my self-restraint is going toward not taking a peek at his half-naked body, my rambling begins.

"Calvin is coming over later. I didn't mean to agree to it, but I sorta did. He's nice enough, right? Cute, I think. Do you think? No, sorry. Well, I shouldn't presume. Maybe you do think he's cute—that's cool with me. That isn't my business, sorry. . . . I'm not sure if it's a date or not . . . but for me, it's never been the way it is in the movies. You know, people go out to dinner or a movie, something cute—or sometimes both . . . then they walk home holding hands. I've never done that. It's always takeout at someone's place. I suppose I might not go out much anymore. Now that I have Willow, I mean . . . I've never been asked out on a real date, before today that is, when you . . . did you mean a date like that? Or—" Warren's door swings open.

He looks at me with widened eyes and a tense, shifting jaw. "Chloe?"

"Hmm?" My eyes zone out over his shoulder at the view of his bed. *I was so close to being in it.*

"Take a breath."

"Sorry . . ." *Too much, Chloe. Always too much.*

"Don't be." Warren licks his top teeth with lips closed. He's looking toward me but not at me. "Look, it was a good kiss—no denying that . . . but you're probably right. It would be a disaster, me and you." *Wait, I didn't say that.* "We wouldn't work. I'd mess it up for Luke and Willow—then what? Scrubs is a much safer choice."

He steps around me and strides down the hall toward the living room. I follow him, feeling rather emboldened by my sincere confusion.

"I didn't say we wouldn't work. I said—" I step around the couch as he walks toward the dining table.

"Well, then allow me. . . . We wouldn't work, Chloe." He picks up the plate of now cold pancakes and places them on the kitchen counter.

He'd only set two plates at the table. Did he make breakfast just for us? Not the usual breakfast either. Was this . . . more than pancakes? I follow him to the kitchen.

"Why?" I ask.

"Are you going to follow me around all day?"

"No." I don't leave the kitchen, though. My question still lingers between us, and he relents, but not without an exaggerated eye roll first.

"You're *you*." Warren spits out the word *you* as if it's an insult. It lands as one. "You're yellow jumpsuits and pink couches. You're sweet. You're a nurse-boy's type. The good girl . . . I don't have a mother to bring you home to. No one will be charmed by your cute dresses or bright colors in my circle of friends. You don't fit, as much as we'd both try."

I huff without meaning to and pull my lips inside my mouth to mask my frown. "So January fifteenth . . ." There's a question there, but I don't ask it fully.

"Consider it canceled." *That was fast.* My first date was four months away; now, not at all. I don't attempt to mask the disappointment that settles into my eyes and threatens tears.

"Someday, *Warren,* I'm going to tell *you* who *you* are." I try to say *you* with the disdain he did—but it doesn't have the same power behind it. It's a sad sound, the voice of a dejected girl.

"Please do! I would love to know!" His body squares off with mine, his nostrils flare as he goes taut all over with anger. There's a twinge of pain in his eyes.

My pathetic retort may have hit a little closer to the mark than

I had thought—or wanted. I attempt to think of an apology but come up short.

Then, a well-timed reminder from whatever gods are laughing at us strikes as Willow begins crying with all the force of her little lungs, and Luke emerges from his room at the same time. *At least they're in sync.* Warren and I break eye contact to look at our hands—which, at some point, had begun reaching for each other.

I slowly put mine into my pockets and turn in quick succession to join Willow in the living room.

NINETEEN

MY JAW DROPS AS I LOOK AT CALVIN, WHO SITS ON THE edge of my bed. *Wow.* "There is no way!"

He laughs and rests both hands on his knees. "Not on purpose!"

"How is that possible?" My voice pitches higher as my amusement slips through.

"I grew up super religious. My parents weren't cool with the whole vampire *thing,* and then I just . . . I don't know! I haven't thought about it this much!"

"Well, it's settled then. We're watching it." I reach for the keyboard on the desk at the end of my bed and pull up *Twilight.* I'm smiling as I turn back toward him. He glances nervously around my room, and I watch him, concerned.

"Something wrong?" He looks up at me as he speaks.

"Nothing . . . I'm not pushing this movie on you, right?"

"What? Chloe, no. I'm cool to watch whatever. I'm a little sad to lose my never-have-I-ever prompt, but I'm glad to find out what all the fuss is about." He gestures to the screen as he relaxes back on the bed, holding himself up with one elbow. "How many movies are there? Five?"

I nod.

"Well then . . . another bonus, four more dates already lined up." Calvin smiles warmly as he speaks.

I pause, making note of the twinkle in his eye. "Want to get drinks before we start?"

"Sure, yeah." He lifts off the bed and does a quick peek into Willow's bassinet as we pass by the entrance to the stairs. I moved her away from my bed for tonight. Not because I think anything will be happening in my bed, despite what Warren and his friend may have thought, but so the noise of our movie doesn't wake her.

Calvin reaches the kitchen first.

"Hey, man," he says.

I turn the last step to see Warren at the stove, watching a boiling kettle. He doesn't turn toward us or speak as he slips a hand out of his jeans pocket and raises it over his shoulder as a form of greeting. *So this is happening.* I offer an apologetic smile to Calvin as I walk to the corner cabinet to get two glasses.

"I'm going to use the washroom. Be right back." Calvin turns down the hall as I open the freezer for ice.

I shut the freezer door. Warren has left his position at the kettle to stand nearer, facing me at the sink.

"What?" I ask.

"Did you notice he has a ring on?"

I snap my head toward him. "That's not funny."

"I'm serious! I think he saw me notice. Probably why he went to the bathroom." He smirks, breaking character despite his best efforts.

"Screw you." I roll my eyes and begin pouring the soda Calvin brought for us.

"Please do." Warren's voice dips down to a lower register. He raises his hand to rest on the edge of the sink, inches away from my right hip.

My eyes fixate on his hand. The same hand that last night picked me up and lifted me to the spot it rests on now. I lower the bottle without looking away from his thumb, which now rubs against the front of the sink. I remember the feel of it on my tongue and swallow. *When did my breaths become shallow?*

Warren's hand tightens around the sink, the veins and muscles of his hand shifting. He knows what he's doing, I'm sure of it. I think of how it felt to cover his hand with mine, like tiny fireworks in my blood vessels. My eyes trace the vein protruding from his wrist up to the elbow where his T-shirt sleeve rests.

I follow the line of stitching to the base of his neck, where it falls into a slight V-shape. His Adam's apple bobs. I look at his face and feel a haze fall around the room, putting us into a bubble where only we exist. He looks down at me with slightly parted lips and bedroom eyes. I suck in a breath as I prepare for whatever Warren is about to say.

"Chloe. . . ." Warren says my name like a prayer.

"Hey-ohh-kay. What's going on?" Calvin's voice slows as he speaks from the corner of the hallway.

My body flushes from head to toe, all the blood rushing to my face. Warren doesn't react other than to reach up to the cupboard in front of me, open it, and hand me two straws from the top shelf.

"Here you go," Warren says matter-of-factly.

"Thanks," I mumble, looking at the two cups in front of me, only one filled. I pour another glass.

Calvin must know what he saw, or what he was about to see, as he appears at my side. He wraps his arm around my waist as he reaches for one of the glasses.

"Thanks, C," Calvin says. *C?* That's new. So is the hand around the waist. Is this what men do? Stake claims? I'm not property or land to be conquered. I don't have to look up to know Calvin and Warren are staring each other down over my back.

"Let's go." I pull Calvin's hand off my waist and hold on to it, using the hold to pull him toward the stairs. His hand fits nicely in mine and is soft to touch but . . . no fireworks.

Once upstairs, I hit PLAY before he has a chance to ask about what went down in the kitchen. Because I don't know. *I really don't know.* The rest of the movie plays as we sit in silence, leaning up against my headboard and not touching. I feel sixteen again.

"All right. Well—I'm excited to see the next one!" Calvin says as the credits begin to roll.

"Good! They get better and better, in my opinion."

"I trust you." He smiles sincerely, and I match it without having to try.

"Can I . . ." He hesitates. "Can I ask you about earlier?" My stomach churns.

"About what?" *As if I don't know.*

"When I came back from the washroom, it sort of seemed like I was interrupting something? A moment?"

"A moment? Oh, no, not at all, no!" *The lady doth protest too much.*

"Okay. I'd rather know now than later. I've had roommates before who linked up. It can get kinda intense when you're under one roof."

"Oh, um. It's nothing like that. . . ." It's everything like that.

Even as I speak, I can see that I'm not convincing him. I want to convince him. I want to convince myself. I grab on to the collar of his shirt and pull him down to my mouth. We bash noses.

"Shit, sorry." I wince.

"It's okay. Just . . . here," Calvin says as he reaches down and holds my jaw, light as a feather. He places one soft, lingering kiss on my top lip. Then pulls away with eyes wide open, as if he's done, instead of pausing before a second try.

"Walk me out?" He stands. *Oh.* He *is* done. I know a pity kiss when I see one. This is one.

"Sure." I take the hand he offers me to get off the bed, and he leads us downstairs.

He hugs me briefly at the door.

"See you soon," I say into his shoulder.

He steps back into the hallway of my apartment building and gives me a curt nod with a slightly bashful smile before heading toward the elevator. I don't think he's ever going to see the second *Twilight* film—at least not with me.

TWENTY

I SIGH AS I LOCK THE DOOR, CLOSING IT GENTLY AND trying not to alert Warren to my presence outside his bedroom. The last thing I need right now is another awkward run-in before I've begun to process this evening's turn of events. Tiptoeing to the living room, I throw myself onto the couch and lie back, tugging on the ends of my hair—an old habit from childhood when I needed to provide my own reassurance.

I may have blown my chances with Calvin. I don't blame him at all. If I'd walked in on *him* having an *exchange* like ours in the kitchen, I'd probably not have been courteous enough to sit through an entire movie or make small talk. I'd have just left. Plus, for as lovely as Calvin is, that kiss did absolutely nothing for me. Maybe, once the dust settles, we can be friends.

I pull out my phone, content to distract myself by scrolling through life updates of people I mostly don't know. I have a few unread notifications, my group chat with my old roommates, a few Twitter news blasts, and an email from my adoptive mother that I open first.

Hello, Darling! Your father and I have booked flights to come visit. Surprise! Flying in on the 19th and will be out on the 24th. We'll be available for a visit on your birthday, but otherwise our schedule is filling up rather quickly. If you aren't available, please do let us know so we can make other plans. We can go out (if you can find a sitter) or have dinner at yours. Anyway, hope you're well—and keeping up with your work despite distractions. Janine said Rodney is still hiring at the firm, if you're interested.

Love, Mom

Someone could write their senior thesis on all the passive-aggressive emails I have from my mother, but this one isn't *the worst*. Even so, I can't help but feel a twinge of hurt rising. They're coming for five days but only want to visit just the one evening of my birthday. And, she didn't ask about Willow—or even name her. Then, there's the mention of work and the familiar offer to work at her friend's husband's marketing firm—totally disregarding my need to work from home right now. I open a reply.

Hi Mom and Papa,

Looking forward to seeing you on the 20th. I will host here. If you guys are still vegan, there is a place around the corner that's pretty good. We can sort that out closer to the time, though. Willow and I are well. She's amazing. I can't wait for you both to meet her. I also have roommates for you to meet. CPS sometimes partners new guardians up to support each other for the first six months—sort of a team approach! It has been helpful so far as I adjust. Hope you're both well. Miss you. Give Abuela a hug from me.

Chloe

My mom had lost her ever-loving mind when I told her about Willow. She told me all the ways I would fail, in literal bullet point format, if I attempted next-of-kin care. The top of her list was my finances. So I'm certainly not going to be honest and tell her that TeamUp was the only way to have Willow here.

I know she means well—they both do.

When I was adopted at seven, I was only beginning the fun of figuring out who I was and what I was interested in. I loved art, mess, blurred lines and loud music, bright colors and my frizzy hair, glitter glue and comic books. Then I was plunged into a family who valued the opposite of most of those things and whom I was desperate to impress. They tamed me.

I heard my mother say that to her friends once as they sat around our dining table. "We've tamed her." Like I was a dog they'd gotten from the pound. The other adults laughed in response, not knowing I was on the other side of the door.

I let that thought pass as quickly as it comes. When I told her I'd overheard, she'd apologized enough for a hundred lifetimes. Still, it burns as brightly in my chest as it did then. I sit up and scan the quiet living room. There will certainly be some cleaning to do before they visit—but I have a month.

As I'm about to get back to scrolling, a door opens from down the hall.

"Hey." Warren's deep voice is soft, so as not to wake Willow upstairs. "Can we talk?"

"Sure." I mimic his tone as I sit up.

Warren sighs with a weary smile. "I'm sorry about earlier. I shouldn't have interfered with your date. I didn't mean to make it weird."

I glare at him playfully. "Yes, you did."

He grins. "Yeah . . . fine. But I wish I hadn't."

That I can buy. "I didn't stop you."

"No, you didn't." He sits at the other end of the couch, his arm draping across the back.

"So, it isn't entirely your fault." I bite my thumb.

We're both quiet, waiting to hear what the other's going to say. I hold out longer—for once.

Warren exhales, rubbing his forehead as he begins to speak. "Whatever you want to do, I'll do it. I'll follow your rules, Chloe. I don't want to mess this up for anyone. Though . . ." His bravado returns ever so slightly. "I could definitely try the same argument I used on Luke to convince him it was a good idea . . . if you'd like."

Don't beg with your eyes, Chloe.

"I should probably factor it into the decision-making process," I jest halfheartedly.

"And Calvin? Is he a factor?"

I shake my head. Warren tilts his chin, looking away from me in what I think is an attempt to hide his mischievous smile.

"So, that argument?" I can't help it; I desperately want to know.

He pauses, giving me a once-over. It's as if he's understanding for the first time that I'm interested in him, like that hasn't been *entirely* obvious. A crooked smile forms, and his eyes fixate on my lips for a second too long. He shakes himself out of it before speaking.

"Luke was angry; you saw that. He felt like it was unfair since, you know, I had been so focused on keeping us all separated." His expression turns concentrated. "I told him that you made it impossible to stay away. That everything about you is pulling me in." He shakes his head, a smile of disbelief spreading across his lips. "I may have referred to you as a whirlpool . . . as cheesy as that may be."

My lips twitch, fighting to hide my amusement, as Warren's expression turns more determined.

"I could resist, try to swim out, try to avoid it—but it would be easier to float. And, for the first time, I'm not scared to." Warren's blue eyes look up, swirling with mixed emotion. Hopeful yet weary. "I've had a lot of people come and go in my life—most of those I was supposed to trust failed me." His eyes close and hold a moment before he opens them. "I'd be an idiot to let myself get hurt. So I make judgments. I put people into boxes. I let my anger get the best of me and push them away. But you keep showing up. You seem to understand."

Did I just get my first declaration speech? *It was perfect.* How do I follow that?

"I, uh, shit, that was a lot more than I meant to say." He rubs a palm over his head. "Please say something." He forces out a strained laugh.

"Wow. Um . . . wow." I bite my lip. "I think, uh." *Say this right, don't ruin it.* "I really like you, Warren. I do. Probably a lot more than I'd care to admit." I smile, but his face remains neutral, like he's waiting on my every word. "I just wonder if for now, with everything hanging in the balance, we just try being friends. I know you said you didn't want to be my friend, and let me tell you, that was quite a swoonworthy line . . . oddly enough. But, I can't gamble Willow."

Warren nods a few times, an expression of regret passing over his face as I take a moment to slow my thoughts.

"I'm not saying no to . . . us. I really want to say yes. But I think we need to wait until we both feel secure that anything more between us would be a safe bet." As the time since Warren last spoke grows longer, so do my insecurities. I try to push them back down, but they absorb me further with every attempt.

"And what you said earlier? About who I am?" I hesitate. "About us not fitting, not working. . . ." My voice trails off.

Warren looks up at me from under his brow. "I don't know why I said those things, Chloe. I'm sorry." A muscle in Warren's neck ticks. "It was stupid. I say stupid things when I'm mad or . . . jealous." He lets out a long breath. "When I woke up this morning, I was so sure we'd slip into this new way of living together. Where we were a *we*."

"I don't disagree. I'm not an easy person. I'm uptight, and I overthink everything. I present this version of myself to the world where I can be condensed. Minimized." I laugh without any joy. "You fell for it too. Just some privileged, colorful, well-to-do girl who doesn't have to try too hard. I tone myself down. I . . . I tame myself."

I swallow thickly. "My roommates, from university, didn't even know I was adopted. How messed up is that? I never once had to share that part of myself with people, because I could avoid the shit my birth mom put me through. I could run away from it." I stop fidgeting and settle in my seat, clasping my hands in my lap. "You didn't have that chance."

"No . . . I didn't." Warren pauses, rubbing his chin. "But we still landed in the same place. Not through any choices we made. That sucks, equally, for both of us." He reaches out to me with an open palm and I give him my hand. "You never have to do that with me. Show me the messy parts, okay? God knows, I've shown you mine." He winces.

I look down at our hands, intertwined and resting between us. *Have I ever fit anywhere quite so easily?*

"We can be friends . . . for now," Warren says as he pulls his hand away. My foolish heart wants it back.

"But you let me know when you're ready for the real thing." He leans in, close enough for me to feel his breath against my cheek. "I'm patient when I need to be, dove."

"Yeah . . . oh-k-k-kay," I stutter, my throat tightening as I try to fight the urge to brush my lips over his jaw.

Warren leans back against the couch and crosses a leg over his knee, ending the moment. I let my shoulders fall with a sigh.

Good things come to those who wait . . . right?

TWENTY-ONE

ANOTHER MORNING BREAKFAST AROUND THE TABLE, another bowl of cereal, another day in this comfortable routine we've crafted together in this last month. It's usually me who interrupts the boys' morning quiet, but they don't seem to mind too much.

"Who are you going to be for Halloween?" I ask Luke.

"I'm fifteen." He emphasizes his age with wide eyes as he signs.

"Almost sixteen," Warren adds from the end of the table, chewing.

"You're never too old to dress up." I shoot Warren daggers.

"Let me guess, you're going to be in costume?" Warren tilts his head at me.

"Yes! It's fun. This building has tons of kids. Last year, I had to run out for more candy."

"What did you dress as?" Luke asks.

"Poison Ivy." *I hope I signed that right.*

Luke spits his cereal back into his bowl as he sputters a laugh.

I swear I hear the thump of Warren kicking his leg under the table as Luke wipes milk off his chin.

"What?" I ask, looking between them skeptically.

"Nothing." Warren sends a warning look to his brother as he signs.

Clearly there's a joke I'm not aware of here. I grow nervous wondering if I'm the butt of it.

"Seriously, what?" I ask, narrowing my eyes at Luke.

Luke side-eyes his brother, and there's a silent exchange of a look that says, *If you don't tell her I will.*

"I may or may not have had a Poison Ivy poster on my wall that got taken away at our last foster home together." Warren does his best to look indifferent as he speaks, but fails.

I grin but push my lips together in an attempt not to tease. *Is he blushing?* Warren embarrassed? I never thought I'd see the day.

"So I should probably retire the costume then." I raise my eyebrows at Luke as he covers a laugh.

"Don't you dare." Warren's voice dips into a bass pitch that sends a single shock up my spine and goosebumps shooting down my arms. He didn't sign his response for Luke either—he meant it only for my ears.

I sigh and shift in my seat to shake the feeling off. We've been on our best behavior these past two weeks since our talk following my date with Calvin, and I'm not going to screw it up. Is it possible that Warren is cooperating because he wants me to break first? Probably. Is it possible that I'm getting dangerously close to breaking? Definitely.

Since the flirting ban, we have operated like a well-oiled machine. Though personally, I feel like the little engine chanting "I think I can" as it struggles up the hill every day.

I drive them Wednesday and Friday mornings—Wednesdays

for errands and Fridays for Willow's appointments. Warren insisted that if I'm grocery shopping for the house, he can't let me walk it. "It'll be getting colder, and Willow shouldn't be out in the cold. Take the damn car." It was his turn to interfere with my parenting—and I didn't mind one bit.

Even while we remain safely platonic, I can't help but consider what will happen when, or if, we both agree it's safe to go on that date. I don't give a lot of thought to the date itself, if I'm being honest.

I find my thoughts wandering past where we stopped in the kitchen . . . what would have happened if Luke hadn't left his room? I think about it a little too much. Mostly before falling asleep in the safety of my loft. I try not to have these thoughts in front of Warren; he's always looking at me so intently. I feel like he'd know. I do wonder what he thinks about at night though. If it's me.

I take my plate to the kitchen and begin preparing Willow's medicines. Warren follows, stands a few feet to my left, and clears his throat before speaking. "What's your day looking like?"

I can't help but smirk at the clear platonic attempt of his tone. He may have slipped at the table, but he's willing to play along.

"I'm having brunch with a friend, then the usual errands. My ex-roommate Emily is back in town for a wedding, but she leaves this afternoon. I'm a little nervous to see her." I place the medicine bottle down and turn to face Warren.

"Why?" he asks.

"Well, Emily is great, but she's someone who wears her heart on her sleeve. She might have a hard time understanding all the things I kept from her. I want to be honest, but I'm scared. I have a lot to own up to. Not to mention, I'll have a very obvious new addition with me."

"If Emily's a friend worth having, she'll be cool about it. You were trying to get by without being labeled—everyone can identify with that."

I raise my brows at Warren as he packs an apple into a lunch box.

"What?" he asks, brow furrowed.

"No, nothing. You just said the right thing. I feel better now."

"Don't act so surprised." He winks at me, and as his back turns, I allow myself a moment to look up at the ceiling in frustration. *Why does he have to be so hot?*

This would be so much easier if he was charming, funny, insightful, and brooding but hideous. Though, who am I kidding? It would probably still be near impossible.

After dropping Luke and Warren off, I pull into the café's parking lot where Emily and I have planned to meet. Willow is crying as soon as the car stops moving, and I hush her as I gather my things from the front seat and exit the car. The new medication makes her irritable. The alternative is worse, of course, but I can't help but feel frustrated that there is only one medication for her to try. If I have a headache, I have about eight different options from a drugstore alone.

"Hey, it's okay, Will. We're moving. Stroller time!" I click her car seat into the stroller, and she settles a little.

I hook the diaper bag around the handlebars and close Warren's trunk. About ten days ago, I started noticing little additions to his car. In the backseat, he installed the car seat's base so we don't have to use the safety belt each time. A few days after that, a mirror that attaches to the headrest and points down at her appeared. Then, the newest addition, an emergency kit in the trunk. Filled with items that would tide us over until he could get to me in the event of a flat tire or some other issue.

Each one filled up a tiny space in my heart. Little gestures that made me feel seen, and more importantly, made me realize that Willow doesn't only have me in her corner.

"Chloe!" a cheerful voice calls out.

I turn to see Emily parked across from me, waving as she pulls out her purse from the backseat of her rental car. Emily is almost as tall as Warren, with an athletic build and dark Bantu knots. As a fashion designer, she's always stylishly dressed in clothes that are one of a kind and fit her like a glove. Usually bright monochrome outfits. Today is all orange.

"Em! Hey!" I lock the brakes on Willow's stroller and turn toward her for a hug.

"It is so good to see you," she says from above my shoulder. We pull apart after a few sways side to side. "And who is this?"

"Ha. Yes. Lots to catch up on." I smooth my hair down.

Emily looks down to my stomach, then to Willow, then back to me—no doubt doing math in her head.

"Nope. She's my sister," I say, answering her unasked question.

"Oh fun! Wow, your mom . . ." Emily met my adoptive mom once or twice, and I can tell by the look on her face that she's trying to figure out how a woman in her early sixties would have a baby. She's getting more confused by the second. *Where to start.*

"Let's walk, and I'll explain." I offer an apologetic smile, and she nods while rubbing my arm.

"Sure, yeah."

We start off toward the café, which looks out over a boat launch on the lake. We used to come here to study.

"So, first off, I'm sorry I didn't tell you any of this before. I'm working on being more open in my friendships moving forward. It hasn't always come easy to me."

She purses her lips, waiting for me to go on.

"I was adopted at seven. My mom, who you met, and my dad—they're not my birth parents. My birth mother, Connie, had me when she was seventeen. For a while, we were okay, but when I was three, my mom got a boyfriend. He was nice at first, but . . . then he wasn't. He used drugs, and my mom started to as well. Then it got bad. I was placed into foster care, and a few years later, I was adopted."

Emily stops walking for a moment, eyes fixed on her shoes. "I'm so sorry, Chlo," she breathes out, moving her gaze to my face.

I start walking again, mostly to keep Willow settled.

"In June, I got a call saying that Connie'd had a baby. She didn't know she was pregnant and asked me to take the baby. And . . . I did. Here we are." I try to make my voice sound light, but this is the first time I've said it all out loud, and it tugs heavily on my heart.

"Wow . . ." Emily nods thoughtfully. "So she lives with you now?"

"Yeah."

"That must be so hard. I mean, I'm sure you're amazing at it, but it must be hard."

"It is." A rogue tear escapes my eye before I can stop it.

"Oh, hey." Emily wraps her arms around my shoulders. "Chlo, you're so strong." She pulls away, one hand remaining clasped on my arm. "I wish you had told us about how you grew up. Honestly, I was always kind of intimidated by how perfect you are—knowing this sorta makes me love you more." She laughs and wipes the tear off my cheek. "I also wish you'd called me as soon as you heard. I would have come."

"Thanks, Em." I blink and sniffle back the rest of the tears.

"I'm coming back to town in a few weeks with Lane. Can we

stop by? I want to catch up when we have more time." She stops, offering me a sincere smile. "I'd love the chance to pick out cute baby stuff! Did you have a baby shower or anything?"

"Oh, you really don't have to. CPS covers that stuff and—"

"No, I want to." She glances over to the car seat where Willow is now asleep. "She is adorable, Chloe . . . she looks like you."

I smile and look at Willow. "She's the best." I turn to Emily. "Hungry?"

"Yes! My treat, mama bear." She turns to open the door to the café, and I still momentarily.

Mama. No one has called me that before. That's what I am, right? Sort of? I mean, I'm her sister, of course, but—the title of *mom* feels so much more fitting. Another thing to talk through with Odette, I suppose.

TWENTY-TWO

MY BRUNCH WITH EMILY WENT BETTER THAN I COULD have hoped. She had a flight to catch, so it was a short meal, but she and Lane will be back to visit in two weeks. I felt a huge relief, finally admitting those hidden parts of my story, but mostly I felt embarrassed. Not about who I am or how I grew up—as I had expected—but embarrassed that I'd kept it hidden for so long. Emily compared it to telling new friends that she's transgender. *No one is owed your history, but there is trust in telling,* she had said. She called it an *authentic exchange*. I liked that.

After lunch, I went to the grocery store to pick up this week's shopping. While there, I received a brief but anxiety-provoking email from Rachel asking for me to call her when I have a minute.

An unfortunate dose of déjà vu hit as I read the message while in line to check out, standing close to the bathroom where I took my first call from Rachel a few months ago. I'm sure it's nothing of importance. It was just the setting playing tricks on my mind.

Now back in my apartment, I dial Rachel's number as I finish unpacking the last of the pantry goods.

"Hello, this is Rachel Feroux."

"Hey, Rachel, it's Chloe."

"Oh. Hi, Chloe, thanks for giving me a call back. How are you two doing?" The sound of Rachel's rolling desk chair sliding across the floor comes through the phone as she speaks.

"Yeah, fine. Nothing new, really. Did you get my email with notes from her doctor? Her medicine change?"

"Yes, I did, thanks. How does she seem to be responding to it?" Rachel must be having a busy day; she's typing as she speaks.

"It's been two weeks, and so far, her blood pressure is trending down, but the artery isn't showing signs of closing further. They're giving it a few more weeks before considering surgery."

I hate thinking about it—her tiny chest cut open; her heart and little body surrounded by a team of towering adults. How do they even have tools that small? I shiver and shove the thoughts far away.

"Well, let's hope it closes then." The typing stops as Rachel's tone shifts to sincere.

"Yeah." There's a weighted pause as I wait for Rachel to speak. The more time that passes—the more I fear what she's about to say.

"Thanks for calling; I actually have some news about Connie. She reached out to me yesterday." Rachel waits for a response, but I don't speak. "Connie has been sober since July, which has been verified by a worker at her residence. She's at a shelter in the city for women in recovery."

"Wow . . . okay . . . that's great." I'm shocked. I lean back on the counter and wait for Rachel to continue. I wonder if Odette has heard from her too.

"Connie is hoping to begin visits with Willow this month. She's open to supervised visits here or visits in your home, depending on your comfort level."

My back hits the fridge, and I slump down to the floor. "Oh" is all I can say.

"I know that this type of news can bring up a whole mix of emotions. I'm sure you need time to process." Rachel sets something down on her desk with a thud, a stack of files perhaps. "I don't need an answer right now, but . . . your mother is entitled to visits. Weekly, for at least two hours. If you were to have the visits take place here, you could choose to be present or not; a staff member would stay with Willow either way."

Rachel stops talking, and I chew my lip ferociously, unsure of what comes next or how to feel.

"Because she has been sober for upward of three months and has put in a formal request . . . we do need to start visits within the next fourteen days," Rachel says, words enunciated in a way that lets me know these are protocols we all must follow.

"Willow has, um, hospital appointments on Fridays. We could do it afterward?" I offer weakly, rubbing my forehead with my free hand.

"Are you leaning toward having visits in your home?" Rachel asks.

I think back to all the times my mother showed up unannounced outside my school and house as a teenager.

"No. I think CPS for now," I answer.

"Okay. That's fine. Whichever you prefer." *I'd prefer not to.*

Visits are one thing, but when my mother had gotten sober and requested visitation with me twenty-odd years ago, it was a matter of months before I moved back in with her, leaving my first foster home forever. I liked them. They had an older daughter who would braid my hair, and they let me watch *Mulan* every day for two months straight.

I need to ask, but I can barely bring myself to. My throat constricts as I go to speak. "Is she—is she considering . . ." I clear my throat. "Is Connie going to contest the adoption?" My teeth clench, the loaded question out in the open.

"She didn't mention it, no. Connie signed the paperwork at the hospital, giving over her parental rights to you. Whatever happens, that would speak loudly to a judge."

I nod but need to be sure. "But she could, right? She could change her mind?"

Rachel pauses, clears her throat, and then speaks. "Yes, hypothetically."

"And if, um, she was to remain sober until then?" My voice is hushed, and my eyes shut tightly, willing tears not to come.

"It would most likely delay the court proceedings for Willow's adoption. Connie would need to meet housing requirements, find work, et cetera. A judge would likely grant her the time to attempt to become suitable for care."

"Then?" I inhale sharply, awaiting the part I dread to hear.

Rachel sighs. "Then they'd weigh up which option would be best for Willow."

I clutch my chest and pull the shirt away from my skin as a hot, stinging rash forms. The world hums louder than before. I force out a breath and inhale empty air. *I can't breathe . . .*

"Chloe? Are you all right?" Rachel asks nervously as I stand and begin pacing in small, frantic circles.

"Sorry. Can I . . ." My tears burn. They're slow-flowing and reflective of the ache in my chest as I gasp for breaths that do nothing to soothe me. "I need to go," I say more forcefully than intended.

"Okay, Chloe. Whatever you need. It's going to be okay. For now—"

I hang up on her before she finishes. I wouldn't be able to hear her anyway. I sink to the floor, then go onto all fours, planting my forehead on the ground. The cold linoleum recenters me some, but not enough.

I count to twenty, forward then backward. It does nothing to prevent the nausea rising in me. *I'm going to be sick.* I pull myself up to the sink and throw up. My hand blindly reaches out for the cold tap on the sink. The water pours, washing my vomit down the drain. I cup my hands under the faucet to bring water to my face.

I let the sound and the coldness of the water take all my focus. For a while, this helps. I'm in a liminal space, between panic and reality, where there is fragile numbness. I shut my eyes as I bring another splash of cool relief to my face and turn off the faucet.

When I close my eyes, I'm transported back in time. I'm in my adult body, standing in the corner of our old living room, watching Connie claw across the stained beige carpet toward my six-year-old self. A police officer and social worker talk to her, standing behind where she lies on her stomach. Another CPS agent is beside Little Me, speaking to them. I don't remember what they said, and I can't hear it now either. I watch as a younger version of myself hugs the leg of the stranger. In that moment, they seemed a more comforting option than Connie.

Connie looks scared. She looks angry. She'd known that was her last chance. She gets a little too close and Little Me hides behind the man. The police officer pulls her back, arms outstretched behind her. I'd had a bathroom accident in my pajamas the night before, and I'm still in them. I couldn't find any other clothes.

I stand there, covered in urine, crying and shaking as my mother is physically dragged away from me. She's yelling, begging the social workers to let her hug me goodbye; her words are slurred. I was so scared but still went to grab my doll from the floor behind the lamp—not sure if I would get to pack my things this time around.

The memory fades, and I open my eyes to nothing but the tiled wall of the kitchen in front of me. I lean over the sink, awaiting another dry heave that doesn't come. Waves of panic break over me, and I do my best to dismiss them one by one.

I step backward, shaking. I have been standing over the sink for seconds, or maybe hours. I pull out my phone to check the time and remember I hung up on Rachel. I open a new email to her, hoping to apologize before she has the time to grow angry with me. I'm going to need her on my team.

Hi Rachel. Sorry for hanging up before. I will email you in the next few days in regards to visits. Feeling a little overwhelmed.

That's as good as I can do right now.

I walk over to the couch and allow my tears to flow. Maybe Connie just wants visits, I tell myself. Maybe she doesn't need more, doesn't need to have custody or attempt it. Maybe she's still going to let me have Willow. I can't imagine not having her. *I won't.* I close my eyes tight and bring my hands to cup my face. *It will all be okay,* I tell myself, over and over, until it feels the tiniest bit true.

My phone chimes with a response from Rachel.

Hi Chloe,
    Don't worry, I have been hung up on an awful lot in this job. You okay? I know it's overwhelming. It's impossible not

to worry about what comes next. But let's remember where we are. Right now, we don't know what Connie is hoping for, but the last time you met, she signed her rights away to you. That's huge. That will be presented to a judge in seven months, and I'm sure they'll see what I see. You're an amazing guardian. You should pass your re-evaluation with flying colors. You've stepped up for Willow and worked so hard. These are only visits. Try to think of them as a few hours to yourself once a week, if you choose to not attend, and nothing more.

I'm here if you have any questions or need to chat it through. Otherwise, I'll need to know what time on Fridays works for you and Willow and whether that can start on the 19th.

I take a deep breath and feel my lungs fill completely like they haven't been able to for the last half hour. Just visits. For now. I can compartmentalize with the best of them.

I reply,

Thank you, Rachel. Fridays at 11—we'll need to leave at one to get back for her nap. We can start next week.

TWENTY-THREE

"MORNING." WARREN SPEAKS SOFTLY FROM THE HALL-way. He is an early bird, sure, but there's no way he is up at five AM by his choosing. I probably made too much noise pacing around the living room for the past twenty minutes.

"Sorry, did I wake you?" I don't stop my laps back and forth across the living room's rug as I speak.

"No. I . . . I couldn't sleep either. Do you want tea?" Warren asks, his eyes following my frantic movements.

"Yes, please. Thanks." I collapse into the armchair that faces the rest of the apartment, knees pulled into my chest. Warren walks over to the sink to fill the kettle.

He sends me a quick sympathetic glance over his shoulder before going about the kitchen making tea. I hug my knees tighter. *Six hours until our visit with Connie.* Today might be nothing, or it could be the start of the heartbreaking process where Connie decides Willow is too perfect to miss. *How could she not?*

A few minutes later, Warren hands me a cup of tea. Instead of setting himself up on the couch across the room, he sits on the floor at the foot of my chair with his back leaned up against the coffee table.

"Thanks." My hands wrap around the warm mug.

"How you holding up?" Warren asks, brow furrowed.

"Oh . . . you know . . ." I attempt to make my voice sound light-hearted, but my tears threaten to pour, and my voice catches.

Something about the combination of Warren looking up at me with concern, the gesture of making me tea, the early-morning quiet, the condensation on the windows blocking the view from outside—it all makes me feel safe to let my emotions run free.

Warren nods, thoughts whirling in those deep eyes of his. He takes a long sip from his mug before speaking.

"Ram has been bugging me about not taking time off. Last year I didn't use any of my vacation days and um . . . I actually think I'm not feeling up for work today. So, if you'd like, I can drive you guys this morning. Stick around outside or—"

As Warren talks, I put my tea down on the side table and go to my knees on the floor in front of him. I shuffle closer until my arms are wrapped around his shoulders and my forehead is pressed into the side of his neck. He took the day off work for *us*.

Warren places his mug behind him, then wraps both arms around my waist. I twist, and with a small look of permission, sit across his lap. I curl myself into him.

I cry. He holds.

Minutes pass—ten, fifteen, twenty. He doesn't rush me by speaking until I let out a shuddering breath as my eyes dry.

"No one is going to take her from you, Chloe . . ." Warren's voice is stern. "I'd love to see them try."

He brings one hand up to my head and does a few long strokes over my messy morning hair, then down my back. I could fall asleep from the calming touch.

"Is this okay?" He shuffles his lap and holds me to him with one arm curling around my lower back, the other across my stomach, both meeting in a firm clasp at my hip.

"Perfect," I mumble. *Like a weighted blanket for my soul.*

Last week, after I got the call about Connie's visits, Luke and Warren sat with me for hours once Willow was in bed. They've had their dad come in and out of their lives—visits here and there. A few times it seemed like their dad would step up, but he never did. Their insight was comforting, and their vulnerability meant so much.

I told them about the day Connie didn't show at the bus, the day she got custody back and we got ice cream, the day she hadn't taken me to school one too many times without checking in, the day she ran out of chances. I bared my soul to them. It felt ugly but real. I hated it during, but afterward I felt a million weights lift off me. *An authentic exchange.*

Warren and Luke held space for my fears, my hurt, and my worries. Not once did I feel like I needed to hold back, diminish, or hide. I had never felt that way before. Even in CPS-mandated therapy sessions, I had always suspected the wrong thing would get back to my parents. More than that, I really wanted the therapist to like me. She once called me her favorite client, and I never wanted that to change.

Show me your messy, Warren had said, and I was starting to believe he truly meant it. This morning confirmed it, once and for all.

"Warren?" I say, voice hoarse from tears.

"Yes, dove?" *That peculiar nickname again.*

"I'm so glad you're here."

I uncurl myself from his neck and sit up in his lap, reaching to place my palm on the stubble that surrounds his sharp jaw. I rub my thumb across the hollow of his cheekbone.

"Thank you," I say, looking into his eyes.

Warren's nostrils flare as he looks around at the carpet underneath us.

"Yeah." His voice is strained and gruff. I know he keeps his words brief to avoid whatever emotions are coming up. He clears his throat with a deep hum and a few coughs. "I know this weekend is a lot . . ." His voice trails off.

A lot is right. Willow's cardiology appointments are always a wild card—like knowing we could hear life-changing news each time. The first visit with Connie, the possibility that she will make her intentions clear. Plus, I still have so much to do before my parents visit tomorrow.

"But we actually have to talk about something else," Warren says with a sigh. "I'm sorry. I've left it for too long. I hate that I waited to talk to you about it, but it didn't feel like a good time after Rachel's call last week and . . ." He rubs his face and leans back on the coffee table. I lift myself off his lap and sit on the floor across from him.

"It's okay. Tell me."

"There's an apartment . . . a two-bedroom, not far from here," Warren says.

Oh . . .

"They accepted an application I put in months ago, and they need an answer from me by tomorrow."

I blink rapidly. "When?"

"The lease starts in November, but I could float both places until December—if that . . ." He shakes his head, knowing that wouldn't solve the problem.

"That doesn't change anything. My re-evaluation isn't until—" My voice is as fast as my racing heartbeat.

"January. I know. . . . Shit, Chloe." He looks up to the ceiling. "I—I don't know what to do. I asked if they could start the lease in January. I asked Rachel if . . . but . . ." He rubs the back of his neck, not looking at me. "I've waited so long to get my own place with Luke. I don't know when, if ever, another apartment will become available around here—one that I can afford."

I can't ask him to pass this up, I know that. Luke spent six years on his own, and Warren has worked so hard to make it happen. But what about Willow? *What about me?*

"I don't know what to say." I pull my bottom lip between my teeth.

He looks down to where my hands rest in my lap and moves quickly, pulling my wrists apart and holding them in his grasp.

"Tell me to stay," Warren says.

Between the lack of sleep, the dizzying effect of his hold, and the urgency in his voice, I feel dazed.

"What?" I ask.

Warren licks his lip, closes his eyes, then speaks slowly. "Tell me we can write up something . . . some sort of agreement. If we can do that, then we can stay."

"But . . ." My voice softens into nothing.

"But what?" Warren's voice sounds winded.

"We'd live together?"

"Chloe, we already live together." His tone is amused, but his face remains focused.

"I know, just—it feels different. What about . . ."

"I think if we can both agree that no matter what, we stick it out here until Luke graduates, then we'd be okay."

Please stay after that too.

"I can agree to that—for sure. Of course." My voice is steadier than it has been all morning.

His hold moves from my wrists to my hands.

"I want to keep all of you," Warren says, blue eyes pinning me to where I sit. He rubs both thumbs over my own.

"I want to keep all of you too." I smile softly.

Warren looks at me from under his brow, his features still sharp as ever but filled with relief and tender warmth.

"I'm sorry I brought it up on an already shitty day."

"No, thank you for telling me. I'm glad you didn't just take the apartment without saying anything."

He jerks back, eyes narrowing. "No way, Chloe. I wouldn't do that. I'm not going anywhere."

Does he know how long I have wanted to hear someone say that to me? To feel *in my bones* that they mean it?

This must show on my face, because Warren's expression shifts, now full of something longing to be spoken in a swelling moment. His lips part as if he can't keep it in a second longer, but he removes his hands from mine and brushes them over his knees.

"Your tea is going to get cold," he says. *Not what I was expecting.*

"It probably already is," I respond quietly.

Warren stands and offers a hand to me. I put my hand in his, and he pulls me into him. Our eyes meet, and I long to kiss him. To feel his firm but gentle lips on mine. But there is something uneasy stirring in him that gives me pause.

"Busy day ahead . . . I'm going to get ready." He lets my hand go and turns away. He doesn't get far before he turns back and speaks. "You okay, though? Do you need—"

"Yeah, I'm okay," I interrupt. "Better now."

Warren nods, turns back around, then walks down the hall toward his bedroom without saying another word.

TWENTY-FOUR

"Good luck today, Chloe. I'm sure it'll be fine." Luke pats my shoulder before he opens the car door and walks to the school's entrance.

"Did Luke know about the apartment?" I ask as Warren looks over his shoulder to pull out into traffic.

"Yeah, I told him."

"Will he be disappointed?"

Warren laughs to himself as we approach a red light at the end of the street. "No. He won't be."

"What's so funny?" I ask.

"Nothing. Just . . . staying was his idea. He made me promise I'd ask you."

"Really?"

I can't help but feel a tinge of disappointment rise—had he only asked for Luke's sake? Would he not want to stay otherwise?

"He knew I'd never ask for myself." Warren looks me up and

down, noticing whatever bit of insecurity must have played across my face.

"But you want to stay too?" *I have to be sure.*

Warren takes his right hand off the steering wheel and places it on my knee. I put my hand on top and follow the hills and valleys of his knuckles with my fingers.

"I want a lot of things, Chloe. But . . . that's a conversation for another day."

He moves his hand out from under mine and to the wheel. *I want it back.*

I turn up the volume on Warren's stereo and hit the CD button. Warren switches it back to the radio without saying anything.

"Hey! Put it back! I actually have been meaning to ask, who is the band? I took it out, but it's just a blank disk, you . . . pirate."

He laughs, then stills, narrowing his eyes at the road ahead. "You've been listening to that?"

"Yeah, I couldn't figure out the stereo the first few times I borrowed the car, and it was on repeat. Track four is my favorite. I've tried googling the lyrics but nothing comes up. Who is this?"

Warren gives me an unfamiliar smile—one of excitement mixed with trepidation. His tongue presses to either side of his mouth as he looks away momentarily.

"Uh, yeah. They're called Leaps and Bounds."

"Huh, cool name."

"Thanks, I chose it," Warren says, amused.

I roll my eyes, but Warren raises one brow, as if he's waiting for me to put something together.

"Wait, what? Do you know them?"

His hands tense around the wheel.

"When I was in high school, I played drums. A buddy and I started a band. We did local gigs mostly, one festival as an opener for this guy who was scouted at the same bar we used to frequent. We had to have fake IDs to play. Anyway, they're not called Leaps and Bounds anymore—they left the name when they left for a European tour."

"What? What happened? Why—"

"I had to get a job as soon as possible," Warren interrupts. "I was half-decent in my auto class, and that seemed like a safer bet." He shrugs. "So when they started touring, I left the band and started working. Luke had waited long enough."

"You gave it up for Luke?" I ask gently.

He sighs and turns the dial down so the music is barely audible.

"The drum solo on the fourth song . . . that's you?"

He licks his lips and his brow is furrowed as he turns to face me, stopped at a red light. "You listened to it that much?"

"Yes. That song's my favorite. The drums especially. Warren . . . you're incredible."

He does a small, shifting glance as he shakes his head.

"Ah, well." His face drops.

"Do you still play? I mean, I know you haven't been since you moved in, but . . ."

"No, I don't have my kit anymore. Sold it a while back to get some money for the car. It doesn't matter really. We can talk about something else."

"Okay . . . I hear you. I do. I just . . . I really want to see you play."

"Someday."

Warren turns into the hospital's parking lot and opens his window to pay for parking.

"A drummer . . ." I mutter to myself, cheeks warming.

He turns to me before the automatic barrier of the parking lot opens, grinning. "What, is that a fantasy of yours or something?"

"Well, it is now." I smile and look away shyly. "Why'd you have it in the car? If you don't like listening to it?"

"I guess I'm proud of it. But I didn't want to be the guy that makes his—" He stops himself. *His what?* "The guy who plays it for other people to show off. I miss it, though."

"Maybe when Luke goes off to college, you could pick it back up."

"Maybe," Warren says with a sigh.

We pull into a parking spot, and I get Willow out as Warren opens the trunk and unfolds the stroller.

"You want me to stay here?" he asks.

"No. Well, if you'd prefer. . . ."

"I'll come with." He locks the car.

Warren pushes the stroller to the entrance, and as we get inside, he reaches for my hand. I'm not sure if it's for my comfort or if it just felt right. *It does feel right.*

I could get used to this, the feeling of not trudging through appointments, difficult days, or fears alone. That thought pulls me out of my body, enough to feel the burden ease as I look down at my hand wrapped in his.

I open the door for Warren to push the stroller in and gesture to a seat in the waiting room while I go to the front desk.

"Good morning, Chloe. How's our Willow doing?" Of all the receptionists, Joy is my favorite—her name personified. She's got to be close to eighty and once told me she's been working at the hospital since before Dr. O'Leary was born. She likes to brag about that to the new patients.

"Morning! She's—"

Joy interrupts me. "And who is that handsome man with her?"

I smirk. *He is handsome, isn't he?* "That's my roommate, Warren."

"Roommate . . . is that what you kids are calling it these days? Okay . . ." She takes Willow's paperwork from me—the charting I do during the week between visits—and makes eyes at Warren.

I look at him as he waves back at her, flirtatious as ever. I stifle a laugh.

"Oh my. Chloe, if you don't snatch him up, someone else might," Joy says, her mouth open.

"I just might," I say through my grin.

"Dr. O'Leary is ready for you in room B." She points to the double doors to her left.

"Thanks, Joy." I wave Warren over and he follows, pushing Willow down the hall and into the small consultation room.

"Talking about me, dove?" he asks, voice barely above a whisper.

"What? No . . ." I answer dismissively. "And why do you keep calling me—"

"Good morning. How is my favorite patient doing?" Dr. O'Leary steps into the room and washes his hands by the front door. "Oh, and we have a new face this morning. Hello, I'm Dr. O'Leary."

"Warren. Nice to meet you." Warren nods politely back at him before taking a seat in the chair closest to the door.

"Good to meet you, Warren." Dr. O'Leary looks toward me as I take Willow out of her seat and back to Warren briefly before speaking again. "I haven't had a chance to look over your charting. How did the week go? And what has her sleep been like since she started the new medication?"

"Well," I say as I walk over to the exam table, "her blood pressure was up Tuesday, but otherwise, it was lower than the week before. Her sleep has gotten slightly better. Actually, she slept through the night last Wednesday—that was incredible."

Warren sputters a cough, and I look over to him.

"Uh, sorry," Warren says. "Does her sleep affect the medical stuff? Would it matter if she slept through the night?"

What a weird question. This isn't really a participatory thing, Warren.

"Well, yes. We're tracking her development alongside her heart health. At four months, we'd hope she'd start sleeping in longer stretches. It would at least tell us if her medication is making her irritable," Dr. O'Leary responds politely to the interruption.

Warren rubs a flat palm over his head. "Okay, so, she didn't sleep through the night last week. I, uh, I got up with her. . . ."

My lips part. *He was in my room?* Wednesday was the day I got the call from Rachel. I really needed that sleep.

Warren looks around sheepishly.

"Well, no matter." Dr. O'Leary speaks, and I drag my attention back to him.

"I'm glad to hear her blood pressure is improving." He clicks open the file with Willow's scans. "Ah, here we are. Okay." He swivels on his stool to face us, grinning from ear to ear. "The scan from last Friday's appointment was uploaded this morning, and I think you'll be elated to hear that the hole in her artery has entirely shut. Surgery won't be necessary . . . she did it herself."

A forceful exhale passes my lips. Relief mixes with shock, creating an open-mouthed smile as I look proudly at my baby sister. *She's going to be okay. We're going to be okay.*

Warren lets out a loud whooping sound from the corner of the room, punching the air above his head.

I laugh, and so does Dr. O'Leary.

"You did it, Willow! Good job, baby girl." I turn her in my lap and lift her up, bringing our noses to touch.

"So we will see you for two more weeks, to make sure her blood pressure continues to trend down, but, as of right now, Willow is no longer a PDA patient. She can go to a pediatrician for her developmental visits like any healthy baby."

Dr. O'Leary closes the computer program and claps his hands once.

"Well done, Chloe. Well done, Willow." He waves to me as he steps out of the room.

"Are the appointments usually this fast?" Warren walks toward us, beaming.

"No, normally there's a scan and bloodwork, but—"

He plays with Willow's hands as I hold her body flush against my front. He is the happiest I have ever seen him, twinkling eyes and broad smile. Because of Willow. Dr. O'Leary should come back to check my heart—it's certainly beating too fast. My mind fixates on a very different type of PDA.

"Warren?"

"Yep?" He barely looks up from Willow to my face before he straightens.

I step forward, then lift onto the tips of my toes. I kiss him, sweet, soft, and brief. "Thank you for coming."

He raises one hand to his lips and smiles. "Anytime."

TWENTY-FIVE

CPS'S VISITATION ROOM IS DECORATED FOR A WIDE variety of families with toys, games, and furniture for kids of any age. It's an inviting space with a large mural of a rainbow and brightly painted walls, a floor-to-ceiling window opposite the entrance and plush carpets thrown about. There is also a red emergency button to call security next to the open door, reminding me of exactly where I am.

Two familiar voices approach down the hall. My heart drops.

Odette enters first, followed by Connie. She stays in the doorway, looking over as I sit holding Willow on one of the beanbag chairs. I clench my jaw and will my trembling breaths to steady. *It will be okay.*

"My girls," Connie whispers, bringing a hand to her lips.

She is much more recognizable now than she was in June. Her hair has been cut to shoulder length and is fading back into her natural color from the roots. She has gained some weight. Her skin is dewy. She looks well, and I'm glad for it.

"Hello . . ." I pause, offering her a gentle smile. "Hi, Odette, thanks for coming." Odette gives me that perfect encouraging nod that makes my shoulders lower.

"I'm not one to miss a reunion, hon." Odette closes the door and props herself on the edge of a table where snacks are laid out and checks her watch—the two-hour countdown begins.

Connie peels herself from Odette's side, cautiously makes her way across the room, and lowers herself to sit in the beanbag next to me. I shuffle Willow to face her.

"Wow. She looks so much like you." Connie blinks, looking between us.

"We get that a lot." I let out a soft laugh.

"May I?" Connie asks, holding out her palms. She looks to Odette, who nods in permission, and then back to me with begging in her eyes.

I straighten, trying to maintain composure, and lift Willow toward her. She cradles her into the crook of her arm. I fight the urge to tell her that Willow only likes to be held upward.

"Hi, baby." Tears flow from Connie just as the first of mine falls. Odette seems to be wiping her face from across the room as well. Connie fiddles with her hand while Willow gurgles, adorable as ever.

I wince. *Don't be too adorable, kid.*

"I chose the name Willow. I hope that's okay," I say.

"It's perfect." Connie reaches one hand over to my knee and taps twice before returning it to Willow's back. "What's her middle name?"

"Jean, like us."

Connie's brows lift in surprise. She nods at me with tucked-in lips and eyes filled with gratitude.

I suppose she didn't assume I'd carry on the tradition of our middle names. My grandmother's name was Jean. I never knew her; but it's also Connie's middle name as well as my own. It didn't feel right to not give it to Willow."

Connie clears her throat and swipes a few of her tears away before speaking. "She looks so healthy. Is she okay?"

"Yeah, actually—we got some good news this morning. The hole in her artery has closed so she won't need surgery . . . she healed herself."

"Of course she did. Strong women, our family."

She hesitates, then we say, barely above a whisper, "Strong brows, strong noses, strong bodies, strong hearts," in unison.

"Strong hearts indeed." Connie sniffles and wipes her face with the sleeve of her cardigan. "Thank you, Chloe. For—for doing what I couldn't."

I nod, wiping some tears of my own. I have to know. Now. "Mom . . . I—I'm really proud of you . . . for getting sober. But—"

"Baby, no," Connie interrupts me. "I know what you're going to say and no. Willow . . . she's staying with you. I promise." She takes in a drawn-out breath, and her chest rises. "I—I miss her beyond measure, as I missed you all those years, but I know I could relapse. I know what that did to you. I know she's better off . . . with you. The stronger version of me."

Calm washes over me like a warm, ferocious wave. My breath is loud and scattered as each of my fears from the last week are purged from my body. I'm speechless and immensely unsure of how I went from resenting my mother for having Willow to being grateful to her for giving her to me. We're silent for a few minutes as Connie rubs Willow's soft hair.

"I'm just so glad you're together," Connie says.

I sit with that, trying to process and untie all the mental knots of tension I've had since Rachel's call about visits. I look at Willow, still reeling from the amazing news from Dr. O'Leary this morning.

A few minutes pass before I speak. "I think we get stronger with each generation. Like we're evolving."

"Well, then." Connie pauses and looks at my face with pride. "The world better watch out for her. Her sister is already the most incredible person I know." Connie reaches out to hold my hand, and I don't move away.

Her hands are soft, like I remember, but trembling. I feel for the scar on her pinkie finger that I used to trace up and down as she read me bedtime stories. It's all much more familiar, much harder to ignore. This is my mom. And she's doing the right thing.

The visit passes quickly, with Willow getting fussier and more vocal before her nap toward the end. Connie got to feed her, which seemed important to her. She asked me four or five times before we left if weekly visits were okay, and she promised to be at each one. I hugged her before she left—the first hug from my mother in six years.

Odette stays back once Connie has left and opens her arms to offer me a hug as well. "Good to see you, hon," she says over my shoulder.

"You too." While I appreciate the calls with her, nothing could come close to the comfort she brings into a room. "Thanks again for coming today."

"Wouldn't miss it. I'm so proud of you, Chloe. You just did a very hard thing. The first visit is so difficult. You gave your mama so much grace. You should be proud."

I don't let the words linger too long. I've cried enough in this room as it is. "Thank you."

"How are things going? At home? With work?"

"Good, yeah. Work is steady. I'm doing one or two smaller

projects a week—trying to make enough to pass the re-evaluation. Actually, I might have an easier time with that now . . . this morning we decided that Warren and Luke are going to stay on as roommates permanently."

"Oh, that's good news! Perhaps then it's time to slow down on work. You look exhausted . . ."

I huff. "Yeah, maybe."

"And things with Warren?" *Where did we leave off the last time we spoke?* I think I had spent a good twenty minutes telling her about the pancake breakfast debacle before she cut me off.

"Huh . . . Well, I kissed him today." Odette leans back, eyes widened and mouth curving into a grin, and waits for me to continue.

I imagine Warren sitting in the front seat of his car in the parking lot, and my heart flutters. Nothing has ever come close to the comfort I have received from him today. This morning in his arms, the firm hand clasped around mine at the hospital. He sees my messy . . . and stays. I shake my head, realizing what I'm about to say is perhaps the first time I've admitted it to myself as well.

"I think I might be in love with him."

Odette smiles in the way an adult does when a child tells them something they already know. "Hon, I could have told you that. You light up like a Christmas tree when you talk about him."

Willow starts crying, and I pick up her car seat to swing it back and forth.

"I'm worried it's too soon. I've only known him for a few months."

"Well, sometimes you just know . . . and you two have already been through a lot together. He sounds like a fine young man."

"He is."

Willow gets louder.

"I should probably go. Can I call you—"

"Call anytime, hon," Odette interrupts. "I love our chats."

She lifts the diaper bag up onto my shoulder, and I carry Willow out to the parking lot where Warren waits. I secure her in the backseat and open the passenger door.

"How did it go?" Warren sits up straight in the driver's seat, turns his body toward me, and studies my face for any visible cues.

"Really well."

His whole body softens.

"She's going to let me have custody. She isn't going to fight it. She—" I choke up. "She seems healthy."

Warren grabs on to either side of my face and presses his forehead to mine, letting out a long breath.

"She hugged me," I say, voice shaking.

"That's so good, Chloe." He pulls away slowly, kisses between my eyebrows, and leans back in.

"Willow is going to stay with me. . . ." I say it out loud for the first time, and it feels real. "I think the worst is over."

"It is, dove. It is. You did it."

I brush my hand over his jaw before moving to check on Willow, who lets out one long cry from the backseat. I gather myself with a steadying breath and buckle my seatbelt. Warren does the same before he pulls out of the parking lot and begins our drive home.

I want to tell Warren that I love him right now and a hundred times after that, but I need to get through my parents' visit first. I've played out twenty scenarios in my mind, going from his best possible reaction to the worst—and none of them are made better by having Warren meet my parents tomorrow.

TWENTY-SIX

"HELLO, DARLING!" MY MOTHER'S ACCENT FORGOES MOST
of her *H*'s, even after forty years of living outside of Barcelona.

She gives me a quick pat on my shoulder before stepping
around me and down the hall of my apartment. My dad pulls me
into a bear hug, and I squeal like a child as he raises me off the
floor and puts me back down.

"Good to see you, Panda."

Panda has been my dad's pet name for me since the day the
CPS worker dropped me off at their home. They had put a stuffed
panda on my pillow, and when I'd told them it was my favorite
animal, they took it as a sign that we were meant to be a family. In
reality, I preferred rabbits. Still, I learned to love pandas. They
were gifted to me by my father after every business trip. Quickly,
a collection began to grow. Snow globes, hats, shirts, stuffed
animals—all panda-related. The original sits on my desk upstairs.

"You too, Papa."

He wraps his arm around my shoulder, and I lead him into the living room where my mother is standing, taking in the space with slightly pursed lips. Neutral expressions are dangerous when it comes to my mother. She will let you know if she's happy. Her boisterous laugh and throaty Spanish accent become louder, her smile more pronounced with a hint of mischievousness. But other than that, it's a guessing game. One that usually ends with someone, often a waiter or hotel maid, crying.

"My roommates, Warren and his brother, Luke, took Willow to go pick up the food. They thought we could catch up for a few minutes uninterrupted."

I pat the cushion of the couch next to me, and my mom settles in. She turns, smiling, brushes my hair out of my face, and rubs my shoulder before turning toward my dad.

"Did I tell you about Chloe's roommates? It may have slipped my mind," she signs.

My dad replies, "The same roommates we met last Christmas? Lane and Elizabeth, was it?"

I take over for my mom. "No, Lane and Emily. They moved out after graduation. My new roommates are Warren and Luke. Warren is also a CPS guardian. We were partnered to make the process easier. Luke, his brother, is fifteen and also Deaf."

"Oh, wonderful, someone new for me to sign with. They will be back soon?" my dad replies, looking toward the front door briefly.

"Yeah, they're picking up the food. Willow is with them."

"Willow, yes. She is, what, six months now?" Dad signs.

"Four." I keep my face in a polite grin. This visit won't be long enough to air out all my feelings. I need to pick my battles.

"And how . . . is it? Being a parent?" My dad tenses, and his eyes remain focused on me, but I can sense my mother trying to get his attention beside me.

"Fine. She is great."

"Oh, happy birthday, by the way! Silly us! Happy birthday, darling."

My mom kisses my cheek and then signs to my dad, but I don't focus enough to watch. I don't know what stings more—my birthday being an afterthought or that the topic was meant to divert the conversation away from Willow.

"Yes, happy birthday . . . twenty-five. I cannot believe it." My dad pulls out his wallet and extends a thick clip of money toward me.

For wealthy people, they're not usually this generous. I look down at the money, then to my father's face, unsure, before reaching out and taking it. I stare at the money in my hand.

According to my parents, my college fund had been eaten up by the tutors and extracurriculars it had taken to get me in because of my "rough start" to life. I fight the desire to count the money here and now. *I'd love to know if it will cover the rest of my car.*

Although that may be something worth talking through with Warren now—maybe we could share his car since he's decided to stay indefinitely.

"You okay, darling? Where did you just go?" My mom speaks but doesn't sign.

"Oh, sorry. Yes. Thank you." I put the money down on the side table next to me. "Thank you, Papa."

"We'll be staying put for Christmas this year, but we'd love for you to come visit for the holidays. That will cover your flight." My dad signs back, smiling.

"Oh, that sounds amazing, but I can't travel until Willow's custody is final. She can't leave the country yet."

My father shifts in the armchair, looking toward my mother, who shakes her head in a *leave it* gesture. He does . . . for now. I let out a slow, purposeful breath. *I need some space.*

"Would either of you like a drink? Water? Wine? Tea?" I stand and begin walking to the kitchen.

"Wine for me, please . . . your father says wine as well." My mom projects her voice toward me.

I pull out three glasses and pour. I take advantage of being hidden from my mother's watchful eye and text Warren.

CHLOE: Please tell me you're almost home. I need a buffer ASAP.

WARREN: Elevator.

I slip my phone into the back pocket of my jeans and take the two glasses over to my parents.

"Warren let me know they're on their way up. You ready to meet Willow?" I try to pitch my voice as excited, but it is forced and full of desperation.

"Well, why wouldn't we be?" *I don't know, Mom—why wouldn't you be?*

My dad offers a less-than-sincere smile.

The door opens, followed by the sound of shuffling paper bags and the brakes of the stroller clicking into place. I nod at my parents, then turn down the front hall.

"It is getting tense in there—fast. Give me the world's cutest baby." I take Willow from her car seat and tuck her in against me so I can continue signing. "Thank you for going."

"Warren got enough food to feed the entire floor, so at least our mouths will be busy," Luke teases.

"You okay?" Warren tries to catch my eye, but I'm too tense to stop moving.

We haven't talked about my adoptive parents a whole lot, other than my dad being Deaf and them living overseas, but he has witnessed my nerves firsthand today. He put Luke to work alongside us tidying the apartment and only teased me when I wiped the top of the kitchen cupboards. "Are they giants?" he had asked. Still, he'd passed me a clean cloth while I was up there.

"I'm fine. Come on, I will introduce you." I nod briskly, gathering momentum.

Warren pushes up the sleeves of his cable-knit sweater and pulls down on the bottom hem as I turn to walk down the hall. *Wait, his cable-knit sweater?* Did he dress up? He isn't in his usual plain long sleeve T-shirt and ripped jeans. These jeans are black and hardly worn. . . . *Are they new?*

"Warren, Luke, this is my mother, Martina, and my father, Tom." I struggle to sign and gesture toward my parents while still holding Willow. My mom smiles subtly, her eyes glancing up and down both of them before extending a hand.

"Nice to meet you both." My mother shakes their hands. Luke smiles blankly—unlike my father, he doesn't force himself to lip-read.

"You too." Warren steps back and nods, then turns to my father. "Pleasure to meet you, sir."

"Please, call me Tom. Nice to meet you both." My dad's large smile is infectious. I think, similar to Luke in the group home, he's been without signing partners other than my mother for quite some time.

My dad shakes Warren's hand and turns to sign with Luke. They begin a side conversation as Warren picks the bags of food back up off the floor and carries them over to the table.

I turn to my mother, who is looking cautiously at the infant pressed into my chest.

"And this . . . this is Willow." I take a step toward my mom. She swallows, and her eyes twitch slightly.

"Hola, pequeñuela." My mother's native tongue has always slipped out when her thoughts are preoccupied elsewhere.

"Do you want to hold her?" I forget to breathe.

"Perhaps after we eat. I'm starved," she says. I bite my tongue and nod, forcing a smile across my face.

"Sure, okay." There's a strain in my voice, and I know Warren hears it since he looks over at me with concern.

Warren waves Luke over, and my dad follows closely behind, paying no attention to me or Willow as he passes us, still wrapped up in whatever Luke is saying. *At least they're getting along.*

I take the seat closest to the hallway, facing away from the living room. My mother chooses the chair on the opposite side of the table, and my father joins her, sitting directly across from me. Luke sits on my right at the head of the table in the computer chair that he brought over from his room and continues his conversation with my dad. Warren sits next to me on my left. He winks at me, out of view from the others, as he sits.

He flirts as a form of reassurance, and it works. He seems to know that what I need most is some of that confidence he has a surplus of. I hold Willow in the crook of my arm as I scoop food onto my plate with the other hand. Warren *did* order the entire menu.

"I haven't had vegan food before, so I just ordered one of everything. I hope that's okay."

"Yes, thank you. It looks lovely." My mother smiles at him as she puts a few items on her plate. "Tell me, Warren, what do you do for work?"

"I'm a mechanic at a shop not far from here." Every time Warren speaks, he glances to see if Luke and my dad are looking at him, checking if he should be signing.

"A mechanic . . . does that pay well?" My mother asks, her tone deceptively casual. I stop chewing momentarily before looking sideways to Warren. He is unbothered.

"It does, yeah. It's an experience-based salary. I'm working my way up."

"And the goal, eventually?"

"Keep spinning on the wheel of capitalism, I suppose . . ." Warren lets out a low chuckle, but when my mother doesn't budge, he straightens and continues. "I'd like to own a shop someday." I choke a little; Warren places a hand on my knee. *I've got this* he says with a squeeze of his fingers.

My mother smiles. "Good for you." She forks food into her mouth, then swallows it down. "Chloe, how's your work going?" *Here we go.*

"Really great. I recently finished this bus advertisement campaign for the city. The payout was great, and it will be cool to see my design out in the real world." *There isn't much to dissect there.*

"So you're still taking the bus, then?" *Never mind.*

"Well, Mom . . . cars are expensive, and I'm avoiding getting into more debt. I have a kid to provide for now. The bus is a more affordable option."

"We aren't going to buy you a car, Chloe." My mother chews as she speaks but still manages to pronounce every syllable of her rebuttal with clarity.

"I didn't ask you to . . ." I breathe out.

"Well, then why are you complaining?" My mother scrapes her teeth on her fork.

I look down at my plate. "Sorry. I didn't mean to." *Don't cry.* "Actually, Warren has a car. He lets me borrow it twice a week, which is so kind of him." I put the attention back on Warren. My mom seems enamored with him. *He's wearing a cable-knit sweater, for crying out loud.*

"Does Warren not need his car for work?" she asks me but looks to watch Warren's response.

His hand tightens around my knee. I hesitate a moment too long, and Warren speaks in my place. "I asked her to borrow it—because she was grocery shopping for the house. Seemed fair. Plus, Willow's appointments are across the city, and the buses here are terrible. Hopefully the new ad campaigns help that."

His chest puffs, as if he has accomplished something, and he loosens the grip on my knee. Poor Warren. He doesn't know his opponent well.

My mother puts her cutlery down and looks down her nose at him. "If you weren't here, then what? Chloe cannot learn to be self-sufficient if she doesn't at first struggle. Her father and I were not born into wealth. We worked hard and sacrificed to get to where we are. Now we can afford cars. We don't need to concern ourselves with borrowing or . . . public transit." My mother waves a limp wrist to the side of her, as if she's gesturing to the peasants below outside the apartment window.

Warren chews his lips and then opens them solely to shovel food in. I think he's keeping his mouth full purposefully.

"Mom, it's fine. I'm close to getting the car, so it won't be an issue soon. Just forget—"

"Well, I hope you don't use your birthday money on it. That is supposed to pay for flights to visit us and Abuela." My mom's expression softens from annoyance to weariness. "She's older now, darling. You may not get many more chances to visit her."

"I already said I can't travel until Willow's custody is final. Then we'll come visit."

"I don't know if traveling with an infant is a good idea. It's a long flight," she says, dismissing my response.

A breathy laugh comes out of me. "Mom, what am I supposed to do? She's—"

"She can't go stay with another family? Constance?" I haven't heard my mother use Connie's name in over ten years.

I take in a short breath without meaning to. "No, Mom . . . she can't. Would you have let me stay with her? When you wanted to travel?"

"That was different."

"How?"

"We weren't babysitting while she got sober. We took you in permanently. We were ready to be parents. We had our time to travel, save money, and enjoy life beforehand. We wanted you. We chose to give up those things. . . ."

"I want Willow, permanently. I'm going to have her permanently."

She raises her hands up as my voice becomes louder. Luke and my father go still at the end of the table, coming back into a room that is tenser than when they left it.

My eyes water, mostly from frustration. "Why can't you support me in this? It has been so hard. You haven't even held her."

"We just got here. Do I need to hold her within minutes of—"

"You should be excited to meet her! She's a part of me!" I'm getting louder, unable to stop it. A tear drops off my chin.

"Do not speak to me like that, *hija*. You want me to be happy to watch you throw your life away?" She scoffs. "I thought you'd follow my example and not your *junkie* birth mother, but now you choose this life? You choose art over success? Pride over wealth? You choose to raise a baby alone? Who will want you now? *Ay dios mio*. We tried so hard! Where did we go so wrong?"

I open my mouth but nothing comes out. I turn to see my father, who I know can lip-read after years of my mother's noncompliance, and wait for him to look at me. *Show me you got that. Show me you're sorry.* He doesn't turn. I push away from the table, and Warren's palm slips off my leg as I stand. I look down at my mother and hold her eyes and tuck Willow closer.

"You are not allowed to speak to me like that anymore." I attempt to hold my voice even. "I'm struggling, sure. It's really hard. But I'm happy with my decision. This is how my life is going to be. Whether you like it or not. So you can either support me . . . or you can go."

My mother looks me up and down with contempt. She lets my words sit for far too long, knowing she's the only person who can speak next. She wants me to squirm—I will not.

She speaks, but not to me. "Do you see how she talks to me? The disrespect . . . would you talk to your mother like that, Warren?"

Warren looks down at his lap, nods once, then stands slowly, his body tense. He looks to Luke at the head of the table and uses his chin to gesture to Luke's bedroom door. Luke nods and leaves the table without hesitation.

Warren takes one slow breath, then signs as he speaks. "Martina, I don't know you very well, but I do know your daughter . . . Actually, I'm beginning to wonder if I know her better than you do." He looks at me and the sleeping baby in my arms with affection. "Chloe is the hardest-working person I know. I don't think I know anyone else who could be a full-time parent to an infant with medical needs and still work. Did you know that Willow has medication she needs to take three times a day? That she requires daily monitoring for her heart? That she barely sleeps? Chloe doesn't complain. Ever. On top of that, she's still a good friend to Luke and me. She's exhausted."

Warren pauses and looks at my dad, then back to my mother, who is leaning on the back of her chair, arms folded over her chest.

"Maybe if Chloe had felt safe to ask for help once in a while, she'd be less hard on herself. It seems, however, that she was taught not to accept help from anyone." Warren looks to me briefly before continuing, an apology in his eyes. "So . . . yes. I hear how she is speaking to you, and frankly, I wouldn't have been so kind."

His shoulders rise and fall on a breath before he looks my mother in the eye without hesitation. "And no, I don't speak to my mother like that because . . . my junkie mother is dead."

TWENTY-SEVEN

I LOVE HIM. THAT'S ALL I CAN THINK RIGHT NOW. I love Warren.

I take his hand in mine. Damn further comments or judgments from my mother. She stands, outraged, and my father reaches up and slowly pulls her back down to her seat. She turns on him in a fury, and my parents share a conversation with glances back and forth.

My interpretation would be that my father is trying to make her see how close she is to losing her only daughter, and my mother stubbornly agrees to give in.

My mother licks her lips, eyes full of annoyance, and signs as she speaks. "I'm sorry, Chloe, Warren. I didn't intend to ruin this lovely dinner. Let's all sit."

We lower into our chairs, still holding hands. Warren grips mine tighter and brings it to his lap, wrapping his other hand around the back and squeezing it between his two palms before letting go.

The four of us load our plates with more food in silence, pausing to pass dishes around.

My father strikes up a conversation with Warren about cars. I relinquish some pride and ask my mother about Abuela's health. We all talk until we've had our dinner, ignoring the scene that just took place. Though I don't forget what Warren said for a single moment. The way he had commanded the attention of the room, defending me from the same judgments he had made of me a few months ago.

After dinner, my mother asks to hold Willow. In her lap at first—at arm's length—but then Willow does her impression of the world's most perfect baby, giving nothing but big eyes and sweet smiles, and even my mom softens to her, pulling her to her chest.

My dad asks Warren to take a photo of the four of us to show Abuela and says they'll get it framed. They leave shortly after I come down from getting Willow settled to bed, exchanging hugs in place of handshakes with Warren and Luke, who had reappeared while I was upstairs.

As I close the front door, I count the visit as a win overall. When I turn, Luke and Warren are in the hallway behind me, offering a group hug. After a long, slightly awkward minute of hugging, we all step back.

"Man, I'm sure glad we weren't adopted." Luke's face lights up with teasing, and I can't help but laugh. Warren shoves his shoulder but smirks as well. "What? I'm kidding. Your dad was cool. He talks a lot, though."

We walk over to the living room as a unit. Warren lands next to me on the couch, our knees touching, as Luke sits across from us in the armchair.

"Yeah, well, my mom can sign but frequently complains about

having to juggle three languages. I think he liked having someone to talk to. Thanks for hanging out with him."

"What happened when I left? Things looked . . . intense."

"Warren stood up for me, literally. Shut my mother up. It was great."

"I wouldn't say that," Warren chimes in, eyes falling to the ground between the three of us before raising slowly to find me.

"No, you did. I . . . I loved it. Thank you." As I look back at him, I can feel myself forgetting to hide what's fighting its way out. *I love you.* My eyes might literally have cartoon hearts popping out of them. Luke coughs, dragging our attention back to the other side of the room.

"Well, I'm going to go to my room now . . . have fun thanking him, I guess. Just don't do it out here." He goes to stand, and I toss a pillow at him. He laughs, and I roll my eyes.

"Good night," he signs to me. "Good luck," he signs to Warren, who raises a hand to rub his chin, smiling and shaking his head.

When Luke's door shuts, Warren clears his throat and scoots a little farther away.

"So," we both say at the same time, then stop.

"You go," I say.

Warren smirks and wiggles his mouth from side to side. "Do you want to talk about it?"

"No." *I have something else I'd much rather do.*

"Sure?"

"Yes."

"Okay." Warren nods to himself, and I shift closer to him on the couch, making my intentions clear. He raises an eyebrow and looks down at my mouth. I watch as the left side of his lip curls up. "Do we kiss on birthdays?" he asks, voice raspier than usual.

"We did on yours . . ."

"So are we kissing now?"

"Like right now? No." I push my lips together, attempting to hide my grin.

"You know what I mean . . ." He's smiling, but his eyes hold steady on my lips.

"Maybe . . ." I pull my lips into my mouth. Warren had told me to let him know when I was ready. Well, here I am. Ready. "What are you doing this Friday?" I ask.

"Putting the final touches together for our date on *Saturday*." His mouth curves into a grin.

"Yeah?" My face glows, and I look away to hide it, feeling shy at how excited a date with him makes me, how active the butterflies in my stomach are. *My first real date.*

"Will Luke be okay babysitting?" I ask.

"Yeah, if you're comfortable with that. I could ask Belle. Or—"

"No, Luke is great with her." I pause, looking up to the loft briefly. "I won't know what to do with myself."

"First time away from Will . . . I promise to make it worth it." He looks at my mouth as he speaks, far more intensely this time. His eyes focus, looking at me as if it's almost impossible for him to hold himself back.

I swallow before I stand. Warren reaches out and grabs one of my hands, twirling me back around to face him.

"Yes?" I look down at him as I speak. His face is all wounded puppy; it's impossible not to laugh.

"Where are you going?" Warren asks, sulking.

"To get us some water. Don't worry." I wink and pull my hand away.

Honestly, the water is to give me a minute to practice what I want to say.

Hey, so—no pressure, but I'm in love with you.

No biggie—but I'm in love with you.

I hope it's not too early to say this, but I love you.

Shit, nothing feels right. As I carry the two glasses back to the couch, the words still don't come.

"Thanks." He takes the glass but immediately puts it on the coffee table, and I follow suit.

Warren places an arm over the back of the couch, his hand behind my shoulder. I place my hand on his forearm and rub my fingers over the knit of his sweater. I know that we're going to kiss at some point this evening . . . but we should probably talk first, right? This was so much easier when we were acting impulsively. Now there's a month's worth of learned self-restraint to combat.

I take a deep breath, trying my best to appear casual as I speak. "So, there's probably a better way of saying this but—"

"Hey, wait. Come here." Warren uses the arm draped across the couch to hook my shoulder and bring me into his lap. I move willingly, placing my knees on either side of his thighs and sitting back, my ass resting above his knees. My hands wrap around his neck. Warren brings his hands to my hips, looping his thumbs through the belt loops of my jeans on either side.

"I kinda"—*Focus, Chloe*—"find it hard to think like this." My mind is fuzzy, straddling Warren. I'm in two places, physically being touched in this new way and position and somehow also in my bedroom—where I have pictured being on top of him time and time again.

I close my eyes to focus on what I'd like to say, but the distracting ache in me grows. I open them, but looking down at Warren is just as unhelpful.

His eyes are dark and full of wanting. His jaw tenses as he looks down at where our laps meet. Then he looks back up to my face and flips one strand of hair behind my back before lazily follow-ing the rest of it down to the curve of my ass.

"Chloe, I'm so sorry," he says quietly.

That's not what I was expecting. "What? No, you don't—"

"I judged you. I . . . everything your mom said tonight? I'd tried to paint that picture too. That must have been awful, hearing your mother's criticisms thrown back at you by a stranger. I hate that I did that. I would—"

"I've spent most of my life having to prove my mother wrong despite wanting to do nothing but make her proud. I'm tired of it . . . done with it. You didn't know. And what you said to her . . . that's everything I needed to hear. Is that how you really feel?"

"And then some." He smiles and brings one hand to my cheek, and I lean into it, the softness of his sweater resting beside the corner of my mouth. "Chloe, I could go on forever about how wrong I was. How incredible you are. . . ." He clears his throat. "How much I love you."

I tense from surprise. *He loves me.*

"You what?" I smile obnoxiously wide, and Warren lifts an eye-brow at me but can't hide his enjoyment of my response.

"I love you, Chloe." His chest falls on a long exhale, and he lowers the hand from my cheek to my wrist resting at his side. "Is that okay for me to say? I haven't said it to anyone other than family before, I don't—"

"Yes!" I interrupt.

He tilts forward to kiss me, and I lean back, remembering I missed my cue.

"Wait!" I say a little too forcefully. I huff out a breath through my nose, taking great pleasure in the way Warren waits for me to speak with wide eyes. "I love you too."

"Well, thank fuck for that." His nose crinkles when he's this happy; I take a mental picture.

We both smile at each other for far too long, like the idiots we are.

"Okay. Stop . . . look away! This is getting embarrassing." I laugh, attempting to cover his face with my palm.

"Oh, this isn't even close to embarrassing. You want embarrassing?"

I gasp as he stands up, holding me against him and shifting so my legs wrap around his waist. He spins us around until I'm giggling and clinging to him for dear life. He kisses my cheeks and chin and neck as we spin and spin and spin, and he repeats "I love you," over and over.

"Okay! Stop! Put me down!" He falls flat on the couch. I land on top of him. He's still smiling—the longest I've ever seen from him.

"Damn," he groans out.

"What?" I brush a hand over his jaw.

"I couldn't even find something to be mad about right now if I wanted to."

"Wow, don't go soft on me. C'mon, this couch must be a little uncomfortable. I could press my elbow into the wrong spot."

I lean down until our bodies are flush, my forehead resting into the crook of his neck.

"I like it here," I mumble against him.

He wraps his arms around me, squeezing me tight before drifting his hands down my back . . . and lower. I look up to meet his face and raise an eyebrow.

He laughs. "What? We love each other, but I can't touch your butt? That's lame."

"See, I knew I could get you to complain about something . . ."

I kiss his lips, smiling against them. He nips at me, and I give it right back. *You're so annoying . . . no, you are!*

Our kiss deepens; lips finding teeth, and tongues finding each other. Warren pushes up to sit, and I settle into his lap again, aware of the scrape of our jeans that separate us so rudely. He reaches for my shirt and pulls it up over my head before he trails kisses across my cheek, to my ear, down to my jaw and neck. He palms my breast with a steady hand, and I reel from the touch, moaning at the firmness of his palm.

"I really love these too," Warren says, his voice gruff and low.

I hook my arms around his neck as he pulls the skin of my throat into his mouth, and the moans escaping me lengthen. The air around us is buzzing, full of kinetic excitement and desire. I pull at the neck of his sweater with my hands until he assists me, pulling it off entirely.

I lean back to look at him. *Mine,* some primal part of my brain hums.

I trace one finger down the center of his chest until I hit the space where my lap meets his. Then I wander back up to his shoulders, cut with muscles that fill my hands so perfectly.

"Is this a good time to say I love you again? Because I really want to keep saying it." I kiss his jaw and feel his cheek raise against me, smiling.

"Never stop saying it." Warren brings two steady hands around my back and runs them up and down my spine, sending tingles through my nervous system. He kisses my shoulder as he wraps his arms around me fully, squeezing my waist between them. As he stands up, I wrap my legs around his back.

"Can I take you to my room?" he asks, voice heavy, but tone sincere.

I kiss him ferociously in response, desperate to show him how much I want him to.

Then, as we enter the hallway and near the bathroom, a sobering thought falls into our path. I pull away from our kiss to speak, missing his lips instantly.

"Warren?" I ask. He pushes his forehead to mine, collecting himself as best as he can, reeling from our kiss.

"Mm-hmm?"

"So . . . I sort of just remembered something."

He comes back into the room, wary eyes meet mine. I look away, embarrassed.

"What?" he asks.

"I'm currently on my . . . period."

"Oh." He shuffles me up his body, his hands still holding me close. *Would he?* No. *Right?* He looks back down to my lips as he pulls his bottom lip between his teeth . . . *he might*.

I stutter, "I'd prefer if-if for our first time . . ."

"Okay, yes. Whatever you want." He kisses my cheek and slowly lowers me to the ground.

I fiddle with my bra strap as I look away from him. My cheeks and chest flush.

"Hey . . . don't do that." He reaches out, taking my jaw in his hand like he did the day he moved in—in almost this exact spot. "We've waited; we can wait more." He smiles, and I can't help but match.

"Okay." I nod hesitantly. *Damn you, Eve.*

"You still want to come in? Lie down with me?"

"Uh, yeah. Let me go get the baby monitor."

Warren nods and kisses me on the temple before stepping toward his door.

I use the washroom, brush my teeth, and pull my hair back for sleep. Still buzzing all the while from our make-out session. I fetch our two glasses of water from the coffee table, the monitor, and a pillow from the couch, trying my best not to drop any of the items as I get back to Warren's door and knock.

"Occupied." He manages to sound sarcastic from inside the room.

I roll my eyes and push down on the handle. He smiles at my full arms and reaches out to take the pillow, switching the one under his head for it—placing his pillow where I will lie next to him. Down the bed is a T-shirt and boxers that, presumably, he's chosen for me.

"I wasn't sure if going to get pajamas would wake Willow," he says.

"Thanks." I unhook my bra and let it slip to the floor before pulling his T-shirt over my head.

Warren's eyes flare wide and he shoots up. "No, no. That was way too fast . . . do it again." His voice strains.

I huff out a laugh and look down at the shirt he chose for me.

"Is this band merch? Damn, this makes me feel like a cool girl. The cool girl sleeps with the drummer of the band."

I pull off my jeans and pull on his boxers as Warren bites a fist and dramatically throws himself back on the pillow to face the ceiling.

"What?" I ask, laughing—at his expense.

"Well, first of all. I saw your breasts for the first time, and they're perfect. Even from the shortest viewing, which you're evil for, by the way . . ." He raises himself to lean on one elbow. "Second, you said you'd be cool for sleeping with me, which is a massive ego boost."

I slip under the covers and turn on my side to face him. His smile is even better up close.

"Lastly, you look so fucking adorable in my clothes that I want to rip them off you." He bunches the fabric at my waist into his fist, pulling me to his lower half, where the evidence of his attraction is obvious through his sweatpants.

I skate my teeth across my lower lip, trying to conceal my prideful smirk. *I've got Warren, man of few words, giving speeches and making lists out loud.* I feel powerful.

"Soon," I say, aching for more.

He relinquishes his grip and lies flat on his back. I curl into his side, hooking one leg across him. Warren's bed is firmer than mine but smells of him; it's like being in a sexy cocoon. My eyes close, despite my best efforts. His body is the perfect warmth against my cramping stomach, and his heavy breaths lull me into an all-encompassing sort of relaxation I haven't felt before. I can't believe I have ever slept anywhere else but here.

He draws circles on the middle of my back. "I love you, dove," he whispers into the still, dark room.

I fight against sleep to mumble out my next words. "When I'm not so tired, I'm going to get you to explain that nickname."

He kisses the top of my head, breathes me in, and relaxes back into his pillow. I drift off to sleep listening to his steady heartbeat, my face resting on his bare chest. *Lucky.*

TWENTY-EIGHT

I WAKE UP SLOWLY, MY OTHER SENSES TAKING IN MY surroundings before my eyes open. The smell of Warren and the feel of his sheets—different from mine upstairs, coarser—a welcome reminder that I slept next to him last night. My eyes blink steadily as the room around me adjusts into focus, but Warren isn't there.

I turn, making sure he's not behind me since I'm currently sprawled out in the center of his bed. The clock on his side table reads 9:57 AM. Two months ago, that would be entirely insignificant, but now that has a whole new meaning. Warren must have gotten up with Willow, letting me sleep in.

I give myself a quick once-over in the floor-length mirror that leans next to Warren's door. I look well rested for once. I also look like Warren's girlfriend. In his clothes and in his room, his kisses leaving my lips swollen, his words leaving my cheeks flushed—even still.

As much as I'd love to stay in his boxers for the rest of the day,

I change back into my jeans. I won't give the shirt back though, that I may never take off—other than to put my bra back on. I step into the hallway and find two of my favorite people in the kitchen.

"Good morning." I wrap my arms around Warren's waist as he stands in front of the stove. *Pancakes, take two.*

He turns, my grip around him remains as he moves.

"You have got to take that shirt off." He looks down at my body, leaned up close to him, and doesn't let up his stare as I speak.

"Never! Mine now!" I hold it at the hem, grinning as I go up on my toes to kiss him.

"No, seriously, it does horrible things to my brain," he whispers against my lips, grinning ear to ear.

"Horrible?"

"Truly despicable thoughts."

I wipe his expression away with my palm and roll my eyes as he nips at it.

"Thank you for letting me sleep." I go back to flat feet, still pressed against him as his hand rests on my waist, spatula in his other.

"Oh, yeah—no problem. We can do that, if you'd like . . . take turns." He moves to flip a pancake, and I step back.

"Wow, if old Warren could hear you now!"

"Willow has the same rule-breaking effect on me that you do. There's nothing I can do about it," he teases from over his shoulder.

"It must be genetic."

"Mmm," he mumbles in agreement.

He flips a pancake onto the stack next to the stove, and I walk over to Willow's bouncer chair. She smiles and kicks her little legs as I approach, making me feel as special as ever.

"Morning, Willow." I pick her up and lean her on my shoulder, giving her chubby cheek a few nibbles.

"She took the world's biggest shit this morning. Don't let the cuteness fool you." Warren points the spatula at Willow.

"Good job pooping on his time, kid. Noted." I wink at Warren as Luke's door opens.

"Something smells good."

"Good morning to you too," Warren signs back.

"Nice shirt." Luke points to me, wearing a knowing smile.

"Thanks." I do a slight curtsy, and he shakes his head.

"So are you two official now?" he asks, looking between Warren and me.

I look at Warren as he looks at me, the same expression on both of our faces, longing to hear the other answer. I owe him one for sparing me from saying "I love you" first and for the lie-in.

"Yeah, we are. Is that okay with you?" I ask.

Warren turns to the stove, hiding his smile, as Luke signs his response just for me.

"Anything that makes Warren this happy is fine by me. Just go easy on him."

"I will." I put Willow down and sit across the table from Luke as Warren brings pancakes and toppings over.

"Thank you," we both sign to him.

This is it, I think. Our new normal. We sit, exchanging light-hearted, teasing blows as we eat delicious pancakes. Luke takes our dishes as we finish up breakfast. I move to feed Willow her bottle on the couch as a slow Sunday morning passes us all by. Warren leans back on the couch, catching the sleep he lost getting up with Willow earlier. Luke lies down next to her play mat as she kicks and tries to push up. *She is so strong.* As midday approaches, I take Willow upstairs for her nap, rubbing her back until she falls asleep.

"Hey," Warren says from the top of the stairs. *He fits up here after all.* "I'm realizing I haven't been in your room during the day before." He looks around, taking in some of my art hanging above my dresser, then turns to look at my bed. He swallows.

"What?"

He snaps out of his thoughts with a quick shake. "Oh nothing, just—not what I pictured."

"The bed?"

"Yeah, I imagined you sleeping on plain white sheets with a wooden headboard. This makes more sense." My floral sheets and white metal bed frame glare back at us both. *Cutesy.*

"You imagined me sleeping?"

"Uh, sure—sleeping. Let's go with that." He winks as he sits down on my bed before groaning and lying down entirely. "Why on earth were we in my room last night? This bed is like a fucking cloud."

"The thought did occur to me." I lie down next to him. "But your bed smelled like you . . . I couldn't give that up."

"So I'm the weirdo who pictures you in your bed to fall asleep, and you're the weirdo who likes my scent more than comfort."

"Love makes fools of us all," I say, sighing. "I've pictured you too." I turn my head on the pillow beneath me as he looks straight up to the ceiling, smiling.

"Yeah?"

"Mm-hmm." I turn to look up too, cheeks burning.

"So, by Saturday . . ." His voice is quieter than usual, awkward and unsure. It's endearing.

"I'll be ready to bring our imaginations into reality." We turn to face each other at the same time.

We smile at each other for a lingering moment, giddy for what's to come before Warren shakes his head and opens his mouth to speak.

"I seriously almost died last night when you flashed me. Next time, you've gotta let me see you longer. Way longer."

I sit up, look down over him, and smile until he meets my gaze. He tilts his head up, resting a hand behind his neck. Smiling curiously—perhaps in reaction to the mischievous grin I wear as I drag the hem of his shirt between my thumb and fingers.

The shirt comes off over my head, and without slowing to feel embarrassed I unclasp my bra, allowing it to fall forward onto the bed between us. He licks his lips before pushing them together so tightly they almost disappear. He parts them to speak but seems to struggle to find words.

"Fuck, wow." He looks up to my eyes, his gleaming. He scrapes an open palm back and forth over his chin. "Damn."

I nod and pull the shirt back down over my head, forgoing my bra.

"How is it that your body turns me into some horny teen-ager? I haven't been this excited just to see breasts in a very long time."

"Well, I consider them a particularly good pair," I say.

"Hear, hear." Warren lies back down, and I join him. We lie side by side in comfortable silence. Comfortable silence . . . a new concept for me, an enjoyable one too. I'm still learning though, so I break first.

"So . . . *dove?*" I ask.

"No, I'm Warren." He turns to face me, grinning.

"Shut up . . . but really, why dove?"

"Well, I, um. You know how everyone at the shop has a nickname?"

I nod.

"Ram used to be called *Beast*. Then he met his wife. He started calling her Belle because she saw him, under all the bad. He switched to Ram because he outgrew the nickname—he wasn't a beast anymore, not with her around." He shuffles the pillow under him and pauses before speaking again. "They call me War, which started out from a shortened version of my name but stuck because of . . . you know."

Warren hesitates, turning to the ceiling. "I've spent so much of my life being angry . . . angry at my mom for dying. Angry at my dad for not sticking around. Angry at CPS for separating Luke and me. Angry at myself for fucking everything up. Angry at people who get to live normal lives . . . angry at pretty girls who make me question why I'm so grumpy all the time . . ." He turns to me, wearing a sincere expression. "A dove is a symbol of peace." He reaches toward me, holding my cheek in his palm. "That's what you are to me . . . peace." Warren softly wipes a tear off my face with his thumb. "Did I say something wrong?"

"No. Not at all. I just . . . I love you a lot."

"So the nickname can stay?"

"Definitely." I snuggle into him, breathing in his intoxicating scent once more—perhaps my bed will do, so long as he's in it too. "But, Warren?"

"Yes?"

"You're so much more than that nickname. With or without me, you're not that guy."

He presses a kiss to the top of my head.

"You might be right." We nap alongside Willow, and I'm as content as I have ever been.

TWENTY-NINE

"CHLOE!" LANE SQUEALS, PULLING ME INTO A HUG BE-fore the door is even fully open. "Whoa—so weird to be on the other side of this door!"

"Lane! I missed you . . ." We pull apart, and she steps around me, removing her jacket and shoes as Emily enters closely behind her.

"Hi!" Emily and I say in unison as we hug. Emily pushes us apart, her hands on both of my arms, and looks me over. She seems to be relieved—I probably look more well rested than I did the last time she saw me. We follow Lane toward the living room arm in arm.

"Well, other than some baby crap, this place really hasn't changed." Lane flops down onto the armchair, blowing a strand of hair out of her face. Lane is the opposite of Emily in so many ways—which is, in my opinion, the best way friends can be. Lane is short and as pale as the moon. Her hair, often some sort of pastel color (currently pink), is usually thrown into a messy bun. She dresses like a teenage girl who never quite left her goth phase—all black clothes, ripped jeans, piercings, and a splattering of tattoos that look more like doodles than art.

"I missed you too, Chlo." I smile at her as she blends back into the apartment, as if these five months haven't passed by at all.

"Where is your precious bambino?" Emily sets down two gift bags on the dining table, and I could burst into tears. *My first baby gifts.*

"She's asleep upstairs, but she should wake up soon."

"Well, then here . . ." Emily extends one bag to me. "This one is for you, mamacita." I take the gift and remove a few pieces of tissue paper to find a bag of coffee, a "World's Best Sister" mug, red wine, and . . . a vibrator. *Classic Em.*

I huff out a laugh. "Thank you, I love it."

"I thought, what would a new parent need? Caffeine, praise, a de-stressor, and . . . I mean, girl, if you're still getting some with a newborn in your room, then props to you, but . . ." I laugh, kiss Em on the cheek, and put the items away in the kitchen, leaving the vibrator in the gift bag on the coffee table.

"Although . . . Emily did mention a certain hot roommate. Perhaps the vibrator won't be necessary?" Lane chimes in as I reenter.

I'd tried not to spend too much of Emily's last visit talking about Warren, but he—and the potential for more between us—had come up briefly. I turn to raise my eyebrows at her, unable to hide the truth written across my face, even if I wanted to.

"Ooh! Tell. Us. Everything." Emily pats the seat next to her excitedly.

"Well . . . Warren and I are together now . . . it's very new . . ." Both women squeal, and Lane quietly applauds. "We had a tough

NEXT OF KIN 195

time adjusting to living together at first, but he is just . . . we just get each other. He makes me laugh. He annoys me—in the best possible way. He dotes on Willow, and he makes me feel . . ." *Sexy. Edible.* "Confident."

"I love that for you." Emily rests a hand on her chest as she looks toward me.

"Okay, stop—too much attention! Ah!" I wave them away, laughing. They both wait for me to continue though. "I told him I loved him . . . after he said it to me the other night."

"Chloe!" Lane sings out. "That is huge!"

"How is the sex?" Emily asks bluntly.

Lane throws a pillow at Emily as soon as the words leave her mouth. "Em!"

"Oh, as if you don't want to know if Mr. Perfect holds up in the bedroom . . ." Em teases, and Lane tilts her head in silent agreement. They turn to me, and I blush, unable to push my smile away.

"We haven't quite gotten there yet. We wanted to but . . . his brother interrupted. Then for a while we decided it wasn't a good idea, and when we were ready, good old Aunt Flo showed up . . ."

Lane gawks. "So you have this man who is . . . hot?" I nod. "Thoughtful?" I nod. "Funny?" I nod but think *he wishes.* "Makes you feel good about yourself?" I nod. "Sees you?" I nod—*big time.* "And he is saying I love you before he's even gotten a taste of your goodies?" I cringe and giggle at her wording, but nod one last time.

Lane and Emily make eye contact with each other, smirk, then, in unison, go to their knees and start bowing.

I tilt my head back, laughing. "Stop!" They both move back to their seats.

"Seriously though . . . brava," Emily says, laughing.

"I'll be taking that vibrator home . . . thank-you-very-much." Lane laughs alongside us.

I missed this. I missed them. "You know, I don't even think I asked . . . why are you guys back in town?"

"Well, good news . . ." Emily does a small drumroll on her lap. "We've decided to move back!" My mouth falls open. "We had planned to come back and visit the old stomping grounds anyway, but after our brunch"—she gestures between me and her—"we talked about it and decided to come back. We're renting an apartment two blocks from here . . ."

Lane finishes, "It may have been the only affordable two-bedroom left in the city. Someone backed out, and we snatched it up. We're here to sign and measure, then we'll be moving our shit cross-country again on November first. Mostly Em's shit, actually—she needs an entire truck just for her clothes."

"Seriously? That is the best news!" I look between them. There is something unspoken here. . . . "Why'd you decide to move back?"

Lane looks at Emily and nods; Emily pats my knee with her hand.

"What kind of aunties would we be if we didn't? We both work from home—it doesn't matter where we live," she says, and I swallow, feeling the tears brim my eyes before I have even fully processed the sincere tone of Em's voice and the encouraging look Lane sends from across the room.

My people were with me the whole time. I just had to let them in.

"Wow . . . I don't know what to say." I sniff back the sensation of tears about to flow.

"Go get that baby, sleep be damned! I'm still pissed that Emily got to meet her first." Lane sends a middle finger across the room to Em.

I stand, thankful for the chance to get some space before my emotions run too high. Upstairs, Willow is nibbling on her fist, not sleeping anyway. *Why can't you wake up silently at night, child?* I bring her downstairs to the sound of clapping from Lane.

"Will, meet Lane. This is the auntie you will call for a midnight ride home after sneaking out." I hand her to Lane, who reaches out with eager, flapping hands.

"Hello, Willow!" She curls Willow into her lap, supporting her back and neck with her palms. "Wow, you have a total mini-me." Lane looks up to me and back to Willow, comparing our faces. Willow drools some milk; Lane holds her out to me, but to her credit, takes her right back once wiped off. "Yes, I like you. Hello."

Emily stands, crosses the room, and crouches down next to them.

"Don't forget who you met first, kid. Auntie Em." She gasps. "Like *The Wizard of Oz!*"

"The auntie you will call for every fashion decision and every school dance or prom shopping trip," I add. Emily beams, nodding in agreement.

I take a few steps back and sink onto the couch as I watch them interact with Willow. I lean into the arm of the couch, consciously feeling the last ounce of loneliness drip out of my system as they stroke her cheeks, hair, and hands, trying to pull smiles out of her. I feel so grateful I could burst.

From behind me, the front door opens as Warren and Luke return home. I speak and sign, facing the hallway so Luke can see. "Hey! These are my old roommates, Emily and Lane. This is Warren and Luke."

As I finish speaking, Warren moves out of the hallway, kisses the top of my head as a greeting, and crosses the room to shake hands with them. Luke nods and signs from the hall.

"He says nice to meet you both," I say on behalf of Luke.

They nod and wave in return before Luke turns into his room, dragging his backpack behind him. I watch him go and notice his brow is furrowed.

For the past four days, Luke has been acting more and more like your average moody teenager. He wants to eat in his room, and his face is buried in his phone—texting ferociously and keeping it glued to his person. I can't help but think it's an obvious reaction to Warren and me. Warren disagrees, but truthfully, I don't see another explanation. I didn't want to mess anything up for Luke. I had thought we had his blessing—but maybe not.

I exchange a worried look with Warren as he sits next to me on the couch and places a hand on my knee.

"Don't worry about him right now," Warren, leaning over, murmurs in my ear.

Right. That can wait. I give him a grateful smile and gesture toward my friends. "So Emily and Lane were just telling me that they're moving back to the city. A few blocks away."

Warren's eyebrows raise as he looks toward them enthusiastically.

"You know the blue building—the really tall one on Fourth Ave?" Lane says as she hands a fussy Willow to Emily for bouncing.

"Yeah, actually, I just turned down a place there," Warren says matter-of-factly.

I watch Lane's expression shift to awe. "Wow! We only got the place because a spot opened up at the last minute."

"Worked out perfectly." Warren looks toward me, smile subtle but real.

Could it be a coincidence? Sure. But I think somehow the universe was on my team this time around—placing my people exactly where I need them. I move my hand on top of Warren's, and our eyes catch for the first time since he got home.

"Well . . . I won't get in the way of your visit. Nice to meet you both." Warren brings the top of my hand to his lips for a kiss, then lets it go as he stands.

We all protest.

"Oh, not so fast. We want to get to know the man who has got Chloe glowing like this," Emily says, bouncing Willow from side to side.

"Yeah, without even giving her an O . . ." Lane mumbles, and I flash my eyes at her.

Warren chuckles. "All right then . . . you ladies staying for dinner? Pizza?" He turns to me, and I clap my approval. "Be right back then." He kisses me, and it's a little too long and sexy to be appropriate for the company of others. I don't pretend to object or attempt to stop him. I think he took Lane's comment to heart ever so slightly.

Lane waits until Warren has left the room to speak. "Damn, Chloe. That kiss got *me* pregnant." I laugh, covering my grin with a hand.

"No more babies, okay? We just got this one." Em snuggles a calm Willow closer.

"Seriously, you better tell us when Aunt Flo heads out of town . . ."

"And here I was being chastised for asking about it moments ago," Emily says, rolling her eyes.

"I didn't know he looked like *that*!"

"He's a mechanic, right?" Em asks, and I offer her a bemused nod. "That means he'll be good with his hands . . ." She winks as Warren's door shuts down the hall.

As he approaches, my cheeks redden, burning brightly at the thought of his hands on my body. He still has a little bit of grease on his face from work, which adds to the sex-infused daydream. *Did I always have a thing for mechanics and drummers, or is it just since Warren?*

"All right, pizza is ordered. Hope you're all hungry." Warren sits. "So . . . who has embarrassing Chloe stories?" Both women throw their hands up to volunteer. I shove Warren's shoulder playfully and send a warning look to my friends, who burst out laughing anyway.

THIRTY

"Okay, her bottles are on the counter, and they're all measured out and ready to go . . . you just need to add formula. If she doesn't finish—"

Luke stops my signing with a wave.

"Then they go in the fridge. I know, Chloe. You've told me . . . and written it all down." Luke gestures to the binder I made that sits on the dining table. "We'll be fine. I'll call you if I need to, but she'll be sleeping most of the time anyway. It's not a big deal." He offers me a polite grin, and I nod in agreement.

This is the most Luke and I have talked in the past week and the most familiar he has seemed since the night of my parents' visit. Polite, willing to help, and not hiding away. Perhaps he's dropped the mopey act and we have no reason to worry after all. *Or perhaps he's about to sneak whoever he texts constantly up to the apartment while we're gone.*

"Sorry, you're right," I sign. "Thank you again."

A deal of sorts took place between Luke and Warren in exchange for babysitting tonight. I don't know the finer details, but I know it has something to do with Luke going out with his friends next month to celebrate his birthday with no curfew. This is a massive trust exercise for all of us.

"No worries. I've got this." He reaches for Willow and, though at first I find my grasp doesn't loosen, I do eventually let her go so I can go upstairs and change.

I hadn't risked getting dressed before Luke came on baby duty—Willow being an adorable spewing machine. I only have about fifteen minutes before the time Warren told me to be ready. He hasn't been home most of today, insisting he had things to take care of, but he told me he'd be *picking me up* at seven-thirty and to dress fancy-ish.

When I'd asked what fancy-ish meant, he'd sent a photo of himself in a suit jacket. I instantly made it my screensaver. *Sorry, Will.* Warren day to day? Handsome. Warren half naked? Achingly gorgeous. Warren in a suit? Devastating.

I pull out two options: one is a deep red velvet dress that is modest in its cleavage and length but hugs my body snugly. The other is a short emerald-green silk dress that scoops low on my chest. I text Warren a photo of them sprawled out on the bed.

CHLOE: A or B?

WARREN: You're going to be the death of me.

CHLOE: What? I can't choose!

WARREN: Red. It looks warmer.

CHLOE: So we'll be outside?

WARREN: Yes.

CHLOE: This wouldn't be so hard if you'd tell me what we're doing!

WARREN: See you in ten minutes.

Truthfully, I actually like not knowing . . . it makes it feel like a real date. However, I equally like giving Warren a hard time.

I slip on the strapless bra that works best with the narrow straps of the velvet dress. I put on my black high-heeled boots and let my hair out of the rollers its been in since my shower this morning. I did my makeup a little edgier than normal—shadowy eyelids, burnt-brown lip, and bronzer instead of my usual pink blush. My hair settles into thick waves, and I leave it down so it hits the arch of my lower back at its longest point. I haven't looked this good since . . . maybe ever.

I check myself out in the mirror after grabbing my leather jacket from the closet—it matches the boots and adds to the sexier look I'm going for. I'm still me under all of this, but I don't look as . . . approachable. Damn, I don't even look sunshine-y. I look like a cool girl. Like the drummer's girlfriend. Like sex in heels.

My phone chimes as Warren buzzes into the building, giving me a polite heads-up as to his arrival. I can't wait to see him—not just because of the suit—but because I missed him today.

As I pass Luke and Willow in the living room, a soft knock comes from the front door. Warren was right, being picked up feels more special. I open the door to his back turned as he waves to someone who is getting onto the elevator across the hall.

His jacket is black, a white shirt collar pokes out over top, and it's tailored to fit him flawlessly. I want to run my hands over his shoulders. I want to peel the jacket off him. He turns, and it's as if I'm truly dreaming.

Time appears to slow as he spins, adjusting the cuff of his shirt on one wrist like James *fucking* Bond. I laugh, because there's no way this man, with his cut jaw, knowing eyes, and ever-present sexy smirk, is here to pick me up . . . in a damned suit. This cannot be real.

There's also no possible explanation for why he's looking at me the way he is. Wide-eyed and lips parted, arrogant facade slipping away as he rubs the back of his neck. He takes his time tracing the curves of my body from head to toe, as if he can't believe every inch is real. My new favorite feeling rises again . . . *the feeling of being edible.*

"I know a chapel not too far from here." He rubs his chin like he's trying to remove a layer of skin. "I mean, I have other plans for the evening, but truthfully, we could call it."

I know he's joking, but something about the way his eyes sparkle as he looks down my body again tells me he could definitely be persuaded.

"Chloe, you're . . ." He leans on the doorframe, and I give him a slow full turn, showing off the back of the dress. "How am I supposed to drive? I meant what I said earlier. You may be the death of me."

As I turn back toward him, his hands flare in his trouser pockets, like he's attempting to hide the evidence of the effect this dress is having on him. I smirk, my eyes holding there.

"You look stunning, dove." He leans toward me and kisses my cheek softly—an innocent gesture in contrast to the glances we're sharing and the thoughts that are flowing between us.

"You clean up pretty good yourself." I unconsciously trace my tongue across my bottom lip, wishing it was his mouth instead. He shakes his head, exasperated.

"No," he says sternly, capturing my attention away from where his shirt tucks in under his belt. "We have to get out the door. Do not look at me like that."

"Right back at you." I move to stand next to him in the hall and shamelessly look him up and down at this new angle as he speaks with Luke. I'm ignoring whatever is being said—probably just instructions anyway. *Who cares about detailed instructions? Not me . . . no, never.*

Instead, I fixate on where his unbuttoned collar hits his neck, the prominence of his Adam's apple from the side and the way it bounces when he looks back toward me. I might try to leave a mark there later.

"Ready?" Warren offers his hand, and I take it.

"For what?" I bat my eyelashes, and he pulls me to him. Luke does his best to act disgusted, but the curling of his lip and the lighthearted roll of his eyes seem to say he's happy for his big brother after all.

"I'm really trying to remember, but I'm drawing a blank." Warren's fingers find my hair above my ear, and he licks his lips.

"Okay, so we may need to reassess. . . . How are we going to get through this date knowing that later—"

"Do not finish that thought. I will Kool-Aid-Man style bust us through that wall to get to my bedroom."

I laugh, but he remains sincerely flustered. "Yes . . . okay . . . sorry." I apologize half-heartedly, grinning from ear to ear.

Warren steps back and leads me by the hand to the elevator, clearing his throat as we step on and pulling me into a hug.

"I missed you today." My voice is muffled by his chest.

"I was just going to say that. One day apart; how lame are we?" he asks. I pull away, and tensions seem to ease. We may get through the date after all.

"So lame," I say, leaning back on the elevator railing as it arrives at the main floor.

Warren takes my hand and leads me to the parking lot where his car waits. He opens the door for me, and I slide in, finding a bouquet of flowers on the dashboard.

"Sunflowers are my favorite! Thank you." I bring them to my nose.

"Yeah, I guessed—you have like six sunflower sweaters." He's teasing, but not in a cruel way.

"Well, no sunflower sweaters tonight," I say, self-deprecatingly, as I gesture to my dress.

"Sunflower sweaters are sexy on you too. . . ." He turns, eyes sincere. "You know, this is amazing." He brushes the back of his hand over my jacket and the velvet on my waist. "But you're sexy as hell when you're sunshine and rainbows too. I'll take whatever version of you I can get." *He said the perfect thing.*

"Okay, good, because this was so much work." I lean over to kiss his cheek before buckling in. "Where are we headed?"

"First? Dinner. Belle's niece is the chef at a fancy Italian place across town that's apparently very hard to get into . . . and she pulled some strings for me." Warren turns the ignition but doesn't take the car out of park.

"Mmm . . . pasta." *A real date. A real date with Warren!*

"The rest of the evening will be a surprise. No amount of flirting will get you answers, so don't bother. I may be in love with you, and you may be dressed like every dirty dream I've ever had combined, but I will not cave," Warren says sternly.

I smirk, narrowing my eyes on him to watch him squirm. *Challenge accepted.*

I unbuckle my seatbelt and scoot backward over the console to land on his lap. I kiss across his jaw and interlock my fingers over the back of his hand, feeling his knuckles press against my palm. I lift our hands, guiding his open palm to my lips before I slide it down the column of my throat until his hand finds my chest. The feeling of velvet—and my breast—under his palm seems to overcome his senses. He lets out a stifled groan that is half annoyance, half arousal before throwing his head back onto the headrest, eyes shut tight.

"You sure about that?" I tease. He opens his eyes and looks down at me; I purposely lick my top lip slowly.

"No . . . you're cruel and unkind, and I truly think this dress has magical powers. But please, let tonight be a surprise. I don't want you in your head all night." His voice isn't his usual slow, arrogant tone but sped up and desperate-sounding. I cover a small grin with my free hand as he removes his from my body.

"Okay . . . you win," I say.

I kiss his mouth as I move away, his lips holding on to mine like a magnet as I turn and fall back into my seat. He whines as he ends our kiss, as if he already regrets every decision he's made that will prolong this evening.

"All right—I'm driving, I'm driving!" He turns, jaw tensing, and reverses out of the parking spot.

THIRTY-ONE

"THIS PLACE IS FANCY . . ." I SING-SONG AS WARREN pulls up to a semicircular driveway where two men in uniforms stand, waiting to park cars. Warren doesn't speak as he hops out and runs in front of the car to open my door. "I can do that," I say as I take his hand.

"Well, yes, I know you can. But I want to." He pulls me onto the curb before handing the keys to the valet with a quick nod of appreciation. He lets out a long sigh as we both look toward the entrance. I turn to face him; he adjusts his jacket and gives me a weak half smile.

"Do you want to go somewhere else? I'm happy—" My voice is hesitant before he interrupts.

"This place is fine."

I sigh, looking at the warm yellow glow from the sign above the doors. It's perfect—a classic date restaurant. "Well, it's great but—"

"Really, let's go inside." Warren fixes his collar, his tone flat and unconvincing.

"Warren, you seem uncomfortable." He stops and turns as another couple exits through the gold-and-glass doors; the sound of a quartet playing comes from inside before the entrance is sealed again. He moves us out of the couple's way, leading me with a hand on my waist. "I really appreciate it but—"

"Chloe, I'm not nervous because of the restaurant." He looks down at me, hands fidgeting in his pockets. "It doesn't matter where we go. You'll still be the most gorgeous woman in the room, and I'll still be the guy trying to figure out how he's with her." He pauses, studying me, then tilts his head and smiles. "People are nervous on first dates. Aren't you even a little nervous?"

"I guess I'm not . . ." *How the tables have turned.*

"I want you to have a good time." Warren brings one hand out of his pocket and tucks a curl away from my jaw, placing it behind my ear.

"Then, let's go in." I smile and wrap my arm through his.

Once inside, we give our name to the hostess standing behind a wooden desk and follow her to a small private table next to a foggy window. The restaurant is lit with dim overhead chandeliers and a single candle on each round table. There is a bottle of champagne on ice and two glasses awaiting us with a note.

"We're rooting for you kids. Love, Ram and Belle." I read it out loud to Warren as he places his jacket on the back of his chair. *Wow, he is beautiful.* The light from the candle flickers and is reflected in his eyes. I catch my breath as the server comes over.

"Good evening. May I open the bottle for you?"

"Yes, thank you." She pours two glasses over her arm, and I

think I truly must be in a movie—at least a Hallmark special of some kind. My first *real* date.

"I'll give you a moment with the menus." She fills two smaller glasses with water, then leaves us.

I open the small menu and catch a glimpse of the prices. My eyes go wide, and before I speak, Warren reaches out and tips the menu down, going over the top of it to grab my hand.

"Do not look at the prices," Warren says, raising a brow. "Promise me."

I nod, lying.

"I'll be paying. Not because you don't work hard and earn your own money, but because I chose this restaurant."

I smile, willing to agree if it relaxes him a little.

"And would you just stop looking so incredible for five seconds so I can finish a thought without wanting to jump over this table? Damn, you're beautiful, Chloe." The sincerity in his tone makes me swallow without meaning to. I don't let go of his hand as I read the menu.

We both order the lasagna—the cheapest item on the menu—and salads to start. Afterward, we share a slice of cheesecake that could've only been made by a deity of some kind.

"You keep moaning like that and I'm going to have to fight this cheesecake." Warren laughs, watching me tilt my head back with another bite.

"Fight it all you want. I'll be in the kitchen finding out who made it." I use the cloth napkin to wipe my lip. He shakes his head as he sets his fork down, leaving me the last piece of cake. "Can I know the next part of the plan now?" I shove the last forkful into my mouth.

The cocky gleam in his eyes shines brighter. "You'll find out when we get there." He stands and puts his jacket back on, throwing an impressive amount of cash onto the table. After slipping his wallet into his pocket, he steps around the table and offers a hand to me.

I throw back the last bit of champagne in my glass. I'm not letting it go to waste—it looks expensive. He slips my jacket over my shoulders, and we head outside, waiting for the valet to return our car out front.

"Thank you for dinner." I kiss him on the back of his hand, still intertwined with mine. He twists our wrists and kisses across my knuckles, and as his hand comes into view, I realize I left a perfect lipstick stain on him. "Sorry." I lick my thumb and reach to wipe it off.

"Don't you dare," he says in that same low tone he used a few weeks prior.

I attempt to calm myself as his car pulls up, shaking off how immeasurably turned on I am by his voice and his willingness to keep my mark on him. My body reacts to things from Warren that I haven't found sexy before. I have a feeling he could read me the phone book and I'd find something to be aroused by.

We drive for about ten minutes before my curiosity gets the better of me. "Really, where are we going?"

"There." Warren points to the top of the escarpment where a large platform sits. I've never been up there, but I know both Emily and Lane have been there on dates. It's infamous for parked-car make-out sessions while you overlook the city below. Romantic, sure . . . but not what I'd expect from Warren. He isn't one to follow a standard formula. If I'm being honest, I'm kind of disappointed, but I try my best to hide it.

He pulls off onto the dirt lot where one other car is parked—

I avoid looking over to see what its occupants are getting up to. I turn to Warren, but he's already getting out of the car. *Oh.* He comes around my side and helps me out, then leads us to his trunk.

"I thought this would be fun, but if it's too cold, we can do something else." He pulls two golf clubs out of the trunk, a huge container of glow-in-the-dark golf balls, and a backpack. *I shouldn't have doubted him.*

We walk over to a clearing where the fence breaks off, and he puts all the supplies down. From the backpack, he pulls out a blanket and places it a few feet back from the edge next to a lantern that he flicks on. He leaves the rest of the backpack's items inside and drops it to the ground with a noticeable thud.

"Ready?" He lines up two balls, and I nod, my smile so wide my cheeks are beginning to ache.

"Three, two, one . . ." I say, and we both hit. I yelp as my swing releases. The glowing orbs travel out into the night sky. His, admittedly, farther than mine. They land somewhere in the forest below.

Warren sets us up over and over until the container is empty and he places the last two balls out in front of us.

"Okay, this time . . . we make a wish," I say.

"They're glowing balls, not shooting stars," he teases.

"Shut up and do this with me."

He raises his hands and smiles. "Fine, okay, yes. A wish. A joint wish or our own?"

"Our own."

He nods, then counts us down. "Three, two, one. . . ." We hit and watch as they soar off into the dark.

I put my club down first and sit on the blanket. He remains at the escarpment's edge, looking out into a pitch-black sky. He drops his club and tucks his hands into his pockets. Since his back is facing me, I can't see his expression, but his jaw tenses as he looks over the lights of the city.

"Long wish?" I ask when he eventually sits down beside me.

"No, I wanted to lock it in. Felt like I had to know it hit the ground for it to work." He turns to me. "What did you wish for?" he asks as I scoot closer to him so our hips and legs touch, too close to turn and face each other. We both look ahead at the city below. There's a reason people come here—it's breathtaking.

"I made two wishes. I hope that's allowed," I say.

"Well, we'd have to ask the golf-ball gods."

"Tiger Woods?" I ask.

"He might be one," Warren muses.

I pause before speaking, quieter than before. "I wished that Willow would be happy with me—that I'd be enough for her."

Warren wraps his arm around my back, resting his hand on the ground next to me. I tuck myself into his shoulder.

"Willow is so lucky to have you. There's no way to be perfect, but I bet if she's anything like you, she'll be kind enough to give you chances when you screw up. She'll be happy." He kisses the top of my head, and I let out a breathy sigh. *I hope he's right.* "And that second wish?"

Right, honesty time. "I wished the same thing . . . but about you."

Warren doesn't pause or hesitate. He pulls away from me so he can look into my eyes. "Me too. I wished that this would be my last first date," he says, and I melt into him.

We hold eye contact as the lights twinkle from the city below and the lantern casts shadows across our faces. I break to look at his lips and kiss him, softly but full of wanting. Wanting more than each other's bodies. Wanting love, wanting loyalty, wanting permanence. We pull apart as Warren tilts his forehead into mine, stopping us before we get too carried away.

"I have one more surprise, if that's okay," he says, voice raspy.

Part of me wants to say no, desperate as I am to go home and finally be together. But how could I not see this night through? *This perfect night.*

"Of course." I kiss his cheek.

He stands, lifts me up by my hands, and places me to the side of the blanket so he can pick it up. He carries everything to the trunk and opens my door for me, then gets in and turns the ignition.

"Ready?" he asks, his cheeky smile pinning me to the passenger seat. I roll my eyes affectionately as he reverses out of the parking lot.

THIRTY-TWO

WE PULL UP TO AN EMPTY LOT IN A FAR SKETCHIER part of town. There are no signs on the brick wall in front of us to identify where we are, and nothing around us other than a dumpster to the right and a set of doors to the left, lit by a motion sensor above. Not exactly the same vibe as the previous two settings, but I've already learned to trust the process.

"Wait there." Warren gets out, then grabs the half-emptied backpack from the trunk before coming around to get me, leaving his jacket in the car this time.

He leads us to the set of black steel doors and presses a key code into the metal handle. There are two beeps and a brief flash of green light before he tries the handle and pushes it open, revealing a dark abyss on the other side of the door. I cling a little tighter to his hand and wrap my other hand around his forearm as we step inside.

"This is the part where you reveal your long con, right? You made me fall in love with you so you could lead me to my death?"

"You're so morbid." He keeps us walking forward. "But yes, sorry."

"It's okay. I should've guessed."

"It's very hard to find an affordable apartment these days . . . this was the only way." He stops. I can barely make out the sight of a wall in front of us. Wherever we are, he must have spent a lot of time here—in the dark—to be moving us around with such ease. "I'm going to turn on the lights now. Don't get scared."

The room fills with muted blue and green lights, revealing a stage beneath our feet.

"This is where my band used to play. It's being renovated right now, so it's emptied out, but I know the owner. He was cool enough to let me bring you before it's all gone." He pauses, lets my hand go, and places the backpack on the floor. He pulls out a bottle of water, a notebook, and a small tin. He puts them on the floor next to a wooden folding chair. "As much as you have a thing for drummers"—he laughs, rubbing the back of his neck—"that's not really a one-on-one serenade type of thing, so I hope this will do."

Warren guides me by my elbows to the chair, and I sit. He disappears around the corner on the opposite side of the stage and returns with a guitar. "Please keep in mind that I was the drummer, not the guitarist, for a reason," he says, eyes lit with excitement but smile apprehensive.

I place both hands in front of my mouth, unable to form words. *This is by far the most romantic thing that could ever possibly happen to me.*

He sits down on the stage and flips open his notebook, opening the tin to grab a guitar tuner and capo. I hate looking down at him like this, so I get off the chair and sit on the ground in front of him.

"But your dress—"

I shush and wave him on, eager beyond measure. I look down at the notebook, which faces away from me. Upside down, I can still make out the chicken-scratch writing at the top of the page. "Chloe's Song," it reads. *Have mercy.*

Warren bites the inside of his cheek, his nostrils flaring as he takes a deep breath and then begins plucking the strings of the guitar in a slow, romantic tune. He is instantly as impressive as he is on the drums. At least from what I've heard on his CD. His fingers move quickly; there's a small scratching as he slides between chords. After a visible swallow, he begins singing. His voice is smooth, even lower than his speaking voice. My eyes close for just a moment, desperate to memorize the sound.

> *Your colors are brighter than I've known.*
> *Rose-colored glasses are all you own,*
> *Limitless smile, but doubtful eyes.*
> *Who else has clouded your skies?*
> *I'm too selfish to hold back,*
> *The indecision that I lack,*
> *Your pain met mine, and I came undone.*
> *All these things I would become.*
> *Kissed me through the clinic doors,*
> *Loved you just a little more.*
> *I'm swimming, let the water take me.*
> *Show me all of you I've yet to see.*

My jaw trembles as I bring my eyes up from the notebook to him—I didn't want to miss a single moment by getting lost in his face. Warren plucks a few final notes, the song slowing as it comes to an end as he repeats the chorus. I wipe a tear off my cheek and shake my head slowly in happy disbelief.

Whatever magic this evening holds is tangible. I wish I could bottle it.

Warren doesn't look up as he rests the guitar beside him on the stage. He closes the notebook in front of him, keeping his eyes on the floor.

I will never be able to convey the way this moment has undoubtedly changed the trajectory of my life. Not to Lane and Emily, not to Willow, maybe not even to Warren. If there was any doubt before, I know for certain now that he has my whole heart. I won't be bold enough to ask for it back.

"Warren, I don't know what to say. I loved it." I throw my arms around his neck, leaning on my knees in front of him. "It was perfect. This night was perfect. Thank you." I kiss his cheek, and he guides me into his lap with hands on my hips.

"Not too cheesy?" Warren speaks into my hair.

"Oh, so cheesy. Unbelievably cheesy. But I love it . . . I can't believe you wrote me a song." I sit across his lap, and he tilts my chin up with his thumb and fist.

"I'll write you a thousand crappy songs if you want." He kisses my bottom lip swiftly.

"Not crappy. Not even a little. I love you. Far too much. It is worrying, honestly."

He laughs as he tucks a curl behind my ear. "I love you too, dove." He pauses, focusing on the hair he holds between his fingers. "Last first date?" he asks, eyes heavy and sincere.

I don't hesitate for even a second. "Yes." There is a bigger promise there, and I'm completely fine with it. "Let's go home." I run my hand along his jaw and kiss him.

"Yes," he repeats eagerly.

I stand and reach out to him, offering to pull him up. He walks the guitar back, picks up his backpack, and leads us to the exit in pitch black. Then, it's as if we hadn't been here at all. This stage might not even exist soon. The moment is ours, existing now solely in our shared memories. It's so much more precious this way.

THIRTY-THREE

AS SOON AS THE ELEVATOR DOORS SHUT, WARREN PULLS my back to his front, guiding us into the corner next to the buttons. I look up at him over my shoulder and spot the camera pointing out above our heads. He's moved us out of view.

"Warren, what are—"

He interrupts me by wrapping his arm around my hips, using a firm hand on my stomach to pull me closer against his body. His other hand comes over my shoulder, the back of his fingers trailing down my neck, collarbone, then down to the edge of my dress. He brushes the velvet edge and uncurls his hand, sliding it into my bra, rough hands finding my bare breast.

I press the back of my head into his chest as his hand plays with my nipple, hard and aching between his thumb and finger.

I moan, raising my hand to the back of his neck so I can hold myself steady as I tremble from wanting. A string of kisses is placed behind my ear as the elevator door chimes, opening to our empty floor.

Warren slides his hand out and twists me around to face him. He kisses me so forcefully I forget where we are until the doors shut and the elevator starts moving again.

"We missed our stop," I say, inches from his mouth. He licks my top lip and brings me back for more. I giggle as shivers run up and down my body. "Hey, wait. . . . Someone might be getting on."

"No one's getting on. I hit the first floor again." He grins, and I look down to see the button turned red. "I wanted more time before our date was over." He kisses my neck, and my eyes roll backward.

"We can't live in the elevator." I hit the button for the third floor.

"Prove it."

He reaches behind me and uses both hands to grab my ass, lifting me straight off the ground and up to his height so he doesn't need to bend down to kiss me. When the doors open, he keeps me pressed to him, my feet dangling at his shins.

My back hits the wall of the hallway next to our front door with force, and Warren's body presses me into place as he continues to kiss me with hard, fierce kisses. I desperately pull at the sides of my dress to allow my legs the freedom to wrap around Warren's hips—I'm no longer able to care about who may stumble into the hall and see us.

"Keys?" He moves his kisses to my cheek to speak, forehead pressing into my temple. It is achingly difficult to tear my thoughts away from the sensation of him between my thighs.

"You don't have yours?" I breathe out.

"I do, but my hands are otherwise occupied." He pinches my ass, and I straighten; he grins. I roll my eyes as I reach into his pocket and pull his keys out.

"Okay . . . put me down," I command.

Warren moans like a spoiled child but lowers me to the floor. He takes the keys from me and unlocks the door. Once we step inside, he turns to block my path beyond his bedroom.

"I'll go check on them—you stay in here, okay? Don't leave this room," he says.

I walk inside, sit on his bed, and cross my legs, putting my chest on display as I lean back onto my palms.

"Yes. Okay, stay like that. . . ." He rubs a palm over his skull. I think if Warren had hair, he'd be pulling it out. "Be right back." He taps the doorframe twice before closing the door, and footsteps sound down the hallway loudly—he might actually be running.

After tonight, after each surprise he gave me, I want to give him one in return. I strip down until I'm fully naked, then fold my clothes on top of his dresser. I turn his bedside lamp on and the overhead light off. I may be bold enough to be fully naked in front of him, but I certainly won't do it under fluorescent lighting. I flatten out his duvet and sit on top of it, crossing my legs and leaning back—as he'd left me. As he asked me to stay.

A soft knock hits the door.

"Occupied," I retort.

There's a muffled laugh from the other side as the handle turns down. Warren is facing the hallway, using his back to open the door while he holds two glasses of water out in front of him.

"Luke said Willow has been great . . . she just went back down a few minutes before we got in, so we should have plenty of—" He turns to see me, and immediately drops both glasses onto the carpet of his room.

"Hi," I say through a faint giggle.

I glance down at the two puddles around his feet as he steps out of the doorway, shutting the door behind him. His hand remains on the door as he looks back at me, eyes flowing up and down my body as his lips drift farther apart.

"Surprise." I smile shyly, covering my chest with my arm.

This was less awkward in my head. Now I'm sitting totally nude in front of a fully dressed man who stands, unmoving, across the room.

"I, uh. Wow." He rubs his face, finally removing his hand from the doorknob. "Sorry." He takes a few steps closer, paying the two spilled glasses no mind. "I was actually speechless for a second there. Do you have any idea how sexy you are?"

Warren unbuttons his shirt and pulls it off. *Do you have any idea how sexy you are?* I want to ask, but remain speechless at the flawless man in front of me.

He unfastens his belt and lets it fall to the floor carelessly—his eyes not leaving my body for a moment. "You're unreal, Chloe . . . your body . . ." He places two hands on the back of his neck, whispering to himself, "What the fuck . . . you—wow. Do you . . ." His voice trails off, and he lets out a long, forced breath.

"Warren, you're not actually saying anything right now," I say, uncrossing my legs and planting my feet on the soft rug next to his bed.

"I can't. I may never speak right again." He steps out of his pants and bends to reach for my thighs, his hands gripping the top of each one. He kneels in front of me and presses his forehead to the tops of my knees where they meet.

"What are you doing?" I ask, stifling a laugh.

"I don't know . . . praying?" Warren says, his grip on my thighs tightening.

I roll my eyes, smiling to myself. "Warren, get up."

"Chloe, respectfully, shut up," he says, looking up to my face, his chin resting on my knee. This is a dangerous angle. The way his eyes appear under his prominent brow makes me instantly wet between my thighs and my mouth dry.

"I'm seeing you completely naked for the very first time right now. Something I plan on doing for the rest of my life." He looks down to the floor, shakes his head, and looks back up. "Did I say that out loud? Yes . . . yes, because your body is truth serum. Damn; your body. Your perfect body."

His hands trail up from my thighs to the roll of my stomach, up to the side of my ribs, and back down to hold on to my hips. His fingers are calloused and rough; I think of what Emily had said—he'll be good with his hands.

Everywhere he brushes turns electric. I can't possibly squeeze my thighs any tighter together; I can't take the need for him anymore. I want him all over me. I use my knee to nudge at his chest until he leans back, allowing me the space to move, throwing my legs up on his bed. He follows and hovers over me, body parallel with mine.

"Truth serum?" I tease.

"I'd tell you just about anything right now . . . don't test it too much."

"Hmm, I think I might," I say.

He kisses my neck and trails a hand all over my chest, shoulder, and arm. I choose to resolve my curiosity instead of focusing fully on the pleasure Warren is already giving me.

"What did you think of me the day we first met?" I ask, my breath catching as he nips at my collarbone. He doesn't hesitate to answer as he soothes the same spot with a featherlight kiss.

"I thought you were beautiful. I loved your eyebrows. Funny but uptight. You called me *Prison Break*—which was weirdly charming. Then you spoke ASL and won me over entirely— though I chose, stupidly, to ignore that."

Wow, truth serum indeed. "And when did you decide you wanted me?"

"Wanted your body in my arms like this?" He wraps a hand around my back, arching it until the tip of my breast grazes his cheek. He teases my nipples with his tongue and licks the entire length of the space between my breasts.

My eyes close, and my lip finds itself between my teeth. "Easy . . . when you hugged me the first time. You fit into my side like you were made to be there. It took everything in me not to get hard. I was literally in pain trying to regain control." He raises himself and switches to the other side of my body, putting his weight all on his right forearm.

"When I wanted all of you?" Warren twists and pulls my nipple between his teeth, and I gasp. He's answering questions I no longer need the answers to. I just need him to keep going. Keep touching. He tenderly places one hand on my cheek and brushes it with his thumb. "The night of my birthday, then more and more every day since."

I wrap my hands around his neck, and we roll until he's flat on his back, and I sit on top of him. He swallows, and his eyes glaze as he looks up at me. "You're incredible."

I lean down and kiss him until my body goes soft all over. Our kisses turn deeper and deeper until he sits up underneath me. He brings one hand to the base of my hairline and uses a single finger to trace the middle of my back, achingly slowly. I lean into the touch, arching on top of him, hips rotating so my bare mound rubs against the top of his boxers. Once his finger reaches the base of my spine, he falls softly against the mattress.

I brush both hands over his chest, abdomen, and hips where my thighs lie. He tenses and writhes under my touch; his eyes are focused on where our bodies touch as I look to his face for his reaction to each movement. I lean to kiss his chest, his shoulders, his neck, before sitting back up—determined to stop soaking his boxers and help take them off.

"Move up." His voice is commanding and gruff.

I look down at my thighs as he tugs on the backs of my knees, trying to pull me up his body. I move up until my thighs rest on either side of his stomach, knees next to his chest—allowing him the space to remove his boxers.

"No," he says adamantly, "up here."

I still, realizing what he actually wants me to do. "I don't know. I haven't—um, I don't think that's a good idea."

"Chloe, please. Don't make me beg," he says, but I still hesitate. Of course I want to . . . but so much of this is still new. I'm not delicate, or light, or—

"Sit on my face. Now."

Something in the deepness of his voice, the plea in his forceful command, stirs confidence within me. I use my knees to crawl up the bed, hovering above his mouth. The exact moment worry begins to creep in, Warren places his hands on my lower back, resting on the curve of my ass, and pulls me down lower than I was planning to go.

"Relax," he whispers against my inner thigh, creating goosebumps. "I have you, dove." He lifts his head, licking straight up the center of me just once. *Whoa.* "By the way, you're perfect here too. So sweet." He attempts to pull me down again, and I give in, but only an inch.

"I don't want to hurt you." My voice is hazy, reflective of my mind. *That one taste was not enough.*

"Trust me, Chloe. I want this." He uses a firm hand on my waist to pull me farther down, and I let him. I lower until I'm truly sitting, the heels of my feet digging into my butt. He hums in response, which instantly sends pleasure shooting through me.

Warren licks, kisses, and sucks until I'm nothing but liquid being reshaped by his movements.

Moans escape my lips that sound unfamiliar, my voice husky and low. I don't attempt to make the sounds higher-pitched or feminine for Warren's sake, as I have with other guys. He wants *me*, not the manufactured version of me.

I take every opportunity I can to use his name, as I had imagined so many nights upstairs on my own. All those nights I spent wishing he was truly there with me. Despite the revelation that it will be as good as I imagined, I'm glad we waited. I feel safe now, safe to show him all of me—body and soul.

Warren turns away from me briefly, for an audible gasp of breath, then dives back in, consuming me beyond what I can stand. Nose rubbing against the top of me as his mouth finds my bundle of nerves, he worships me without mercy.

"Yes . . . Warren, I'm so close." My hips begin rolling unconsciously as I feel an orgasm within reach, coming closer and closer as Warren pins my hips down, resisting my frenzied movements.

I go over the edge as he continues to hold me in place against him, his hands grasping my hips, and his neck straining to meet my pleasure. I whisper out his name one final time as my body stills, and I roll onto my back to lie next to him.

"Thank you," Warren says, licking his lips.

It's selfish, not answering him—or thanking him—but I can't seem to speak. I smile wistfully at him as my body shudders a few more times, like aftershocks of an earthquake.

THIRTY-FOUR

WARREN PULLS OFF HIS BOXERS AND LOOKS OVER AT me, eyes focused. "If you want to stop, that's completely fine. I just—it was getting tight in there," he says.

I nod, looking down at his hardness. I should have known this part of him would be as incredible as the rest. My lips curl inside, and I bite down on them. I want him. *Now.*

"I'm on the Pill," I blurt, voice still hoarse from my panted breaths and exclamations of pleasure moments ago. "And I've tested negative."

"Me too." He nods eagerly.

"Warren, please fuck me." My voice is barely above a whisper, even still. His eyes go wide, and within seconds, he's on top of me, hands resting on either side of my head.

"Say that again." He lifts his hand to brush a strand of hair away from my mouth.

I grab his chin in my fist, pulling his head down until his eyes lock on mine and our noses touch. "Warren . . . please. Fuck. Me."

I punctuate each word. His face is hypnotized and tense. He reaches down between us and guides himself into me. His eyes flare before they shut tight in response.

"Fucking hell, dove." He grunts as he pushes farther in.

I don't respond. All my attention is focused on adjusting to the feeling of him inside me. My mouth shuts tight, wincing slightly from the warm pressure. I let out a single, pained breath as he finishes filling me, our hips now touching and bodies completely intertwined. After a moment of stillness, I open my eyes.

"You okay?" He pants softly as his heavy eyes find mine, fusing our connection further. I have never been a fan of eye contact during sex—but that doesn't apply to Warren.

"Yeah," I reply, watching my hand as I bring it over his jaw, past his ear, then up to the back of his neck, hooking my fingers around him. I look over his shoulder at my hand, saying a silent prayer of thanks that I get to touch him, feel him like this, know him intimately. And then our eyes meet again.

"Hi." He smiles softly down at me.

"Hi," I whisper back.

There is a familiar energy between us, similar to the night of his birthday. The first moment I felt a channel open through our stares. The place where we could exchange our pain with each other. Ease some, if we chose to. Now, we're exchanging something entirely different. Pleasure for pleasure. Wanting for wanting. Giving ourselves over to receive from the other.

"I love you," I say through trembling lips as Warren begins moving his hips, slow and circular.

He stills, and his bottom lip juts out. "No one has ever said that to me during sex before."

I look up to his gorgeous face and wonder how that's possible. If I had been with any guy capable of making me orgasm like Warren just has, I'd be picking out china patterns the next day. How could those other women resist? I couldn't hold back around him even if I wanted to.

Oh, no. Don't think of the other women he's been with. Don't start imagining their bodies under him. Don't picture their flawless skin or flatter tummies, their manicured hands or—

"Dove . . . come back." I turn my gaze from where I'd been ruminating over Warren's shoulder to his face. "Do you want to stop?" he asks.

I wince, eyes closing as I form my next words as best as I can. "No, no, I don't want to stop. Just—what you said, *during sex before* . . . I started thinking of the other women you've been with and if I'll measure up."

Warren's brows knit together as he shakes his head. With a series of quick movements, he lifts me onto his lap, holding both our weights as he moves backward until his shoulders rest on the headboard. He takes my wrists into his hands and brings them to either side of his face, placing them on his jaw.

"That was a dumb thing for me to say in this moment . . . truth serum, remember?" He tilts his head until my shifting gaze lands on him. "I'm sorry. It meant a lot to me to hear you say that, and I blurted it out. I hate that you're thinking about . . . no. I hate that you're thinking at all right now." His nostrils flare as his eyes focus on me. "I want you out of your head," he says forcefully.

Warren releases my wrists, but I keep my hands on his face. He leans forward and kisses me, slow and sultry. He uses his bite on my lip to pull me closer to him as he leans back on the headboard. The longer we kiss, the quieter my thoughts become, until I can't even remember what I was worried about.

When did I start writhing against him? I'm certainly not in my head anymore.

"You're it for me, dove. You're going to be my last everything. My body knows that as much as the rest of me does. I've been aching for you for so long." He groans as my fingertips dig into his shoulders.

Can a person orgasm from words alone? My inner walls tense and tighten at the thought of getting to do *this* forever.

"Shit . . ." Warren hisses through his teeth. "Have you been aching for me too?" he asks. I nod, my breath louder through parted lips. "Let me take the ache away, dove. Tell me to take care of it for you."

I lean in to kiss him, our mouths open for each other before we even connect. I begin raising and lowering myself on top of Warren as he sets our pace, his hands tight on my hips.

"Nothing will ever compare to this. Do you hear me?" Warren says, his breath hot on the side of my neck. I tilt my head back as his words swirl inside my emptied mind.

"Yes," I force out as Warren's pace becomes slower but deeper.

I'm aware that I'm barely assisting in raising or lowering myself at this point but can't bring myself to care. It feels too good.

The pressure and rhythm from Warren are perfect, but I know I won't be able to find release from this alone. I lower one of my hands off his cheek, gliding it down his front, where a light sheen of sweat has begun to form, and bring my hand down between us to assist in my pleasure.

"Need more?" Warren's hazy blue eyes bore into me. My lips part on a shaky breath as I nod.

Without hesitating, he lifts me off his lap and lays me down in front of him. He remains on his knees, wraps my legs around his hips, and wraps his arm around my knee to find my point of pleasure with his thumb. Once he finds a rhythm I obviously love, he fills me again.

"This right?" he asks.

Oh, god. "Yes," I whine out. "Harder."

"Me or my thumb?"

"Both," I cry out.

Warren responds with a dark laugh, a knowing type of laugh. *A warning.* He gives me exactly what I asked for; unrelenting thrusts and pressure from his thumb sends me skyrocketing toward an orgasm within seconds.

I feel myself tightening around him; he twitches in response. Our eyes meet as my mouth opens in bliss, finishing with his name on my lips.

Warren follows closely behind, alternating calling out *Chloe* and *dove* between grunts and bared teeth. He lands on top of me, his body pressing me into the mattress. I don't mind at all. He's exhausted from a job well done, and his weight on top of me feels glorious.

Warren's chin burrows into my neck as he finds his breath. I bring a hand over to the back of his head, brushing his almost nonexistent hair with my fingers as he relaxes. Once he lets out a low groan, he lifts himself, arms more wobbly than before.

"Didn't know you had it in you." I wink at him.

The teasing gleam in his eye returns. "I think you mean to say . . ." He puts on a mocking voice. "'Gee, Warren. Thank you for the two orgasms. I have never known such pleasure.'" I cover my smile and laugh as he raises his eyebrows, waiting for my sincere response.

"You're right . . . thank you, Warren, for the best sex of my life and—"

"Say that again," he says darkly.

"What?" I ask.

"The first part."

"You're right?"

"Ooh," he moans, voice dripping with sarcasm. "Yes. Again, baby."

I shove him until he falls next to me on the bed. As he lands laughing, my heart swells. *I love him*. I can't muster any other teasing with that pesky thought lurking around.

"Really though, that was incredible," I say.

"Yeah, we really brought it." He raises a fist in the air, offering it to me. I bump it with my own as I roll my eyes at the gesture.

"Do you think it will always be that good?" I blurt before analyzing what could be taken from such a question, what it implies. But he's made his own declarations tonight in regard to the future; why shouldn't I?

"I think it will always be good—maybe not *that* good. I won't be trying to impress you as much fifty years from now."

"Fifty years, huh?" I roll on my side to tease him, but he nods sincerely, eyes fixed on the ceiling.

"Yeah, I'll try for at least forty." He's so earnest it actually catches me off guard. I feel my cheeks flush.

"You really mean that?" I don't entirely know what I'm asking, but it certainly isn't just about sex. Warren turns his body toward mine, wraps an arm around me, and pulls me to him, our bodies flush.

His chin rests on top of my head and presses into me slightly as he begins to speak. "I thought it was obvious . . . I plan on keeping you forever. If you'll have me."

I'll have you. Yep. Forever. Done. "Yes, please."

"I love you," Warren says, pressing a kiss to the top of my head.

"I love you too." I lazily brush my palm across his chin, curling into him further, before I let sleep close in.

THIRTY-FIVE

LANE AND EMILY SPENT THE LAST TWO DAYS SETTLING into their new apartment. Tonight we christen it. Just us, a cheese board, and a few bottles of red wine. Warren has Willow at home, and I have a tote bag over my shoulder, the contents of which are 90 percent dairy products.

"Welcome, welcome!" Emily kisses both my cheeks and hands me a glass of wine.

"Ah, yes. Wine before I have even removed my shoes. I have missed living with you, Em."

Handing Lane my bag, I say, "I come bearing cheese!" She arranges cheese boards like it's her religion—it would be offensive to her if anyone else attempted. She makes salami rivers for crying out loud.

"Thank you, my liege." Lane peeks inside the bag as she speaks. "Come see the kitchen. Yours is way nicer, but we have a dishwasher."

"Jealous!" I follow her to their narrow galley kitchen and nod approvingly at the appliance. "There she is."

"A beauty, isn't she?" Lane takes a sip of wine, looking lovingly at it.

I huff out a laugh and rub a hand over her back as I pass behind her toward their living room, where Emily is waiting to give me the rest of the tour.

"She only cares about the dishwasher, but let me introduce you to my walk-in closet. She is the true star of the show," Emily says as I follow her down the hall to her bedroom.

Once the tour is finished, we all reconvene on the couch, gorgeous charcuterie in front of us on the coffee table.

"To you being back in the city!" I hold out my wine, and we all clink glasses.

"To roommates, old and new!" Lane raises another toast, winking at me.

"Real casual segue there, Lane." Emily sips some wine, smirking into her glass.

Lane rolls her eyes. "Okay, I've been plenty respectful, but Chlo . . . Did it happen?"

I assess how much is left in my glass and throw it back in a few large gulps. *Courage.* It isn't that I'm a prude or that I don't want to talk about it, because I *really* do. I simply don't know how. I always was more of a listener when Emily and Lane would talk hookups.

"Yes. It happened . . . and happened . . . and happened some more." I pour more wine into my glass as the women squeal. "I've never had it . . . happen . . . this much in one week."

"Every night?" Emily ogles.

"First time was our date last Friday, and . . . twelve times since,"

I say, and Lane audibly gasps. "He is . . . thorough." I bite my bottom lip, smiling despite myself. "He gets the job done every time."

"Well, damn. Cheers to that!" Emily says.

We all clink glasses again, giggling.

"It hasn't been like this for me before. Is this normal? Was I having bad . . ." My voice trails off.

"You've had sex twelve times in one week but can't say it out loud?" Lane pokes at my knee, and I stick my tongue out at her. "But no. No guy has ever made me come twelve times in a row. You have a superhuman on your hands and should probably get a ring on that man's finger as soon as possible." She pours wine into her glass as Emily nods in agreement.

"Well, Warren has made at least one reference to marriage every day since our date"—*not that I'm keeping track or anything*—"so I'll keep you posted," I say with a wink.

"Dibs on maid of honor." Emily raises a hand, beating Lane to it. I roll my eyes but smile.

"When do you ladies go back to work?" I change the subject.

"Two more days for me," Emily answers.

"I started back yesterday," Lane says. "I'm looking for something closer by. I like freelancing, but I need people to interact with. I'm driving Em insane." Emily's eyes widen, and she nods, her lips quivering on an *almost* laugh.

"There's a local tech company that paid me to do their business cards. They were hiring in-house, but I needed to stay unattached. I can send you their info," I offer.

"Mmm!" Lane says, mouth half-filled with Brie and cracker. "Please do," she mumbles, crumbs spewing. Emily hands her a napkin, shaking her head affectionately. We all nibble at the cheese board until Lane speaks again. "How have the visits with Connie been going?"

"Pretty good. She seems to be doing well. I like seeing Willow with her, but—a part of me feels sad when we're there. Right now, Willow has no idea who she's with, but still, I can't help but think about when she's older. Whether she'll hate having to go, or hate me for keeping her if my mom stays sober."

Both women nod thoughtfully, and Emily lowers her glass to the table before she speaks. "I think the fact that you're already worrying about the decisions you're making for Willow down the line means you're probably making the right ones. Or at least the best ones you can. Her life will never be entirely normal—but she'll be loved. By you, by your mom, us, hopefully Warren and Luke. No one with all that love around her could have hate in her heart, especially not for her big sister."

The room stills as Emily leans back in her seat, her soft eyes gently holding contact with mine. My heart swells at her words, and I try to form a response, but Lane speaks first.

"Damn . . . what she said."

I laugh softly as I wipe a warm tear off my face.

"Thanks, Em," I say as Lane places a hand over my shoulder and brings me into a half hug.

"You're doing a great job, Chlo," Lane says with uncharacteristic sincerity. I pat her knee in thanks, and she takes my silent cue to change to a lighter topic. "Let's talk about something else—like why Emily got the bigger closet."

Emily huffs as she reaches for the goat cheese. "Okay, well, when you decide to stop dressing like My Chemical Romance let me know, and we can start sharing clothes. Until then, I have the burden of being fashionable for the entire household. Therefore, the bigger closet is mine."

"You know, I will never understand how your clothes can be so expensive but be ripped and cut in so many weird places. When did peek-a-boo waists become a thing?" Lane retorts.

"You want to talk about rips? Do you own a pair of pants without them?" I blurt at Lane. Both of my friends turn to me, wide-eyed and smiling.

"Ladies and gentlemen . . . Chloe has entered the ring!" Emily laughs as Lane makes a *ding-ding* noise. I cover my mouth with my palm.

I've never been one to join in their bickering before, always afraid to overstep and offend. They've always been a lot closer, and I've taken my place as third runner-up in our small group. Perhaps it's the battle training with Warren these past four months, or merely the confidence I've seemed to develop—but I guess I'm ready to join in.

"I knew you had it in you, bi-atch." Lane raises a glass to mine. "And yes, I have two pairs without rips . . . my mother bought them for me."

Emily raises off her chair. "You know what this night needs, ladies?" We both shake our heads with creased brows. "Music!"

She pulls out her phone and clicks a button. In typical Emily fashion, things seem to happen around her like we're in a movie. A speaker begins playing "That's Not My Name" by The Ting Tings—the song we declared as our household anthem in our first few months of living together.

We dance while sporadically diving down for cheese and wine for at least an hour before the two bottles are empty and our stomachs are beyond full. After a final lip-sync battle to "And I Am Telling You" between Lane and Emily, Lane begins to tidy up—the bitter loser.

"Behold, the beauty of a dishwasher, ladies," she says, taking my plate from me.

"I should get going—my cab is almost here." I uncurl myself from the couch and regretfully shed the throw blanket.

"Ooh!" Lane brings me into a hug—tipsy Lane is admittedly much more affectionate. "Thank you for coming, Chlo! I love you . . ."

"Love you too, Lane." I kiss the side of her head as Emily steps beside us. "Love you, Em." I bring her into a hug.

"Mmm. Have fun with lucky number thirteen tonight!" Emily snickers over the top of my head as I pull away.

"Good night, ladies." I slip my jacket on and turn as I step into the hall, taking one last mental image of my two beautiful friends, who smile back at me from their doorway. I let out a contented sigh as I make my way down the stairs to their front entrance.

There is no loneliness left inside me. I'm all filled up. It's a feeling I never want to forget.

THIRTY-SIX

"HEY YOU," I WHISPER, SLIPPING UNDER THE COVERS next to Warren. We've gone to bed together every night this week, but I haven't found him in my bed without me before. I love how normal it feels to see him sleeping here.

"Mmm. Hello." Warren reaches out, eyes still closed, and brings my face to his so he can kiss me—he misses and kisses my nose. "Have fun?" he mumbles.

"Yeah, I did."

"Good." He moves his hand under his pillow, settling back in.

My cheeks warm. "Are you awake?" I ask, raising a brow in the dark.

"Nope." *How does he manage to sound sleepy and sarcastic?*

"All right, I guess I'll put my pajamas on then."

Warren opens one eye, which makes me giggle. As he reaches a hand over my back, his eyes flare.

"You're naked!" he exclaims, still attempting to whisper.

"I am." I stifle a laugh.

"How presumptuous." His voice lowers in pitch, and he brings my body a little closer with a grasp on my hip.

"How can you be sleeping one minute and using words like *presumptuous* the next?" I tease.

"How can you still be horny after the week we've had?" *Touché.*

"Oh, just me then? Shucks, okay . . . I guess I'll—" I'm interrupted by Warren tightening his hold on my hip and pulling me until I land on top of him, straddling his thighs. "You're also naked!" I laugh.

"I'm very presumptuous." He sits up, speaking inches away from my mouth as our smiles meet for a kiss. "Mmm. Hey." Warren firmly clasps my jaw, tilting me back from the kiss I'm insisting doesn't need to end. I grumble in response. "You taste like wine, dove. Actually, you taste like a whole barrel. Are you drunk?"

"Not drunk . . . tipsy."

Warren sighs, the heat in his eyes cooling off. "Well, then perhaps we should call it a night."

"I take it back. I'm stone-cold sober," I say through exaggeratedly pouty lips.

"Sorry, dove . . . I'm not taking advantage of wine-drunk you."

I roll my eyes. "I, Chloe Jean, am of sound and sober mind and am *really* hoping you take advantage of me."

Warren scoots up to sit against my headboard. "Prove it." He lifts a brow.

"Seriously?" I say, frustrated.

He nods, amused at my annoyance, as usual. I bring my arms out to the side of my body and touch my nose with my fingers in sequence.

"Good enough?" I glare at him in the dark.

"Alphabet . . . backward." Warren's voice is low again, a timbre that suggests we're about to begin *very* consensual activities after all.

I move up his lap until his hardness is pressed against my lower belly.

"Z." I lick the section of skin between his earlobe and jaw that always makes him suck in air through his teeth. "Y." My fingers wrap around the base of his throat, squeezing in the way he's told me turns him on. "X." I kiss him gently before biting down on his bottom lip, dragging it so he sits at attention, leaning into me. "W."

Warren's tongue darts out to my upper lip, and I open for him gladly. "V," I say, pulling away. He made this a game. He should regret all twenty-six letters.

"You've made your point." He wraps a hand around my shoulders to bring me flat against his chest.

"Uh-uh-uh." I shake my head. "U." I trail one feather-soft finger down the center of his chest. "T." I lean back as far as I can bend, my shoulders resting on Warren's legs. "S." He watches my hand curl up my inner thigh and groans like a man being tortured.

I smile slyly in response as my fingers find my pleasure and begin moving in small, delicate circles. Warren knows as well as I do that I'm toying with myself alongside him—this touching won't bring me to an orgasm. Though combined with his pained expression, it might bring me close.

"R," I elongate through a moan. "Q," I say, voice pitchy. "P."

Warren sits up, reaches toward me, and fists my hair at the base of my skull, cradling my head. The grip sends my thoughts spiraling. "You win . . ." he nearly whines. *Enough teasing*.

"O, N, M, L, K, J, I, H, G, F—" I attempt to finish, but when he sits me up and licks from my collarbone to my jaw, I admit defeat. "Satisfied?" I bite down on a cheeky smile as he rolls us until he's on top of me.

"You're about to be," he replies before guiding himself into me, soliciting a gasp from both of us. I would roll my eyes at his overarching confidence but—*dammit*—he's right.

Warren rolls his hips as I tilt upward, creating an angle that allows him to be deeper inside me. He wraps his forearm under my neck, bringing his face close to mine, and despite the pumping of his hips, it's like I'm being held.

It's a hold I hadn't known before him—one that sends me skyrocketing toward orgasm each time from the feeling of safety alone. I make a sound that's more like a whimper than a moan, and it reverberates with each sinfully deep thrust.

"I know, dove." Warren kisses my chin before resuming. "Let it build."

"Shiiiiit." I lengthen the word by at least three syllables.

"Yes . . ." Warren hisses out as I begin contracting around him. "So good."

"Yeah?" I ask, voice scattered as my orgasm becomes impossibly close.

"Perfect. You're perfect," Warren groans. "Come, gorgeous. Right now," he commands.

"Warren!" I cry out. *"Oh—"*

Warren places a hand over my mouth, silencing the cries he's come to expect. The ones I hadn't known I was capable of before him.

"Good," he whispers against my forehead. "So hot."

As my body winds down, though my legs still shake, Warren's smirking mouth finds my parted lips.

"Dove . . . you've got to be quieter."

No one wants to be thinking about the sleeping infant on the other side of the room right now, but it's a necessity.

"Though I do love hearing you . . . fuck, I really do." He soothes my lips with gentle kisses as his thrusts slow to almost nothing, his hips circling against mine.

I let out a breathy laugh. "I like when you cover my mouth. It's like you're capturing my moans for only you to hear."

I gasp, and my half-closed eyes widen as Warren plunges forward in one shocking full tilt of his hips.

"Oh . . . you liked hearing that?" I ask. "That my pleasure is only for you to hear?" In an almost mindless response, my legs hook around his lower back, bracing against him as he relentlessly pounds into me—building my pleasure again alongside his own.

"Well, it is. Only for you. I am . . . yours," I say desperately.

"All. Mine," Warren says through gritted teeth, his sharp blue eyes finding mine as he watches me writhe with laser focus. "And I'm entirely yours."

A minute or an hour or seconds pass, filled with rapid, desperate thrusts that have us covering each other's mouths as we finish our *incredibly lucky* number thirteen.

THIRTY-SEVEN

I LIE FLAT AGAINST WARREN'S CHEST, MY BODY CURLED up against his side. Thanking my lucky stars—*and glowing golf balls*—for how the second half of this year has unfolded.

I'm so fortunate to have found a partner in Warren. I like to think that without all these straining circumstances we would have still found each other—call it kismet, soulmates, fate, whatever. But I wouldn't take back a single hard day. I wouldn't trade all those lonely nights if it meant I didn't get to be right here, right now, in his arms.

Warren and I might not have a single clue what we're doing, but we have each other to carry some of the heavy load.

"Can't sleep?" Warren asks, brushing his calloused palm in circles across my shoulders.

"Thinking about how lucky I am." I tilt up to see his face, resting my chin on his chest. "How much I love you."

Warren chews his cheek, lost in thoughts of his own. "Can I

ask you something?" he says as I lower my ear back to his chest, listening to my all-time favorite sound.

"Of course."

"Do you ever have an aching sense of dread when you feel this happy?" He laughs softly, without joy.

I lift my chin to see him again, studying his weary expression as he continues, "It's just . . . whenever I feel like I do right now—content—I think . . . it's as if my brain tries to tell me to expect the worst. To brace for shit to hit the fan."

I sigh, nodding. "Sometimes, yeah. I think that's normal, considering how much you've had taken away from you."

"Maybe . . ." He turns his face away.

I shift off him and sit cross-legged next to his hip. I pause, choosing my next words carefully. "Whatever comes, we'll deal with it together."

Warren blows out a gust of air that makes his lips trill. An uneasiness washes over him that I recognize well as doubt. "What if—"

"Anything . . . together." I try to ease his worries before he can truly name them.

He nods, looking through me, not at me. "It's really fucking scary, Chloe."

I exhale, then lick my lips. "It is."

"It's like . . . I can't imagine my life without you, so I don't want to. But then it's worse to not think about it, because then it's like I won't be prepared to rebuild."

"You don't need to be prepared." I rub his chest, and he places his hand on top of mine.

"I'd fight for this, dove. . . . You know that, right?"

"I do."

"To the ends of the earth," he says, voice determined.

"That would make a great band name . . ." I'm rewarded with a slight grin on his face. I bring his hand to my lips and press a soft kiss to him. "I would too." He nods absentmindedly. "You okay? Is there something else that's bothering you?"

"I'm worried about Luke." Warren's swallow is audible.

"I know . . . me too," I say.

"I talked to Rachel the other day about maybe getting him some counseling, but she seems to think he's acting like your average angsty almost-sixteen-year-old. And it's a long list."

"She could be right. I mean, he's never been safe enough anywhere else to act out."

"Right. But I thought I'd have more time with him. To hang out, do shit together, be . . . brothers. He's totally uninterested." Warren tugs his hand away and wipes it across his jaw.

"There's still time. He's adjusting. We all are. Maybe for his birthday the two of you could do something special."

Warren nods hesitantly, and I lie down, curling back into him. He strokes my hair for a few silent minutes while my thoughts hold on Luke, worrying that the more he pulls away, the guiltier I'll feel for occupying his brother's time. I want to assure Warren it will be okay, and I hate not really knowing.

I shift positions so we can see each other's faces in the dim light. The gears in his brain are almost visibly turning.

Warren clears his throat. "After Willow's custody hearing . . . will you be changing her last name?" He bites down on his bottom lip as it curves upward on one side.

"Yeah . . . I think so," I answer, voice slightly hazy from fighting the need to sleep.

"Do you want to change yours too?" he whispers, pressing his forehead into mine.

"Ha ha." I let my eyes fall closed as his warm breath tickles my cheek.

"Hear me out. I've been toying with the idea of changing my last name and creating a new one. I never loved the idea of carrying on my father's name. I think I'd like to start fresh." He speaks purposefully but with obvious uncertainty.

"Okay . . ." I open my eyes. He has my curiosity piqued now—sleep be damned.

"What if we made a new one . . . together?" Warren's voice slips back into its usual confident tone, but at a whisper.

"Would we be sharing a last name or . . . *sharing a last name*?" I ask anxiously.

"You tell me." I hear his smirk.

No, you tell me. "Are you asking me something, Warren?" I let my eyes fall closed again.

"Not right now. . . . That would come with a ring and a grand romantic gesture of some kind . . . but would you be open to the idea? Of the last name, I mean . . ."

I hesitate but can't fight the reply burning its way out. "Yes."

"Okay, start brainstorming last names, then . . . make a list."

"Oh, any reason to make a list," I mumble sarcastically against my pillow, knowing full well I'll be making said list starting tomorrow.

"So far I have McAwesome and Bond," he says, excitement like that of a puppy clear in his voice.

If I had the energy, I'd quip back. But I don't. "Good night, Warren." I groan.

"How do you feel about Buffett? Give the other Warren a run for his money . . ."

"Go to sleep, Mr. Buffett." I turn away from him.

"Oh, so you like it!" He moves closer, his arms wrapping around me from behind, enclosing me in the world's warmest safety net. "Good night, Mrs. Bond."

THIRTY-EIGHT

"Happy Birthday!" I sign to a half-asleep Luke, who's blinking at the daylight as he appears from his cave-like room. I couldn't convince Warren to wear his, but Willow and I have our pointed party hats on proudly.

Luke looks between us, smiling as he sees the two balloons next to the couch. A giant *one* and *six*.

"Good morning," Warren signs before grabbing Luke into a classic brotherly hug, one arm wrapped around his neck until he relents and gives in.

I get my own hug after. A group hug, I guess, since I'm holding Will.

"I know you're leaving this afternoon to be all cool, aloof, and sixteen with other cool sixteen-year-olds, but we made waffles and have gifts. Tolerate us for two hours?" Warren gestures to the table, filled with toppings and freshly made waffles. I contributed the sliced fruit, but he did the rest—from scratch.

"You had me at waffles," Luke replies, smiling.

We all walk over to sit around the table, and I prop Willow up in her high chair. Now that she's close to sitting up on her own, she gets to be involved a whole lot more.

"So you don't want the gifts, then?" I wink, and Luke laughs, but not with his usual warmth. Something is weighing on him. Perhaps birthdays are as difficult for him as they are for Warren—a reminder of all the missed ones before.

Warren places two gifts and a card I made in front of Luke. It features a picture of Luke dressed up on Halloween. Well, it can only be assumed that it's a picture of Luke since his face is hidden. I'd convinced him to get dressed up with me to hand out candy, which felt like a win, and he chose a T. rex costume that inflated. He was barely able to get through the door. The kids in the building loved it though; he chased a few of them around the hallways. The card reads "Have a Dino-Mite Birthday."

He smiles, shaking his head at the card as he slips it out of the envelope. After putting it aside, he tears the wrapping paper off the first gift. A smart watch with a text-to-speech feature, the practical gift Luke had requested from Warren.

"It's great, thank you."

"This next one was Chloe's idea—my apologies in advance," Warren warns, and I shove at his shoulder. He rubs it as if he's wounded.

"If you don't like it, we can return it," I sign to Luke as he reaches for the gift bag. After taking out the tissue paper, he reaches in and pulls out items one by one. A compass, multi-tool, flashlight, and a tin of matches with a gift card to the local outdoor sports store attached. Luke holds a few of the items in his hands as he looks at me for an explanation. "Warren told me that you guys have never been camping. I thought it could be fun. The gift card will cover a tent or sleeping bags, the bigger stuff. If you don't want to—"

Luke stands, lowers the items to the table, and walks around to where I sit. He stands a foot away, then waves for me to stand. When I do, he gives me a hug—a proper full hug. My first ever from Luke. I gloat at Warren from over Luke's shoulder. *I knew he'd like it.*

Luke pulls away, stepping a few feet back to sign, "Thank you, Chloe."

"It can be just you and Warren, if you'd like."

"No . . . we should all go." *As a family.* I look at Warren. Had he seen?

"Okay, great." I play it cool, but internally I'm overwhelmed with relief.

Once the waffles and toppings are gone, I offer to clean up, insisting Luke get the day off for his birthday. Warren was going to ask Luke if he wanted to go out this morning to put the gift card to use, just the two of them. I hope Luke accepts—Warren could use the win.

Once I'm done cleaning a good twenty minutes later, I turn to find Warren and Willow sitting at the table, Luke not around. Warren is flushed and has two hands fisted in front of him.

"Everything okay?" I place a hand between his shoulder blades as I move past.

"No." His voice is cold.

I turn back to him. "Did something happen with Luke? Did he go out?"

Warren places two palms over his eye sockets, elbows resting on the table as he leans into them. "He's been talking to our dad . . ." *Shit.* Warren sits up, looking toward me, hurt and anger mixing in a heartbreaking combination over his face. "Luke has been going to see him after school. Apparently, my dad found a place nearby and . . ." His voice trails off as I lower myself into the chair closest to the stairs. "He asked Luke to move in with him."

I close my eyes, willing it to be untrue. Warren's dad has drifted in and out for years, sometimes leaving in the middle of the night—often with bets left owed or someone's angry husband coming to find him the next day. He's done nothing but hurt Warren and Luke, and there's no reason to think his dad would be any different now.

"Shit . . ." I start, reaching out for Warren. Warren jolts his hand away, placing it on his knee under the table as his leg bounces. *That's not about you. Don't get upset.* "Luke won't . . ."

"Luke is a kid. He doesn't . . ." Warren's tone shifts to anger, his voice like gravel. "Asshole thinks he can show up now? Where the fuck was he when I was in high school and Luke was stuck in that hellhole?" He pushes off the table, his chair falling backward as he stands in a fury, rubbing his chin as he paces. "Making Luke lie to me." He moves as if he wants to crawl out of his own skin.

I take a deep breath in, telepathically willing him to do the same. "We can figure this out. Luke is a good kid. He'll—"

"Don't tell me about *my* brother." Warren turns to me, leaning over the table to where I sit. "Sorry—just—fuck!" I hold my breath until he takes a step back and turns, still pacing. "He wants to. Luke wants to move in with him. He—" Warren stills. *Double shit.* "That's why he has been holed up in his fucking room—he was counting down the days until he could . . ." *Leave.* Warren doesn't have to say it for me to hear it.

"Why don't we just catch our breath, then come up with a plan? Your dad will probably not get CPS-approved anyway. We can talk to Luke, we can—" I stop at the sound of a fist hitting drywall.

There's now a large hole at the end of the hallway where Warren stands. Willow cries loudly in response to the sound. I run to her. "Hey, it's okay, baby." I pull Willow out of her high chair and bounce her from side to side. Her cry grows louder.

Warren approaches us, regret pulling down on his face, and I reactively take a step away from him. He stops dead in his tracks, horrified.

"I didn't mean to—" His voice cracks.

"Warren, you need to go calm down. Now." I don't look at him. I can't bring myself to.

"I would never—"

"Just leave!" I shout in reply.

A dreadful silence floats around the apartment as no one moves. I slowly lift my eyes off the floor and turn to Warren. Even from across the room, I can make out the tears that roll down his cheeks. His eyes fixate on the floor. His face is tilted as if he's been slapped. I told him to leave—the worst possible thing I could say to someone who's never been allowed to stay.

"Warren, I'm sorry. I didn't mean that—" He raises a palm, and I stop.

"Don't do that. Don't apologize right now. It's all my fault. I should be . . ." He licks his teeth as his body grows even more tense; there's a slight shake to his hands. Without another word, he turns on his heel, rushing down the hallway.

By the time I unbind my body from its position and move toward Warren, the front door closes behind him. I'm left standing there, speechless, with Willow heavy in my arms.

THIRTY-NINE

I DO WHAT WARREN ALWAYS DOES—OPEN LUKE'S DOOR, count to twenty, switch the light on and off, then step inside. I assume it's for privacy reasons, but today, I'm also grateful for the opportunity to spend my time counting so I can calm down before entering.

Luke is in his loft bed, hunched over with his forehead in his palms and elbows pressing into his knees. He removes his hands slowly and turns toward me. He must have seen the door open since he isn't startled to see me there. He slowly drags his head toward me. His face is wet with tears, deep lines formed between his brows.

"Hey, I need to talk to you. Can you come sit?"

"It's nothing to do with you, Chloe. Or Warren. I tried telling him that." He looks exasperated.

"I know, but please—can we talk out here?" Looking up to Luke's loft bed is not a comfortable way to have this conversation.

"I've said what I wanted to say."

"Warren left." I pause, collecting myself before the stinging in my eyes turns into full-on tears. "Can you please tell me what is going on?"

Luke's brow creases as he nods, scooting down toward the ladder at the end of his bed. We silently enter the living room, and I take Willow, now calm, to her play mat as Luke takes a seat on the couch, restlessly tapping his foot.

"So your dad wants you to move in with him?" I ask.

"Yeah."

"How is he? Sober, I presume?"

"I guess, yeah." His eyes shift, unsure of his own answer.

"Okay . . . when did he get in touch?"

"Rachel told me when I moved here that they let my dad know. Nothing specific, just that I was moving in with Warren. He reached out online, and then we started texting."

"Okay . . . right. You've been visiting?"

"Yeah, for about two months."

Two months? My eyes close. I take a deep breath, centering myself as best I can.

"And he has a room for you? In his place?"

"Sort of. It's empty right now. I'd have to move my stuff." Moving Luke's things into his father's home might actually destroy Warren. Surely Luke can sense that.

"Luke, this may be a stupid question . . . but does your dad know ASL?"

"He's trying to learn. . . ." The watch he asked for makes more sense.

"Okay . . ." I inhale deeply, trying not to let my frustration show. "Why move in straightaway? Why not wait until the new year, or perhaps split your time between here and his place?"

Luke looks to the ground. "Dad . . . Dad needs my help."

"What do you mean?"

"Well, he rented the apartment so I could live with him some-day, and the cost has gone up. He knows that Warren gets money from CPS, and that would help with rent. It doesn't seem fair that he'd be homeless because . . ." He stops, resting his hands on the back of his neck.

"Because what?" I ask.

"Because I want to stay here." He looks at me with heavy eyes.

"Did he tell you that? That he'd be homeless if you don't move in?"

"Not completely. He said he'd have to move out and find a new place, probably not near here. So I wouldn't see him anymore . . ."

Asshole.

"Luke, we could drive you to see him wherever he ends up. For visits." My chest rises and falls with a deep breath.

"I know . . . but he'll be mad at me. Won't he?" Luke signs slowly.

"For what?"

"For not moving in?" His shoulders climb up to his ears.

"Maybe. But that's not fair. You want to stay?" I ask. He nods. "Then I think you should stay."

A few moments of stillness pass, neither of us moving or sign-ing, just exchanging glances of empathy and smiles that don't reach our eyes.

"I didn't mean to upset Warren." Luke runs his fingers through his hair. It flops back down to his face.

"He's not mad at you. He's mad at your father. There is a lot of hurt there. You know that."

"Yeah." He doesn't seem to believe me—Warren will have to do the convincing.

"So, what do you want to do?" I ask.

"What are my options?"

"Well, you could wait until you're supposed to see your dad next and talk then. We could come with you, or you could go alone. You could also text him if the idea of talking in person makes you uncomfortable."

Luke nods slowly, full of concentration. "I think I'll wait for Warren to get home, then call my dad. I can sign to Warren and he can translate for dad."

"Sounds like a great idea." He chews the inside of his cheek, the same worried tell his brother has. "You okay?"

"I feel sort of stupid."

"What? No. Luke, you love your dad . . . he . . ." *Choose your words carefully, Chloe.* "He cares about you, I'm sure. But he doesn't get to manipulate you for his benefit. You have a big heart for wanting to help him, but that is not your job."

"Isn't that what you did for your mom? Gave up your choices to help her?" Luke signs. His eyes are sincere.

"I suppose so, a little. Except I got Willow out of the deal . . . you'd just be getting a new bedroom." I tilt my head with a grin.

"It smells like cat pee." He winces.

"Yeah, not a fair trade." I smile gently. "You want me to call Warren? Let him know the plan?"

"Yes, please."

"Okay . . ." I hesitate but trust my instincts. "I think it is best that you don't go out with your friends until Warren is home, okay?"

Luke nods. "Yeah, okay." He stands and pulls out his phone. "I'm going to cancel," he signs before going to his bedroom.

The phone rings five times before Warren's voice comes

through the line. "You've reached Warren Davies, leave a message" is followed by a beep.

"Hey, Warren, it's me. I talked with Luke. He's not going anywhere. I think your dad confused him, but he really wants to stay here. Come home. Love you." I hang up and text him.

CHLOE: Left a voicemail. Luke doesn't want to move out. Come home so we can talk. XO

I wait for the little check mark to appear, letting me know he's seen the message, but it doesn't come. Perhaps he's driving. I call again, but it goes straight to voicemail. *Answer, dammit.*

I pace the apartment for three hours, my phone faceup on the counter, checking it every few minutes. When Luke reappears from his room, he attempts a few calls and texts as well. All go to voicemail, none read. It's too early to worry, right? He was so upset when he left.

"He's probably turned off his phone to think. The minute it's back on he'll feel silly and come home," Luke signs.

"Right . . . yeah."

Two more hours pass with nothing from Warren. I have a thought that I can't seem to shake off. I tap Luke on the shoulder to get his attention as he stands in front of the microwave.

"Did you tell Warren where your dad's place was?" I sign rapidly.

"Yeah, why?" Luke tilts his head.

"Like a rough idea or the exact location?"

"He knew the building when I described it. Why?"

"Okay. Can you give me the address?" I pull out my phone, ready to write it down.

"Forty-three Watford Ave. Apartment five."

The GPS on my phone says it'll be a thirty-minute walk, which isn't so bad—but it will be longer in the snow, and I can't bring Willow. I pick up my phone and hit CALL before my brain has fully embraced the idea of asking for help.

"Hey, Em, are you busy right now? I have a big favor to ask."

"What's up?" Emily turns down some background noise as she speaks.

"Can I borrow your car? And can you come watch Willow? Warren is MIA. There's been some family drama and—"

"On my way." Emily hangs up before I have a minute to thank her.

I turn to Luke, who is looking more and more confused by the second.

"I'm going to find Warren. I have a feeling he may have gone to find your dad. My friend Emily is going to come watch Willow. I need you to stay here, okay?"

"Yeah, okay . . . is Warren going to beat up our dad?" *I hope not.*

"No . . . I don't think so. I'll have my phone on me. I will keep you in the loop—okay?"

I rush upstairs and grab a warmer sweater and socks, ready to face the snow outside—unsure of where the rest of this day will take me.

Please let me find you, Warren.

FORTY

AFTER I PARK EMILY'S CAR, I PAY THE METER FOR AN hour, locking it twice as I turn toward a dilapidated building—dirty moss and graffiti cover most of the brick, cardboard in almost every window. I take a deep breath in, cringing at the thought of Warren having to imagine dropping his brother off here.

I find the main entrance unlocked. The first floor only has three apartments, so I run up the first flight of stairs. There are distant sounds of a baby crying and a couple arguing. The whole place reeks of smoke and mildew. Luke's father was going to make him live here. I approach the door of apartment five cautiously, then knock three times.

A thin man wearing an oversized gray T-shirt and khaki shorts opens the door. Not exactly weather appropriate—it's freezing in here. I know it's Warren's father instantly, their brows and noses identical. Whatever warmth Luke has that Warren lacks is nothing in comparison to the coldness behind this man's eyes, which are brown, unlike both of his sons. With a violent flick of his chin, he sends wisps of long gray hair flying from his face.

"What?" the man says.

"Hello, we haven't met yet. I'm Chloe. I—"

The man scoffs, interrupting me. "He left a few hours ago."

"Oh, okay." *Charming.* "Any idea where . . ." I stop talking as Warren's father walks away from the door, farther into his apartment and out of view down a long hallway. He leaves the front door open. I presume so I can follow. I text my location to Emily from the door before I step inside, just in case.

"Fuck!" His voice follows the sound of a metal object falling.

"Um, sorry . . . Mr. Davies?" I step through the doorway and down the dimly lit corridor, past an open door that leads into a bathroom that needs a *deep* clean—or possibly a detonator.

"Call me Al," he shouts from the narrow kitchen at the end of the hall.

"Um, Al, did Warren tell you where he was going?"

"No. The bastard was too busy telling me how to live my life," he mumbles as he lights a cigarette and blows smoke out the small kitchen window. "Kid thinks he knows better than his old man. I fuckin' tell ya . . ." He puffs out smoke, almost directly into my face. I take a step back. "You looking for him?"

"Yes."

"Don't bother. He isn't worth the time." He puffs out more smoke.

My jaw tightens in response to his hateful words. He couldn't be more wrong. I would turn around and walk away, but this man is likely the last person to have seen Warren, and I have a feeling he could be useful.

"What did he say right before he left?"

"'Go to hell, Dad,' I believe." He leans back onto the counter, and for a second, Warren's arrogant persona is in his place. His eyes hold the same teasing gleam, though Warren's is actually charming.

"And before that?"

"I don't fucking know." He drops the cigarette into the ashtray, and my teeth grate against one another. "Listen, I don't know you, but you're wasting your time. This kid is a magnet for disaster. Not even his own mother, God rest her soul, could find it in her to stick around. You're better off—"

I don't let him finish. "You know, you're a real piece of shit." I can't control the words that tumble out of me, and I let them linger between us as Al blinks, stunned.

This man is not my father, or my mother, and he'll probably never change—but fuck it. I'm done. I'm done holding back my anger toward people who don't care about the impact their decisions have on others. The manipulation, the emotional immaturity, the narcissistic tendencies . . . I'm done with it all. Warren and Luke are my family, and I refuse to let this man take any more of our happiness. Him or anyone else.

I lift my chin and look him dead in his wide eyes. "You have two incredible sons. They're some of the best people I know, and you choose to come in and out of their lives when it's convenient— leaving nothing but hurt and broken promises behind you. Screw that. You don't get to have an opinion about them. So if you have any helpful information, I'll take it now . . . please."

Sure, I added a *please* at the end, but the rest of it was not polite at all. I give myself the win and stand a little straighter in response.

Al pushes out his mouth, lips turned upward. "Well, I see why the kid fell for you, though he didn't seem to think you'd come looking."

"What?" I ask as he crosses his arms in front of his chest.

"Something about it being my fault that he gets so angry. About how he scared you . . . lost you like he loses everyone—because of me. It's always my fault, you see. Boy can't take any of his own . . ."

I close my eyes, blocking out whatever nonsense he's spewing. I told Warren I'd fight for him—why didn't he believe me? *Why won't he answer his phone?*

"Did he say anything about where he was going?" I interrupt his rambling.

"All he said was that he wasn't going to be around to help Luke move into this"—he uses air quotes—"shithole." He lowers his hands back to the counter behind him. "Something about his kid . . . which I didn't even know he fucking had, by the way. Am I a grandpa?"

"What did he say about a kid?"

"'I won't get to see her grow up because *you* had to show up.'" He points at himself, acting out Warren's part. *He wants to see Willow grow up.* "'I was going to be happy, you asshole.'" He finishes the scene with an unnerving curtsy.

This is useless. I spin on my heel to head toward the front door.

"Chloe, wait." Footsteps get louder behind me. "I'd check where he works. He'd make himself useful if he can't be happy—that's the Davies way." Not a terrible suggestion, but I see why Warren wants a name change.

I hesitate but give a polite nod. "Thanks. Bye, Al." I descend the stairs and take a deep breath of fresh air as I exit the building. Next stop, Ram's shop.

FORTY-ONE

I PULL INTO THE PARKING LOT OF THE GARAGE. WAR-
ren's spot is empty. My stomach twists in knots. Still, I park and
get out to check—I drove all this way. I approach the entrance,
where Belle sits behind a service window.

"Hello, darlin'! What can I do for you?" Belle's voice soothes
me, even on this shitstorm of a day. But if she isn't sure why I'm
here, then Warren isn't here.

"Hi, Belle. Um . . . I'm looking for Warren." I twitch my lips.

"Ah . . . come on in, girlie." Belle leaves the service window and
steps around to the side door, opening it just enough for me to
step inside the reception office. She pats a chair and sits across
from it. "Did something happen?"

"Yeah," I mumble.

"Wanna talk about it?"

"I'm not sure I should . . ." It could reflect badly on Warren,
and Belle is sort of his boss, isn't she?

"Oh, darlin', it's perfectly okay. You tell me what you'd like or nothing at all. But know this—there ain't nothin' you could tell me that'd make me turn my nose up at that boy. He's a sweetheart. I know you know that too."

I smile softly. "Yeah, I do."

"Me and Ram have known Warren goin' on three years now. I've always thought he was someone special, but lately . . . Well, honey, he shines brighter because of you."

I tilt my head and chew my lip. *Then why'd he take off?*

I swallow before speaking, then tell Belle everything from the beginning.

"Do you feel like you were ever in any danger?" Her tone is sincere and concerned, despite her previous statement on behalf of Warren's character.

"No. It was just a knee-jerk response. I know he wouldn't hurt us."

"All right. I assume you've been to his daddy's place?" she asks, and I nod in response. "Well, I could give you Bryce and Matt's numbers, see if they've heard from him."

"Maybe I'm overreacting. Maybe he's somewhere calming down. I don't want to embarrass him."

"Well, that could be true. But in my experience"—she leans forward, finding my eyes as she offers a gentle smile—"if someone runs away, it's 'cause they want to be searched for. Warren has wanted someone to care about him this much for a very long time. You know he calls you dove, right?"

"Yeah, he does that at home too."

"Honey, that boy is head over heels in love with you. Has been for quite some time. Hell, I don't even know if I'd seen him smile before he told Ram and me about you and that little girl of yours. He was smitten from day one. You go get yo' man. You show him he matters."

Renewed confidence surges through me. I stand. "Can I have those numbers, please?"

Belle leads me behind the desk and pulls up a contact list for each employee on the computer next to the desk's phone. I hope I don't have to call Bryce, but I doubt Warren would go to him anyway. I dial Matt's number.

"Hi, Matt, it's Chloe. Warren's . . . girlfriend."

I hear a creaking sound, like an old door in the background, then what seems to be footsteps on wooden stairs. "Hi, Chloe. I assume you're calling to see if he's with me."

"Is he?" I ask eagerly.

"Not anymore. He came by about two hours back and told me what happened. He left about thirty minutes ago."

I huff. "Shit . . . do you know where he went?"

"He said something about going to a motel for the night. I told him he could stay with me, but he said he needed the space."

"Any idea what motel he might be going to?"

"No, sorry. Although . . . I doubt he went far. He mentioned his phone was dead, so I guess somewhere he could easily get to without it."

"Okay. Thank you, Matt."

"Hey, no problem. If you find him, tell him *I told you so* from me."

"Pardon?" I ask.

"I told him you weren't finished with him."

I smile into the phone. "Okay . . . I'll tell him."

"Good luck, Chloe." Matt hangs up, and I turn to Belle, who is standing far too close to have missed what was said. She bites down on her long acrylic nails.

"Motel . . ." I mumble, pulling up a list on my phone. There are three not too far from here. I'll start with the closest. "Thank you, Belle."

"Of course, darlin'! Lemme give you my number . . . I want to check in later, okay?" She takes my phone and puts her number in. "All right, well, go get 'im." She pats my back with a firm hand and passes my phone to me with her other.

I normally can't stand to drive without music playing, but it's silent in the car as I drive fifteen minutes to the motel by the water. It's closed—as in boarded-up and half-burned-down closed.

Okay, one down, I guess . . . according to my phone, the second motel isn't too far. I scan every black car that passes me twice, hoping to see Warren behind the wheel. The second location is open, but his car isn't in the parking lot. Still, I park Emily's car and run to the front desk.

"Hello," I say to the female employee behind the desk. She's a little older than me and has straight brown hair and a serious expression.

"Hi." She flips a page in her book without looking up.

"I was wondering if a guest named Warren has checked in?"

"We don't give out guest information. If they're expecting you, you can go right up to their room," she answers, boredom heavy in her tone.

"Right, well . . . sorry, what's your name?" *Time to lay on the charm.*

"Stevie . . ." She looks up from her magazine suspiciously.

"Hi, Stevie. The thing is . . . my boyfriend and I got into a fight, and he stormed off. It was a misunderstanding, really. I'm just trying to find him to let him know he should come home."

Stevie nods slowly, pulling her bottom lip into her mouth. Her eyelids close with sarcastic glee. "Uh-huh. Totally hear you on that. The thing is . . . this is a motel. We would not be in business without runaway dudes or affairs. It's sort of our thing?"

"Got it." *That was a bust.*

"Hypothetically, though, there is nothing stopping you from going and knocking on each of the guests' doors . . ." She shrugs.

"Uh, thanks." I head toward the exit. "Have a good one, Stevie."

"Yup!" she calls out as the door shuts behind me.

I pull out my phone before getting back into Emily's car. I could use the minute to stretch my legs though. The temperature has dropped as the sun begins setting. I send a quick text to Luke, letting him know I spoke with Matt and have one more motel to try. He sends back a thumbs up as a car pulls into the parking lot.

A black car. *Warren's car.*

FORTY-TWO

MY SIGH OF RELIEF CREATES A PUFF OF STEAM IN THE cold air around me. Warren pulls into a spot right outside the entrance. With the falling snow and the hood of my coat blocking my face, I don't think he notices me leaning up against Emily's car across the lot.

"Hey!" I shout at him as he gets out of his car. The wind picks up, and a gust of snow swirls with a high-pitched whistle. "Hey!" He doesn't turn to me as he reaches the door and enters the lobby.

I jog across the parking lot and follow him inside.

"Name?" Stevie is asking as I shut the door behind me and pull off my hood.

"Warren Davies." She looks immediately at me, her lips twitching. Her expression says *this oughta be good.*

Warren follows her line of sight over his shoulder, and I offer a half-hearted but hopeful smile as he turns. Gorgeous somber eyes find mine across the room. His head drops, brow furrowed and lips pulled inward. His jaw tenses as he opens his mouth to speak, but I beat him to it.

I turn to the front desk. "One room, please." Stevie nods and slides a key across the counter behind Warren's back. He doesn't move, stunned. "You know, I tried to get your attention outside." I inject as much levity into my voice as I can manage, taking a step toward him. *It's okay, I'm approachable, I'm safe.*

He plays along cautiously. "Yeah?"

"Yeah . . . you can't park there." I gesture to the parking lot outside. "That's a loading zone."

A small smirk appears at the corner of his lips. "I'll just be a minute," he says, slipping into his part in the script of our origin story. He grabs the key off the desk, then takes a few steps toward me, stopping out of arm's reach.

"Listen, *Prison Break,* you're blocking the entrance." I tilt forward, projecting nothing but reassurance from my eyes.

Stevie clears her throat. "Um, actually . . . your car is fine there."

I stifle a laugh, and Warren grins crookedly as he closes the gap between us.

"You came to find me, dove?" His deep voice is a whisper. His eyes pleading.

"We agreed to the ends of the earth, right? This isn't so bad . . . only the other side of the city." I shrug, faking confidence.

"I'm so sorry." Warren gives one loud sniff, and I notice his eyes become glossy.

"Hey . . . let's go to the room, okay? Willow is with Emily. Luke is home safe and sound. He rescheduled his friends. It's all sorted. Let's go talk."

I wave a hand to thank Stevie, who looks confused but thoroughly entertained. Warren and I don't speak as we walk along the front of the motel, passing several rooms before we get to ours.

We brush the snow off our jackets as we enter. It's not the gross, seedy motel room I'd presumed, but a quaint, simply decorated room with one bed, a kitchenette, and an en suite. I slip my heavy jacket off and leave my boots by the door. I watch Warren hang his jacket and stay facing the coat rack for far too long, his shoulders rigid.

"Warren . . ." I say, hoping to snag his attention from the thoughts that hold him in place away from me. When he finally turns, I reach my arms around his neck and pull him into a tight embrace. "You okay?" I mumble into his shoulder.

He shakes his head.

I pull away enough to look up at the man I love. He looks worn, like he's been battling hard throughout the day. I want to kiss the sadness right off his face.

"I'm so sorry, Chloe," he says. He chokes back a few tears. "I'm so sorry. I let my anger get the best of me and—"

I stop him with a kiss, gentle and swift.

"I know, baby, it's okay. You're allowed to make mistakes." I remove my arms and sit on the edge of the bed. "I went to see Al, who looked remarkably untouched. You didn't take your anger out on him—that matters."

"You met my dad?" Warren leans forward.

"Yeah, super fun guy . . ." I joke but wince at the memory. "You described him well." Warren slumps down on the bed next to me, a person's width away.

"And Luke?" he asks warily.

"Luke's okay." I offer him a reassuring nod. "He doesn't want to move out. Never did." A heavy exhale passes Warren's lips, pursing them as he presses his forehead into his palms. "He thought he had to in order to keep your dad from moving out of the city. We talked about it, and he knows now that it wasn't the right call . . ." My voice trails off.

"I hate that I did this on his birthday. I'm a shitty brother for that." He sits up.

"Warren . . ." I don't have the right words.

"This is the first birthday Luke's had while with me and I ruined it. Then I scared Willow . . . and you." He rubs a flat palm across his head. "I'm really sorry."

"I know you are and I forgive you. But . . ." I exhale slowly and choose my words carefully. "You're right, you did scare us. Next time, you need to take a lap or sort yourself out before it escalates that far. We can't do that in front of Willow as she gets older. We have to show her better." I rest my hand on top of his, his knuckles pink and sore.

"But I do understand. You've given up a lot for Luke. Your music, your privacy, your whole adulthood has been about getting Luke out of the system. It must have felt like it was all for nothing. And for it to be your dad who tries to ruin what you built? I cannot imagine how awful that must have felt."

Warren's nose twitches as a single tear falls down his cheek. He looks toward me with the quickest of glances, but his lips tremble as he looks away, and a suppressed sob makes its way out.

"Luke will have other birthdays," I go on. "You did make it special . . . the breakfast, the gifts, the balloons. He'll still go celebrate with his friends another day. You'll both just have to talk it out."

His free hand rubs his chin. He nods, then turns away, bowing his head. "I saw Will's face when she started crying and—" He cuts himself off, voice shaking. He clears his throat. "I'll never do anything that stupid again."

"The stupid thing was running away, Warren." I scoot closer to him, leaning my head into his chest as his arm wraps around my back. "I love scavenger hunts as much as the next girl, but please don't leave like that again, okay? Or, if you do need the space to cool off, bring a charged phone along for the ride." I lean back to see his face.

Warren looks down at his lap. "When you told me to leave . . . I thought you meant forever."

I reach out and brush his cheek softly, turning him to face me until his eyes meet mine. "Nah." I smile timidly. "You can't shake me that easily." I rub my thumb over his jaw. "I love you. That means something." I take a deep breath, hoping to relax us both. "You know, you once gave me a very convincing argument mixed in with a very romantic declaration."

"It didn't work as intended," Warren interrupts, a small smirk forming.

"Well, maybe not—but I hope this one does." I sit up straighter. "What is my most annoying habit?" I ask.

"This feels like a trick question."

"Answer."

"The key thing?" he asks, as if it's not the thing he's teased me about the most from the start.

"You notice that's not so much of a problem lately?" I ask. He nods thoughtfully in response. "I only have two keys now. One to our place and one to the car . . . not so easy to get those mixed up." He tilts his head—I don't think he knows where I'm going with this. "I kept every key from my life before. Eight keys to eight different homes . . ."

I gather myself. "I never even really knew why I kept them. But then you came along and teased me about it . . . and then you stuck. And then you loved me. And more than that, you became the only home I've ever really known. The only place I've ever really felt safe to be me. And then I didn't need to hold on to them anymore. Those little remnants of my past didn't seem to matter."

Warren brings one hand to my face. We stare back at each other for a full heavy moment. "I love you . . . so much." He brushes my cheek.

"I'm peace to you?" I ask.

He nods, pulling his lips into his mouth with a creased brow.

"Well, you're my home."

Warren lets out a long, shaky breath, as if he finally believes that everything will be okay after all. "Thank you for finding me," he says as he places his chin on top of my head and presses a kiss on my hairline.

"Ready to go?" I ask, pulling away to look up at his face.

He smiles softly and clears his throat. "Yeah . . . let's go home."

EPILOGUE

WILLOW SQUEAKS AND CLAPS AS WARREN PLACES A CUP-
cake in front of her. It's not her first cupcake—that was given to
her by Odette when we met at Connie's place yesterday for their
little celebration. One year of Connie's sobriety, one year of Willow's life. Both amazing reasons for cake.

Willow grabs two fistfuls right away. One hand stays in the
icing, and the other finds her chubby face, stuffing her mouth.
The dozen people crammed into our living room cheer as they
finish singing "Happy Birthday." Lane snaps a photo as Emily
brings out the rest of the cupcakes for the guests.

"Warren, Chloe, go stand behind Will for a photo!" Lane says.

I look over at Warren, who is unknowingly ignoring Lane, content to soak up Willow's giggles. His nose crinkles as he pretends
to nibble at the hand she reaches out toward him, and they both
laugh.

He's entirely wrapped around her finger. Not just on her birthday but every day. I give in to the spoiling mostly, since she's al-

ready been through so much in her short life. But, seriously, what one-year-old needs their own miniature drum set? It does look good next to Warren's though.

"Photo?" I get his attention with a kiss on his cheek and guide him into place behind Willow's chair.

"Ready? One, two, three . . . cheese!" Lane says.

"Cheez!" Willow exclaims. Warren and I turn to each other, wide-eyed.

"Willow! Your first word!" I applaud, and she looks so proud, shimmying side to side and covered in yellow icing.

I look around at the crowd of people watching, and my heart swells. Luke and his girlfriend Stephanie, Lane and Em, Belle and Ram, Matt, and my parents—who flew in entirely unexpectedly. Of course it means the world to me that they'd come, but it seemed like a big trip for a first birthday party.

"Cheez!" Willow says again, and we all clap.

With everyone's attention focused our way, I take the cue to begin the obligatory "thank you for coming" speech, but just as I clear my throat, Warren begins to speak and sign to the group.

"Hello, everybody. Thank you all for coming to celebrate Willow's first birthday. We are grateful you came and for all the gifts . . ." He points teasingly to Matt, who is still holding a teddy bear the size of a fully grown adult. "Willow is lucky to have you all in her life, and so are we."

Warren continues as I reach out and put my arm around his lower back. He looks down at me, pausing as his eyes focus lovingly on my face. "Celebrating Willow's birthday is a lot more than another calendar year passing by. You all know what a challenge it has been for Chloe and Will to get here. All the doctors' appointments, the long nights, and the court hearings. . . ." His voice trails off, as if he's unsure of how many struggles to list. "But yesterday, we got some news . . ." He tilts his chin toward our family, silently telling me to take over with a warm smile.

"Willow is officially adopted!" I exclaim.

The room explodes into joyful chaos. My mother hugs each person surrounding her, including a shocked Luke—who, of course, already knew and is trying his best to pretend he was none the wiser.

A line forms, all the guests coming to congratulate us one by one. Emily and Lane charge at us and bring us into a group hug. Everyone stops by Willow too. Some for a high-five, others with applause. She loves every second of it, giggling, clapping, and signing "more" to try to swindle another cupcake.

Once the commotion settles, I address the room again. "Thank you all again for coming. Help yourself to food and stay as long as you can. We—" Warren kisses my temple while patting my shoulder, and I turn to him, confused at the interruption.

"Actually, there is one more thing . . ." Warren takes both of my hands and sinks down to one knee.

All the air leaves my lungs—and perhaps the entire room. *It's actually happening!*

"Chloe, I—"

A nervous giggle escapes me, stopping him. I push my lips together, trying to quiet the giddy noises threatening to spill out. "So sorry, go on!" I feel my cheeks flush and glance at Emily and Lane, who look like they could burst from anticipation.

Warren smirks, then resets. "Chloe, I love you more than words could do justice, but I will try. Our paths have not been smooth or easy, but I'd do it all again, a million times over, to get back here. By the grace of the golf-ball gods and the whim of

CPS, we were thrown into each other's lives, and I have spent most of the last year wondering how I got so damn lucky." He clears his throat and rubs his thumbs on the backs of my hands.

"You're the most resilient, dedicated, and beautiful person I know. To know you is to love you, and I consider myself privileged to know you." He lets go of my hands and reaches into his back pocket, pulling out an understated wooden box.

The box opens with a slight creak to reveal a stunning solitaire sapphire ring—the same one I showed Emily and Lane a few months back. I gasp and bring a hand to my mouth.

"Chloe, may I please be your husband?"

"Yes! Yes, please!" I say through a gentle sob.

He stands up and picks me right off the floor until my legs are swinging out behind me. I wrap my arms around his neck and hold on for dear life, wishing to memorize every bit of this moment.

"I love you," I say into his ear as he lowers me.

The crowded apartment bursts into clapping and cheering for the third time today. Warren slips the ring onto my finger, and I squeal at the sight of it. I've never owned something so beautiful.

My mom rushes over and kisses us both on the cheek twice, and my dad gives Warren a firm handshake before pulling us both into a hug. They flew in—*I should have known*.

I flash my hand over my dad's shoulder to Lane and Emily— both crying, though Lane is definitely trying her best to hide it. They give two thumbs up as Warren leaves my side to hug Luke.

As the two brothers hug, Matt sets down the teddy bear— finally—and joins the hug over the top of their embrace. Both brothers laugh and bring him in.

Belle practically skips over to me, holding out her hands to see my ring. Ram pats Warren on the shoulder in passing, then follows his wife over to where I stand. I hug them both, feeling like I could burst with gratitude.

All these people, *our* people, in one room—on our *team*.

"Oh my darlin' . . . that is a beauty!" Belle moves my hand from side to side, seeing the light glisten off the ring.

"Kid did good," Ram chimes in.

"He sure did." Warren joins the three of us, wrapping a hand around my shoulders and kissing my cheek. I couldn't stop smiling even if I wanted to.

"So, Mr. and Mrs. Davies, eh?" Ram asks.

"Well, actually . . . we haven't decided yet," Warren replies.

"Yes, sweetheart, this is what the young folk are doing." Belle hits the back of her hand softly against Ram's chest. "They hyphenate or keep their last names these days."

"We want to make a new name. Something for only us," I answer, looking up at Warren as he smiles down at me. *My fiancé.*

"You know . . . I did have one idea," Warren says with hesitation.

"Oh, yeah?" I remember his list—McAwesome, Bond, Buffett . . . *no thanks.*

"It's a little cheesy . . ." He tilts his head.

"I love cheese."

"Cheez!" Willow pipes up from next to us, still working on her cupcake that has now decorated her party dress. I brush a strand of hair away from her mouth before turning my attention back to Warren.

"How about Mr. and Mrs. Dove?" he asks softly.

How did I not think of that before? "Chloe Jean Dove . . . I like that. Willow Jean Dove. Warren Michael Dove . . ." Each name rolls off my tongue, and I nod more confidently each time. "I'm in." Warren beams in response, holding me tighter.

"Well, congratulations then. To the soon-to-be Mr. and Mrs. Dove." Ram raises his cup to us, and the room follows suit.

"To Warren and Chloe!" Emily exclaims, wrapping her arm around my mom's shoulder. My mother winks at me, and I smile in return. Maybe she sees it now. The life I made for myself is a beautiful one.

Warren turns and kisses me until I forget about the circle of people around us. Nothing is as important as this kiss, this moment. Warren has always been good at that, creating a moment where nothing else seems to exist or matter. Where time pauses. Where loneliness disappears.

Filling me, body and soul, with total, familiar, and sensational peace.

BONUS EPILOGUE

FOUR YEARS LATER

Warren

I NEARLY ROLL OFF OUR BED WHEN I TURN, HALF-awake, looking for Chloe. I groan my disapproval into her empty pillow and inhale the scent of her flowery shampoo like I used to do in the shower before we officially began dating. Though the term *dating* never worked to sum up what we were. Teammates? Roommates? Co-parents? Inevitable?

I should've been embarrassed to have done shit like that, even though I never got caught. But I wasn't and never will be. Because the second I allowed myself to truly *see* Chloe, a switch was flipped. The armor I had built around myself fell apart at a startling speed. There was no use fighting it. So, I did the unthinkable . . . I let her in.

I was carved from rage and built by heartache with a chip on my shoulder the size of Russia and an ocean of fears under a thinly veiled surface. Ready to explode at any given moment. Chloe's lips tasted like a way out. Like fate. Like nothing—not my failures, my past, no amount of stacking regrets—would matter if I could just keep kissing her.

So, I kept kissing her.

Four years of waking up next to the only love I've ever known and I can barely recognize that person I was before. Now, I lie in bed at night and thank *whoever's* listening that she's next to me while she slurs her final witty phrases before letting sleep win. Four years of daydreaming, fucking, teasing, planning, and living as if we were never those two broken kids who had to grow up too fast.

Our type of love is a mirror, she says. Reflecting all the best parts back to each other. Chloe sees me as a person who's deserving of good things. Someone worth a damn. Slowly, I've started to see it too. That's a gift I can't thank her for. Not properly. Never enough.

It's unsurprising she didn't make it to bed last night. Willow was having some pretty serious night-before-kindergarten nerves, and the last sound I heard from her room was begging for one more book. One *last* book. Yeah right, it's never just one more book with her.

I get dressed and follow the winding steps down from the loft, stopping briefly to turn on the coffeemaker. The apartment is silent as I make my way down the hall to Will's bedroom and open her door.

With a small bit of light filtering in through the star-patterned curtains, I can make out the shape of my two girls curled around each other in the twin-sized bed. My shoulder hits the doorframe with a contented sigh. This view never gets old.

Two of the three people I love most in this world, under one roof. Safe. With me. With one another.

It's an honor to have lived in the only home Willow's ever

known—and for as long as she has. I've gotten to experience every first. Steps, words, teeth, tantrums. There's not a single part of me that doesn't recognize it's my daughter lying in that bed. She might not look like me, but she sure as hell acts like me. Grumpy little thing.

I know it's been different for Chloe in that way. Navigating the dynamics of her relationship with Willow has proven challenging. She wishes it could be more straightforward, that she could just label herself "mom" without reservation and call it a day. But she wants Willow to do that herself, when she's ready. *If* she ever is.

I cross the room to kneel next to them. When I touch the blanket covering my wife's hip, the crinkling sound of the feather-filled duvet is met with her wistful sigh.

"Dove . . ." I press a kiss to her nose. "Chlo?" I whisper a little louder.

"Mmm?" She blinks awake. Even after all this time, I'll never be prepared to see her eyes. Green like holding a leaf up to the sun—and just as bright.

"You girls have a wild party last night?" I ask as Chloe tucks a hand under her head and smiles softly at me. Her lazy morning smile I love to kiss away.

"Oh yeah . . ." She scoffs. "Big time." Her eyes open wider as they adjust to the light. "Ow." She kneads her neck and groans as she twists it to stretch. "This bed is not made for an adult-sized body."

"I wouldn't call you adult-sized," I tease with a smirk.

"Ha, ha." Chloe sits up gently, trying not to stir Will. "I think I fell asleep reading to her." She rubs her eyes and yawns while I kiss her neck. "Morning," she whispers, her greeting nearly lost as her lips press into mine before she lies down again.

"Today's the day." I sigh, grabbing Chloe's hand and giving a quick squeeze. I brush her knuckles with my thumb, taking in the way she's nervously nibbling her bottom lip.

We both turn to our little girl with weary expressions. Willow's curls are sticking up in all directions and she's snoring softly—as her big sister often does. She clings on to her favorite stuffed animal with a vise grip. Ever since her third birthday party, when Luke gave it to her, "Puppy" and Will have been inseparable.

Luke sends a lot of gifts, actually. I think it's partially out of guilt, but I'd be lying if I said I didn't use that to my advantage to get him to call more often. I know he can look after himself—he has for most of his life—but I like knowing he's okay.

When Chloe and I had our wedding in Barcelona the week after he graduated high school, Luke fell in love. Not with someone—he still won't talk about that with us—but with seeing what the rest of the world had to offer. Chloe nearly had to talk me off a ledge when Luke withdrew from the local college in order to take a gap year touring southern Europe.

I wanted him to go to college. He's a smart kid. But Chloe was right—he just needed some time. Last year he found his way back to Barcelona and enrolled in university there to major in journalism. He's living with Chloe's parents, both of whom adore him and spoil him more than we ever could. Case in point: He drives a Vespa to class. They're not perfect, but Chloe's parents try. Hosting Luke and watching Chloe and I parent from afar has helped heal a lot of wounds. It's just unfortunate that it wasn't until Chloe no longer needed their approval that she finally got it.

Right after he began classes, Luke started a blog about traveling the globe as a Deaf person. What began as a school assignment blew up online. A few months ago it got picked up by a pretty big travel magazine and they paid him to spend his summer exploring Australia.

Not to sound like Martina, but knowing the sacrifices I've made have helped get that kid a decent life has made everything worth it and then some. Now it's Chloe's turn to see some of her hard work pay off.

Chloe watches with heavy eyes as Willow sleeps. "I don't know if I'm ready . . . maybe we wait till next year?"

"She's ready." I press my forehead to hers, flattening her anxious expression. "She's more than ready." I pull away and huff a laugh. "She'll be running that school by the end of the day."

Chloe rolls her eyes affectionately. "Probably." She untucks herself from the blanket and dangles her feet off the edge of the bed as she stretches, arms extended toward the ceiling. Her shirt lifts on the right side, revealing the subtle scar from her appendix surgery. I trace the raised skin with my thumb.

Chloe was so determined not to miss Lane and Matt's wedding that she didn't tell anyone—including me—how much pain she was in the entire day. It wasn't until after midnight that she whispered we had to leave and go straight to the hospital. That was probably the worst argument we've ever had, when I was driving her to the emergency room as she groaned and clutched her side in her bridesmaid's dress. I promptly made her swear not to risk her safety for her loved ones, which she did, even though we both know she'll do it again. Chloe's selfless to a fault and it's hard to not admire that about her.

"I put the coffee on. I'm going to make Will's favorite breakfast, and Luke is going to FaceTime around eight to wish her luck before we need to head out." I sit next to her on the bed. "So . . . all we have to do now is wake her up."

"Five more minutes," Chloe says, leaning into my shoulder.

"She might be having the best dream ever, and then she won't forgive us for interrupting it."

I chuckle, shake my head, and press a kiss to the top of Chloe's messy morning hair. "Five minutes."

"Em's girls are both going to be in her class. Did I tell you that?"

"What? No, you didn't. That's great. See?" I bump her shoulder with mine. "She'll already have two friends." I raise a brow, trying to persuade my stubborn wife that it will all be okay.

Emily and her partner Amos have recently begun fostering three siblings. A set of twins a month older than Willow, and their baby brother. They were the first of our group of friends to buy a home, but they made sure to stay nearby.

"I feel really bad I can't go with you guys." Chloe pinches the bridge of her nose. "Why'd my stupid presentation have to be the first day of school?"

"I am going to take *all* the photos, dove. Her cubby, her teacher, her outfit, her classroom—it will be the most documented first day in history." I rub her shoulder. "And you'll be there after to pick her up and hear all about it."

Chloe was hired by Child Protective Services two months ago as their marketing and design consultant for their programs, fundraising, and initiatives. It's basically her dream job. Even though we have a framed copy of the TeamUp brochure on our bookshelf for sentimental reasons, it's also a visual reminder of how much work needed to be done. She's killing it so far—obviously.

Willow stirs and I watch over my shoulder as she rolls onto her side. Still completely asleep, she licks away a bit of drool that's dribbling down her chin. I smile to myself. "We got a good one."

"The best one," Chloe replies adamantly.

"Bet we could *make* a pretty good one too." I turn to face her with a grin.

Chloe's eyes widen at my suggestive remark. "You're relentless." She giggles.

"Let me get you pregnant, woman," I hum against her neck before nipping at her jaw.

"What's the agreement?" Chloe pulls away and crosses her arms with a playful smile.

I shrug in an attempt to rile her up. I know the deal, the list of all that has to happen before Chloe will reopen the baby conversation. She's been preaching it to me for months. Willow has to start school, Chloe has to work enough hours at the new job to qualify for maternity leave, and I need to hire enough new guys at the shop to keep up with the demand so I'm not working as much. That last one is proving difficult.

"How's the new guy working out?" Chloe asks, reading my mind.

"Matt likes him but . . . I don't know."

"I know when Ram sold the shop to you guys he asked you to take care of it, but you also have to take care of yourself." Chloe catches my eye. "Because I want to keep you. For a long time."

I roll my head away with a soft whine, mimicking Will when we tell her it's bedtime. Chloe's laugh fades to a sigh.

"You need to stop firing people, Warren. Let them prove you wrong. . . ." She curls her hand around my neck and tilts my chin back toward her. "Like *someone* else did."

"You're way hotter than the dudes I work with," I argue.

"Well, I'm glad to hear that." Chloe pats my shoulder.

I choose to let it go. Just like my many attempts to propose before I actually did, I knew that when the time felt right for

Chloe, she'd say yes. She hadn't wanted to be married until Willow's adoption was finalized and the moment it was, I asked. So now I'll just wait for her to give me the signal again. It'll come. I've seen her walking slower through the baby aisle at the grocery store and she can't hide the way her eyes light up when she holds Emily's foster babe.

"Ready yet?" I ask her, gesturing to Will with my chin.

Chloe nods with a frown and scoots off the bed.

"Low?" I brush a curl off her cheek. "Will-low," I sing out, rubbing her shoulder. "Time to wake up, Tiny."

"I'm *not* tiny," Willow mumbles into her pillow. I knew that'd get her attention.

"No, I guess not, now that you're going to start school with the big kids."

Willow groans then swats an arm out. I catch it before it hits my chest. "You're going to have to be faster than that, kid." I blow a raspberry on her wrist and she giggles. "C'mon, time to make pancakes."

Willow rolls onto her back, and with eyes squinted and nose scrunched, she studies me skeptically. "With sprinkles?"

Chloe opens a drawer on the other side of the room.

I lean in close to sign out of view of Chloe. "Only if you wear whatever LoLo picks out."

"Dad, no, please," she protests as she sits up.

"Be nice, kid. We like her," I sign back.

"Sprinkles?" She bargains with one word.

"Sprinkles." I nod.

"What do you think?" Chloe asks from across the room, holding a bright yellow dress and a striped top to go underneath. *She'll look like a bumblebee.*

Willow gives me a glance with a sassiness of which *no* five-year-old should be capable. "Love it," she says through gritted teeth.

"So many sprinkles," I whisper, and we exchange excited smiles. "Hey . . ."

"Hmm?" Willow says through a yawn, turning to me and folding onto my lap.

"I'm proud of you, sunshine. It's a brave thing you're doing today." I brush her hair in long strokes.

"I think I'm going to like school." She fiddles with the strings of my hoodie, pulling them back and forth. "I get to have a backpack. And it has a matching water bottle."

"And lunch bag," Chloe adds enthusiastically.

"I think you're going to *love* school." I smile at Chloe as she crosses the room to us and kneels down, placing a pile of clothes next to us.

"I think so too." Chloe taps her finger to Willow's forehead. "Because . . ."

"Strong brows, strong noses, strong bodies, strong hearts," they say in unison, though Willow yawns halfway through.

"And strong minds," I add.

"The strongest, biggest, most genius mind ever." Chloe presses her forehead into Willow's.

"It's too early for this." Willow lifts off my lap, picks up the clothes, and struts across the hall to the bathroom.

Chloe and I turn to each other in shocked amusement.

"She's a piece of work." Chloe shakes her head.

Kid's five going on fifteen—we're definitely screwed. Still, I can't help but laugh.

"I think she'll be *just* fine," I scoff. "Maybe we should be worried for the other kids."

"And the teacher," Chloe adds with a wince, before sitting across my lap and wrapping her arms around my shoulders. I lean into her touch and find her eyes deep in thought. I wait, knowing that she needs a moment to say whatever she's rehearsing in there.

She clears her throat. "Keep the new guy on payroll for three months and we can start trying."

Fucking finally! I nod enthusiastically and kiss all over her face until she squeals. "Done!" I proclaim. "He'll be the employee of the month." He can have the whole shop.

"Do you even have an employee of the month?"

"We do now."

Chloe rolls her eyes and bites down on her lip, poorly hiding her smile.

"So, are the months retroactive? Since he's already been working for one . . ."

"You're pushing it," she warns with a laugh.

"And, we can still practice trying . . . until then."

"That can be arranged." Chloe checks the doorway then kisses me with a little *too* much passion for this early in the morning—especially because we're on our five-year-old's bed.

I cool her off with a tap to her hip and she relents with a soft sigh. "It feels like a long time since we did the morning-rush-to-school thing," Chloe says, looking around the room that used to be Luke's.

"Yeah . . . remember that time I caught you feeding the couch?"

Chloe laughs. "Ew, yeah. I never did get the smell of formula out of the cushion."

"What happened to that couch? I don't even remember getting rid of it."

"We gave it to Connie when she moved out of the shelter."

"Right!" I snap my fingers. "I wonder where it is now that she—"

"I don't know if . . ." Chloe checks to make sure Willow is out of earshot. "If nudist hippie communes have a *need* for furniture."

"Well, what are they sitting on?" I ask, then raise a hand. "Nope. Don't answer that. Too many visuals already."

"If I've said it once, I've said it a hundred times." Chloe closes her eyes with a smile. "At least it's not drugs."

"Amen to that."

"I like the memories we have on the new couch too," Chloe says, blushing.

"You're all riled up this morning, Mrs. Dove." I lick my lips as hers drift apart.

"We've still got it." She shrugs and kisses my cheek. "You still got it."

"You say that like it's been decades. . . ." I laugh.

"We've had enough life happen for a decade or two."

I place an open palm across her stomach. "I have a feeling the best is yet to come though." I wink. She pulls my hand off and narrows her eyes at me. Her grin, however, tells a different story.

The bathroom door opens and Willow emerges, skipping toward the kitchen, singing to herself.

"That's my cue." I lift Chloe off of my lap and press a kiss to her hair before following my littlest dove down the hall.

"Okay! Who wants my world-famous pancakes?" I shout after her.

ACKNOWLEDGMENTS

First of all, a massive thank-you to *you,* dear reader. If you enjoyed the book, and I hope you did, then please leave a review wherever you purchased or elsewhere online.

Thank you to Ben, my best friend and husband, for always being my first reader and a *very* good kisser. Thank you for your patience when I got too deep in the writing zone to notice if our children were screaming, for your renewed interest with each and every draft, and for your countless pep talks when I wanted to quit many, many times. I love you. *You're simply the best.*

A massive thank-you to my mother, Joy, and my sister-in-law, Kim, who have listened to each of my books as ideas rambled over a video call and seen them through to the finish line. Your honesty and excitement spurred me on like nothing else could.

Thank you to Abi, who never reads but made an exception and truly made me feel like I had something great to share with the world. I hope you know what an inspiration you are.

To my writing partner and literary soulmate, Christina. You're the reason this book is ready to go into the world and why I have not had a full meltdown in the process of writing it. Thank you for befriending some weirdo on the internet and becoming one of my all-time-favorite people. When your books are published, I'll be the first in line with ten copies.

To all the wonderful ladies in the Happy Romancing Group, and the organizers of NaNoWriMo for bringing us together— thank you. You've been so persistent in your support for me and my writing, and without all your extra sets of eyes and surplus opinions, this book would be a shell of what it is. I cannot wait for the day we all get together in person.

I want to especially thank each sensitivity reader who worked on this project. I am humbled by your support and grateful for your time pointing out my blind spots and helping me correct them.

Beth, from VB Edits, I cannot thank you enough for whipping my manuscript into shape. You've been patient and professional, and I could not recommend your services more.

Lastly, to anyone who has struggled with substance abuse, past or present, and is turning their life around: I hope you get the love and grace that Chloe gave to Connie. You deserve it. I'm proud of you. Keep going. As well, to all the social workers, care providers, guardians, foster parents, and siblings who have had to step up for a child in need of care—you're the best of us.

Upon Rerelease:

I'd be remiss if I didn't add to the Acknowledgments to include the teams and support systems behind *Next of Kin*'s rerelease. Thank you to my agent, Jessica Alvarez, Sophie Sheumaker, Madison Werthmann, and the entire BookEnds team. Jessica, from that very first phone call I knew that you were going to change my life and you absolutely have. Thank you for taking a chance on me and my stories and for all your hard work and dedication. I also want to extend a massive thank-you to everyone at Dell and Penguin Random House for taking my humble indie release and giving it the opportunity to be on booksellers' shelves—namely, my incredible editor, Shauna Summers, and her assistant, Mae Martinez, who've been so kind and patient with me as I transition into this new space. Thank you to Leni Kauffman for this stunning new cover as well as Talia Hibbert and Chloe Liese for their generous words of support. This is a dream come true, made possible by my passionate readers. Thank you all for reading my books and coming along with me on this journey. I'll be forever grateful for you all.

Keep reading for an excerpt of Hannah Bonam-Young's
second book in the Next series:

Next to You

PROLOGUE

ONE HOUR UNTIL I CAN LEAVE. WELL, MAYBE ONE HOUR and three minutes, so as not to appear rude. Midnight is the minimum expectation at a New Year's Eve party, after all. But the time beyond that is all mine.

Chloe's apartment throbs with the bass from a stereo that should be called "neighbor's nightmare." That's what I'd market it as. I can see the design I'd make for the ad if I shut my eyes.

The music playing is unfamiliar, but the playlist I threw together this morning was hoisted off the auxiliary cord around ten. The TV and speakers have been playing *Rockin' New Year's* something-or-other live from New York ever since—and right now, it's a DJ who's pumping up the crowd, saying we're about to have the best year *ever*.

Yeah, right.

I steal two bobby pins from Chloe and Warren's bathroom cabinet and pin my bangs out of my face. The purple hue of my hair is beginning to fade at the roots, revealing a pale brown. I canceled my hair appointment a few weeks back for the third time in a row. It always seemed too big a chore. Too far from home. The only place I want to be these days.

I'd hide out in the bathroom forever, but there's only one in the apartment, and I'm sure by now there's a line forming at the door. All the other guests are probably wondering if I'm taking a massive shit. *Nope.* That smell, dear friends, is the scent of fear.

My piles of self-help books would suggest I ought to evaluate. *Get to the root of the issue,* they'd say. But I can't be bothered. *Let the fear live,* I proclaim! It's what's kept the human species alive. Survival of the fittest, baby! Perhaps I'm a *little* drunk.

I step—and almost fall—out of the bathroom into an unexpectedly empty hallway. Chloe and Warren's friends have impressive bladders. Speaking of, when did they even acquire this many friends? There have to be twenty people crammed into the apartment Chloe, our other best friend Emily, and I used to share while in university.

Life was simpler then. When all I had to do was complete homework and assignments from the safety of my room, occasionally coming out for air and food. It's expected of university students to be shut-ins. Hermits. Recluses. Homebodies. All words that are affectionately used until you reach a certain age. Or meet a certain doctor. Then it's "agoraphobia."

Agoraphobia . . . I always thought it sounded like a fake country from a Disney movie, like *Genovia.*

"Prin*cess* of Genovia," I say to no one in particular as I reach into the fridge for another vodka cooler. My fifth, if you're counting. Which I am not.

"Pardon?" a soft, deep voice asks as I shut the door.

I turn to walk toward the loft's spiral staircase, hoping to find a private perch away from the other guests. Like a nosy owl.

"Guess not," the same low voice says from behind me, hitting me in the gut. I turn to find the source.

Familiar dude. Handsome. And we've definitely met before. I think he's Warren's friend or co-worker. Basic name . . . Steve. *No.* John. *Nope.* Kevin?

"Matt." He points to his chest, wearing a quizzical expression with one raised brow. He's got a warm, welcoming smile, like he's hearing one long joke—but not at your expense. His light brown eyes have a certain kindness to them that puts me instantly at ease. His dark beard isn't particularly tidy, but it's full and fluffy-looking. His nose is ragged, like it's been carved out of rock, and his hair is longer than mine, thrown haphazardly into a bun on top of his head.

And, *goodness me,* his lips. I could curl up on them with a good book.

"I'm Lane." I raise my glass to him before turning to take three steps up. I fumble back onto the stairs, my palm finding the step just before my butt does. The cool metal touches bare skin a fraction below my underwear, eliciting panic that I've flashed my backside to everyone below the stairs. I reach under my bum to tuck the black fleece skirt under me and tug it farther down my thighs, keeping my knees tightly pressed together. My black turtleneck shirt is new and itchy around my throat. I have to actively fight to stop myself from adjusting it every few seconds. This outfit is cute but not conducive to settling nerves.

"I know, Lane. We've met. . . ." He smirks into the top of his beer as he takes a sip. His lips look even better that way. "Here alone?" He asks this as if he is an adult who's found a lost child. *Your mommy around, sweetie? Let's go find her.*

"Alone," I confirm. "And you, Matthew?" Surely a guy with silky black hair, full lips, and a strong dad bod is here with someone. Guys like him are *everyone's* type.

He huffs out a quick laugh. "Yeah, me too."

Ah, well, he must be deeply flawed then. *Just your type,* my inner saboteur hums. *Shut up,* I quip back. *So why is he talking to me and not someone else?*

"Is it me, or does everyone at this party seem to know everyone else at this party?" I sigh, looking down at the large group of people strewn about the apartment below.

"I'd have thought you'd know most people here, being Chloe's best friend." Matt takes another sip of his beer.

"Mmm, but you see, Matthew, I do not venture out much." *Ever.*

"Introvert?" he asks, standing at the bottom step, a firm grip on the metal railing.

I bite the skin around my thumb just once before I remember I'm no longer alone and that habit isn't the slightest bit attractive. I let out a nervous laugh, placing both hands around my cup. "No, actually. I'm an anxious extrovert. We are a rare but not extinct breed."

Matt nods, his eyes narrowing, causing happy, wavy crinkles on the outer corners. "I didn't know there were others. I've been living underground."

"Aw, well, we do like to hide." I chug my drink and stand to fetch another.

"You know what's great? Ice water," Matt adds as I sidestep him and make my way toward the fridge. "Have you had some today?" His voice is cautious, like he's approaching a street cat. "Can I get you some?"

I nod, grinning ear to ear as I look up at the curl that looks like an upside-down question mark resting on his remarkably tanned forehead. "D'you work outside, Matt?"

"I work with Warren." He takes my glass and places it on the counter, turning his back to me.

"I do not understand the mechanics of mechanics."

Matt looks at me over his shoulder, not laughing but obviously amused—a small tug at his lips and inquiry in his eye.

"I work inside the shop mostly." He uses tongs to place a few cubes of ice in my glass before pouring water from the tap. *Tap water?* My mother is somewhere clutching her pearls.

"But you're so tan . . ."

"Built-in skin tone." He hands me a full glass of water, and I take it with two hands, trusting neither to do their job alone in my inebriated state. "My mom's Samoan," he adds.

You dumbass. Why'd you ask such a stupid—

"Got any straws back there, barkeep?" I ask, hoping to swiftly move past my blunder.

With a smile and a less-than-sincere eye roll, he turns and grabs a straw off the counter and drops it into my cup.

"Thank you, Matthew." I bow slightly, trying to capture the straw with my tongue as it dodges me and spins around the rim.

"It's Mattheus." He chuckles under his breath, scratching where his cheek meets beard.

"Huh?" I turn and walk back to the stairs.

"You keep calling me Matthew . . . but Matt is short for Mattheus," he says, following close behind.

"Oh, sorry." I sit down, careful not to spill my water.

"Don't be." He gestures to the stair below mine, a question in his rich honey-colored eyes.

"Have at it." I signal to the step with a flourish.

"Is Lane your full name?" he asks, lowering in front of me. His body is so broad all over that he barely fits on the step, so he sort of hovers, balancing himself against the railing.

"Elaine," I answer. "But I've never suited *Elaine*. Maybe I should try it. New year, new identity." I push an invisible pair of glasses up the bridge of my nose. "Hello," I say in a hoity-toity accent. "I'm Elaine . . . the third. Charmed." I hold out a limp wrist that he shakes lightly, his lips curled between his teeth.

Matt's laugh seems to burst out of him. It's deep and full and shocking. I focus on how his Adam's apple bobs while he does it and the way his lips part. *Cute.*

"Wow, uh . . . thanks," he replies, looking down between us with a subtle, pleased grin.

I said "cute" out loud, apparently. He studies me and then looks off to the crowd, glancing side to side. Still trying to find my keeper, I think.

There's an ease to him in total juxtaposition to the liquid energy that seems to be rushing through his veins. No part of his body appears to stay still for long—a knee bouncing or a foot tapping. But the smile that's yet to fully fade has a calming effect. I wish I could bottle it like a perfume. I could use a few spritzes throughout my day when my brain won't cooperate.

I'm still staring at him, with no words being said. I don't even think I'm smiling, just blankly looking at him like art in a gallery. Yet he doesn't look uncomfortable. He just looks about the room, his gaze landing nowhere in particular.

Attempting to look away from him feels like swimming against a current. I start up the conversation again so I don't have to. "Any New Year's resolutions?"

He turns back toward me slowly, his shoulders raising and tensing a little. His eyes shift from side to side for a moment, then he shrugs. "Not really. I'd like the shop to do well."

Right! This is Warren's friend who will be running the shop with him when their burly boss guy retires. That is soon, I think. "When do you and Warren take over?"

"My uncle Ram retires at the end of January, then it's all ours." His jaw tics as he throws back his beer. He blinks a few times too. He's either nervous about this takeover, or I'm far more drunk than I thought and misreading him entirely.

"You worried?" I ask.

"Little bit," he replies with a dim smile. "What about you?"

"Constantly." I blow out a breath, trilling my lips.

"I meant, any New Year's resolutions?" he asks, voice sincere.

"I—uh." *Where to begin?* "This year hasn't been my best. There's . . . a lot to improve on."

He pouts his lips but stills, waiting for me to go on.

"I'd like to start by being a better daughter," I offer plainly, but I'm not sure—even if I was sober right now—that I could stop the emotion tensing my expression. "My mom has stopped asking me for things. I'd like her to ask again."

"What sorts of things?" he asks.

"She's on a board for this charity, and they have a gala every year. I used to do the designs for it—invitations, posters, stuff like that. Now? She hires out. She doesn't want to ask me."

This change only happened about eight months ago, directly after a phone call with my sister. I mentioned, in passing, that I was going to the pharmacy to pick up my anxiety meds. Since then, it's been near silence from my mom. Fewer phone calls, texts, requests, and questions. Instead, I get care packages in the mail. Bath bombs with lavender, an oil diffuser, self-help books, a weighted blanket, sleepytime tea . . . you get the idea. Like get-rich-quick schemes but for fixing mental illness.

Matt nods thoughtfully, slowly. It spurs me on.

"I'd also like to call my sister more. She isn't much of a texter, but she gives in because I hate talking on the phone, but that's not fair." I rub the back of my neck. "I miss her," I nearly whisper.

"That's a good one. I'm stealing that," Matt says.

"You have a sister?" I ask.

"I have five sisters." He lowers his emptied bottle from his face and watches me with a knowing smile.

"Five?" My lips part into a wide *O*. "You have *five* sisters?"

"And three brothers," he adds, grinning.

I slam my drink down beside me and bring two hands in front of my face, raising five fingers on one hand and three on the other, then adding one for Matt. "Nine of you?" My voice is quickly approaching a pitch only audible to dogs.

"Nine."

"Your poor mother!" I laugh, and so does he. Thank god— I hoped I hadn't sounded rude. "That's a lot of phone calls," I add.

"Well, I guess I'll call my parents more, then," Matt replies. "What else is on your list?"

"I'd like to take my job more seriously. I'm . . . not the best employee. I show up late, I call in sick when I'm not. . . ." *Technically.* "I do the bare minimum."

"I'm sure that's not true."

"That's sweet—but it is. I started over a year ago, and the person I trained last spring just got a promotion to be my supervisor. It's a tech company, and people bounce around. There's lots of room for upward growth—if you're trying." I mime climbing a ladder and falling to my death, and Matt watches me with a subtle smile. I should be embarrassed, but I'm not. The alcohol is working.

The television in the living room catches my attention as the presenter begins speaking over cheering crowds. "We are just ten minutes shy of midnight, and what an incredible night it has been. . . ." My focus falls to the ice in my cup, and I stop listening, watching the ice cubes dance around one another until my brain goes quiet.

"You okay?" Matt asks, leaning into my view to catch my eyes.

"Hmm? Yeah." I smile weakly.

He sits back and looks across the room to where Chloe and Warren stand near Emily and her boyfriend, Amos. They're all laughing, except for Warren, who shakes his head and smiles into the top of his glass.

"They seem happy," Matt says, petting his beard absently.

"They do," I answer, my voice not hiding the jealousy that creates an ache in my throat.

It's not that I'm not happy for Chloe, I am—she deserves the world. All I could want for any of my friends is a guy like Warren. He worships the ground she walks on and lets her shine, unafraid of being in the shadows. Emily deserves it too. She and Amos have only been together a few months, but they make a gorgeous couple. Stylish, tall, and equally striking, they get a lot of head turns walking down the street. I know this because I'm usually trailing behind them, cementing my third-wheel status.

"Three things . . ." Matt says, dragging my attention away from our friends. "The shop, calling my parents, and finding someone who looks at me like that." He points with the tip of his beer bottle toward the happy couples.

"Single?" I ask.

"Perpetually." He blows out a long breath.

"That's an eighteen-pointer," I say before cracking an ice cube between my teeth. *A bad habit,* my mother would say.

"Eighteen?"

"*Perpetually* is worth at least eighteen points on a Scrabble board," I explain.

"You play a lot of Scrabble, Lane?"

"Used to. With my dad." A trapped sigh comes out. I rarely talk about my father—and when I do, it's not with people I'm attempting to flirt with. It's not just a difficult topic; it's one I still can hardly speak about—without crying, that is.

"Oh. I'm sorry," Matt says, rubbing his eyebrow as he looks down between us. I guess my face said what my words failed to.

"It's okay. Long time ago now." *Three thousand and forty-two days, to be exact.*

"I'm still sorry," Matt says, his eyes searching mine.

I look away quickly, suddenly shy. "I'm going to get another one of these. Want something?" I rattle the lone ice cube in my glass.

"Let me." Matt reaches for my cup and walks to the kitchen. I watch him move about from my elevated position. He turns to narrowly pass through a group that's congregated near the kitchen island and makes conversation with them as he fills our cups. I can't hear what he's saying, but I hear his laugh as he sidesteps them again on his way back.

I check the time on my phone—four minutes till midnight—as he returns.

"Thanks." I take the glass of fresh water from him.

"So anything else on that list of yours?" he asks, eyes softening as they meet mine. "Or are you already seeing someone?"

I scoff. "No, the girl I was recently hooking up with called it off when she procured herself a sugar daddy." *Can't say I blame her.* "But yes, another one on the list. I'd like to be a better friend too."

"How so?"

"Well, I should probably be helping with wedding stuff? I feel like Chloe doesn't ask because . . . well—" I sigh. "She knows Emily will pick up my slack." I take a deep breath, my chest rising high.

"Right, the wedding. I keep forgetting. It's coming up fast." Matt looks toward our friends briefly. "I should probably do stuff too, right? What do groomsmen usually do?"

I shrug. "I think you get off easy until the week of the wedding."

"Right, still . . . I'll add that to my list." He clears his throat and checks his watch in quick succession. Then he raises his cup toward me, and we cheers. "To a new year, new chances, new lessons, and . . . new friends."

"To calling family and not dying alone." I raise my cup, smiling.

"To succeeding at jobs and taking charge," he responds, voice louder, as we clink glasses again.

"To you, Mattheus." I lean forward and wink.

"To you, Elaine." He matches me, and a rush of excitement has my bottom lip pressed between my teeth, biting down on a giddy smile.

As the clinking of glass sounds between us, our eyes meet and hold.

"You know, you're cute *too,*" Matt says as his eyes briefly glance over my face. "Too bad." He leans back onto the curved railing behind him.

"Too bad?" I ask, voice hesitant. What does that mean? Cute but a mess? Cute but not my type? Cute but a basket case?

He freezes, as if he's said the wrong thing. His brow is furrowed in confusion, and only then does it dawn on me that I mentioned it was a *woman* who recently dumped me.

"I'm bi—" I'm cut off by every other party attendee when they begin counting down from ten. The room explodes into chaos all around us, but it blurs out of focus. I'm tunnel-visioned, looking at Matt. He's so still. Steady. His eyes hold on me in an unreadable gaze.

"Nine, eight, seven . . ." they chant.

"I'm into everyone," I say, a little too loudly and cringe at my urgency to tell him he's a possible candidate. Even though no one else can hear us from up in our little nest, I look over my shoulder, blushing.

"Oh," he says, bringing my attention back. He wipes a hand over his beard and mouth, but I can see the grin he's hiding. He drags his hand from his chin to the back of his neck and tilts forward as he rubs it like a sore muscle. All the while smiling down between us.

I can't help but smile too. The embarrassing kind where you absolutely *have* to because someone's joy is being reflected onto you.

"Three," we say in unison with the crowd. My nose twitches, and he swallows, his throat working.

"Two." His chest rises as he takes a deep breath, but I can't seem to breathe at all.

"One." The hand he has splayed across his thigh twitches, and I fight the urge to lay my palm over top.

"Happy New Year!" the crowd shouts, but not us.

The sounds of noisemakers and confetti poppers fill the room, and I turn over my shoulder to the sudden influx of sound. Couples descend upon each other's faces like wolves on the hunt. I look up toward the ceiling as confetti falls slowly.

When I look back to Matt, he's staring up at me, eyes curiously narrowed as a stray piece of silver confetti drifts between us.

"Happy New Year, Lane," he says, his smile faltering.

He looks disappointed. For some reason, I *hate* that. I make a split-second decision and throw caution to the wind. I place my cup down on the stair beside me and put two palms on his cheeks, scrunching his face together like I've done to Chloe's sweet baby girl so many times.

"Happy New Year," I say, pulling his face toward me, his lips squished and opening for a laugh as they land on mine.

A firm palm lands on the edge of my jaw, and I lean into the touch. His hand is cool from holding his drink, and the pads of his fingertips are rough on the edge of my hairline. My hands around his face soften, and as they do, his lips follow suit. I was totally right. They're lips you *could* curl up on.

A few beats pass while I'm locked into the sweetest kiss I have ever had. Time slows—as if the confetti is floating around us instead of falling, voices dropping low and drawn out, "Auld Lang Syne" stretching like a vinyl spinning at half speed.

Pulling away from Matt's lips feels like an abrupt reminder that the world is *not* so still. The party continues and—surrounded by people and noise—isn't where I want to be.

Still, as we settle back against the stairs, my pulse races and the butterflies in my stomach take off in flight like never before. I mindlessly brush my thumb over my bottom lip. It's warm and buzzing. When I notice him watching me, I play it off—using the same hand to brush hair behind my ear. He clears his throat to speak, but I'm looking for a quick escape, not more conversation.

I've been with lots of people—*kissed* lots of people, but I've never felt *shy* after. Like a part of me was exposed the moment our lips broke apart. And I don't like it. At all.

Home, my anxiety demands. *Agreed,* I reply.

I stand and raise my chin as I try to step around him without toppling.

"Heading out?" Matt looks up at me with sad-puppy-dog eyes, getting up slowly as I pass him. A twinge of guilt rises, but I shove it down.

You'll see him around. You probably shouldn't go home with your friend's friend, anyway. It's hard to ghost someone you'll see at birthday parties for years to come.

"Got a new life to start, Mattheus." I shrug playfully. *Casual, unaffected, unbothered.* "No time like the present."

He nods, his polite smile masked by confusion. "Right, well, good luck."

I look over my shoulder, stealing one last look, and nod. "You too."

Goodbye, lips. I'll miss you most of all.

CHAPTER ONE

15 MONTHS LATER

I HAVE BEEN PROPOSITIONED FOR A THREESOME FOUR times this afternoon after being on the lovebite app for only six hours. This has to be some sort of record. People read "interested in anyone" and take it to mean *everyone* and *all at once.*

And while in college, I would have perhaps been more than happy to oblige. The difference now is that it is exclusively couples asking for *me* to join *them.* Which just about sums up my life these days.

Emily and Amos are newly engaged, and Chloe and Warren married last summer. When the five of us hang out, I'm watched over like a child, talked to like a sweet, innocent newborn on the teat of life. *Someday,* they all hum merrily into their drinks, *it'll be your turn,* patronizing me as they feed one another grapes. That last part is an exaggeration, but only slightly.

But today—the day I signed up for my first ever dating app because I admittedly may be having a hefty dry spell and a crisis about said dry spell—is my twenty-seventh birthday. The end of my "mid" twenties, and the dawning of a new era of "full adult-hood."

So, in the words of Taylor Alison Swift, this is me trying . . . to get laid (Taylor's Version.)

My computer chimes with the sound of *another* message from my boss—but I ignore it while on my smoke break.

I don't actually smoke, but in the interest of equality, I take a ten-minute break every few hours, as my co-workers might.

This break has been met with an onslaught of incoming notifi-cations, and I've yet to put my phone down. Other than the threesome requests, I have a few comments on Instagram, a text from Emily about how excited she is for my surprise-it's-not-a-surprise birthday dinner, and an email from Matt.

Yes, an email. I'm insistent there was a mix-up with Matt's driver's license, which I *made* him show me, and they incorrectly printed his birth year as 1995 instead of 1959. He emails almost exclusively. The guy actually texts with a single finger and signs his name on each message, so, honestly, email is less painful. That he can type out on his *desktop computer* at work.

Instead of opening the email, I click on the "you have a match" notification. Ah, yes, the pretty brunette, Valerie. Twenty-nine, single, interested in women, Gemini. Her bio reads, "*here for a good time, not a long time,*" which makes me wonder if it's a *Walk to Remember* situation or if she's *that* cliché.

I message, "Stop making a fool out of me. Why don't you come on over, Valerie?" and pour one out—hypothetically, because my coffee is piping hot—for my girl Amy Winehouse. I screenshot it and send it to my group chat with Em and Chloe.

CHLOE: Make sure to ask if she has a good lawyer.
EMILY: Tell her you miss her ginger hair!

I love them.

LANE: What are you wearing tonight? How fancy do I have to be?

CHLOE: What's tonight???

EMILY: She knows.

CHLOE: What?! Dang it! Ugh . . . I'm probably going to wear my yellow dress.

Emily sends a photo of her in a fuchsia two-piece pantsuit.

LANE: Gotcha. Effort required.

CHLOE: It's your birthday, Lane. If you want to have a sweatpants party, then we can do that.

LANE: Hmm . . . Thoughts, Em?

Emily sends a GIF of a forced smile and a twitching eye.

LANE: Effort is fine. I have that vintage jumpsuit I've wanted to wear.

CHLOE: Ooh! I love that one!

LANE: I gotta get back to work. See you ladies tonight.

A few hours later, I finish my packaging design idea and send it off to my supervisor. A box that will house the newest, most rugged, most hardcore, most extreme, most badass, underwater, 360-degree, high-definition camera with a battery life longer than my will to live. I sign off and begin my grueling commute home, shutting my laptop and taking twelve steps from my dining table to the couch.

"What a day, huh, Simone?"

Simone is the rabbit I bought to replace Emily when she moved out of our place and in with Amos. I was having a vulnerable moment when I opened Marketplace, and there she was. She *and* her three siblings. I feel like the siblings are worth mentioning to reflect that I had some self-control. I only got one!

"I don't want to be rude . . . but you've yet to wish me a happy birthday." I sit up, looking at the bunny condo that cost me more than a month's rent. "Simone?"

Fuck. The cage's door is open.

"Simone!" I look around frantically. She's a little Houdini on the best of days, but she couldn't have gotten far—typically she just burrows under a blanket or laundry pile.

My phone rings, and I answer without thinking. "Hello?" I say, voice hysterical.

"Hello?" my sister responds in obvious confusion at my urgency. "Everything all right?"

"Sorry, yes . . . I thought you were someone else."

"Who?"

"Simone."

"Your rabbit?"

"No, Simone Biles! Yes, the rabbit! She's missing."

I hear a soft sigh and a shuffle that sounds like Liz moving the phone to her other ear. Shit. She's annoyed. I forgot to call her back yesterday. Or today.

"Happy birthday, Lane," she says haughtily.

"Oh! You remembered!" I tease, attempting to lighten the mood. "Happy birthday, Pudge."

"I asked you to stop calling me Pudge. We're too old for it. Especially now."

Pudge was the nickname my father gave her because she couldn't pronounce fudge. A silly little thing, but it stuck.

"Do not remind me how old we are." I stand and lift a blanket off the floor. No Simone underneath.

"Mom call you yet?" she asks.

"Yeah, this morning before work."

"Good."

I don't love that my twin sister is making sure *our* mother called me on *our* birthday to check that *she* shouldn't feel guilty for being the favorite and undoubtedly getting the same deposit into her bank account this morning. I look at the doors to each bedroom and the bathroom, all shut. Simone has to be here somewhere. Unless she could fit through the vents? Shit. Can she?

"Can rabbits do that thing cats do and fit through small spaces?" I ask.

"I don't own a cat," Liz says, matter-of-factly.

"I'm wondering if Simone escaped through the vents," I explain.

"Oh, I hope not. Your building will kick you out if the forced air starts smelling like decomposing rabbit."

"Elizabeth!" I gasp.

"What? Sorry . . ." She huffs.

"My rabbit ran away on my birthday." I slump into the chair. "I've never been lower."

"Really? Are you sure about that?" she asks flatly.

"Ow," I whisper.

Liz can't help it. She's always been . . . ~~a bitch~~ curt. My mother loved to say that we were left brain and right brain personified. Liz is the pragmatic, logical, detached one. I'm the impractical, creative, emotional one. Together we'd make one fully formed being.

I never settled into the idea of being half of anything. My brain *felt* whole—just different from Liz's. But hers is similar to my mother's, and I'm more like my father. My parents were a great team as the left and right melded together, so I know it was with endearment that my mother considered us twins the same. But when Dad died, it made the family's score uneven. Lonely on the right.

Suddenly, qualities that I had been celebrated for—spontaneity, imagination, empathy—began to make me feel alien in my own family. That, and my feverish desire to get away from my own personal haunted mansion, had me applying to arts college far from home. When I arrived here, I found creatives again. I found acceptance. I found my people.

But now they've both found *their* other halves, and I suddenly don't feel whole again.

Then there's Matt. Sweet, handsome, kind Matt who flew through the stages of *a crush* to *too risky* in the span of one brief New Year's Eve kiss.

Turns out our first real encounter, when I was drunk, complaining about my life and listing off my many failures, was *not* the sexy type of impression that would score me a date or a shag, regardless of my own intentions.

He started calling me "kid" shortly after our kiss and has even noogied me once. The universal gesture of the friend zone. It's very disappointing to Chloe and Warren, who are enthusiastically hoping we get together, but I'm glad for it.

Matt isn't the type of guy you hook up with—he's practically got "commitment" written across his forehead in permanent marker. Between his caretaking tendencies following years of helping to raise his ridiculous number of siblings and his general dad-like physique, he's begging to make someone a wife and mother. Which is the *opposite* of where my life is headed. So, a friendship is best—and it's a good one.

A few weeks after that fateful New Year's Eve, I learned that

Matt grew up on Vancouver Island almost entirely off the grid. I decided to take it upon myself to introduce him to all the music, television, movie, and pop culture references he'd missed out on.

I'll be scrolling on my phone and see a reminder of some fantastic, cinematic masterpiece late one night—previous films such as *The Breakfast Club* and *The Lizzie McGuire Movie*—and I'll immediately send him a text. He'll agree the situation needs to be remedied, and, based on my level of intensity, we'll choose a time for him to come over with pizza. Often the next day.

We watch the movie with bowls of snacks, pizza boxes, or even a pillow as a buffer between us—because we do *not* need a repeat of the accidental hand brush incident of last year. Then he leaves at a respectable hour.

"Lane? You still there?" Liz asks through the phone.

Shit. "Hey! Sorry. Looking for Simone. Uh . . . what are your birthday plans?" I ask, continuing my impersonation of Elmer Fudd on the hunt for a rabbit.

"Phillip is taking me out for dinner."

Elizabeth and Phillip—never not funny. I stifle a laugh, but it comes out as a soft snort from the back of my throat.

"Don't," Elizabeth warns.

"I didn't say anything!" I protest.

"Your fascination with the British royal family is bizarre."

"Sorry . . . your majesty." I grin into the phone, lifting a chair to check under the dining table. What *the fuck,* Simone? You have a swanky bunny condo! Two stories! Why would you leave?

"Well, I'll let you go. I'm going to call you tomorrow."

"Could . . . we text?" I hesitate to ask, but damn, I'm tired of this calling every day *thing.* What started as a New Year's resolution has turned into a massive, self-inflicted pain in my ass. We don't talk about anything real, mostly bouncing between small talk and passive-aggressive remarks about each other's lifestyle. I miss her, sure, but it's not fun. And there are way better uses of our time than forcing a relationship, right?

"I guess, but I thought telling you over the phone that I was engaged would be more appropriate."

I drop the pillow I was looking under. "Pardon?" I glitch. "Who's what now?"

"Well, tonight Phillip is taking me to my favorite restaurant. Last month he asked for my ring size, and Mom asked me to go get my nails done with her."

"Well, damn . . ." I blink rapidly. "Congrats in advance?"

"We'll probably get married in the next few months. No use waiting. It will be at his parents' estate, so late spring is ideal weather-wise." She's completely calm, her voice level, while I can't pick my jaw up off the floor.

"Few—few months? Liz, are you sure? You've been together less than a year."

"Nine months. Surely enough time to grow a new human is enough time to decide to marry one."

She's got me there. "Okay . . . yeah. You're not growing a human, though, right?"

"Not yet."

God, my mother will be unstable. A grandchild. A Hargreaves, nonetheless. The only family my mother considers richer, superior, and more well connected than her parents—who, though dead, she still tries to impress. And now my sister is marrying their eldest son. Truly, they *are* like royalty.

"All right, well, yeah, call me tomorrow then," I mumble.

"Will do. Happy birthday, Lane."

"Happy birthday, Liz." She's right. She's too old to be called Pudge now. *We're* too old.

When she hangs up, I stare at my phone until something moves in the corner of my eye, capturing my attention.

"Simone, you little asshole, get back in your cage!" I dive for her, catching her by her back foot mid-hop.

We struggle momentarily, but I manage to get hold of her without injuring either of us. "I should have gotten your sister. Betcha she wouldn't pull this crap." I stop dead in my tracks, horrified. "No . . . that was cruel. You're great. Your sister is *different* but not better. I'm sorry."

Damn. We truly do become our mothers eventually.

I nuzzle Simone as I lower her into the cage and check the time. I have a little under an hour to get ready before Emily comes to pick me up. Actually, she said she'd be picking me up *after* everyone else, but I'm not sure who *everyone* is. Chloe, Warren, Amos, and Emily for sure but . . .

LANE: Who all is hanging out tonight?

EMILY: Everyone.

LANE: Just wondering if we'll all fit in your car.

EMILY: Change of plan, Warren's driving the six of us in their van.

LANE: Cool!

EMILY: So, yes, Matt is coming ;)

LANE: Not what I was asking, but that's great!

I immediately sprint to the shower.

An hour later, I finish my makeup while practicing my affirmations and take my 75mg of Sertraline, prescribed by a random, well-mannered doctor at the local walk-in clinic. I keep my pills in my makeup bag and my affirmations on a Post-it on my mirror.

I can always come home, but going out is fun.

I'm safe wherever I choose to be.

An environment I can't control is a memory in the making.

I added a new one, just for tonight and *not* on paper.

I will not flirt with Matt, no matter how tipsy I get. Even if he wears that gray button-up. Even if he does that thing where he flicks his wrist a few times to get his watch back in its place.

These reminders are necessary. I'm well aware of the many reasons Matt and I wouldn't work, but I'm also a raging flirt. I'll flirt with a lamppost if it flickers the right way. But with Matt, when it does slip out, there's an awkwardness afterward. Like I've stripped naked and run into a public fountain. No one dared me to, and I've made it weird. So I try my best not to flirt with him at all . . . but *shit,* does he make it difficult sometimes.

I zip myself into the tight black velvet jumpsuit and let my electric pink hair out of the rubber band I used in lieu of a hair tie this morning. With a little fluff, it actually falls quite nicely, the longest point tickling my collarbone. The good hair day is extremely lucky because I'm almost out of time to get ready.

My body is small in stature and height, but I've come to accept it in a neutral sense. I celebrate that I don't have to wear a bra if I don't want to, and being a size small makes thrift-shopping a lot easier, but often I still have to shove the cruel words of my high school classmates down when I take in my lack of hips, breasts, or ass.

Little boy, twig, flat, skeleton—they weren't very original, but the labels stuck.

It's probably why I always lean toward wearing baggier, darker clothing that hides me well and have a healthy splattering of patch-work style tattoos all over that are *mostly* seen by only me. But no baggy clothes this evening. Tonight, this jumpsuit is doing *wonders* for my self-esteem. I look hot.

My phone chimes with a message from Chloe that they're waiting out front. I allow myself one last glance in the mirror and give a thumbs-up to my reflection.

You can do this, I tell her. *It's going to be a great night.*

I point at her sternly. *Don't flirt with Matt.*

CHAPTER TWO

EMILY IS A CELEBRATOR AT HEART AND A TOTAL CHEER-leader for her people—she also has a tendency to go overboard. Chloe matches that energy—when she *has* the energy. Having a toddler at home while being self-employed and in a near constant state of flustered means that she's as thoughtful as she is forgetful. So, powered by perhaps a bit of pity and a whole lot of enthusiasm, they've put together a *beautiful* evening.

The back room of the trendy, dimly lit bar is decorated with silver and purple decorations surrounding a pair of black balloons in the shapes of a *2* and a *7* that are almost as big as me. The room has whitewashed stone walls and warm chandelier lighting, and a large oak table in the center creates an intimate, charming atmosphere.

"Oh my god!" I say, probably for the fortieth time as I brush my hand over the decorations. "You guys . . ." I whine, pouting my lip as I feel tears spring loose. "This makes me feel so special. Thank you."

"You *are* special, Laney." Chloe gives me a hug, squeezing a little too tight.

"Happy birthday, babe." Emily wraps her arms around both Chloe and me and shimmies us side to side.

Warren, Amos, and Matt find our private room after parking down the street and grabbing us the first round of drinks. Warren hands Chloe a pink cocktail, kisses her cheek, then immediately pulls out his phone. Chloe gives him a teasing smirk, whispering something about trusting the babysitter and assists him in putting the phone away. Amos performs a similar exchange, except he grabs Emily's ass after handing her a martini. She looks at him with a flirtatious smile that makes *me* blush. I turn away to see Matt standing in the doorway with two drinks.

"One . . . er . . . sex on the beach." Matt extends the fruity cocktail my way with a cheeky grin.

"Thanks." I take it and allow myself only two seconds to appreciate that he *did* wear his infamous gray button-up.

"Happy birthday, kid." He raises an arm around my back, patting my shoulder with his hand. Matt's not a particularly tall guy, I'd guess five-eleven, but to my five-foot-nothing—that's huge. Everything about him is *strong*. His wide frame, his broad shoulders, his working hands with veins that must be a nurse's wet dream.

I take a sip of my drink. It's stronger than I anticipated, the alcohol burning the back of my throat on its way down. I sputter a cough. "That is *stiff*." I look up to Matt's face, wincing.

"Gimme." He takes the glass without a second thought and throws back a sip. "Damn . . . it is." He tsks. "Guys love to say women are lightweights, but I'd like to see a man drink three of those, then walk home in heels."

"Totally," I agree mindlessly, looking at the smudge his lips left behind on my glass that overlaps with my lipstick stain, just *a little*.

He chases my drink with his own, something honey-colored in a short glass. "I watched another one of your movie suggestions last night," Matt says.

"Which one?"

His brow furrows, and then he reaches for his back pocket. He palms his drink while untucking some sort of paper from his wallet. "*Dead Poets Society*," he reads, then lowers the paper. "It was great. Probably my favorite of your suggestions so far."

I snatch the paper from him and try to make sense of what I'm holding. Reading it over, it becomes obvious. There is a list of all the movies I've referenced or we've watched together since we became friends squished together at the top of the page. The bottom half is a chart of sorts. He's filled in the date, the title, his rating—he drew actual stars—and his favorite quote or scene.

"Matt, have you been taking notes?" I feel myself losing all sense of self-preservation. Cartoon hearts attempt to fight their way out of my eyes.

"I take my homework assignments seriously." He snatches his notes back with a wink. "I also learned how to spotify to keep all the songs in one place." He folds the paper delicately and tucks it back into his wallet.

"I sort of want assignments too," I say reflexively. Our friendship suddenly seems totally off-balance. Sure, I suggested he watch the movies and listen to the songs, but I didn't think he'd *actually* do it. Certainly not all of them or, at least, not when I didn't make him come over to watch. This is hours of dedicated time.

He pockets his wallet and crosses his arms in front of his chest before flicking his watch into place. *Striptease, why don't you.*

"What could I possibly teach you?" He laughs, a smile creasing his cheeks.

"How to build an engine," I offer, leaning to one side.

He nods with pursed lips. "Do you have a *need* for an engine?"

"Not at the moment, but you never know." I bat my eyelashes before catching myself. "How to grow a garden?" I suggest, extending an open palm between us.

"Lane, you don't even have a balcony." He shakes his head while looking over my shoulder at the cozy room.

"True," I mumble, bringing my hand to my chin and tapping as I think.

"What about . . . books?" he asks, his attention directed back to me. "Dickens?"

I feign shock and offense. "Pardon me, *sir*? Dick-what?"

He rolls his eyes. "Austen?"

"Texas?" I shake my head internally at the stupid series of jokes I've now attempted. Still, Matt seems to find me amusing—his smile growing lopsided and sincere. "But yeah . . . I could definitely read some of your favorites. Seems more than fair. Where do I start?"

"Well, what haven't you read already?"

"I think what I *have* read would be a shorter list . . . as in, none. I read *Twilight* in high school, though. *Oh!* And *Twilight* fanfiction. *Lots* of that. There was this one where Bella gets her period and—"

"I'll bring a few over. I'll have to think about it," Matt interrupts, probably for the best.

"Not a fan of *Twilight*?" I glare playfully, baiting him.

"What? Nah, books are books. And it helps narrow down the type you may be interested in. Gothy, angsty stuff. Romance, maybe."

I want to pry as to what books that might be, but I'm interrupted by Emily grabbing my arm and hip bumping me.

"You want to split the Brie starter?" she asks, wagging her eyebrows suggestively.

I hum my agreement. "Chloe?" I call to get her attention from across the room. "Do you have a Lactaid?"

Chloe thrusts her drink at Warren without so much as looking at him before she begins rifling through her bag. She pulls out *Sesame Street* Band-Aids, two different pill bottles, a children's thermometer, a pack of baby wipes, and a package of tissues and places them all on the table one by one before her eyes light up. "Yes!" She tosses the little packet to me with shocking accuracy.

"Let's cheese it up!" I throw back the pill and down my drink with a sputtering cough before looping my arm through Em's and walking to the bar to order together.

*   *   *

Somewhere between the piece of seven-layer chocolate cake with one candle in it, the fumbling walk to the karaoke place down the street, and Amos's fierce rendition of "Somebody to Love," I've decided this is the best night of my life.

"Who's next?" Amos shouts into the microphone, sweat dripping off his chin as he uses the corner of his untucked shirt to wipe his brow, revealing the eight-pack that Emily has described *well*. She walks over with a hanky and kisses him sweetly as she dabs his face dry.

I raise an eyebrow at Warren, who's doing his best to disappear into the booth seating. His chest falls with a sigh, offering a look that says if I ask him point-blank, he'll do it. But he's begging me not to.

I contemplate how *badly* I want to hear his notorious rendition of "It's All Coming Back to Me Now" that Chloe describes as the best seven minutes of their honeymoon—much to his annoyance. I let him off easy and turn to Matt instead.

"Mattheus!" I sing out, gesturing to him with jazz hands.

He looks around enthusiastically, like he's on a game show, pointing to himself. "Me?" he mouths.

I nod like I'm Simon Cowell giving him the chance of a lifetime. He stands and takes the microphone from Amos. "What's the song, birthday girl?" He smiles at me, beaming like a damn spotlight.

I scroll through the tablet's list of songs, quickly realizing that most of them are love ballads. Or at least love-adjacent. I stammer, scroll some more, and feel my brain begin to shut down. "Performers choice." I hand him the tablet. He won't know many of them anyway.

Matt makes quick work of selecting his song, places the tablet down, and grabs the second microphone that has remained in its holster on the stage. "C'mon." He holds it out to me just as the beginning notes of "Ain't No Mountain High Enough" begin playing.

Lord have mercy.

"Listen, baby," he sings to me, taking my hand in his and spinning me around. I giggle as I'm moved about like a collection of helium balloons tied around his wrist.

We're both awful singers. He can't hold a note without losing his breath, and I can't match pitch to save my life. But it's possibly the most fun I've ever had.

With one hand on his microphone and one clasped around mine, he glides us around the small platform. He tugs me to and fro until I'm laughing so hard I'm half out of breath trying to sing. All the while, he keeps his eyes locked on me, wearing a mischievous grin.

I'm two drinks too deep to stop myself from getting lost in the moment and the giddy feelings rising in my chest.

Dangerous, my brain hums. *Live a little,* I retort.

When the song ends, we bow, and I look out to see Chloe and Warren exchanging wide-eyed, hopeful glances. I glare at them, promptly plucking my hand away from Matt's and wiping it down the seam of my thigh, as if I could remove the memory itself.

"Duets!" I exclaim. "We all must do duets!" I throw Warren a quick that's-what-you-get smirk while handing him my microphone and claiming his seat.

I curl into myself, downing the last of my drink.

Matt's not a fling type of guy, I remind myself. And god, what a guaranteed way to ruin our friendship sleeping with him would be.

I want to, though. I'm drunk and woman enough to admit it. I *really* want to.

My heart rate is approaching the speed of a hummingbird's wings, so I attempt to think of anything but Matt naked on top of me.

The smell of burning hair, feedback from a speaker, people who keep pigeons as pets, stale-coffee morning breath.

Matt, apparently unaware and entirely unaffected by our proximity, falls into the seat next to me as Chloe makes her way to the stage, joining her husband.

"You're the One That I Want" from *Grease* plays as Chloe spins circles around Warren, doing a near perfect Sandy. I can't help but smile as Warren's grin grows wider until he's also doing his best Danny Zuko.

I feel Matt's eyes on my profile, so I break the silence. "They're so cute it's disgusting."

"I like it." He shrugs, settling back into the booth.

"Of course *you* do. You've got no shortage of romance in your life. I'm bitter."

Every once in a while, I'll do this stupid thing where I make a generalized statement about Matt's love life to see if he'll correct me. It's the least embarrassing way to bring it up, but he never dignifies it with a response. It's fucking infuriating.

"Still no luck with the apps?" he asks.

"Bit the bullet today and finally joined one. Not going well."

"No?" He leans, raising his arm to rest along the back of the booth. His hand hovers above the back of my neck, and it distracts me momentarily. "How?"

"Well, I've gotten *some* messages," I reply, looking at his wrist over my shoulder before forcing myself to look away.

"So what's the issue?" he asks.

"It's been mostly couples looking for a third."

"Ah." He brushes his nose with his knuckle, and I notice a piece of his hair has broken free from his bun and rests alongside his cheek. I resist—with *everything* in me—twirling it around my finger.

"Are you seeing anyone?" I ask boldly—and unexpectedly. I need to drink some water. Or eat some bread. Bread absorbs the alcohol in your stomach, right? I think I've read that somewhere.

If I wasn't watching him so carefully, I might not have noticed his expression fall. The happy lines on either side of his eyes soften, and the upturned corner of his lip dips too.

"Nothing serious," he says, unbothered.

As in he's sleeping around? As in he's not looking for commitment? As in . . . "And that's what you . . . prefer?" *What the fuck am I doing?*

"I'm not sure." He leans back, scratching his jaw. "If I worked less, maybe I'd look to settle down." He smiles softly, lifting his shoulders.

"You don't work *that* much. I mean, you're here right now." I point around us, as if he's unaware that he isn't elbow deep in an engine.

Chloe and Warren pass their mics to Amos and Emily, and a new song starts up. A ballad I don't recognize and can't seem to focus on.

Matt presses his lips together and tilts his head. His eyes narrow on me until I fidget in my seat.

"What?" I laugh nervously under his stare.

"I made you something," he says, voice hushed.

"For my birthday?" I ask.

That snaps the tension. He licks his lips as they transform into a smirk. "No, for Hanukkah." He laughs, then it fades to a shy sort of smile. "But yeah, for your birthday." He raises off the bench slightly, reaches into his back pocket, and pulls out a tiny wooden object. "Here." He lays it in my open palm, his fingers brushing my wrist *far* too lightly.

I look at it for a moment before my eyes translate what it is, though I'm still not *entirely* sure. A simple carving of wood in the shape of a peg doll. It's smooth as I rub my thumb over it. I glance up at him through my eyelashes.

He moves his hand from his mouth to speak. "My dad made these for my siblings and me. They're called worry dolls. Or maybe he made that up, I don't know." He rubs the back of his neck and chuckles slowly. "It's, uh, yeah. For worrying. Or, stopping it, I guess."

"You made this for me?" I ask softly.

He nods.

"Like you carved it from wood?"

He nods again.

"So when I'm anxious . . ." My voice trails off.

"You take it out, and—well, I used to sort of fiddle with mine. Run my fingers over it, squeeze it in my palm." I mimic his instructions as he explains.

"Do you still have yours?" I ask.

"Yeah, it's on a shelf somewhere at my place."

"This is such a *you* gift." The words tumble out of me.

"Cheap? Boring? Peculiar?" He crosses one leg over his knee, which is bouncing.

"No." I find his eyes and hold his stare. "Thoughtful, careful, beautiful."

His leg stills. He blinks more than a few times, then swallows heavily. "Well, I'm glad you like it."

"Thank you." I tuck it into my bag. "I really do."

Amos and Emily finish their song. We all decide to call it a night when Chloe announces that they need to go relieve their sitter.

It's a contentedly silent car ride home, followed by a chorus of *thank yous* and *love yous* as I exit the car and make my way upstairs. I drag my balloons behind me and place them in the center of my living room. In the middle of my empty, silent apartment.

The tears come quicker than I expected them, though they're not a surprise. I've cried on every birthday. All the ones I can remember, at least.

I'm a crier at my core. I try my best to hide it now that I'm an adult and recognize big emotions scare people off. But if I'm above a seven or below a three on the emotions scale—I'm crying.

And sometimes I'm at a ten and a one all at once. Especially when drunk, as I suspect I might be as my living room whirls in and out of focus.

It could be a number of things. Relief at being home mixed with loneliness following a night of chaotic, constant company. Gratefulness makes me feel guilty about what others don't have. An awareness of another birthday passing without getting a hug from my dad. Knowing he'd still be here if I had just stayed home that night.

That last one can cause tears even on the best of days.

I strip and get into the warm shower, allowing my makeup to be washed away as the last tears evaporate with the steam.

When I get out, dry off, and find my coziest pajamas, I get into bed. My entire body hums its approval like a cat nuzzling against its owner, purring in satisfaction. A warmth in the back of my neck, a dense, heavy feeling in my bones dragging me down, down, down. When my bed curls around me like this, when my body melts so naturally into it, I know getting out the next day will be challenging.

Anxiety creeps up in many forms, but most often, it feels like exhaustion. I'm an electric vehicle running on two AA batteries. Sure, it could run for a little while—but it's not a permanent solution.

You had a good time, I tell myself. *Quit complaining.*

I attempt to shake off the feeling and reach for my phone. I *like* the posts shared by my friends tonight and the comments on the photo I posted earlier. Me and my giant 27 balloons. It's the first time I've ever considered not including how old I am in a birthday post, but the only photos of me before I got a little sloppy feature the balloons—so *whatever*.

I don't think it's so much the age itself. Most of my friends are in their late twenties, and it doesn't look so scary when I watch them go through it. But combine being twenty-seven, working a job I don't particularly like, going without sex for over a year, living in a shitty apartment, and basically being entirely direction-less . . . that's a different story. There's some shame there.

Here. There's some shame *here*.

I know what my dad would say. No direction means no limita-tions. A job you hate? An opportunity to find something better. A place you're not tied down to? A chance to go somewhere new. Lonely? Learn to enjoy your own company.

I'm stuck, and deep down I know I'm the only one who can do the *un-sticking*—but I feel resistant to change. Change requires ef-fort, innovation, energy . . . which I have little of these days.

So, instead, I scroll and scroll until optimum numbness is achieved. Video after video passes, all of them fitting into neat, distinct categories. You've got your funny animal videos—that's a given. Your political hot takes and news updates that I usually watch all the way through out of a sense of obligation. Plus the professional content creators who've found their niche.

I follow a hot dude who only posts cooking videos and appar-ently doesn't own a top, a woman who films herself thrifting home goods and renovating her finds, a pair of friends who tap dance to pop music in unison so precisely it makes my brain go quiet. But one video ends my scrolling and sends me into an internet research tailspin.

I spend the next hour watching videos of a couple buying, emptying, fixing, renovating, and then decorating their school bus conversion. Between the camera-lens flares of the adorable yellow bus and peppy, up-tempo music, I'm sold.

It's a bright, colorful world. It's freedom from rent and land-lords. It's being on the move while also going back to your *own* space each night. A space you designed to your *exact* specifications.

They seem happy.

One Google search later, and I'm on an auction website. One click, and I'm looking at the bus I'm convinced fate has brought to me.

$27,000

2013 International 48 Passenger School Bus
- Low Mileage
- Rear Air Ride Suspensions
- 39 Foot Length makes this bus perfect for a skoolie conversion

Call Carl for details. It won't last long!

Twenty-seven thousand dollars. An obvious sign. Less obvious, the year of the bus is the year my father passed—the $50,000 he left me still sitting unused in a savings account.

My dad would've loved this idea. He'd have insisted on taking it for a test drive. He'd tell my mother jokes until her weary, tight lips turned to a smirk, and she'd come around to the idea of her daughter living on wheels.

My sister used her inheritance to fund research at her alma mater—stating that her education had been covered by my parents' vast wealth already, and she didn't need much else since she was choosing to stay near home. But I know our dad. Knew him better than she did. He separated that money from our education funds because he wanted us to use it for something joy-giving. Something impractical. Something fun and just for us. Like he would have done.

I wouldn't be a single almost-thirty-year-old in a half-empty apartment, depressed and alone with her rabbit. I'd be an adventurous nomad, living in a home catered to her needs, experiencing a simpler way of life . . . with her rabbit.

I'm emailing the seller, Carl, as the sun begins to come up. He's two hours ahead and responds immediately. Quickly, phone numbers are exchanged, and I'm receiving a request for a video call. I keep my video off, as I'm still in bed. Once my tour is complete, I send him a deposit. He sends me the address, and then we hang up. Carl, the happy salesman. Me, the proud owner of a bright yellow, forty-eight passenger bus.

Then, at just after six, I go to bed.

ABOUT THE AUTHOR

Hannah Bonam-Young is the author of *Next of Kin, Next to You, Out on a Limb,* and *Set the Record Straight*. Hannah writes romances featuring a cast of diverse, disabled, marginalized, and LGBTQIA+ folks wherein swoonworthy storylines blend with the beautiful, messy, and challenging realities of life. When not reading or writing romance, Hannah can be found having living room dance parties with her kids or planning any occasion that warrants a cheese board. Originally from Ontario, Canada, she lives with her childhood-friend-turned-husband Ben, two kids, and bulldog near Niagara Falls on the traditional territory of the Haudenosaunee and Anishinaabe peoples.

hannahbywrites.com
Instagram: @authorhannahby
TikTok: @hannahby_writes